RUNNING BLACK

Thank you,

Peter

RUNNING BLACK

It's nothing personal. It's just business.

***

Euro Cybernetics Integrated. Toulouse, France. New European Union.
Same night - 02:59 a.m.

> *It was overcast and we came in from a mile up. On a moonless night,*
> *with our new drop rigs, the six of us were inside their perimeter like*
> *vampires in the mist. It was that clean. We hit the ground, dumped*
> *the packs, and waited. The security routines for the complex had just*
> *been raped blind, so we supposedly owned every null space and*
> *nanosecond, but we were now officially trespassing.*

PATRICK TODOROFF

Running Black Copyright 2010 by Patrick Todoroff

All Rights Reserved. No part of this publication may be reproduced, stored in a retrieval system, or transmitted in any form or by any means digital, electronic, mechanical, photocopying, recording, or otherwise, or conveyed via the internet or a Web site without prior written permission of the author, except in the case of brief quotations included in critical articles and reviews.

ISBN: 978-0-578-07071-1

Various quotations from the Holy Bible and the Quran. In the attempt to depict a credible near-future setting, real-world nations, companies, politics, and parties are mentioned. However, this is a work of fiction and no challenge or offense is intended. All the mistakes are mine.

For my wife, Rachel

PROLOGUE

OUTSIDE

Gibson: I am alone in the black. Below me, a million strands of light skip with data, blue and white, like a vast spider's web humming with motion. The net is alive, even at this hour, and this is just homes and small companies here in Toulouse. I decipher the routines: email and music, vid-bits and late-night purchases, transfers and automated memos. Nothing exciting. I spy lime green flashes around the business nodes; crackers riding the lines, probing for holes. They creep along and hop from strand to strand, pounce, flare, and vanish. I watch them until I get bored, which isn't very long. They never do anything new; just re-script packet sniffers to snatch numbers or names. Besides, they're slow, much slower than me. The staff all says I'm the fastest yet.

Big, bright shapes sparkle in the distance. On my level, I can see the giant honeycomb structures of other corporations, the red military nets, and the tangled green branches of the government. They pulse and twirl, and it makes me want to leave, to explore, but I can't. Dr. Evans says I'll go soon enough. He seems sad when he looks at me lately. I'm going to look through his files and try to find out why.

I got another headache and couldn't sleep, second night in a row. There are no more pain tabs in the med-station upstairs, and no one's here in the lab to talk to. The security guards aren't even allowed in my area. I keep remembering what Dr. Evans said about my final trials next week, how directors from the Head Office would be coming and I need to be at my best. I hope I don't have a headache then.

I wanted to walk out on the plaza, but all the doors are locked for the night, so I jacked in and left through the messaging system. I'm not going to tell them about the hole; it's my escape hatch. They'd only close it, and then I'd be stuck here on nights like this, and watching takes my mind off the pain. Besides, I'm outside now, at least in some sense.

I'm still not sleepy, so for now, I'll stay in the lab Grid. I'm going to tap into the security cameras and follow the guards. I make it a game to see which one finishes his rounds first.

INCURSION

CHAPTER ONE

LIKE CIGARETTES

Dawson-Hull Conglomerate Regional Offices. London, England.
New European Union. 2:18 a.m. Day One.

He wasn't going to make it. His mind kept nagging him with that fact, but a primal part much deeper inside snarled back and kept him running anyway. The slip-in had been so smooth too, everything going flawlessly right up to the last seconds of the download.

It should have been a simple loot and scoot: prep work for some other mission. They'd even received Tier Two pass codes that let the four of them voodoo through the building's security like wily ghosts. Floor plans brought them straight to the mainframe hub. They'd been told exactly where to search there too, and after a crypto-crack and a quick cable to the terminal, they watched the flash drive fill up and passed a smile around in the stillness. The buzz of easy money. But someone in D-H Cyber-Division must have strung a tripwire in the transfer executable, because right at ninety-seven percent an alarm went off, the thick dark exploded, and a perfectly good break-in was shot to hell.

Now the air quivered with sirens and every light in the complex glared stark phosphorus. The freelancer was alone, flying through the maze of offices back the way he'd come, his world compacted by the tyranny of rage and fear.

He'd jabbed all his speed-stiks at once, and the adrenaline cocktail hit him like a freight train. Everything tumbled together in a rabid blur: steel gates slamming down over windows, the drop and swivel of ceiling turrets, nightshift guards shouting, popping out in front of him like cartoon targets in a kill house. He focused on them long enough to double-tap holes in their tailored uniforms, then ducked, weaved, rolled and ran on.

The intimate dead urged him on, raw in his mind. Riko buried under a wave of first response spider 'bots; Mahoud shredded by flechettes, choking on his own blood. Even Daffid, so cool and precise, had bought him these last seconds, pushing him through a kill sack before he ended up spattered all over the lower parking level. Lives stubbed out like cigarettes, littered in a trail behind him. He was the only one left.

Somewhere in another hallway, his brain reminded him about the U.A.V. The mission contract stipulated that his team had the stealth drone circling overhead for the duration, ready to relay the files once they got clear. Talk about a clue. It had been the first item on the load-out list. Corporate pass codes or no, whoever hired them hadn't counted on a clean getaway. They'd been so right.

A squeeze on the trigger folded up another guard, then the *click, click, click* of an empty magazine registered in his mind. Now even his ammo was gone.

What's the use? his brain nagged again. But there was twenty-five million on his flash drive, and the contract stated *no files—no funds.* Four minutes ago, he'd wondered what was worth so much, but now all he wanted was to get outside so it could be passed to whoever was up next in this horror show. The data pad was blue-toothed to the drone, but he got no signal inside the building. He needed clear sky, so he kept running.

He darted down a sharp left, bouncing off the walls. He was almost there. At least Mira and the kids would get five percent, plus benefits.

The final stretch was empty, and for a second, he imagined he'd actually survive. He almost laughed, but his lungs were heaving, his muscles burning out on the ragged edges of the chemical overkill. As he burst through the basement double doors onto the service road, he instinctively looked up for the drone he knew he couldn't see. The night sky was littered with stars, and the air was heavy with the reek of garbage and bio-diesel.

Someone shouted, but he didn't stop. He was out.

Still at full speed, he raised his arm and thumbed the "Send" button. He saw police lights, men braced behind car doors, their helmets silhouetted against the muzzle flashes. Rounds tore through him, but they were too late. He heard the electronic bleat and knew the machine valkyrie was bearing the files onward. He did laugh then, deep and wet. He'd made it.

Tri-bursts scoured his body, punching his forward motion back until it stopped in jerks and shudders. He tumbled to the asphalt. Blood was running now. The freelancer lay there, looking up as every ounce of overdue pain came crowding in. It was finished. He saw the sky, the stars, and thought of Mira. Then everything winked out.

CHAPTER TWO

FULL INTRUSION PACKAGE

In the sky over French airspace, New European Union. 2:37 a.m.
Same night.

Droning. Engines droning and the hiss of stratosphere outside the compartment always made me sleepy. Soldiers sleep anywhere, anytime. I guess if you do anything for long enough, any familiar sound can become a lullaby. Tam and I knew this Bulgarian in the Balkans who had nodded off in his foxhole just before an attack. He slept through the whole firefight. Not a scratch on him either. He got pulped the next day when the AI on one of our drones failed to recognize his IFF tags. Bad mojo, but still…

A gust of turbulence rocked the suborbital.

I opened one eye. It was dark. Tam was still at the command and control station, waiting. I heard his boots shift on the steel decking. The crew of Eshu International had been on standby, contracted for the second phase of a possible mission. If he got the green light, we'd only have a three-minute jump window. There was a lot of money on hold in this contract, and if the mystery crew botched the first stage, we wouldn't see any of it. Too many moving parts made Tam edgy. He wasn't keen on missing a payday and losing face with corporate sponsors.

I looked back to see the green cast of the holo-display on his face. The black Mitsubishi sneak suit absorbed the light and made his glowing head look like a bakemono ghost had floated in from the netherworld to haunt the transport.

Christ, I needed more sleep.

"Jace."

I opened my other eye. "Yeah?"

"They prepped back there?" The head nodded toward the cargo compartment.

"Of course. Jeeze, Tam, not like we haven't done this before. Been wheels up every night for a week waiting on a go."

"Corp dime—Corp time. They promise payments like this, I'll do it as long as they like."

"That sounds dirty."

He laughed. "Call me easy. Better than getting shot at."

"I read that." I shut my eyes again. Then I opened them. "So those authorizations are real?"

"The money?" Tam stayed focused on the displays. "Yep, they're real. Triple mission rates, even equipment reimbursements and bonuses. Rao thought it was a U.N. phish at first."

I let out a low whistle. "You know what they say about 'too good to be true', right?

Tam looked up at me. "Yeah. Yeah I do. Our backup gear is still onboard, right? Tell me you brought our gear."

"Yes, mother. It's in the back. I'll need sixty seconds once the ramp drops." I settled back to doze again. "Probably a no-go tonight too. If you're still worried, I can do a search when we get back. Find out who's footing the bill. If it is an UNdie sting, their fingerprints are out there on the net."

"Nah." His ghost head smiled. "Your web-fu is Amish. I already said something to Poet. He's on it."

"Amish? Ha, funny, ha. I don't know why they say Koreans lost their sense of humor." I closed my eyes for a third time, hoping it was for good until we landed back in Belfast. "If there's a data trail leading back to the Security Council, Poet9 will sniff it out."

"Rao says all signs point to Tokyo, which is good, because it's been months since we've seen any action from them."

"Contract like this, seems like they're making up for lost time," I noted.

"Absence makes the heart grow fonder. Besides, not like there's a pile of other outfits that could pull this run off. They need us. And if what the contract brief says is true," I could hear the smile in Tam's voice, "after we deliver, I'll be packing my bags for that vacation."

"You and your vacation," I grunted.

"Gotta have goals. I hear Belize is nice."

"Nope. Shining Path hit it last month with the Marburg virus. Still a Q'd zone."

"Hell. What about Disneystan then? Some of the resorts are secluded. Separate from the parks."

"You want secluded, you're better off with Cancun or Cozumel."

"Well sure," Tam snorted, "If Rao can grease us past the North American Border Grid. Clearances are hard to come by."

I shifted around, trying to find a vaguely comfortable position. "Jaithirth Rao is Mr. Wizard. He can do anything. Just follow that yellow brick road."

Ten seconds later. "Jace?"

I opened one eye again. "Yes, Tam?"

"Go back and make sure Poet and the Triplets are all set. Just in case."

"Just in case," I echoed, getting to my feet.

The back compartment was bathed in ruby half-light and hard shadows. Our gear was perched on skids waiting patiently for the jaw of the drop ramp to open. Tam had made us bring all three of our Raytheon "Whisper" remotes. They were top-grade surveillance drones; I could see the tiny green status lights winking. Multiple sensor lenses peeked out from under the blue-black wing shapes like the shining eyes of ravens. Between the drones, our Mitsubishi armor, and a full ECM suite, it was obvious the sudden corporate largess hadn't allayed Tam's trust issues just yet. Freelance teams had been left out in the cold before, and no one wanted their beneficiaries haggling with the pond scum from legal over the fine print of a contract's death clause.

Poet and the Triplets were huddled together. The small Mexican was saying something, and the three hulking soldiers were repeating after him. I stood there for a moment and watched.

Devante Peres, or Poet9, as he liked to be called, was our Splicer. Born and raised in the Mexico City Sprawl, he cobbled his first deck from dump parts when he was eleven, hot-lining the public access for the next six years. He became something of a slumdog celebrity making candy runs: tracing deadbeats for dealers, wiping police files for MS-13 and La Eme.

Then one sweltering night one his seventeenth birthday, he jacked in and went poking around the Ixe Grupo Financiero domain. Somehow, he managed to spoof his way in through the foreign currency exchange. He later said it was sheer luck, crank, and tequila. Now if he'd stayed calm, been smart, he might have gotten away with it, but with all those dólares floating around, the barrio punk, he treated it like a smash and grab. He siphoned off a hundred million, tagged gang code everywhere, and ran. Loud and sloppy, I.G.F. counter-intrusion tagged him in minutes and traced him back to his cinderblock hut. They kicked the door in the next morning. During the interrogation, the lead security officer saw past the gang tats, acne scars, and cheap bling and gave him an option: life in a Mexican prison or an entry-level desk in their firewall department. He took the job, got a twenty-year indenture, and wound up with a Cybernetic Interface Unit wet-wired to his cortex.

The Triplets were a different story. Our team's gunboys, they were Pretoria Series Seven combat clones, and the last remnants of General N'kosa Mambi's fever dream of an African empire. Gene-modded to their eyeballs, literally, Mambi's scientists had ramped up the stock soldier template until they broke it, reducing mental capacity to autistic levels and introducing albinism into the sequence. But that was fine by the general's syphilitic racist logic. The extremely Causasian Series Seven clones had only two imperatives: total loyalty and killing with startling efficiency. They were lethal savants, and the general fed thousands of his new shock troops into the savage brush wars. Under his command, they slaughtered everything in their path and burned through the surrounding Sub-Saharan nations for almost two years until E.U. forces brought the hammer down.

After the battle of Victoria Falls, all Series Sevens were declared illegal. Every one they could find was rounded up and executed, their bodies burned by the hundreds in deep, slit trenches. Veterans say the veldt around the Zambezi River smoldered for weeks. Somehow, these three Series Sevens had stayed hidden and alive until Tam found them and smuggled them out on an old friend's boat.

They'd never been given names, so we called them Flopsy, Mopsy, and Cottontail, our killer bunnies. Now every time our resident doctor, Ibram Kalahani, came around, he'd say, "Death awaits you all with nasty, big, pointy teeth." He'd then laugh to himself for minutes. He still hadn't told us what was so funny.

My boot hit the door kick plate and all four heads swiveled my way.

"Hey, boss," Poet sang out.

"Hi, boss," the Triplets called in unison.

"I'm not the boss. Mr. Tam's the boss." I frowned at Poet. "You're not teaching them Spanish again, are you?"

He threw up his hands. "Just a couple things. All tactical stuff, I swear."

"You swear is right. Doc Kalahani will have your balls in a vise, you teach them any more. He's still mad about Lisbon."

Poet laughed. "Buenas épocas!"

"Good times." The three big soldiers thumped their fists on their thighs.

I shook my head. "Tam sent me back here to make sure we're good to go tonight. Are we?"

"Same as all the other nights." The little Mexican tapped the C.I.U. on the left side of his head. The gray electronics were partially hidden under a knit cap, but the "Brain Box's" awkward angles made the graft look like a geometric contusion. "I've got the Whispers slaved on a high-band channel on our heads-up-displays. Anyone of us can access their camera views on the helmet visors. And they'll start singing loud and proud if anyone violates our space." He threw me a sly grin. "Seven flights so far and you still haven't told me what we're stealing."

"Who said anything about stealing?" I smiled back.

"Jace, mano, it's got to be a big party, or..." he waved a hand at our drones, the racked weapons, our H.A.L.O. drop rigs, then placed it solemnly on his Mitsu's armored chestplate, "...we wouldn't be bringing all our toys."

"Asian Pacific wants us to jump on some labs in Toulouse," I explained. "Some other crew is supposed to squirt pass codes and schematics up to us, but we don't know exactly when. That's why we've been in the air every night. Tam's up front still waiting."

"But we must be picking up a souvenir while we visit, right?"

I pondered before answering. "We're after an N3," I finally added.

He raised his eyebrows at me.

"I know, I know... but the mission brief states the Brits actually developed one. It says these labs actually have a working prototype."

"Horseshit," he observed.

"Mierda del caballo!" three deep voices boomed in unison. The albino giants looked over at me, big expectant grins on their faces. I burst out laughing, but Poet9 was still serious.

"The Nanotech Neural Network is a myth, Jace. Can't be done. The human body rejects the little machine bastards. Madre de Dios, this thing almost killed me." He tapped his C.I.U. again. "Everybody and their cousin had lab geeks running R and D for years. The bank even looked into it. Every one of those projects flat-lined. All they got was bloated bodies." Poet9 shook his head.

"Well, Rao says someone on high in the Asian Pacific executive is fronting our little expedition. From the money being thrown around, it looks like whoever that diamyo is, he's a true believer."

Poet9 sat back with a grunt. "Fine. As long as they pay up when we come back empty-handed and say I told you so."

"We say that, we might not get paid anything. And Tam wants that vacation," I told him.

"Still with the vacation?"

"He'll get it someday." I turned to leave. "I'll tell him we're ready."

"As always," Poet9 called out.

Tam was standing in the same place when I got back up front. No flash traffic yet. "I told Poet about the N3. He thinks we're chasing ghosts."

He glanced over. "Chimeras actually; literal and figurative."

"You're a barrel of laughs tonight." I sat back down. "They're ready, by the way."

"I figured."

I'd almost made it back to sleep when the command and communication station warbled abruptly. I stood up. A large yellow cube appeared in the center display, rotating in the holo-field. It blossomed into strings of code, COBOL3 encryptions unfurling, arranging themselves to coherency. The top field was blinking lime green.

"Relayed traffic coming in," Tam noted. "It's on. We're going in right now." I grabbed a handhold as the suborbital banked hard to port, going south. Tam was downloading the data, transferring the target schematics to his forearm pad, synching them with our crew's command net. He scanned the projection as a message played out. "Damn, that didn't come cheap."

"What didn't?" I asked.

"This is a full intrusion package. Somebody just nicked proprietaries and overrides for the entire Toulouse facility. Tier Two, at least."

I headed back to Poet9 and the Triplets. Tam was right behind me. Ahead, I heard the ramp whine open and the wind come howling in.

CHAPTER THREE

VAMPIRES IN THE MIST

Euro-Cybernetics Integrated. Toulouse, France. New European Union. 2:59 a.m. Same night.

It was overcast, and we came in from a mile up. A moonless night, with our new drop rigs, the six of us were inside their perimeter like vampires in the mist. It was that clean. We hit the ground, dumped the packs, and waited. The security routines for the complex had just been raped blind, so we supposedly owned every null space and nanosecond, but we were now officially trespassing.

Not just anywhere either; this little research campus belonged to Euro-Cybernetics Integrated, the lead biotech division for the Dawson-Hull Conglomerate. Black contract jobs are always touchy, but this bordered on psychosis. No Geneva Convention for us. Get blown in the 'Glom's backyard, due process would be a bullet in the head. Tam held us back by a row of concrete planters and signaled me to confirm our Mitsubishi stealth gear was working, and that all three Whispers were overhead and online.

So far, nothing had exploded or started wailing, so I figured that was a plus.

I dialed up the frequency and got another bonus: the little remotes were squirting real-time video from their flight paths seventy-five meters above. I cycled through each one, getting a God's eye view of the entire facility from three different angles in night-vision green. The only signs of our presence were minor distortions, six man-sized absences that quivered like heat demons over desert sand. Our equipment was working as advertised. For someone to get a bearing on us, they'd have to know we were on-site, and exactly what to look for. And if they knew that much, we were in deep *kimchi* already. I gave the thumbs-up. Tam motioned the Triplets ahead.

I watched them rise and do a little tactical ballet, synchronizing into positions further out on the plaza. Limited vocabulary or not, every time I saw them in motion I thanked the war gods they were with us.

When they'd settled, Tam's voice came over the helmet radio. "Poet9, I want a splice in their surveillance net. There's a node in that security station. Jace will go with you."

I slipped out, and we ran towards the guardhouse. It was really a bunker, a thug-ugly shape trying to hide behind a couple of coiffed hedges and a manicured walkway. I could make out the thick poly-steel plating and the dish array on the roof, and from experience, I knew pop-up turrets were stowed behind the big flat screens that displayed the D-H icon. Their light threw a shifting glow on the lawns around the station. There was no other movement.

I checked the time and the stolen schedule. Perimeter patrols in this part of the facility weren't due for another seventeen minutes. That meant all four guards were still inside, biding time against the night's chill. We approached the double doors.

"*Muy liso*, Jace,"Poet9 whispered.

Crouched next to the slab mass of bunker, my hands started itching. That only happened when I was nervous. "Doesn't feel smooth, *mano*, my Spidey sense is tingling."

"*Cálmelo*. We're *como la seda.* We'll be gone in no time."

Poet9 took off his helmet and zipped two cables from sockets in his C.I.U. to the door keypad. While he overrode the lock, I peered into the dark like something was going to snap. I caught myself squeezing the grip on my sub-machinegun, but that just made the flex stock clasp tighter. It made my 6mm Blizzard look more like an alien insect was trying to mate with my hand. My worry stayed with me.

Poet nudged me. "Jace…"

I brought the Blizzard up, flipped on the holo-sight, and nodded. He only grunted, put his helmet back on. Seven seconds later, the doors slid open and the first guard was dead at his desk.

We were in.

Multi-spectrum imaging, area denial, micro-drones, laser trips, smart mines… all ultra-tech, all lethal, all precise, all predictable. And predictable is good for freelancers like us. Hired to do nasty things, we are deniable, deletable, and disposable. Our only hope is to be fast and devious, to get in and get out without rippling the pond. Automated systems, however precise, can be hacked with hot codes, bounced with newer, faster tech, sometimes just unplugged. The intrusion/detection race is a fevered constant. We manage to stay one step ahead because we have to, and because Poet9 is one of the best hammerjacks alive.

Which brings me to people: people are the problem. No matter what the Maginot Systems sales rep says about their latest perimeter envelope, there's no subroutine for suspicion. A good human guard, a veteran with training and combat experience, has instinct: that visceral feeling something's just not right. Any security executive that forgets this basic rule of combat loses the ability to read the ground, read the moment, and if you fixate on the latest chromed out, automated defense network, it's a sure bet you'll wind up emptied out, or dead. There's plenty of hardcore bush war leftovers who come cheap and can shoot, but that's not the real reason smart managers keep them on the payroll. It's intuition.

There's only one countermeasure for that kind of primal radar: running black. That means more than buying mimetic camo-suits, or investing in the hottest I.C.E. breakers. It's more than training day and night on how to ghost through a dozen of the most common security formats. It means going blank, void. It's the ability to slow everything down and draw it all in so you null down your psychic profile. Someone running black becomes empty space. There's no sense of person. It's a monkey skill, some sort of primate stealth gear that can't be taught or drilled into you. Either you have it or you don't. I have it, and so does Tam. And that's the main reason we're still alive.

So far, we hadn't reached into that bag of tricks. Between our tech-toys and training, we'd weaseled inside the facility's defense loop undetected. Now all we had to do was stay that way, fetch the item in question, and go. Easy.

I left Poet9 in relative safety at the desk while I moved down the hall for the last three guards. He'd have to jack in uninterrupted in the station's control room, so there was no skipping them. Schematics put the armory just down from a break room, and with a patrol due, I figured that's where they'd be. I dropped a blade into my left hand—just in case—and I moved with the Blizzard straight-armed and sighted.

Sure enough, two of them were suiting up, half-dressed, with helmets, shotguns and radios all neat on a table. I closed the door with a click, and they turned, looking for their partner. The Blizzard coughed and they crumpled, disappointed, on the floor.

I switched off the light and slipped back out into the hall. One to go. Where was he—sleep or food?

I radioed Poet9. "Two more down. Desk monitors got eyes on the fourth?"

A few second later, "Nothing on screen. Find him fast, *mano*. I need access before the next rotation. Want me to call Tam?"

"Just be ready. I'm on it." I slipped right, towards the break room and kitchen. Call it instinct.

He was eating, an older guy with a rank badge and cold eyes that said "veteran". He was definitely modded because he was up and moving at warp speed the second I spun in through the door. He crash-flipped a table for cover and dodged left towards the communication panel on the wall. I put a burst of three shots where he'd just been.

I moved to cut him off, the Blizzard making rapid spitting noises as it put lines of holes into the tabletop, but he came up on my right with an ugly snub carry piece. Definitely a vet. Two shots roared in the small room, and the panel splintered next to my head.

My turn to dodge.

I tumbled, slid into some chairs, and came up hosing the area until the breech locked open. As my thumb hit the ejection and the empty magazine slid down out of the grip, he came up again with those eyes and that backup piece lasered in on me. I didn't even think. My left arm whipped around and the knife sprouted from his neck. He went down and backwards and out of sight.

Just in case.

Suddenly, Tam was in the doorway with his visor up and a sliver of a smile on his face. "You finished?" He yanked my knife out, wiped it and tossed it back. "Poet's in their Grid, and we have to move on the labs now."

We entered the control room. The opposite wall was stacked with monitors showing grainy black and white exterior sweeps with thermal views winking in at random. It was enough to give you seizures. Poet9 was spliced in at the desk, cables from his interface unit running into the station terminal. He was talking off hand, distracted, trying to keep focus on two worlds.

"We're still clear. No increased traffic on their nets. Over in the lab, there's no staff, just guards, two, three, total—yeah, three inside... He closed his eyes for a moment.*"Campus patrol is three bots and six guards. All right where they're supposed to be: doing routine sweeps in overlapping eights. There's one Cerberus-'bot and a single guard doing the walk around the lab buildings."*

He jacked out and his eyes cleared. "I'm not quite done. I'll set this terminal to give its standard 'all clear' to the next system security query. They're every thirty minutes, and next ping is in just over nine. According to the schedule, we have eleven minutes until this station's guards have to be out on fence patrol. My patch will bluff once, but not twice. We have to be gone before the second check."

Tam lifted his helmet visor and nodded at Poet9. "We can do that as long as we move fast and stay subterranean. We've got floor plans and key codes for the lab building, but I want you to access the defense network in the lab area itself. Sift the system to see what's online in there. You know how I hate surprises." He glanced at the station terminal. "Can you crack it from here?"

"Not in a half-hour." Poet9 said. "Their intranet has centralized control, but each building is separately zoned. With the time we've got, I'd have to splice at a specific site to mess around with its local grid. The only way is through a terminal in that building." Poet9 squared off in front of Tam and patted the oversized Walther 11 holstered on his hip. I'd swear he even lowered his voice a bit. "You want it down, boss, I'll have to go in with you."

"Stop with the *machista grande.* You're a data rat, not a slum gunner, remember," Tam sighed. "Jace and I will clear the way. Scan the bodies and dig out their chips, then have Flopsy and Mopsy walk the fence. That'll keep the alarms quiet. Make sure they prep some EMPs in case those 'bots show up. You hang back and only come in the lab when I say it's clear. Got it?"

Poet9's eyes gleamed as he coiled up his data cables and tugged the knit cap back over his misshapen head. He unsnapped the pistol holster at his side."Sure thing, boss. We're good."

Tam and I headed for the door. "*Machista Grande*? What is that, a coffee drink?"

Another faint smile."Don't even start."

"He's got a name for that hand cannon, you know," I whispered.

"I'm not listening."

A minute later, Poet9 was carrying two bloody RFID chips from the guards' hands. Tam re-deployed the Triplets, and I checked the feed from our drones. No sign of a response. The action inside had bled off some tension, but something still gnawed at the back of my mind. I looked to see if Tam felt it, but he'd gone into mode and was all crisp. The Triplets were moving, so I sprinted towards the tangled geometry of the labs. We were running all the way to the end.

CHAPTER FOUR

SHOPLIFTERS

Dawson-Hull Estates, London, UK. New European Union. 3:03 a.m.
Same night.

The Lear shuttle dropped from the black of space straight into the pallid sky over the London Metro Zone. A luminous haze clung to the city night like a shroud, and the shuttle slid shark-like in the murk, ionized gas flaring off its hull. Then with a twitch, it plunged down into the canyons of glass and steel. Threading past tall offices, industrial units, and row after row of apartment blocks, its wake rumbled, shivered windows in passing and sent echoes thundering in the distance. It darted south, and knots of late-night traffic scattered, third shift commuter transit and massive cargo transports surrendering the right of way as the shuttle arrowed closer to restricted airspace.

Within moments it passed into the exclusive districts and turned back its engines so only the merest trail of turbulence shuddered behind it. Now approved ID codes cleared the way, and one by one, missile locks blinked off—a recognition of peers. Beyond one roll of hills, an estate opened up, the grounds hemmed by walls and trees and towers. The distinguished lines of a manor house were illuminated by landing pad lights on the rear lawn. The Lear dipped its nose like a tip of a hat and settled there with fluid precision. As the pinging engines shed waves of heat into the night, a slim flight attendant opened a side door, and Asian Pacific Consortium Regional Manager Avery Hsiang strode down the waiting stairs and stood before a Dawson-Hull corporate security detail.

One of the guards, a lean, hard-faced man in a midnight blue suit, approached Avery and bowed. "Director MacKinnon appreciates you coming on such short notice, Mr. Hsiang. Because of the urgency of the situation, he is unable to greet you personally, but if you'll come with me, sir, he's expecting you in the third-floor conference room."

Avery Hsiang didn't bother to answer the man. After all, he was only a guard dog. Avery frowned and waved for the man to proceed. As he followed, the rest of the security team fell in step on either side of Avery and escorted him up to the main house.

Euro-Cybernetics Integrated Facility, Toulouse France. 3:19 a.m. Same night.

Crouched outside the light cone of a walkway lamp, I could make out the nameplate beside the door of our next target. *Dr. Eric Drexler Building. Research Labs 3-5.*

"That's it," Tam nodded.

"End of the rainbow, eh?"

"'That's what the brief says." Tam tapped his data pad. "D-Wing. Secure area. The N3 is somewhere in there."

"And all we have to do is find it. Which, by the way... what exactly does a Nanotech Neural Network look like again?" I whispered.

"Hmmm," Tam's helmeted head turned back toward the building.

"You don't know, do you?"

"It's a top secret prototype, Jace. That data's not in these files. You expect a picture?"

"A description would be nice," I said. "Just so we don't nick someone's PS9 by mistake."

"The mission brief only says it's in D-Wing. I'm hoping it'll be obvious. Sort of a, *'we'll know it when we see it'* thing," he shrugged.

"Couldn't make it too easy, right? OK, Einstein, next question. How are we getting in?"

"Now *that* I can answer." He pointed up to the roof where a layered jumble of HVAC and atmosphere control units squatted together. "Maintenance panels are unlocked, not wired into the alarms. Schematics show the ductwork will get us close to the restricted area. Then all Poet9 has to do is crack the doors."

I checked the ammo count in my Blizzard. "You know it's going to change everything."

"What is?" Tam asked.

"Working nanotech, especially cyber-ware. Poet9's brain box makes him what, twenty times faster than your average console jockey?"

"Devante's faster than that."

"Yeah, yeah. But this could make someone a hundred times faster than him. It's inside the brain, direct processing at synaptic speeds. No more electronics. Grafted hackers like Poet will be dinosaurs. Once Asian Pacific gets their hands on it, they can write their own ticket. They'll be the *mal hombre* of their own comic book."

Tam turned back to me. "If this technology is really in there, and it really works, then yes, it'll put Tokyo light years ahead of everybody." He checked his data pad again. "Which is why Tam Song and Associates is getting large money for this run... Speaking of which, you ready to get back to work here? The patrol is supposed to stroll along any minute."

"Sir, yes, sir!" I threw him a mock salute as we rose to our feet. "Ready to make history, sir."

"Jerk. You'll thank me when we're on the beach in Cancun." We ran towards one of the brick brown walls and activated the Gecko pads on our suits. It took us all of six seconds to get onto the roof.

The security patrol passed beneath us two minutes later. Tam and I watched the sensor lights blink steadily on the hulking sentry 'bot as it shuffled by. The guard accompanying it kept his eyes glued on the Cerberus' displays. He never even glanced up. Tam and I were up and moving as soon as they went around the far corner of the building. In a few quick motions, we levered the panel aside and slid into the interior gloom of the maintenance space.

Tam called on his helmet's radio. "Poet? We're in. Give us a few minutes to secure the hall into D-Wing. Once I call, I'll need you most Rikki Tik to override the doors. Clear?"

"Loud and clear, boss. I'm going to set some mines. Pop goes the weasel on these 'Glom *bastardos* if they come running, eh?" Poet's voice crackled back.

"No, leave the mines. That's what the Triplets are for, remember? You want to do something, drop back in their net and double-check for surprises. Tam out."

A grunt and a double click cut the link. Tam looked over at me and shook his head.

"Hey, at least he tries," I said.

"At least he's good on the Grid." Tam tapped his data pad again. "Let's move."

We fast-crawled through the narrow space toward D-Wing following ceiling struts laden with cable bundles and vent ducts. My palms were still itching, so I kept switching between the drone feed over the facility and the building blueprints on my visor H.U.D. So far we were still clear.

Poet9's data hack back in the guard station put two badges at the only junction leading into the Research lab. The third was making rounds checking doors. All we had to do was cross them out, grab this thing, and go.

Hot damn—maybe I'm wrong, I thought. This run really might be dirty easy money.

Light filtered up through the grate into the cramped darkness as we approached the point marked on our displays. A quick drop, then eighteen meters of hallway would bring us into the only entrance to the secure labs. If there was trouble, here's where it would be waiting.

On cue, Poet9's voice whispered in our ears. "Problem."

"What?" Tam hissed back.

"Sorry, boss, I just found it. Security logs here mention a bio-ware link in that zone. A mobile one. I'm guessing the lead guard on each shift is wet wired to the alarm system. Probably linked to his heartbeat, or brainwaves. Maybe coded to his RFID chip. Either way, that's pretty smart for the 'Glom."

"And your point is?" Tam asked acidly.

"My point is that the guy is constantly monitored. He goes offline, as in "dies", it initiates a total lockdown. Then every drone and clone within fifty klicks will be coming to the party on full auto. You two are gonna have to find him, and keep him alive at all costs."

"Great. Just. Great," Tam said.

We lifted the grate and dropped down onto the hall carpet.

Dawson-Hull Estates – London Metro Sector, England. New European Union. 3:37 a.m.

Avery Hsiang caught himself staring at his reflection in the window across the room. He had what most Westerners called a "Laughing Buddha face": full, round and sincere, with thick black hair sprinkled with gray—the congenial features of a typecast Asian grandfather. When he was younger, he'd hated his appearance. Now he used it to whatever advantage he could.

He realized the man across the table had stopped speaking. Avery looked up, leaned forward slightly and put a wan smile on that face. "We've come full circle, again, Mr. MacKinnon." He shook his head slowly. "I flew here because you demanded an emergency meeting in the middle of the night. You invoked confidential protocols and the communiqué stated this crisis affected both our companies. Now all you do is stand there and vent preposterous accusations. How many times must I repeat myself? Asian Pacific Consortium denies any complicity in tonight's intrusion into your London facility. It's quite simple."

Jackson MacKinnon was Avery Hsiang's opposite: a trim, almost lean, elderly man with a fine featured face and pale ice blue eyes. He was Dawson-Hull's UK District Manager, as well as their Assistant Secretary of the Exchequer, and although his voice was low and even, his ears were red beneath his impeccable white hair. "Our sources indicate those mercenaries were associated with your company. As I understand it, they have previously been in your employ on several occasions. It is obvious—"

"It is obvious," Avery interrupted, "that your *sources* confirm what you wish to hear. I suggest your security division is anxious to shift scrutiny away from a serious lapse in vigilance." He leaned back, adopting his most reasonable tone. "Why accuse Asian Pacific? Our companies have shared several profitable ventures in the past. What of the Americans? Your successes in their Argentinean markets must offend them. You know how territorial they are. Perhaps this clumsy burgling is their way of lashing out."

Avery smoothed down the puckered silk of his jacket sleeve. "From your description, the attempt seems rather amateur. Your security services aren't even sure of the extent of the systems breech." Avery let his gaze travel over the rich wood paneled walls of the conference room, and he conjured a mildly irritated look on his face.

"The *attempt*," Jackson MacKinnon bit off the word, "was carried out by a highly skilled freelance outfit, Mr. Hsiang. Their equipment was far too sophisticated for simple shoplifters. Most damning of all, their ability to penetrate that far inside our facility so rapidly betrays an uncomfortable level of privileged intelligence."

Avery raised his thick hands toward his rival."Betrayal might well be the issue here. But I suggest you look to your own house before casting aspersions on the Consortium." He paused. "You haven't even told me what type of data was compromised. Is there something that directly concerned Asian Pacific? If so, do you require our assistance? These thieves, these spies... whatever they were... you stated they'd all been killed, am I correct?"

Avery knew full well the first mercenary team had been killed. His secretary had confirmed it. He'd demanded a totally sterile operation, and Avery was assured not one shred of tissue or scrap of equipment could implicate his office. Jackson MacKinnon and the Dawson-Hull Conglomerate had nothing but a ransacked database, four dead mercenary contractors, and empty allegations.

Outwardly, Avery looked patiently at his frayed counterpart, who could only glare back. Inwardly his mind leapt. His agent had been telling the truth: the prototype must be real. Otherwise, why would Dawson-Hull react so swiftly?

He is scared, Avery thought. *Jackson is scared someone is after the Nanotech Neural Network.* He glanced down at the stark face of his Movado. *In fact, someone is. The second phase of the operation should be underway right now.*

Jackson MacKinnon made a noncommittal noise in his throat. Avery responded with smile and continued. "Well then, if there is no direct threat, then perhaps this may be of some consolation: I promise, first thing in the morning, to relay news of this incident to the appropriate departments at Tokyo Head Office. I'm confident our directors stand ready to render all possible assistance."

Jackson rose to his feet, signaling the meeting was at an end. "Mr. Hsiang, our investigators are going to sift through every speck of evidence. Forensics experts arrive from Brussels tomorrow, and the London Board has granted me full authority in this case." He snapped his briefcase shut. "When we find the perpetrators, Avery, reprisals will be severe." He let that hang in the air over the polished table.

Avery Hsiang nodded sagely and proffered another sad smile. "I trust your forensics teams are a bit more accurate than your *sources*, Jackson. Again, speaking on behalf of the Consortium, I would remind you Asian Pacific prides itself on the skill and dedication that render such dishonorable practices unnecessary. However, we sympathize with your dilemma and fully support you in apprehending these criminals. The problem of illegals is a concern for every corporation."

Avery stood up as well. "Now, if you'll excuse me. It's been a long night." He picked his briefcase up from the floor. After another angry glare from the Dawson-Hull manager, he left the conference room.

Only when Regional Manager Avery Hsiang was back in his Lear shuttle feeling the steady thrum of twin engines through the back of his chair did he permit himself another smile. But this was a different smile. He leaned forward and hit one of the buttons on the armrest.

"Have the second team of mercenaries reported in yet?"

"Negative, Mr. Hsiang." The reply came from the tiny speaker near his hand. "The flier's transponder is inactive. They must still be inside the compound."

"I want to know the instant they're airborne. Remind Colonel Otsu he is to personally attend the rendezvous and confirm delivery." Avery paused, his eyes tightening, "Once he's in receipt of the item, he is to settle the contract with them. Understood?"

"Yes, sir. Absolutely."

Avery cut the secure channel without another word and closed his eye, freezing the moments. Whoever said ambition was the last infirmity of noble minds was a fool. He savored it on the tip of his tongue. This was like fine wine, like voltage, like sex. This would change everything.

Nine months before, one of his intelligence agents had come to him with rumors about the N3, mere hints sifted from snooping in the Dawson-Hull data stream. Avery was incredulous at first. Complex nanotech applications were fatal to human beings. Yet, as implausible as such technology was, clues about the prototype persisted. The English were trying to conceal something and the information remained so credibly elusive, so tantalizingly plausible, Avery was intrigued.

Weeks went by, and Avery's informants inside Dawson-Hull insisted something huge was indeed moving in the undercurrents of the British multinational. Evidence kept trickling in. So Avery watched, and waited, and began compiling all the data into a personal file. Then, after the third agent confirmed Dawson-Hull's activity at a Toulouse biotech facility, a plan brushed against his mind—barely tangible strands as delicate and intricate as a spider web.

The annual Directors' Assembly had been scheduled the following month in Tokyo.

On the agenda was a discussion of potential new Board members.

Initial candidates were selected from high performing regional management.

Operational neural nanotechnology would be worth billions, if not trillions of dollars.

The next day, Regional Manager Avery Hsiang made a dangerous decision. He withheld the intelligence regarding the device from Tokyo Head Office, encrypted his files, and contracted the finest freelance operatives available. He would acquire the prototype on his own.

From that day forward, he began siphoning off funds from his office accounts as well as his personal fortune to set things in motion. An operation like this jeopardized his career and brought him to the brink of personal financial ruin, but he kept reminding himself that *crisis* and *opportunity* were the same word. And this opportunity demanded to be seized.

The plan was all his own: its risks, and its rewards. And right now, in this moment, it was coming together. He was on the cusp of the greatest corporate espionage coup in a century, and the rewards would be his alone. Avery watched the landscape slide by in the early morning darkness.

Jackson MacKinnon stood at the window as Avery Hsiang's shuttle rose into the air on tiny daggers of hot blue flame. No sound carried through the thick insulated glass, and its sleek form paused above the trees like a dark specter. Then the thrusters swiveled, the main engines flared, and it darted off into the sky. Jackson considered the receding glow of the Lear's engines until the night swallowed them up. For several moments, everything was still and silent. Then he spoke over his shoulder to the blue-suited security officer. "I'm ordering a full lockdown: offices, factories, all corporate properties. Everything. I'll notify the Board, of course, but I want all our security forces on high alert. Do you understand?"

"Yes, sir. Immediately." The man turned to leave.

"Sergeant..." The man stopped. "Order two Rapid Response units to the ECI facility in Toulouse. Bureau Three, S.D. platoons."

"Sir?"

Jackson turned to face the man and repeated his orders tersely. "I said I want two Rapid Response units. At the ECI Labs. In Toulouse. Now. I want Major Jessa Eames to lead them personally. Tell her they're to seal the facility, but I'll brief her en route with the particulars."

"Yes, sir. Immediately, sir."

MacKinnon turned back to his reflection in the huge glass window and stood perfectly still.

CHAPTER FIVE

LIVE WIRED

Euro-Cybernetics Integrated Facility, Toulouse, France. 3:43 a.m.
Same night.

The clock was ticking, so Tam and I moved fast down the halls with our Mitsu suits humming at full power. Drifts of static, we ghosted under camera domes, over laser tripwires, until we hit the entrance to the D-Wing lab. No alarms sounded.

Coming around the last corner, the hall opened up into a reception room with a huge desk and tastefully sterile waiting area. Two big interlocking steel doors set in the far wall led to the lab itself. Poet9 had radioed that the bio-ware would show up as a hot spot in the human body, so we'd switched our visors to thermal view. We needed to ID the wet-wired guard as fast as possible. The two soldiers in the lobby read negative. Silenced headshots left them slumped in their chairs, cooling to room temperature. Tam and I then switched our visors back to normal view and went prowling for our live-wired friend.

We found him in the bathroom of all places. Tam kicked in the stall door and dragged him out zip-cuffed and gagged. Another vet, his face had old splash scarring from an acid burst, but it is kind of hard to look intimidating with your pants around your ankles. He thrashed around and growled, trying to play hard core and break free. After a couple of attempted headbutts, I chopped him on the shoulders and yanked his head close to my helmet. "You play nice, you'll be alive when this is over…" He could finish the sentence on his own. Not that it was much comfort: our run was definitely not good for his long-term career plans, but he quieted down. At least until he spotted his two friends in the lobby. He threw himself toward the desk panel trying to trip the alarm. I kicked his legs out and sat on him while Tam called Poet9 on the radio.

"OK, now we got the wired guy, but he wants to be a hero. You sure we have to keep him alive?"

I looked down and saw him biting on the gag, so I bounced his head off the floor. He stopped.

"Just until we're on our way," Poet9's voice came back.

Seven minutes later, the little Mexican dropped in from the ceiling vent and went to work on their intranet. Another fifty-eight seconds and he'd burned through the security grid like a plasma torch. He grunted when the vault-like doors hissed open. "Stupid executives—always six months behind."

We all went in. Poet9 ran point, the big black Walther bobbing in an outstretched two-hand grip, while Tam and I frog-marched the guard between us. Private Ugly started sweating the moment we crossed the threshold, his eyes wide above the gag. I saw the dim notion of bolting or going limp flit behind them, but apparently, he still had enough functioning brain cells to realize we weren't in the mood for more half-assed escape attempts or stall tactics.

Twenty meters down the hall, we entered a large room with sharp white walls, lights, glass and chrome, alive with the purr of dozing electronics. It was the main lab. Even through the helmet filters, I tasted fuzzy ozone on my tongue and the backwash of bouncing signals.

"This must be the place, right?" I asked.

Poet9 approached one of the computer terminals and unzipped his cables. "Ho, nothing gets by you."

"Well I'm clever like that."

"Head of the class, I bet. Here, take this." He slung a black nylon pack off his back and tossed it toward Tam. "You're looking for a cold safe, a minivault, even a stasis canister. Nanotech can't be that big, right? I'll sift their daily logs and see if I can find something." He stopped, his long skinny fingers poised over the workstation."But when you find it, let me at it first. Don't go fondling it until I've looked it over, *que*?"

He didn't wait for us to answer, just plugged in his leads and sent his fingers staccato on the keyboard. As his eyes glazed over, Tam and I started combing the main room, checking every desk, locker, closet and container we could find. I dragged the guard with me, hoping for some kind of reaction as we made a circuit around the room, but just he seethed, all surly and tight. When we came back around to Poet9, I plopped him in a stray chair and stood behind him with my hand on his shoulder. "Stay."

"Jace," Tam called through the helmet radio."This seem easy to you?"

I was silent for a second. "Ummm… yeah, now that you mention it. Security feels wrong for cutting-edge tech. I mean, the perimeter's tight, there's modded guards, even the bio-alarm. But there're no turrets, not even motion sensors past the big doors. You thinking we're in the wrong place? Dawson-Hull move it somewhere else?"

"The intel package said D-H is going public in two weeks. The N3 is here for the shave and tweak stage. They want to work out the kinks for the big debut."

"So what's wrong with this picture?"

"Dunno yet. But seeing as we're here…" he said.

"…we might as see what we can find." I finished.

Poet9's head jerked up. "I have something! Cyber-activity in that room." The bulky muzzle of his Walther 11 pointed at a set of double doors on the west wall. "In there."

Tam brought his Tavor 24 rifle up. "Another security guard?"

"Not supposed to be," Poet9 said.

I yanked the guard to his feet, and with Tam leading the way, the four of us slipped through the doors into an observation room. There were desks full of screens and idling computer equipment, their yellow lights winking at us. A large medical station was tucked into a corner, recessed pin lights focused on its red cross, bright and clear. On the right, a metal staircase led down into the gloom of a lower floor, and directly in front of us a row of large glass panels angled out and away, overlooking the darkened floor below. I hung back, holding the guard as Tam and Poet9 moved forward and peered through the glass.

"I saw you," a voice said. It came from the speakers at one of the computer station. All of us froze.

"You tried to be sneaky, but I saw you," the speakers sounded again. Poet9 twitched his pistol up. Tam tensed.

"I saw one of you in the net too. You're fast, a lot faster than the others around here. I tried to show them how to improve the security, but they wouldn't listen," the voice continued.

Poet9 leaned closer and stared down through the glass. "*Virgen Maria, Madre de Dios!* Someone's down there."

"I'll turn on the lights if you want. Here." The area below suddenly flickered to life.

Poet9 brought up his magnum, but Tam put a hand on his shoulder. I pushed the guard forward in the chair and looked through the glass myself.

The room below us was plain, like an army barracks. Tan colored, with a bed in the corner, drawers in one wall, and several items scattered on a faded red rug. In the center of the floor was a large u-shaped desk with a single workstation and three oversize screens. And someone was sitting at it.

"A kid," I heard Tam whisper in my helmet. "There's a kid down there."

Poet9 craned his neck, scrutinizing the scene. Tam started down the stairs. My grip locked on the guard's shoulder and I could feel the Blizzard's stock digging into my forearm.

It was a boy. No more than nine, maybe ten, years old, he was dark-skinned with cropped black cut hair and a small round face. He was dressed in khaki coveralls and sitting at the computer looking up at us with clear, green eyes that jumped out at me even from a distance. He swiveled in his seat as Tam came out onto the floor. "What do you want?"

"Are you the only one here?" Tam asked, as he walked slowly toward the boy.

"Right now I am. Dr. Evans and Dr. Heinrich are here with their staff in the daytime. Sometimes they stay late and have me do things with the computers, but that's been less and less lately. I couldn't sleep though, that's how come I saw you."

"What's your name?" Tam was halfway across the room.

"Gibson. Who are you?"

"That's not important right now. Gibson, what do you mean 'you saw us'? When?" Tam was nearly at the desk now.

"On the security grid. I told you, I was awake, so I logged into the facility intranet to watch through the cameras. That's when I saw you, sort of. The air was shimmering, so I got curious and followed the shimmers. Now you're here." He paused, looked at one of the screens, then back at Tam. "You killed those two men. Why?"

Poet9 broke in over the radio link. "Hate to interrupt, but we've got a job to do. And... only eight minutes to do it in. Does he know where they keep it or not?"

Tam was at the computer now, his gloved hand on the edge of the desktop. He stood there looking down at the boy.

Gibson just sat there unafraid and looked up into the stealth suit's matte black visor. "Look at him," Tam spoke over the radio. "Look at him, Poet."

"What? I see a kid. I want hardware. Just put him to sleep, and let's *vámonos*."

"No. Look at his head," Tam said.

I stepped forward, gripping the guard until he winced, and cranked up the amplification on my visor. There, on the back of the boy's neck, just at the base, was a vat-tat: a gene series shotcode imprint. The kid was a clone. And right next to it, a single thin black cybernetic jack snaked up from the computer terminal and disappeared behind his left ear.

"Could you turn off the lights for me, Gibson?" Tam asked.

"Sure."

The lights went out. The room snapped right back to gloom and shadow, but it took another second for the realization to hit me.

"I think I just found the N3," Tam said.

And right then, Cottontail's voice broke in over the radio channel.

"We have contact."

"What?" Tam said.

And a whole lot of unpleasantness came crashing in at once.

Outside on the E.C.I. Facility grounds. 3:45 a.m.

C.U. 5901 and C.U. 5902 walked along the fence at a brisk, steady pace. C.U. 5905 lagged back in the darkness, shifting twenty left to right to cover their flanks. It was the simplest patrol pattern, one of the first the Triplets had ever learned, but the master/leader had ordered them to impersonate the enemy guards and they always did their best for him. 5901 and 5902 hoped this was close to the perimeter security procedure, sloppy though it was. Back in Africa, anything this careless would have earned a disciplinary beating. A second time and they'd have been shot where they stood. Still, the master/leader ordered it, and eager to please, the Triplets loped on, hoping they looked like security guards on patrol.

They were halfway back to the labs when the facility's emergency signal went off. Their suits' scanners grabbed it from the campus security frequency: a braying alert in their headsets. Someone had tripped the alarm. Nothing visible changed around them, no sounds erupted, no lights started flashing, but something shivered in the air and burst. 01 and 02 froze mid-step and brought their rifles to the ready. C.U. 5905 stopped, looked up and lifted his visor, sniffing the wind. He radioed Tam.

"We have contact."

"What?"

The assault carrier burst out of the night sky, engines screaming in rage. A massive wall of air and sound and steel rolled over the Triplets. Landing gear and ramps unfolded like giant wasp legs, and it started disgorging figures from a back ramp while it was still in midair. The cyclone haze of heat and matter rose up under the downdraft of the turbines, rendering enhanced vision impossible. Without a word, the three of them knelt and fired into the swirling mass anyway. Unable to distinguish targets, they simply fired, anticipating a standard air/ground assault dispersal pattern, and men started dying.

The boxy carrier touched ground, bounced twice, and started to lift. In a blur, 5902 whipped the Balor-3 rocket launcher off his back and fired through the open drop ramp. There was a sharp crack, a flash within. The transport flinched, then flipped sideways out of the air onto the concrete plaza and exploded.

Without a word, the Triplets switched out new magazines, rose up and shifted right, firing with each step. Like breathing, like a heartbeat, a battle pulse coded in every cell of their bodies propelled them, a howling core emergent and savage in its clarity. Fire move, fire move, fire move, again. The surviving armored troopers ducked and scuttled frantically like black beetles against the white inferno backdrop, one falling with every shot. Fire move, fire move, fire move. Stop.

There were no more.

"Contact end. Engagement finished. Orders?" C.U. 5905 breathed out to Tam.

"Head to the rally point and cover for exfil. We're coming out."

"Acknowledged." The three clone soldiers turned and ran together back across the plaza, flames towering in the sky behind them, black phantoms loosed fluid and vicious into the night.

I hit Ugly at the base of the neck, and he dropped like a sack of rags. Poet9 ran to a terminal and speed-jacked in. "Shitshitshit—we're busted! Base net just bloomed to full alert. Gimme a second. I'll dump some Luna-C in their system." He fished a thumb drive full of custom virals from a pocket and slotted it into the machine, his fingers flying across the keys.

"No time. No time!" Tam was yelling. He yanked out the boy's cable, snatched him up like a doll, and took the stairs in three bounds. I span and sighted the double doors behind us, half-expecting a Cerberus 'bot to shatter through right then.

I turned back to Poet9. He staggered as he slammed through the net, eyes rolling back to white. His fingers blurred over the deck as he hot-loaded malware into their security grid. Blood trickled from his nose. "I'm opening exterior doors... mimic a breach at their north gate too," he gurgled.

He swayed again, his body reeling under the data torrent in his brain. Blood was dripping onto the clean white tile floor now. Tam motioned to me, and I caught Poet9 under my arm.

"Wish you'd let me... drop those spider mines now. I'm. Almost done. There." His finger slammed the final key as I pulled his leads and turned, half dragging him toward the door. Suddenly the muffled roar of a massive blast shook through the walls. I dialed up a tactical map on my visor. Three dots for the Triplets were still blinking green and moving fast. A tangle of red ones that weren't there before were disappearing faster.

"Surprise, surprise," I said.

Tam chuckled. "Shoot and scoot, baby. Shoot and scoot."

We ran outside.

CHAPTER SIX

STARTLED RAVENS

In the air over the E.C.I Facility, Toulouse. Dawson-Hull Conglomerate Special Deployment Detachment Team Two. 4:01 a.m.

"**M**ajor! Wraith One is down. I repeat: Wraith One is down."

Major Jessa Eames turned in the cockpit and snarled, "Down? What do you mean *down*? How *in hell* could they be down?"

The co-pilot swallowed. "Something just plucked 'em out of the sky. Looked like a portable SAM—a Stinger 3 or Balor. Over there." He jerked a thumb to his right, and Major Eames bent to look out the starboard view port. The smashed heap of the other assault transport was blazing like a beacon down on the central plaza.

"How did these bastards get Balors? We don't even have them." She savaged the tactical vest tighter around her chest. "You got any targets yet?"

"Negative," the co-pilot responded. "We detected three recon drones and dispatched hunters. Scans around Wraith 1 are fragged from the wreck, but we're sweeping the south quadrant on all frequencies. Wait! Jesus..." he stared at one of his screens. "I... both... both squads from Wraith One are gone too!"

"What?"

"ID chips for squads Charlie and Delta are offline. They're dead, ma'am."

"Goddamn it! MacKinnon dumps us neck deep in shit and ties our hands." She clapped the pilot on the shoulder. "Vector away and approach from the south side. Tell both Fury gunships to stay with us, but they're to *hold fire!* Weapons are *not* cleared hot. Confirm?"

"Confirmed, Major. Furies in formation—northeast approach. Weapons are not cleared hot at this time," the pilot drawled back at her.

"And tell Base Security to wake the hell up!" She ground her teeth as the transport banked, gripping the steel rim on the pilots' seatbacks to steady herself. *Someone is going to pay for this*, she fumed.

E.C.I Facility, Toulouse, France. On the ground.

The four of us slipped through a side door into a wide alley cluttered with crates and oil drums. I was on point, Tam was still carrying the kid under his arm, and Poet9 had recovered enough to be waving his big Walther around again. The crackle and roar of flames rolled through the night, and the mangled heap of a burning assault transport was neatly framed in the far end of the passage. We stopped and stared.

"Ooooh, Kodak moment," Poet9 said. "Killer bunnies have been busy."

Rifle fire barked out, chased by the rapid *crumps* of bursting spider mines.

"Still are," Tam said.

I flipped to the drone feed: one was static hiss, another the spastic blur of evasive maneuvers. The third, lacking new orders, apparently defaulted to circling the downed transport, panning for signs of life. I looked at Tam and pointed to the blazing wreck. "I'm sure they weren't alone. More company's right behind them… if they aren't already here. Time to color us gone."

"So much for being coy," Tam said. "Our ride out is a Gaki Swiftship. APAC stashed one three klicks east. We're supposed to rendezvous on the coast in forty minutes."

"Right now, I'll settle for anywhere but here," I said.

"Roger that," Tam replied. "No matter where we end up, I'm sure Asian Pacific will come for us. For him," he motioned to the boy. Tam accessed our squad command net. "I'm marking Rally Point Three on everyone's H.U.D. Triplets are close enough to secure it."

I called up the mini map on my visor display and found a yellow square winking near a corner of the east wall. A thin blue line marked the shortest route there. I nodded at Tam and moved into point position. We'd made it three steps before a Cerberus 'bot heaved around the corner, its hunchback form filling the walkway. The sensor stalks on its wedge-shaped head spun, the lenses extending, dilating, in an accusation of whirrs and clicks. Then they locked rigid, pointing right at us, and shoulder-mounted halogens snapped on with a blinding *thunk*.

In the air

Major Eames turned and faced the transport's rear compartment. Two full combat teams stretched away in the seat webbing on both sides of its armored bay, straining like dogs on the leash. Emergency lighting bathed everything the color of blood.

"All right, listen up," she shouted over the roar of the engines. "Wraith One just got splashed, so this situation is now officially Alpha Mike Foxtrot.

Problem is there's an asset down there that's tier *ultra*—high as it gets. The facility's already been breached, and rumor is someone's here to snatch him. We're not sure they have him yet, but he's the reason we live and breathe. I've forwarded his image to your tactical comps. Engrave it in your brains."

She paused and swept her gaze over every soldier. "I have no idea who he is, but we put a single bruise on him, we're hosed. Secretary MacKinnon himself waved me and spelled it out. Our first order of business is to lock the place down fast and find him. If you spot him with hostiles, it's non-lethal only. I repeat, non-lethal only. Understood?"

"Yes, ma'am," the answer came back.

She gave a curt nod. "Time to embrace the suck, gentlemen. We drop in five." Turning back to the co-pilot, she snapped. "Where is Base Security?"

On the ground

"You are in violation. Remain where you are. Security personnel will arrive shortly."

This blared out of the Cerberus' chest speaker in a rapid succession of Anglo, Spanish, and Mandarin. I guess anyone speaking Arabic or Hindi was pretty well screwed. Not that you couldn't figure out what six gaping barrels of side-mounted rotary chain gun were saying. Or the tangle web sprayer on the steel-fingered mauler arm. Weighing half a ton, and three meters tall, Cerberus security robots were as subtle as a brick through your living room window. I fingered an EMP on my belt, but between our suits and Poet9, it was a dumb idea. We were too close. An electromagnetic pulse could snow-blind our Mitsu suits and fry Poet9's brain box. Not good options.

"Now would be a really good time for the Triplets, I muttered. Eyestalks swiveled my way. Tam moved one step backward.

"What are you doing?" Poet hissed.

The Cerberus turned on Poet9 now, reacting to the sound of his voice. The recording cycled again, and Tam used the opportunity to take another step. The Cerberus seemed to hesitate. "Playing our only card right now," Tam said. "I deployed with 'bots in Seoul during Pacification." His voice came over our helmet radios, sounding low and steady. He was still holding Gibson, and the Cerberus weapon mounts were tracking him.

"Use of non-lethal restraint is authorized. Remain where you are. Security personnel will arrive shortly."

"That's all I wanted to know." Tam took two more steps then froze. "This'll have to do. Poet, Jace… get ready to run. Jace, limpet an EMP on this heap when I say. I'll be right behind you."

"Are you *muy loco*?" Poet grew furious nervous, dancing from side to side. "*Fuera de su mente?*"

Tam risked another step to one side. "Ready…" The machine shifted after him, extending its servo-arm into firing position. The mantra sounded again.

"Okaaaay," I said.

"Steady…" Tam was leaning sideways, toward the wall, keeping Gibson in sight, but back and firmly under his arm. Maybe it was because of the boy, but the Cerberus' programming seemed to have discarded Poet9 and me as low priority targets. The robot was following Tam's every move. My hand drifted down to my belt and unclipped the charge.

"Oh shit…" Poet9 said.

"*Now!*"

Too many moving things at once...

I snapped the grenade out with one hand and grabbed Poet9 with the other. As the EMP arced through the air, I started running, dragging him with me. I was trying to get both of us out of blast radius before it popped. But Poet was too astonished to think, let alone move. I saw the grenade stick fast next to the speaker grill on the robot's chest, and Tam, cradling the boy, dove behind a stack of crates. The robot's sensors blinked, and it lumbered after them.

As I turned away, the tangle web launcher belched wetly. I managed a few more steps, pulling Poet9 along, before the EMP went off. There was a loud crackling sound, and a sharp blue flash scrambled my display. Poet9 cried out, staggered and fell. I went down with him, skidding on the duracrete.

I lay there for several seconds too long, dazed, expecting a piston leg to stomp my spine into the pavement. Finally, I shook my head to clear it and looked around. Poet9 lay next to me, tangled and unmoving. His visor was up and there was blood seeping out of his ear. A cold feeling dropped into my stomach.

"Jace." Tam's voice.

I gritted my teeth and rolled over. Back down the alley, Tam appeared with Gibson under one arm. There were masses of stringy adhesive clotted all over the crates, draped like green-glow vomit. The Cerberus was motionless at the end of the alley; a sizzle of little sparks witching across its slumped chassis.

Right then, its handler peered around the corner of the building looking for his robot. He saw us instead, and his rifle came up to the ready. Tam fired his Tavor 24 twice. The guard dropped. Gibson yelped, clutching his ears at the sharp sound. Poor kid looked on the verge of losing it.

Tam pointed at Poet9. "Grab him. We need to move."

I didn't look. I didn't think. I reached out and slung Poet9 over my shoulders. He wasn't moving.

I need to check him. I need to check Devante. Why do bodies always feel lighter, like a sack of sticks? Even in armor.

My emotions threatened to hemorrhage, but I clamped down hard. We didn't have time for that. I chinned the displays in my helmet and took off after Tam. The visuals flickered back, skittish and blurred. My meters climbed sluggishly, critical reds edging into orange before they stopped.

My trouble had dropped in after all, quick and brutal.

As we jogged across the broken ground, I heard breathing in my headset. Tam was angry, coiled tight. Good training locked everything down, brought it to a single white-hot point. Stay focused, stay alive.

"Rally point Three," Tam spoke.

"Acknowledged. Securing Rally Point Three." Cottontail answered.

In the air

"Major," the co-pilot called out."Base Security is all bunched up at the north gate."

"What are they doing there?" Major Eames said. "They corner the intruders?"

"Scans are up, but no signs yet."

"Take us there." she ordered.

Suddenly the co-pilot called out. "Wait... I've got a thermal. A single target. It's small, heading toward the east wall. Christ, I've got signal bounce too. I'm reading multiple stealth shimmers in the same vicinity moving fast. Looks like they're running, ma'am."

"Forget the north gate. Bring us around. Go, Go, Go!" Major Eames yelled back into the troop compartment. "We got 'em. Get ready."

The pilot yanked the flying yoke and the big transport banked hard. Jessa Eames' thin features went taut as the view outside the windscreen pitched sideways. She set her jaw, leaned into it, and held on.

On the ground

The Triplets met us at the eastern perimeter wall. Tam handed Gibson off to Mopsy. The kid was visibly shaking now, but he didn't utter a sound. He simply watched, those bright eyes absorbing everything. He stared at me and Poet9 for what seemed like a long time before Mopsy wrapped his arms around his small figure and huddled over him. Tam set det-cord on a vertical seam in the concrete wall. Some desultory fire strayed our way, but it slunk back, chased away by Flopsy and Cottontail's replies. Tam stuck the last charge in place and set the timer.

"Ninety seconds."

He ran back and knelt beside me. He stole a glance at Poet9's form draped on my shoulders, and I heard breathing again. I gripped Devante tighter and counted the seconds down in my head, trying to beat off the fear that stalked me like a jackal. At fifty-seven seconds, the deafening shriek of turbines swelled around us. An assault transport, a large C-class Wraith, flanked by two black gunships, plunged down at us.

Tam stood and pointed. "Drop them."

In the air

"I got them, Major," the co-pilot exulted. "Ninety meters dead ahead. Looks like six probable suits and one civilian. They're stationary... shit! I've got missile locks." He slammed a series of buttons on his instrument panel. "Hostile launch! Hostile launch!" he screamed at the pilot. "Two trails. Evasive. Evasive!"

Major Eames was thrown back into the troop compartment as the world wrenched under her feet. Alarms erupted, shrill and frenzied, a counterpoint to the howling engines as the blocky transport thrashed, trying to sidestep the two rockets. The Fury gunships panicked, jinking up and away, popping bright clouds of flares and chaff. One of the rockets hesitated then looped into a sizzling cluster of flash and foil. The second doggedly followed the transport in its turn and burrowed in the starboard turbine. Jessa Eames heard a bang then a snap. The sound of pieces shredding away.

"We're hit! We're hit! Wraith Two is hit! We're going down!"

The transport slewed and started spinning. The major slid across the steel decking, everything blurring faster and faster around her until the transport slammed flat into the ground. Pain and darkness spiked into her and everything stopped. Overhead, the two gunships flitted back and forth like startled ravens.

On the ground

Flopsy and Cottontail rose to their feet, and a split second later two Balor rockets hissed up threads of fire. The aerial formation jumped apart. One rocket spiraled into a cluster of tinsel and heat, the other augured in and blew apart one of the Wraith's engines. The massive profile hung in the air, then gyrated off-center, spinning, spiraling downward until it hammered flat on the ground. Our charges blew at the same time and the ground shook like a wet dog.

We were up and moving before the rubble settled. Behind us, the gunships swarmed, confused and spiteful over the fallen carrier. We ran until we couldn't hear their furious buzzing anymore.

CHAPTER SEVEN

CRISIS AND COOPERATION

Three kilometers east of the E.C.I Facility, Toulouse, France.
4:47 a.m.

It was an advanced model sneakship: a Mk. 5 "Gaki", all low and sharp, and sexy. With its sinuous trademark twist of dull black carbon composites that enfolded two turbofan engines, the stealth jet was nestled in the clearing, sucking light and sound out of the air like a sliver of black hole. Kawasaki Aerospace had designed the first ones for covert incursions over the deeply paranoid People's Republic mainland. They were incredibly fast, nearly invisible to airspace defense grids, and best of all, capable of transporting commando teams. During the Taiwan Crisis in '35/36, the Taipei government used them to fend off advances from their cousins in the "Glorious Worker's Paradise". They worked quite well, until Gakis emblemed with little Red Stars and packed with North Korean mercenaries started showing up in their own night skies. It seemed someone in Tokyo saw the opportunity to make even more money. In fact, the first time I saw Tam, I was deployed with the 3rd North American Peacekeeping Unit, and he'd been dragging himself out of a downed PRC Mk.2 on a beach in Changhua.

Tam walked right up to this one and punched in an entry code on the lock pad. The hatch popped open, and the seven of us climbed in. Squeezing down the aisle, I laid Poet9 out on a back bench, and after I got his helmet and torso armor off, started searching for the first aid locker. There wasn't one.

I did find an old autodoc jammed in the back of one of the overheads. Setting it on the floor of the cabin, I dusted it off and flipped its dented top open. It was practically antique, but it powered up, and I started sticking sensors on his chest and head. Most of the leads were worn and bent, and several of the wires pulled right out of the side. I swore as the small screens blipped to life, willing them to read positive.

Tam was over my shoulder. "Is he…?"

"Breathing? Barely. Heart's weak. Cortical waves are barely rolling. Crap equipment like this, I can't tell what's going on. We need to get him to Doc."

Tam pursed his lips. "No time. We have to make delivery. APAC will get real nervous if we don't show. And I bet Dawson-Hull is going into full-blown panic mode, especially after the mess we left. They'll want the boy back something fierce."

"This is Poet9, Tam, not some meat shield we hired off the street. He could die," I said.

"I know who it is, Jace. But if APAC thinks we skipped out, they'll take *all* of us down. He's going to have to hold on. Make him comfortable and do what you—"

"Look at the read-outs!" my voice rose. "Look at this!" I held up one of the frayed cable ends. Gibson and the Triplets turned to stare. "This gear isn't even mil-spec. It's a refugee handout from India or the Pak five years ago. His gear might be *fused*, Tam. This is way over my head. Screw APAC, we need Doc Kalahani. Right now." I glanced furiously around the Gakis's sleek, lean cabin. "A four-hundred-million flier with no medical station: real asset prioritizing there. Miserable bastards."

Tam looked at Gibson then at Poet9's thin, brown features. They were drawn, waxy, and his breathing was broken and shallow. "All right, I'm listening. You got anything that resembles a plan?" he asked quietly.

"I can stabilize him, but we need to go to ground fast. Somewhere safe and close by; the Gaki doesn't have the legs to get us back to Belfast. Once we're under wraps, we call Doc and have him come to us. We can reschedule with the Japanese in the new location," I said.

"So where's close and safe?"

"Barcelona's the only place I can think of right now."

"Fuck," Tam sighed.

"What?"

"I don't want to deal with that on top of everything else."

"With what?"

"You know… religion."

"Jesus, Tam. They're not that bad, and you know it. It's close, and it's safe. We can trust Al and Carmen totally. You know that too."

It was several seconds before Tam responded. "Yeah, I do know that. Not like there's much of a choice either."

"Right," I said.

Tam looked at his watch. "OK. How fast can you weasel around the autopilot?"

"I can have us wheels up inside two minutes."

"OK, do it." Tam frowned. "We've been sitting here too long." I started up the narrow aisle.

"Jace…" he called out. I stopped and looked over my shoulder. "I'm going to bounce a message to APAC. I'll send it through Jaithirth back in Belfast."

"Hiding usually works better when people don't know where you are," I said.

He gave me a shrug. "I have to keep them in the loop. I won't mention Al and Carmen. Barcelona Metro Zone is big enough to hide in for a few days. I have to assure our employers all we're doing is changing the delivery time."

I didn't answer, just raised my hands and hurried toward the cockpit. At least I'd get to rip something apart, even if it was only the flight panel. Gibson's gaze followed me.

"I'm sorry about your friend," he said.

I halted mid-stride, something smart and tough on the tip of my tongue. I turned back and looked straight into those startling green eyes.

"Yeah. Me too," I said.

E.C.I. Facility. Toulouse, France. 5:38 a.m.

"Tell them to quit dicking around at the north gate, now, or I'll shoot every goddamn last one of them!" Major Eames shouted into the radio.

She grabbed the steep flank of the armored vehicle to steady herself. The sounds around her made her head pound more, and the world wouldn't stop wobbling. The left side of her face had ballooned up brown and purple from where she'd slammed onto the flight deck, and her lip was split. She was spitting blood every minute just to talk intelligibly.

She turned to the radio handset clenched in her other fist. "I said, where's my satellite cover? I need D-H Aerospace to skywatch everything inside two hundred klicks, even if it's goddamn seagulls. Ground civilian flights if you have to. We're cordoning off the facility now, but I'm telling you, that transponder echo was them. Get it done and patch Aerospace through to me."

When they found her in the wrecked transport, medics had insisted she remain stationary until they could check her out, but she'd pushed them away, climbed off the stretcher, vomited, and staggered off to find the base commander. It didn't matter that she felt like she'd been run over by a truck. "I don't have time for pain right now," she'd told them.

"I don't care," she shouted again. "My status? You tell Madrid the Dawson-Hull Conglomerate just invoked the Crisis and Cooperation Act. The Special Deployment Division is starting an investigation, and that means I'll be apprising them of *their* status until further notice." She paused and listened for a second, then growled. "My name is Major Eames of the D-H Corporate Security Services, and I'm in charge of this task force. And right now, you need to shut up and give me what I need."

She swallowed two pain-tabs, and spit out more blood. A SD lieutenant passed by. "Have Fury One and Two refuel and stay on station for a possible intercept. And find me some ground transport!" She looked back at the handset. "Why am I still talking with you? Get me my satellite cover. Now!" She slammed the unit back into the cradle and looked back at the lab building.

The glimmer of dawn was starting in the east, drawing pale, drained colors into the scene before her. The flames from the transports had been doused, and poison trees of brown smoke blossomed up into the air. Bodies were stretched out in front of her, a parade row of glossy rubber lumps on the black tarmac, their white identity tags troubled by the limp morning wind.

The facility had been breached, its security force neutralized, an Ultra level asset snatched, two assault carriers downed, and half her men had been killed.

She gritted her teeth against another wave of throbbing and rage. Whoever had done this just made first place on her shit list. It would be better if they shot themselves right now.

Over New European Union Airspace, 5:49 a.m.

Avery Hsiang leaned forward in his chair. "What do you mean, *vanished?*"

The voice of his secretary, Peter Kanang, came through the small speaker. "We tracked the jet's transponder as far as the Pyrenees, Mr. Hsiang, but lost it right before the mountains. They never showed up at the coast. It seems the autopilot malfunctioned, or they found a way to override it."

A sharp jolt of pain shot up Avery's neck into his clenched jaw. "Do you have any idea where they were headed?"

"Last heading indicated a south-east track. We received a message from their agent in Ireland that they're heading to the Barcelona Metropolitan Zone, sir. Do you want me to mobilize security services in pursuit?"

"No," Avery hissed. "Why would I want to advertise a covert operation by storming into Spain? How is it Colonel Otsu failed to plan for the very real prospect of treachery?"

"Sir, the colonel had no way of—"

"You are not salaried to make excuses, Mr. Kanang. I expect results for my money. And one minute ago you informed me a significant expenditure had vanished."

Avery let his words impact on the other end of the line before continuing. "I am gravely disappointed in Colonel Otsu's performance. Inform him he is to stand by until I have further instructions. Do you think you can carry out that task?" he asked.

"Yes, sir, Mr. Hsiang."

"Good. I expect this mercenary team's personnel files to be on my desk when I walk into my office. Everything we have on them."

Avery cut off the secure line without another word and stared out the Lear's view port. The shuttle was soaring through lowspace, and at this height, the bright crescent of the rising sun creased the blue black of the horizon, its brightness expanding over the curved earth. It was magnificent, but all Avery could see was his plan unraveling.

His mind was churned. The Director's Assembly convened six days from now. This one item would unlock his ascent to the height of the Consortium's leadership. If he brought functioning nanotechnology to the table as a *fait accompli*, a seat on the Board was virtually guaranteed. Director Hsiang. That thought sent a warm rush through him. He must possess the prototype.

Six days. He still had time, but how to acquire it quickly and quietly, in Barcelona no less? He could order Colonel Otsu and his unit to Asian Pacific's Trade Legation at the Port Complex, passing them off as a security upgrade. But they were too conspicuous to go searching in the city, and apparently incompetent. No, Avery Hsiang needed guarantees, loyal agents who would execute his orders ruthlessly, without question, and above all, blend in. He stared out the window and cast his mind over the skein of events. Suddenly another strand fell into place. Avery jabbed at the armrest button again.

"Kanang, get me the Chishima Lab authorization codes."

Dawson-Hull Estates. London, England. New European Union. 6:00 a.m.

Jackson MacKinnon watched the sun creep into the new day. In the gaining light, there were many options, opportunities, moves, and countermoves. His mind fastened on one in particular, and with a start, he turned around. Moving deliberately to the head of the huge conference table, he touched a recessed button underneath.

"Yvette," he said into the air.

"Yes, Mr. MacKinnon? The computer's voice filled the room, full and proper British, with a hint of sensuality. "What can I do for you?"

"Secure the room. Code blue three five five. Engage SCIF protocol."

"Yes, Mr. MacKinnon."

Instantly, the large glass windows hazed opaque white, and a low ambient hum filled the edge of Jackson's awareness as the Sensitive Compartmentalized Information Facility measures took effect. He waited another moment. "Open a secure sat-link with channel 00597. Maximum encryption. Audio only."

"Right away, Mr. MacKinnon. Sat-link engaging... Online."

After a small static whine and hiss, another voice filled the air. Clipped and British as well, but it was very human.

"Brenton, here. Jackson, I take it you met with Asian Pacific?"

"Hsiang left over an hour ago, smarmy little toad. Practically seethes with ambition. APAC denies complicity in the break-ins. But you knew that, yes?"

"Yes. It's his ambition we're counting on, you know," Brenton said.

"I know." MacKinnon paused."Was the prototype stolen?"

"Initial reports indicate the boy is missing," Brenton answered. "The Toulouse base was certainly breached. The two Rapid Response units you sent were neutralized as well. Both their transports shot down with one platoon wiped out completely. Most of the casualties occurred when the infiltrators fought their way out. No one knew they were there until then. Whoever APAC hired did extremely well. No losses on their account that we could determine. Very thorough, very professional."

"And the major? Is she—?" Jackson asked.

"Eames is alive. Frothing mad, of course, out for blood."

"Good. Any leads?"

"Seems the local air defense net picked up signals from of an unidentified transponder at one point, a small craft heading south toward the Pyrenees. A possible flight path into the Barcelona Metro Zone. Your dear major jumped on that, invoked the C and C with Madrid. She intends to go jack-booting in there, loaded for bear. She'll have the whole of the BMZ flex-cuffed and up against the wall if she gets her way."

"That's why we pay her, Brenton. She's the best man we've got. One platoon wiped out, you say? Who performed the infiltration?

"Yes, an entire platoon. And a third of the security force. We're still working on the mercenaries' identification. Not much to go on, I'm afraid. Just footprints and a few drops of blood. I'm not concerned about that, however..." Brenton's voice hesitated, "... final trials were underway. The boy made absolutely remarkable progress, better than anything else thus far, but it was obvious the technology hadn't developed into its final phase. From the earlier versions, things cascade rather quickly once the critical point is reached."

"You're saying things were delicate, I understand," Jackson replied. "But you were going easy on him, said you wouldn't risk triggering an advanced state prior to the window of opportunity. All the reports indicated the nanites were stable. Advanced stage activity was dormant."

"He wasn't ready, Jackson... We've spent over nine months preparing him for the next phase. For the boy to be taken now, it could ruin—" Brenton caught himself.

"No matter. The thing's in motion. There's a new variable introduced, that's all," Jackson said firmly. "Barcelona, you say?"

"Yes, as best we can tell. Eames is sure. 'Gut feeling' and all that. Intel division says it's credible."

"I want to contact Hester and bring him in on this jumble. I'll brief him personally. It's a rather... diverse target package this time."

"Hester... really? Why bring him to the surface? What about Buenos Aires? Terrible mess, that was."

"Not his fault really. It was self-defense." Jackson sniffed.

"I know he's your agent, Jackson, but eliminating two cartel families seems a bit of a stretch for preservation instinct."

"Good thing we were present to take advantage of the market shift afterwards, I say. Regardless, this is the single most critical venture we've undertaken in a decade. It could sway affairs completely in our favor. We can't risk failure, Brenton. The Board is well aware of the gravity of the situation. Hester is a necessity."

"Very well, Hester it is. I'll have the lads in the dark room locate him and drop him off in Barcelona on the double. He'll be in touch, no doubt."

"No doubt."

"Keep me apprised," Brenton said.

"Of course. MacKinnon out."

CHAPTER EIGHT

STOLEN

Gibson: It's all my fault. I jacked in without permission, and now I'm in trouble. Dr. Evans told me to pay attention, told me not to go alone, but I did. The jet is moving, we're lifting, the engine roars so loud it's making my headache worse. I'm not supposed to leave.

I'm scared. There was noise and fire and running. One of the big men carried me, and now I can barely breathe, cramped inside their black jet with them. The men are scared too, angry and arguing. Something went wrong, and one of their friends is hurt. They're mad and scared for him, and for themselves I think, because they can't do anything about it. His head is almost in my lap, the one from the Grid, and they're scared he might die.

Two of them went up front and the three big pale men are here with me, dressed in armor suits black like the jet. They don't speak, just hold their guns and watch me. I'm so cold my hands won't stop shaking. Dr. Evans isn't here, but I'm not going to cry. Breathe, he'd say. Focus. Focus. I'm trying, but the tears make everything blurry. One of the three, the one that carried me, sees me gulping for air. He sets down his rifle, takes my hand and holds it. The other two move near, their bodies closing in around me. Their breathing is warm and the jet is loud, and I am moving fast to somewhere I don't know.

I've been stolen.

CHAPTER NINE

LOOSE ENDS

Asian Pacific Consortium N. EU Division Regional Offices,
Amsterdam, Netherlands Zone. 8:05 p.m.

Avery Hsiang's office was large, befitting his position. Nothing ostentatious, it was a calculated understatement of satin black and brushed steel that emitted a sense of power like radiation at a Siberian nuclear site. The stark minimalism of a single desk under high vaulted ceilings, back-dropped on three sides by panoramic windows, was all calculated to emphasize executive transcendence by blunt subliminal. Beyond the tall armor glass, the city dropped away, pulsing veins of light and motion entwined among smaller black towers. The restless tracery of arrhythmic urban glare below him, it was a precipice of dizzying authority, but Avery Hsiang was bent forward under the desk lamp. He never looked out the windows anymore.

The hardcopy report compiled by his secretary lay stacked in two neat piles in front of him. He rubbed his eyes and continued reading.

...while these agencies act as intermediaries for any number of subcontract outfits, both legitimate and covert, Asian Pacific Consortium's security department has determined that Eshu Export, [Belfast Metro Zone, Ireland sector, principles: Jaithirth Rao and Matthew Dengler—see Appendix 1A] are the exclusive handlers for two elite level clandestine operation teams: Black Friar and Eshu International. It should be noted that Eshu International has been engaged on numerous prior occasions with a high degree of success and profitability. Due to the very nature of our dealings, much of the information following is partial and speculative. However, several known Black Friar operators were injured in a recent mission in the Singapore Maritime Zone, making it likely Eshu International is the team currently engaged in this extraction operation. Knowledge of team members is sketchy, and to be considered unreliable and out of date. [BF & EI Personnel Profiles attached—Appendix 1B &1C]

He yanked out the attached profiles and grunted, thumbing through them quickly. As he suspected; typical outcasts, zone trash. All military and corporate failures.

Tam Song: North Korean. Raised in State military orphanage. Drafted into NK ground forces for the Unification War '38; served 18 months with distinguished service citation during Pacification and Withdrawal phase. Selected for NK Special Response Unit. Advanced training in urban combat, surveillance, and demolitions. Combat citations in Malaysian Counter Insurgency, Thai, Cambodian & Indo-Pakistan theaters. Suspected Military Assistance Advisor Group in Philippine Revolution. Battlefield promotion to captain. Last known action during Taiwan Crisis, D day +1. Missing, presumed dead.

Jace Manner: North American Union, Canadian Sector. Volunteer, Canadian Armed Forces. Two tours in Canadian Ranger regiment. Expert arctic and survival training. Recruited for the 427 Special Operations Aviation Squadron (SOAS) at CFB Petawawa. Two years fixed wing, VTOL, and helo training. Meritorious Service medal for Siberian Operation in '40. Volunteered Joint American/Canadian Drug Interdiction Task Force. Advanced CQB and Surveillance cross training with US Delta force. Stationed to Detroit-Windsor-Cleveland Metro Zone '41-'43. Wounded four times. Deployed with N.A.U. forces to Taiwan Strait '45/46. Wounded in action. Dishonorable discharge: Gross Insubordination. Court-martial transcript sealed.

Devante Galeno Perez, alias "Poet9" North American Union, Central American Sector. Mexico City Sprawl. Child prodigy in computer systems and programming. Convicted in '33 of e-fraud and grand theft. Sentence commuted. Employed by BioGen International under 20-year indenture, System Security Division. Surgically fitted with advanced model cortical cybernetic interface. Disappeared while on loan to Dawson-Hull subsidiary in '51.

Eshu International has been thought to hire from a pool of experienced former military and police members as tactical parameters dictate. However, unconfirmed rumors persist of two, possibly three Pretoria series combat clones attached to their permanent roster. If verified, this represents both a considerable force multiplier and a serious hazard to any potential adversary, not to mention a breach of numerous international laws and U.N. Resolutions. Advised to proceed with caution.

Avery shoved the file aside in disgust. Employing illegal, substandard clone units... Colonel Otsu was a fool. These were exactly the sort of degenerates that would renege on a contract. He was surprised they'd managed to acquire the device. No question they were offering it to a higher bidder. The mercenaries, the sloppy infiltration in Toulouse, Colonel Otsu... loose ends, that's what they were, and Avery wasn't about to risk unraveling his presentation to the Board the following week.

Avery Hsiang opened up a secure link to the Chishima Lab.

PURSUIT

CHAPTER TEN

Barcelona Metro Zone, Spain. New European Union. 6:00 a.m.
Day One

I kept the Gaki moving fast as we threaded through the snow-flecked Pyrenees down into the Barcelona Metro Zone. Dawn was coming over the Mediterranean, and I wanted to touch down before BMZ AirNet caught a glimpse of us. The old city of Barcelona sat high on its plateau, clean and separated, gleaming in the sun's first rays. Old Barcelona, or UpCity, was the region's exclusive district and corporate capital. Through the cockpit window, I spotted the Collserolla communication towers twinkling like Mardi Gras sparklers, and the barbed spires of Santa Eulalia. In the east, I spied the dark hunchback of the Montjuic Administration Center. It perched on the cliff edge like one of the cathedral's gargoyles, brooding over the Barcelona Port Complex below.

The Port Complex was almost a city in its own right. Splayed out over the oil black harbor, the massive North and South Docks were long collisions of craggy gray steel streaked with orange rust, bright with the actinic glare of thousands of halogen lamps. Even at this hour, the twenty-story labyrinths were crawling with the ants of commerce diligently eviscerating stacks of colored cargo containers. In the waters below, white shoals of packing foam and twisted plastic threaded the girth of support pylons, rising and falling with the rainbow-sheen tide, shifting with the endless procession of cargo ships.

We'd flown here to hide, so I turned toward the outer districts. The sprawls were the UpCity's opposite: dark, mottled scabs that spread out below the plateau like a crust of industrial run-off. Over them, a haze of smog was smeared like grease on the pale film of the morning. There was no way to get an exact count, but Madrid authorities estimated twenty million people were crammed into these feral, failing slums.

To the south, I could make out *Las Tres Vergüenzas*, three deep scorched craters that pocked the district's center. Massive explosions had marked the last stand of the Separatist Revolt of 2027. Madrid's official word was the Basque terrorists had craved martyrdom over defeat, triggering old American fuel-air bombs they'd stolen from air bases in the Gulf. Survivors told another story: *Mossos d'Esquadra* units driving semis into the contested

Esplugues de Llobregat district then abandoning them in the dark hours before dawn. Apparently, the Montevedo administration had demanded the military set an example and put an end to the insurrection. They did. Nothing had been built there since.

I swung north, into the Sant Adrià de Besòs district, and after a few minutes searching, dropped onto a tar-veined, parking lot hidden in the middle of a cluster of abandoned factory ruins. The Gaki settled barely blowing trash, and we climbed out.

Signs on the fence warned off trespassers, while a large hologram billboard propped over the broken-down office building announced the construction of another subsidized housing project. The impossibly tidy apartments popped out at us next to the smiling face of the prime minister, who sported an Armani suit and matching hardhat. The start-up date was five years past.

As the Triplets scoured adjacent buildings for life forms other than weeds and rats, Tam searched out a place to stash the ship. He found a suitable dank and far corner in the burnt-out skeleton of a decrepit steel foundry. I taxied in, shut it down, and the Gaki vanished in the thick shadows. Tam took Gibson by the hand as I carried Poet9, and we walked back out to the lot following a procession of enormous smelting cauldrons caught in dense tangles of chain. It creeped me out, this cascade of iron tonnage frozen in mid-tumble, perpetually falling like some kind of pending judgment. I picked up the pace until we got outside.

"No word from Doc. K yet, but the Garcias say they'll let us stay as long as we need," Tam said. "I told them we had a WIA. Didn't say who." He looked at Poet9, pale and limp on my shoulders. "Doc will come in time, Jace."

"Don't doubt it. Now would be good though." I shifted his weight and found Gibson staring with those startling bright eyes. I tried to return his gaze, felt another smart-ass line fail to materialize, so I gave him a wink instead. A little smile flashed back.

"All clear," rang in our headsets. The Triplets were headed back our way at a steady jog. Tam was staring at the empty buildings.

"What?" I asked.

He shook his head once. "Nothing."

"Yeah right. What is it?"

"Reminds me of the last time I was in North Korea, that's all."

"When was that? Fifteen, sixteen years ago? Right before Unification?"

"Yeah—all seven weeks of it." He laughed with a soft bitterness. "They drafted the whole school into the "glorious drive" south." He looked around again. "Damn, this place almost looks *better* than that state orphanage."

"Well, then here's to ghosts and the glory paid to ashes," I said. "Both come too late to make a difference."

"Here's to the wet dreams of psychotic dictators," he countered. His eyes traced the building's scarred profile a moment longer until he finally turned away. "Come on. Let's get the hell out of here. Real people and downtime will do us good." The six of us walked away from the chill of those brick and iron husks into the smog and light and rising babble of a new day.

The Garcias lived in an anonymous block of concrete tenements, amid a hundred identical slab-sided, soot-grimed buildings. Crowded together on the edge of the Northern District, they made a warren of narrow streets, markets, and slip cuts called *Callejón del Apuro:* "Trouble Alley". We entered through a dented steel door in a sliver of an alley and descended into a large cellar where Alejo, and his wife, Carmen, were waiting for us. Warm spice and bread smells filled the air, rising from covered dishes on a long dining table made from two battered wooden doors. Their eldest son, Curro, propped himself in the stairwell across the room. It took me a moment to recognize him; he'd been Gibson's age last time I saw him. He waved as we entered. I spotted a number of faded military lockboxes stacked in a corner, and a simple unadorned cross was mounted on the wall above them. Reminders of where the Garcias had come from, and who they were now.

Carmen let out a little shriek when she spied Poet9, and immediately shoo-ed me toward a bed off to one side. There was a first aid kit and a newer model autodoc propped open on a sheet metal stand beside it. I laid him out on the covers.

"No wounds?" Her eyes scanned his body rapidly, her hands checking for broken bones.

"EMP blast." I nodded toward his head and cyber unit. "Got caught on the edge of it. I don't know—" my voice choked.

"He'll be fine. Just fine. I'll see to him. Go now." She waved me off with a dishcloth and went to work, snapping switches, setting leads, fine-tuning the monitors in quick, efficient motions.

I backed away softly and turned in time to see Alejo limp over and embrace Tam and the Triplets each in turn. Tam was his usual understated self, but I could tell he was relieved to see Alejo, relieved to be here in this dingy cellar. Despite his reservations about Alejo and Carmen's conversion, I watched his tension drain out.

The Triplets returned Al's hugs with huge wraparound arms, lifting him off his feet three times. They were careful not to squeeze too hard. It was Alejo who had smuggled them out of Africa during the final bloody spasms of the Consolidation Wars. He and Tam had found them, cornered, starving, cut-off and alone. The two of them realized what they were and disguised them as best they could among the other refugees hidden in the hold of Alejo's boat. The old Spaniard had been the first person to ever hug them.

At last, Alejo came to Gibson. "A ho! What have we here?" He pinched the boy's cheek then nearly smothered him against his belly. The old Spaniard bent down and peered full into the boy's eyes. "You travel with serious company, my little friend. You must be very strong and fast to do so."

He grabbed Gibson's arm and made a show of flexing it. "Ah! but surely a boy as dangerous as yourself must be even a little hungry, no?" A huge toothy smile appeared under Al's walrus moustache.

Gibson blinked, and smiled back. "Sure."

"Good! Very good!" Alejo patted the boy's stomach. "We can eat then!"

And we did.

Research Facility 5. Asian Pacific Consortium Black Lab – Chishima Islands, Japan. 8:45 a.m.

A delicate two-tone chime sounded from the computer that made Dr. Iso Shoei set down his data pad and peer over the top of his glasses. Across the desk, a pop-up warning flashed from red to green on the flatscreen, a signal that the decryption algorithm was complete. He frowned and hurried over in small steps, hunched and still gripping the pad's stylus. He keyed his password and a secondary window blinked open. It was an order from an executive in the European Division for a clone unit requisition.

He sighed and scratched the side of his nose with the stylus. Nothing unusual there, it was probably some executive requesting Comfort series units for a conference. Dr. Shoei remembered the Director's Assembly was scheduled for the following week. So predictable, these managers.

Activated clones were illegal now, of course. They had been ever since the African Wars, but every government and major corporation had kept their genetic engineering and genetic research labs. They'd simply tucked them away in remote locations, like this one. Regardless of United Nation mandates, specialized biological units—bio-forms—were still created for in-house use, and what was termed "possible extreme contingency deployment". Cached in biogenic suspension tanks, the clone series batches were replenished in eighteen-month cycles to assure top performance and offset storage atrophy.

Dr. Shoei tore off a Post-it from one of the many pads scattered about, and with a pen poised over the paper, he read the order. His brow furrowed as the text slid past.

… activation of three (3) Type Five units.

The message ended with the phrase: *"Immediate deployment for operations critical to corporate interests,"* and was bracketed by executive authorization codes. He fell back in the chair, blinking at the screen. Type Fives? Dr. Shoei was confused.

We made it clear in the last report. Don't they realize...?

He scrolled back to re-read the main portion of the message. It was very specific. They wanted three units, of the Type Fives. He double-checked the authorization. It was valid.

A single bead of sweat crept down behind his right ear into his shirt collar, his breath coming in small pants. He gulped his mouth shut and touched the intercom on his desk. "Dr. Hatsumi, meet me in Replication right away. We just received an order for three units. Tier Two approval."

"I'm in the middle of a gene sequence here. Can't Hiru take this one? I'm about to—."

"It's for Type Fives. You're the only one in this rotation with proper clearance. Meet me in the tank room in three minutes. Dr. Shoei out." He cut the link and stood up.

A timer in the message window was counting down to auto-delete, so he transferred the order details onto his data pad, then turned, grabbed his key card and headed out the door.

As he hurried down the central corridor, the steel-ribbed ceiling suddenly seemed low, and the distant throbbing of geothermal processors only added to his apprehension.

Three? Why in God's name do they want three?

Carved deep underground in volcanic rock of the Chishima island chain, Dr. Shoei's lab was a "black" facility: classified, isolated, and heavily guarded. The Japanese consortium enticed the best and brightest from every university and scientific firm in the region in the relentless pursuit of cutting edge biotech. Dr. Shoei ran Asian Pacific's entire bio-form department, and had developed all four of their current stock series models: medical testing, labor, soldier, and comfort series. He was the father of the corporate giant's clone division.

But the Type Fives are still too volatile. Their physiological capabilities are undeniable, yes, but the neural-restraints are tenuous—at best. Released into society they'd be sociopaths. A very high-risk product.

He stepped up to the elevator, the heavy doors opening with a brisk hydraulic sigh as he waved his card. His right hand in his lab coat pocket clutching the data pad now. He felt the merest nudge as he started descending.

Tier Two authority. What choice do I have? Really?

Seconds later, the floating sensation ceased. "Yellow Section. Level Four, Unit 731," the elevator announced. He stepped out and headed left to the clone banks, his mind racing. The other four gene-sets were stable, perfect. But it had taken time to work the bugs out. He'd told them that. He thought the directors respected him, had listened.

They are not mature yet.

These units—*shinigami* designation—would be his finest work yet. Infiltrator units with configurable cosmetic morphology, Type Fives could be produced resembling any human racial type on the planet. Perfect for assassination, sabotage, and espionage missions, they'd also rank among the best tactical units ever manufactured. Better than the quirky albino series Pretoria spliced for the African Civil Wars. Dr. Shoei just needed more time with them. But it didn't look like he was going to get that, not with an immediate requisition in his pocket.

His forehead was pebbled with perspiration as he pushed through the faded blue double doors into the Replication wing. Dr. Hatsumi was already waiting for him, nervousness etched on his face as well. He bowed low. "Are you sure they want Type Fives? Now? At this stage? They can't be serious."

Dr. Shoei waved the data pad in front of the younger scientist. "They are serious. The order's green stamped for extreme contingency deployment. I confirmed the authorization codes. They're Tier Two—a District Manager with the European offices. We have to comply and fill the order."

"Yes. But three?"

"Three."

"That's... Dr. Shoei, the Fives are still in the developmental phase. Your Q1 report stated their conditioning hadn't rooted. The behavior patterns were still highly erratic. Even when complete, they should only be activated in cases of extreme necessity."

"Well, Dr. Hatsumi, someone upstairs feels this is an extreme necessity." He looked wearily at the younger man, and gestured with the data pad again. "Are you saying we refuse to perform this procedure? You know what that would mean, yes?"

"I... well, no. I mean... Dr. Shoei, it's just that they are dangerous. I was simply expressing some professional reservations. My apologies." He bowed.

"No, no, no. None of that. You are right. But we have orders," the older scientist said. "Once they leave the facility, however, it's out of our hands. You start the de-tank process, and I will switch on the automated defense systems for this area. As a precaution." He bent over a security terminal and started logging in. "And we are not going to stimulate their tactical and combat enhancements until the pheno-imprint is stabilized. Even then, we will instruct Operations to only inject the neuro-chemical triggers when they're deployed in the target environment. Agreed?"

"Fine. The less we handle the units, the better. What are the gender and imprint requirements?"

"Two male, one female. Latin phenotype. Engagement area is Spain, Catalonian region. Occupational covers are lower-class laborers: courier and dockworker for the males, medical orderly for the female. Initiate the pheno-imprint chemicals simultaneous with the thaw to speed up the process. I want them out of here as quickly as possible. Once they're defined, forward the details to Operations so they can insert cover profiles into the Barcelona Metro Zone population database."

"Of course, Doctor. I'll select appropriate units and start the de-tank sequence right away."

"Very good," the older man said. "Let's get this over with."

CHAPTER ELEVEN

EL TACTO DEL FANTASMA

Barcelona Metro Zone, Spain. New European Union. 9:05 a.m.
Day One.

Eleven armored personnel carriers crouched in the walled lot behind Barcelona Metro Comisaría de Policías 137, engines idling, waiting. The turbine purr strained the morning air, blocking out the city sounds all around them. Their drivers had activated their mimetic camouflage, making their hard armored edges fuzz into dingy blurs against the surrounding buildings. To Major Eames, the vehicles seethed like a brood of giant crocodiles, thick and anxious to menace the new day, and she liked that.

The back hatches were slung open and armed men peered out from their interiors, stone-faced and still. Their commander, a *Mossos d'Esquadra* colonel, was standing at attention in the middle of the lot; his face was flushed red as the British corporate commander yelled two inches from his nose.

"You think? Think, Colonel? That's not in your job description! You read the orders: Madrid says you and your men are seconded to me! To me. For. The. Duration! What don't you understand about that? As long as this operation is running, this is my unit! My command! I do the thinking around here!"

She looked up and yelled even louder, her voice rebounding off the tall, ashen walls. "Listen up, because I'm only going to explain this one time. The Crisis and Cooperation Act is now in force. This operation is considered a matter of national security, so all corporate and governmental forces in the BMZ will coordinate under my command until the situation is resolved. This case has priority over routine law enforcement. Is that understood?"

"Si, Major," came the dull answer.

Major Eames grunted at the lame response. "I'm not leaving your city to the dogs, if that's what you're thinking. I'm saying pack your bags, gentlemen, because you'll be living at the stations until further notice. I've mandated double shifts for everyone until we get what we came for. I don't want to hear any whining either—you'll be getting standard overtime pay."

That statement brought a few groans mingled with murmurs of approval. Extra credits were always good, particularly when a corporation was footing the bill. Eames noticed most of the men were sitting up straighter. She had their attention now.

"The fact is, D-H Corporate Security has been tasked with apprehending some illegals, a crew of sprawl scum that heisted a piece of proprietary technology. Our intel division believes they're in your city. Right now."

She began pacing, looking into each of the carriers in turn. "Now, my men and I are here because these aren't your usual dump-raiding scabs. They're better equipped, better trained, and armed to the teeth. Most likely ex spec-ops or top echelon security from some rat's ass country. They made the fatal mistake of breaking into one of our research labs then killed a bunch of people on the way out."

She paused for effect. "So here's the deal. First, any soldier who secures or terminates one of these mercs gets a pay-grade jump and six-month bonus. Tax free. Second, you recover the asset in question, there's an added transfer benefit: you and your whole family, anywhere under the D-H umbrella. Now that right there is more than enough incentive to keep kicking in doors until we find them. And we will find them. In fact, I'm going to get our property back and put these mercenary fuckers in the dirt. And you're going to help me. Do I make myself clear?"

"Si, Major!" A chorus of whistles and laughter barked out of the darkened interiors, then a rhythmic thudding as the troopers started pounding their boots on the steel plate floors.

"Outstanding," Major Eames said. "I'm confident you men won't disappoint me. Section leaders have their orders, now let's roll."

Major Jessa Eames spun on her heel and stalked towards her command vehicle. She motioned the colonel alongside. "*Mossos d'Esquadra* units are going to seal the main checkpoints in each district. Nothing flies, floats, or rolls in the sprawls without us knowing. I've also ordered Grupo Especial de Operaciones and Guardia Civil units to assist with the search phase. We're going to lock down and sweep districts in turn. The G.E.O. will act as reserves for major incidents. My Special Deployment units are on twenty-four hour stand-by for any solid leads. Understood?"

"Si, Major Eames!"

She stopped abruptly and looked at the Spanish colonel. The name on his uniform read "Estevana". "Colonel Estevana, the BMZ newsnets are going to start running terrorist alerts as part of our cover story. We've profiled up an Afghani narco-terrorist gang, an al-Qaeda offshoot, that's targeting the port with pocket nukes. Story is they're staging and recruiting in the zones, so make sure your men stick to that. We're offering the usual perks for info leading to arrest, suspicious activity, all that. The phones and net are going to go crazy at first, but we can sift out the cranks and get solid leads. We wave enough credits around, sooner or later some scab will drop a dime. In the meantime, I want you and four of your units with me. I've got forensic teams with gene sniffers waiting at the airport. We're going to start sweep operations in the southern district. Sprawlers there are still pissy about the Tres Vergüenzas, right? We don't want the Basque scabs to think we're ignoring them."

Tam and I were mopping up the last of our eggs when Alejo slid the small white box across the table to us. It was a RFID chip for the BMZ population database. "Here, this is a good one. Fresh from the factory. Nothing high profile, it's out of a run designated for low-level laborers, domestics, people like that. You still with Rao in Belfast?"

Tam nodded, his mouth full.

"Good! He was always smart at cover IDs. I'll send him the serial number so he can construct one and paste it in to the database. Then you should have no troubles for food and clothing while you're here. I know where we can get you some clothes, things to blend in." He winked and waved toward the old military crates along the wall. "And, I bet I have some old equipment kicking around somewhere... in case you need it."

He hunched forward over the scarred top of the door table. "You must be careful going out on the streets. Things here are difficult, even more these days. There are many who would sell their family for a corporate chip. Always the UpCity offers rewards, bonuses, even citizenship, to those who inform on criminals, smugglers, suspicious activity. It is tempting for many."

He gestured over to the Triplets, who were clustered around Gibson and helping him finish his breakfast. "They must stay in. Their size and color would give them away in a second." He snapped his fingers. "But that is obvious, no? What of the little one?" he smiled slyly. "You are bringing him to his family?"

Alejo figured Gibson for the child or relative of some corporate defector who wanted their family brought over to them. A common enough job, it was easy to assume we'd run a snatch to reunite him with a mother or father. Any other time he'd have been right. Tam shook his head.

"He was our target for this run, yes... but he's the asset, Alejo. Big time."

Alejo looked at the boy through narrowed eyes. "And so little, he does... what?"

Tam and I smiled at him.

"Sorry. Old habits. You're right, of course." He shrugged and leaned back. "You know, I thank God every day now. I'm happy to be here, to have lived to be old, to be with Carmen."

"Here we go with a life choices sermon..." Tam said.

Alejo grinned. "What, you get a lot of those?"

"Hell no, look where we are," I said.

Alejo laughed. "You know I still dream of diesel and cordite? Sometimes I close my eyes and see the open sea in the moonlight. I remember the electricity of slipping past an UNdie blockade."

"You're not getting all sentimental in your old age, are you?" I asked.

"No, no. But we did many things, some of them even good." He gestured toward the Triplets.

"Some of them even good," Tam nodded.

Then the old Spaniard frowned. "Carmen gets angry when I tell the children about Greece and Turkey, the towns on the coast, the mountain roads in the 'Stans. She wants them to stay in school. Become doctors, relief workers… Leave the past behind, she says. She's afraid the children might talk, let something slip to the wrong people. But I know…" he tapped the side of his nose with his finger, "she does not want them to get ideas. She thinks what we did was dangerous."

"Ummm… Al?" Tam looked intently at him. "It was."

"Yes, Yes. It was. You're right, of course." He glanced over at his wife, who was now busy defending Gibson against Flopsy and Mopsy's predations on his breakfast plate. "Now I am called to *overcome evil with good,* as the Scripture says. We still know so many from that life, and we tell them how we changed. Some listen and they walk with God now. But others… I have to remind them of old times, use old tricks, and get them to do good in spite of themselves, you know?" He chuckled darkly. "Whatever it takes, yes?"

"Whatever it takes," Tam echoed. "Where are you going with this, Al?" I asked.

"We used to say it's good to be prepared, remember? So keep a few old things around here in the basement, and I teach my children how to look out for themselves, stay safe in the sprawl. But Curro over there," he jutted his chin at his eldest son, who still stood in the doorway, "he is very capable. I even think Curro has *el tacto del fantasma*—the touch of the ghost." He lowered his voice so Carmen wouldn't overhear. "I think that boy could run—run for what is good, that is." He looked at me and Tam. "He would need more training, of course."

I almost squirted coffee out my nose. "What, and have Carmen gunning for us? I'd rather be darkside on Luna."

Alejo barked out another laugh, and even Tam cracked a smile. Our old friend looked at us expectantly, but neither Tam nor I were willing to pick up that line of thought. The moment hung in the air, then moved on, and suddenly all the noise and smells and chatter of the big cellar room rushed back in. After a few minutes, we poured out the last of the strong black coffee, cleared the plates and started working on enjoying our little seaside vacation.

Still, later that morning, I caught myself watching the dark-haired Curro, watching the way he moved, spoke with Gibson or the Triplets, carried away the trays. Oddly enough, I caught Tam doing the same.

CHAPTER TWELVE

Asian Pacific Consortium Trade Legation. Barcelona Port Complex,
South Dock, Section D, Level Five. 11:30 a.m. Day One.

Colonel Keiji Otsu kept his face neutral. Three thousand kilometers away, Avery Hsiang's sneer was a slap, even through the video link. His father had once said that bureaucracy was a giant mechanism operated by pygmies, this man's blindness and arrogance was as solid as an iron mountain. Grateful for the distance between them, Keiji knew he must take particular care to avoid being crushed by this one.

Still, the man was his immediate superior, so he endured and remained at attention, staring at a point over the top of the screen. Avery Hsiang was still speaking.

"…derelict in your obligations, Colonel. Consequently, I am remanding you to an assignment you *can* handle. I've ordered three clone units to Spain. These are *shinigami* designation, highly valuable prototypes, sent to accomplish the mission you, apparently, could not. I have ordered them to keep you informed, but they are deployed on my authority and answer directly to me. Do you understand me?"

The colonel's mind halted. Three of the prohibited replicants deployed in one area together? New prototypes at that? Two clone units was the maximum permitted short of unanimous Board approval. There was too high a risk of exposure and U.N. censure if they were discovered. He'd known Mr. Hsiang considered this venture important, but what exactly had the zone mercenaries stolen?

The manager continued. "You and your men will be reviewing the security measures at our Barcelona Port interests. You will use this position to support the clone agents in any and every possible way. Do you think you can perform those duties adequately, Colonel?"

"Of course, Mr. Hsiang."

"I hope so. These *ronin* completely disregarded the terms of our agreement, missed the rendezvous, and fled to the Barcelona Metropolitan Zone. I've been informed there was a message outlining their intention to disappear until they felt more secure, but I suspect a more devious motive. They're attempting to sell the item to another buyer, some other corporation."

"Sir, we've employed this outfit in the past. They've always delivered per terms. Why think they'd break a contract now?" the colonel asked.

"They are mercenaries," Avery Hsiang sighed. "You cannot trust their kind. Without honor, self-interest is their guiding star, and even they understand how valuable nanotechnology is. Like whores, anyone with credits can entice them. The prototype must be obtained before they can sell it. Secondly, I've ordered the *shinigami* to eliminate them, but not at the risk of their primary objective. Consequently, you and your men must be ready to eliminate this zone trash once the replicants have completed their mission."

"Mr. Hsiang, if I cross that line, other contractors will refuse to undertake jobs with us."

"Colonel, I want to send a clear message to their kind: Asian Pacific does not tolerate duplicity. Besides, with this technology, we won't need sprawl whores to service us anymore. Expect the clone units tomorrow and see that my orders are carried out."

He cut the link without another word, and Colonel Otsu found himself looking at a blank screen.

He was small, quiet, nothing obvious. Fit perhaps, with dark hair, but not out of the ordinary to cause you to remember him one way or the other. He smiled at the very pretty, very Spanish customs constable, and she smiled back, scanning the back of his hand. She checked her screen. He waited. Just another tourist, she thought. An Anglo. American or UK perhaps. No, not American, he was certainly a N.EU citizen. His scan said so. The accompanying profile pop-up warranted no attention, raised no flags. He was suitably boring, nobody special. A business traveler, probably something with the Port Complex, the constable thought. She punched a few more keys on her computer console.

"Have a pleasant stay in Spain."

"Thank you. " He smiled again.

But she was already looking away as the next arrival stepped up to the counter.

The man called Hester walked slowly past the lounge area, put on his sunglasses, and stepped out into the bright Mediterranean warmth of Barcelona. In the distance, the bells of the Cathedral of Santa Eulalia began their noon chimes, and he waved for a cab.

CHAPTER THIRTEEN

THE GOLDEN RULE

Barcelona Metro Zone, Sant Adrià de Besòs district. Callejón del
Apuro, "Trouble Alley". 2:18 p.m. Day One.

Later in the day, the team had settled in the Garcías' cellar. Our Mitsu
suits were stacked in a corner, and most of our gear was sealed away
in two of Al's ubiquitous old military crates. Alejo and Carmen had
gone off, doing whatever they did for work here in the northern sprawl, while
Tam and I took turns watching over Poet9. I guess I could say his condition
was "stable" in that it was unchanged. There was still no word on Doc
Kalahani.

Gibson was my other concern. On some level, I knew being a clone, the
boy wouldn't be "normal". I'm not sure what I expected, but he certainly
wasn't a "kid" the way I understood them. He didn't whine, or cry, or try to
run. Except for the escape at the labs, he never even appeared frightened. He
simply watched, listened, and took everything in. Whatever he was feeling,
he kept it all inside as if he was processing the whole event. Other than to
Carmen, or the Triplets, he barely spoke a word. That afternoon, he sat
watching the three big soldiers fieldstrip their assault rifles.

Before Alejo had left, he'd gotten through to Jaithirth Rao, our agent in
Belfast. Our chip was now in the BMZ system, and we could access our front
accounts for cash. As long as D-H or Spanish Security didn't trace us, we
could stay underground indefinitely. Carmen's calls had paid off too. It
wasn't long before bundles of clothes started coming in through the side
cellar door, and since I'd volunteered to get chipped and be the outside man,
I got first pick from the goodwill racks.

I grabbed loose, drab-colored khakis and a suitably dingy denim jacket
with Kevlar under-weave. Al said between police patrols and the zone-wide
surveillance, it wasn't wise to carry any kind of weapon, but if I was running
errands in the zone, I at least wanted some kind of protection—just in case.
The jacket would only turn away blades and small shrapnel, but it was better
than nothing. I was fitting the side straps when Curro ducked in, all
concerned.

"Sorry, but the newsnets are 'casting emergency flashes, level Orange.
They say there's narco-terrorists going after the B-Port with a nuke, and that
they're hiding in the sprawls, signing up volunteers for the seventy-two

virgins tour of Paradise. UpCity execs are offering big rewards for any information, suspicious persons... all that stuff. It's coming on every channel, every half-hour."

Tam grinned. "Don't stress. No one traced us here. We're transparent, and the last thing we want to do is endanger your mom and dad. In fact, Jace is on his way out to contact our agent. We'll be gone in a couple days. I promise."

Curro nodded and disappeared back up the stairs. "That didn't take long," I said after the door shut.

"Nope. Guess D-H wants their stuff back. On top of that, Jaithirth said Asian Pacific wasn't too happy about our missing the rendezvous. Sent him a nasty response when he told them what we'd done. All the more reason to make delivery asap."

"Well, from the money being thrown around, I guess the suit that hired us is out on a limb. He's bound to be touchy about his expenditures."

"Yeah, well, they should know us by now," Tam said. "We're practically on retainer with APAC for Christ's sake. Something this big, they have to allow for contingencies."

"And we have a man down," I said.

"And we have a man down," Tam nodded. "When you go out, have Rao tell them no worries. This is a detour. Eshu International abides by the contract. Always. Their tech is on the way."

I zipped up the jacket and edged in closer to him. "Tam, you think they realize this tech is a kid?

"A clone?"

I glanced over to see Mopsy all serious, trying to explain to the boy about the workings of the upper receiver and bolt assembly on his 10mm H-K assault rifle. "Yeah... a child clone," I said slowly.

"Couldn't say," Tam shrugged. "Nothing in the contract brief or tacticals hinted at it. C. B. sets the payment terms, while the Ts provide target data." He thought for a second. "Am I supposed to care here?"

"I'm asking," I said.

"My guess? They probably had no idea about a bio-unit. Then again, they wouldn't tell us everything. No 'need' in the 'need to know' loop. Doesn't matter as long as we deliver the package and get paid, right?"

"Except this time the kid is the package."

"He's a clone, Jace." Tam's face went serious.

"So?"

"He's a package. Blonde, brunette, clone or little black box, we do our job." He stared at me. "This isn't another one of *those* conversations, is it?"

"Maybe it is. So?"

"So we always end up talking in circles. Stay focused."

I looked over at Gibson, who was laughing as Mopsy reassembled his rifle, blindfolded. His large hands were moving in precise, fluid motions, making the weapon reappear as if by magic. When he finished, the pale soldier tore off the bandanna and made a little bow. Gibson clapped.

"You have to admit this is a first," I said.

Tam had watched the little show with me. "Custom cloning isn't new, look at the Triplets. The fact that it's a kid is new ground, I'll give you that. And if it helps, it's not like I'm enjoying this." He shook his head. "But we finish the run. That's our secret to survival."

"We go through with this, what does that make us?"

"Ummm… a lot of money?" Tam said, irritated. "Why the sudden attack of conscience?"

"Well, no one's shooting at me right now…"

"My point exactly. Employment-wise, we've got very limited skill-sets here. Black contract work is our only option."

"There's always work for guys like us—" I started.

Tam shook his head. "Like the Bunnies are going to be mall security... No, we need corporate coverage. Period. Otherwise, we're no better than some scab standing in line for a handout. I'm not giving the bastards the satisfaction."

"So we're going to hand over the kid and ghost off screen?" I said.

Tam's face hardened. "We're going to contact APAC, arrange delivery, and request an extraction. In the meantime, Doc Kalahani will come and fix up Poet9."

"What do you think APAC is going to do to him?"

"How would I know that? Damn, Jace, listen to yourself. We're not even with Al and Carmen one day and you go all soft and cuddly."

"Piss off, Tam! We're talking about a kid."

"No, we're talking about the future." He was adamant. "It's 'The Next Big Thing', remember? First it was robotics, then genetics, now it's nanotech. If what's inside that clone is real, it's the key, and the corp that holds that key stands to make billions, even trillions, over the next decade. Once that happens, the Golden Rule kicks in: those that have the gold make the rules. You don't piss off people like that. Especially not Execs."

"Those Execs are going cut him open, squeeze him dry and toss the husk in a dumpster. You OK with that?"

"Suddenly you know what APAC is going to do?" Tam asked.

"Call it a guess."

"Well here's a fact: we're not welcome in polite society. We drop a contract, we might as well roll over and die right here. We'd be useless to any corp on the planet."

"So we're useful as long as we do their dirty work, but how long before we get labeled a liability?"

"And here's our chance to stow a pile of credits away against that day," Tam said. "We can't burn bridges now."

I kept silent and went back to watching Gibson and the Triplets.

Tam sighed. "Look, we're not the black hats here, Jace. We didn't develop the technology, we didn't grow the kid, we didn't play God and weave the stuff into him for a higher quarterly return. We're just delivery guys."

"How Eichmann of us…"

He grabbed my shoulder. "Life's tough; get a helmet. If it wasn't us, some other crew would step up, and who knows how that'd go down? At least we'll deliver him in one piece."

"I've got a bad feeling," I said. "Had it right from the drop."

"The contract doesn't give a shit about our feelings. Like Alejo used to say, we're 'between the sword and the wall'." He grinned at me. "Remember that song 'a scab's gotta cover his ass…'?"

"You're not helping," I said.

"Sorry, them's the cold, hard facts, brother. Survivor's guilt will kill you."

Now Tam had seen every shit storm combat zone on the planet in the last eleven years, not to mention a major chunk of heavy black ops, and made it out alive. Right then, he was bone-tired and worn to the core, but his eyes had that hard brightness to them. He was right. He knew it. I knew it. Stay focused, finish the job, move on. That's how it was done.

I had nothing else to say, so I changed the subject. "Speaking of scabs, any change in Poet9?" I moved over to the corner where our friend was lying on the bed pallet. The autodoc beeped faintly.

"No way of telling," Tam said. "Carmen looked him over and says he's fine except for the brain box. She thinks it shut down, and it's got him in a shallow coma. Patching up a body is hard enough, but cyber gear is way past her. She can't tell if the neural fibers got damaged, or if it's permanent. How close were you?"

"Right on the edge," I said. "I grabbed him, threw him down as the EMP popped, but it still frazzled my onboards. They rebooted right away, but—"

"Carmen says she'll pray for him," Tam interrupted. "Every little bit helps I guess."

"Now who's all soft and cuddly?"

A tiny smile played on his lips. "She better pray Doc K gets here fast."

"You tell her that?"

"No. That's your job. She always liked you better. 'Darkside on Luna', eh?"

"Hell, yes!" I laughed. "Remember that time off Qatar, on the boat? Those Muj came after us in Swifties with M60s. Alejo went down, and damn, Carmen could shoot."

"Well, they wanted to see Allah, and she wasn't going to disappoint them," Tam said.

We both laughed, but the smile dropped off Tam's face. "We're going to make it through this. We'll finish, fix up Poet9 better than new, and take some time off. A month or two, like we said. Then we can have Jaithirth flush out the next job. With a cash reserve, we'll be in a better position to pick and choose. We won't step in it like this again. OK?"

"There another choice? Maybe I am getting soft. I'm still not into handing a kid over to APAC, uber-tech or not."

"Choices are for rich people," Tam said. "Us? We're sharks. We have to keep moving or we die."

"Stop with your homey analogies. Most of the sharks are dead from the dumping. The only ones left are in reserves or aquariums."

"That's part of the point," he said.

"Yeah, great. Somehow that makes it even worse."

Tam said nothing, so I moved past him for the side cellar door. "I'm going out, do a walk around and grab some food. I'll go to the café Alejo mentioned and check in with Rao. See what APAC has to say about an extraction team. They'll probably want to take it out of our finals, cheap bastards. I'll be back in a flash."

I went out the metal door into the narrow alley and slipped into the current of people moving on the sidewalk.

Hermano had a pounding headache. He leaned over, washing his socks under the tap, and the throbbing only increased. Another bad shift at work, unloading container after container of things he could never afford for the Old B corporates he would never see. His supervisor, Señor Vandarm—an anglo—had yelled at him, called him slow and stupid. Well if they paid better, Hermano would work better. What did they expect? A man couldn't feed his family on such piss-poor wages. There was barely any to buy a few drinks after work. They did that on purpose to make it just enough to crawl back the next day and stand in line at their gates, groveling like some beggar. Hermano wasn't stupid. He knew what was going on. Well, as long as they pretended to pay, Hermano and the other dockers would pretend to work. And if that greasy little *punta* yelled at him one more time, he'd show him. He'd smash him in his greasy little face. Hermano twisted the thin damp cotton in his hands, wrenching out a few more soapy drips.

He jerked his head at the thought and the drums hammered faster inside. Groaning, he was clutching the sink to steady himself when the stranger stepped out into the street. Hermano stopped and peered through the window with bleary eyes. It was another anglo, clean and fit, wearing an old jacket. He'd never seen him before, and Hermano knew everyone in his neighborhood. This man was walking tall, all proud, not weary and hunched over like a decent working man.

Ever since Hermano had got home, the news had been blaring some special story about a group of druggies hiding in the zones. The newscasters said this gang wanted to detonate explosives at the B-Port. Put Hermano and his friends out of what little work they had. That made him mad. Hermano had already lost two daughters to drugs; turned them into prostitutes. His beautiful girls. That anglo must be one of them. The 'cast mentioned a reward. A large one. With that kind of money, he'd be able to buy some nice things. And some decent drink.

He'd get recognized too. Finally. The dock management would realize Hermano was no dummy, not just some oaf driving a lift. He'd be promoted to shift supervisor and that greasy little rat Vandarm would be fired. He could almost see the look on his face when the big bosses came down and patted Hermano on the shoulder, saying what a fine fellow he was and how they were so glad to have him watching over the shift. Señor Vandarm would slink off, sad and scared, escorted from the premises by security, and the big bosses would speak among themselves and nod at Hermano, knowing things would run smoothly on C level, South Dock 16 from now on.

Hermano saw the anglo's back disappear around the corner. Filthy druggie fanatic. He snapped the socks twice in the air, flicking drops into the smoky light, then laid them on the edge of the sink to dry. He had a call to make.

CHAPTER FOURTEEN

BOKER BLADES

Barcelona Metro Zone, Sant Adrià de Besòs district. 3:47 p.m.
Day One.

I found the café *Antojitos* on a hectic street near the district's market square. The yellow, green and black awning marked it out for me. Alejo had said it catered to the local mob circuit, so the clientele was mixed and questionable, which was good because that meant the local *policía* were paid off and a stranger wouldn't raise too many eyebrows. It boasted bitter hot Arabian coffee, decent curry, and most important, several Public Access terminals. A couple of swarthy muscle boys at a corner table watched me when I came through the door, but I waved for coffee and went straight to a booth. After a few seconds, they realized I wasn't an issue and went back to muttering over lunch.

The monitor was locked away in a battered steel cabinet behind a lexan panel, the keyboard and optical mouse on a slide out tray underneath. I swiped the back of my hand under the scanner, and the new chip registered one 'Abuyen ibn Hadiz. Islamic Republic, Moroccan Zone. Electrical Engineer Forth class', logging on to Public Access.

Now, like any other decent contract outfit, Eshu International had high-tech gear for secure communications. Encrypted squirts are instant and nearly unbreakable, perfect for a tactical net in a combat zone, or emergency use. But if someone's balls-out hunting for you, the burst transmissions show up like flares at midnight on surveillance networks. They're a dead giveaway. We needed to stay out of sight, out of mind, so I went to Plan B.

Over the years, we'd developed a simple system of communication with our agent, Jaithirth Rao, and various other handlers and contacts. We hid in plain sight.

Most of the time, we used barely coded ads on various business and hobby message boards to stay in contact. There were hundreds of thousands of forums with millions upon millions of members and posters worldwide, so unless you knew exactly where and when to look, and could understand the jargon, intercepting our communications was like trying to find a needle in a stack of needles. On top of that, we changed location, boards and identities at random intervals. One month it might be a cooking forum, another it was robotics, and another might be dating personals, gambling, or some sleazy

Thai porn site. This month was automotive, and "geargreaser313" had parts to trade. I clicked through to the forums. Jaithirth was online and I opened a chat screen.

"Item off the shelf and packed for delivery."

"Sorry to hear about your family problems. Everyone OK? The part's still available? In good shape?"

"Of course. Our cousin is very sick though, and the weather is bad. We'll have to deliver it some other way."

"My client says he has friends coming to the area who'd be happy to pick it up and pay you."

"Has friends near me?"

"Yes. Says they love Esqueixada de Bacallà. Says it'd be no trouble."

I sat back in the hard plastic chair. Agents on our tail—that was goddamn fast. I knew APAC was hemorrhaging credits, but this was huge if they were coming to get it themselves. Gibson's face flashed in my mind. *Him, they're coming get him.* I typed again.

"Well sure. If it's no trouble. Let us know when his friends will be around, and we'll arrange to meet up. Any word on my O2 injector? My cousin's ride is in bad shape."

"Shipped out this morning, so it should be there soon. It'll need aftermarket parts once it gets there though. Can't fit everything in the priority box."

"Understand. Looking forward to it."

"Let me know ASAP when/where, so I can tell my customer. He's all hot and bothered on getting his car up and running. Excitable type. Stay cool and play safe. Out."

"You too. Out."

I logged off and leaned back, staring at the gray screen. I downed the rest of my coffee in one gulp. It was scalding, harsh all the way down, but what shook me more were the thoughts burning in my head. I got up and hurried out the door. Tam and I needed to talk to Alejo.

After dinner that night, Carmen washed the dishes, and we listened to the tiny voices of their younger girls saying their prayers upstairs. I'd told Tam and Alejo about my little net chat, and the old Spaniard sat quiet for several minutes nodding, stroking his moustache, then nodding some more. I could almost see his brain scanning through options. Finally he spoke up.

"A place with a crowd, multiple exits, and no police surveillance? I know of three such spots nearby. I haven't been to any of them since I came to Jesus. They are not good, these places. *Deporte de la sangre*—blood sport, understand? And the people who run them..." He shrugged. His shabby leather chair creaked as he leaned forward, smiling grimly. I saw the former pirate breach the surface for an instant. "There is one that will work better than the others. I will go and make arrangements. You can rendezvous there safely," he said. "Well... safer than the others."

He leaned back into his chair a contented old man, grinning under his huge moustache as he scribbled on a scrap of paper. "Here is the address. Tell these Asian Pacific agents they must come in two nights. At sunset. And now..." he pushed himself to his feet using his arms, "...one more thing."

I looked at the paper. "You're sure we can meet at this place?"

"Yes. The Arif family runs the place, and the Turks still owe me... for a couple of things." His eyes hard-edged at a memory then softened as he saw Carmen.

He'd walked stiffly over to one of the battered military trunks lodged in the corner and started rummaging through it. We watched curiously, listening to him murmur as he went through its contents item by item.

"Aha!" He turned back to us. "Now, they don't let spectators bring weapons inside of course. There are guards, and a Russian scanner at the entrance. But I still have these." He tossed a musty, stained cloth bundle onto the door table in front of us. "Could come in very handy." Tam unwrapped it with several quick motions and a dozen sharp, flat gray knives spilled out.

"Funny, the souvenirs you kept from the old life. Thought all you needed was faith," Tam asked.

"Trust God. Keep your powder dry," Alejo answered.

I picked one up. "Ceramic?"

"*Si*, Boker blades. Old C.I.A. stash, no metal at all." Alejo winked. "So they don't show on older detectors."

They had a dull stone smoothness, and I hefted the one in my palm, admiring its fine edge and evil point. It had such perfect balance I tossed it thrumming into the doorjamb across the room.

"Hey!" Carmen hit me with her dishtowel. "You're going to fix that!"

CHAPTER FIFTEEN

LAND OF OPPOSITES

Gibson: I don't know what to do. There's no terminal here, no wireless, no Public Access, not even a flat screen for normal vid-casts. I want to contact Dr. Evans, tell him I'm all right, tell him to come and get me, but I can't. I don't know where I am.

Before yesterday, I'd always been in the same place. Separated from other people, monitored in a restricted area, kept busy with tests, lists, instructions, schedules, examinations, more tests, every day was divided up into half-hour slots. I don't remember my life any other way. Only nurses touched me, only doctors spoke to me, only scientists came to see me, and always there was another assignment. But I've been dropped in a land of opposites. Everything in this place is dirty and dark and loud and warm and up close. There are people touching, hugging, talking, eating, laughing. The three big men want to play games and show me their rifles, their equipment. The older man and woman are nice, always bringing food, getting me to smile. Even the other two soldiers try to be kind. I am lost. And happy. This is the first time I've ever had nothing to do. It scares me a little.

The one they call Poet9 is still sick. He was the man on the Grid, and he's lying on the other side of the room, not moving. It has something to do with the grafted unit on his head, and everyone is worried, especially the older man and woman. They smile and say it will be all right, but I think it might not be. I've seen that look before on Dr. Evans' face. The men are waiting for their own doctor to come and make Poet9 well. For some reason, it's difficult. I think because people are searching for me.

I'm not sure I want to be found.

CHAPTER SIXTEEN

GOOD INTENTIONS

Barcelona Port Complex, Asian Pacific Consortium Trade Offices,
Bureau D. South Dock, Level Five. 9:03 a.m. Day Two.

The guard snapped to attention as Colonel Otsu approached the black armor-glass entrance. He returned the boy's salute and entered the security office.

They seem younger every deployment. Or am I really that old now? he thought wryly. He made a mental note to learn the young corporal's name and welcome him to the unit. He wanted to let him know his commander wasn't so ancient as to not be on top of things. Yet another thing to do later. The bedlam of the dockyards snapped off behind him, replaced by the steady hum of air-conditioning and the array of computer systems. A small mob of Asian Pacific traders swirled around large-screen monitors, shouting into satellite phones, sending their clerks scurrying off in random directions every few seconds. Compared to the twenty-four-hour racket of the Port Complex, it seemed positively blissful. His secretary was waiting, hot tea and several data pads in hand. She came alongside him instantly, matching his stride.

"Good morning, Colonel. Captains Asaki and Girin-Taga want to speak with you this afternoon about the Libyan longshoremen. They say it's urgent. Please sign here. And here. The Traders Collective has pushed up the monthly meeting to tomorrow morning, 0800. And here too, sir. Sergeant Hashimi requested an order of one hundred new cameras to extend the coverage on levels three, four, and five. And there's a secure line waiting for you, sir. E.U. Regional Office. Again."

His brow furrowed. "How long?"

"Less than five minutes."

"Route it to my office. No disturbances."

She nodded and moved off as Colonel Otsu entered his small office. Latching the door behind him, he saw the green light was flashing on his desktop monitor. He steeled himself with several deep breaths, took his seat and pressed the "Accept" button. Avery Hsiang's plump face snapped into view.

"Colonel Otsu. You have kept me waiting."

"My apologies, Mr. Hsiang. It was unintended. I returned to the Trade Office moments ago. For added plausibility, my unit is conducting a security audit here at the Docks. The cover story you devised is ingenious, but quite demanding. It's necessary we maintain appearances."

"I have no time for excuses," the manager fired back. "Tell me about the mission. Have the Type Fives arrived yet?"

"Within the hour, sir. I've sent one of my men—Lieutenant Kaneda—to pick them up and get them to a safe house. In the meantime, we've made contact with the mercenary team's agent and have made arrangements to meet."

"When?"

"Soon, sir. Our initial contact is tomorrow night."

"Perhaps I have failed to impress on you the imperative nature of this mission. I want that technology now. Not 'soon.' Now, Colonel Otsu. Avery Hsiang said dryly. "I didn't hear from you last night. I want updates. Why are my orders being disregarded?"

Colonel Otsu frowned inwardly, but bowed low.

This man is far too anxious about this mission. Is he simply uneasy about the funds? Or is it something more? "Mr. Hsiang, I meant no disrespect. This morning's sit-rep will outline our plan and mission details. I will compile pertinent information for this evening's report as the situation develops."

"I want up-to-the-minute reports. Just what do you deem to be 'pertinent information', Colonel?"

"Sir, nothing substantial has changed since yesterday. The Type Five clones will arrive shortly. We have an apartment in a sprawl neighborhood near the Docks that will act as a temporary base for their operation. My lieutenant will support them in every possible way, and I have transport standing by once the item is in hand. My entire unit stands ready to assist them."

Avery Hsiang scowled. "You are restating the obvious, Colonel. I want specifics. Tell me specifics on the operation."

"A preliminary meeting between the clones and the mercenaries is scheduled for tomorrow evening," Colonel Otsu said.

"Where is this meeting?" Hsiang snapped.

"At a public location in the sprawl's northern sector."

"Northern sector? Is that where the item is?"

"Mr. Hsiang, it is a rendezvous spot. The mercenaries could be holed up anywhere in the slums around the city. The Type Fives are simply going to work out the details of getting the device. The mercenaries are professionals, Mr. Hsiang. It is highly unlikely they'll have the technology with them."

"Professionals would have delivered the device on time. Get that device, Colonel. Nothing else matters," Avery Hsiang said.

"Yes, sir, we're moving as quickly as possible, despite the increasingly complicated situation." The Colonel spoke quickly.

The manager's round face creased with impatience. "Colonel, your excuses are taxing."

"Sir, I'm stating facts. The Regional Threat Level has just been raised based on the possibility of a terrorist attack here at the Port Complex." Colonel Otsu consulted a data pad from his desk. "Spanish government troops and Dawson-Hull Special Deployment units are conducting district by district sweeps, presumably in search of the terrorists. We believe the story has been manufactured as justification for Dawson-Hull's efforts to regain the device. Nevertheless, the entire Barcelona Sprawl is under restriction, with a corresponding surveillance and security increase."

"You thought a declaration of martial law was not pertinent?"

Colonel Otsu bowed his head. "The state of emergency is on all the Euro-newsnets, sir. I had no intention of wasting your already valuable time."

"Colonel, your good intentions are irrelevant." Avery Hsiang breathed out a heavy sigh. "Perhaps you're too obtuse to appreciate the delicacy of this matter. I neither know nor care. I want this operation brought to a successful conclusion, and I'm going to inform the *shinigami* they are free to act on my authority. I'm even considering granting them 'maximum sanction', anything so long as they get the device."

Maximum Sanction? To a clone unit? Colonel Otsu was shocked. "Sir... maximum sanction. Is that wise? The risks of a covert operation like this are large enough without adding—"

"Colonel Otsu," the Executive Manager interrupted. "I'm not accustomed to subordinates questioning my decisions. You are there to facilitate this operation, not complicate it. Do I have to spell this out for you, Colonel? Tokyo Head Office considers this critical to the company's global strategic interests. Get your head on straight, and quickly, or you will be seeking new employment. In the zones."

Tokyo Head Office... Colonel Otsu ignored the threat and focused on that phrase. A shadow of suspicion flickered in his mind. "Should I be forwarding my reports to the Directorate and Central Operations as well, sir?"

Avery Hsiang slapped that idea away with a wave of his hand. "That's only more time wasted. This mission is streamlined and red-stamped 'Top Secret', and is being run through my office. Duplicate channels only give opportunity for bureaucratic interference, and create a potential security breech. I will make a full disclosure to Central after the matter is successfully concluded. Your only concern is acting to that end: success." Avery Hsiang tapped his finger on his desktop, emphasizing the last word.

"Very good, sir," the colonel bowed toward the screen, suspicion brushing his thoughts again.

Obtuse am I? Mr. Hsiang, you are trying to fly under the radar... Why?

The manager's face relaxed somewhat, and he took on a more conciliatory tone. "Colonel, before us is a rare window of opportunity, an opportunity for everyone involved. Be assured, in the future I will not neglect those who recognized this for what it was and acted appropriately. I expect you and your men to do your duty." The older executive suddenly glanced off screen. "Colonel, I have an incoming call. I will contact you later. Hsiang out."

The connection cut.

"Of course Mr. Hsiang," the colonel answered, but the image had already faded. Colonel Otsu turned, grabbed his black and red uniform jacket and headed straight out the door. His secretary was waiting for him, more data pads stacked in her arms.

You and your men…

The face of the young corporal came unbidden to his mind. What was his name? The colonel mentally added another item to his agenda for the already long day.

The hanging ceiling bulbs divided the large cellar room into smaller lit portions, each separated by thin walls of dimness. After breakfast, the Triplets played a loud card game with Gibson and Curro: two-deck Scum. They'd learned it onboard Alejo's ship. It was also the only one they knew, so they took great delight each round changing seats and teasing the loser. The three large clone soldiers played with a simple, unaffected joy, snapping cards down, roaring with laughter or groaning with each discard. Curro sat smiling, but saying little, one eye always on the stairway, while Gibson picked up on the game's strategy quickly and had retained his "king" position the last three rounds. At a break, Gibson slipped off his chair and entered into a lit fragment of a corner where Carmen sat next to Poet9's bed pallet.

The autodoc was beeping at a calm, steady pace, tiny columns of green alpha-numerics bouncing in time on its small gray screens. Carmen sat on the edge of the bed, one hand on Poet9's head, murmuring a soft singsong cadence. He shuffled closer, curious, but reluctant to interrupt her. After several minutes, Carmen switched the monitor volume off and smiled at him. "Yes?"

"Is he… Is he going to get better?"

"Yes. Yes. He'll be fine," she said. Another smile.

"Really?"

Carmen sighed and pushed back a stray lock of thick black hair. "Well, *pequeño,* I hope and pray so. He's not getting any worse; he just isn't getting any better. Out doctor friend will know what to do."

"That's good then." Gibson shifted his feet but didn't move away.

"You want something else?" Carmen asked.

"I want…" the boy faltered. "I want to go back."

"Back?"

"Yes. Back to the labs. I don't know why I'm here. Please."

Carmen hesitated, watched hope, confusion, and fear trace across his little face. That look dredged up a montage of memories: screams, fire, blood, and bodies. She closed her eyes and shook them away. The old life was over, buried with Christ. And thank God because some things were better left buried. She remembered the Scripture: *"As far as the East is from the West, so has He removed our transgressions from us."*

Alejo had warned her. The boy would be gone in a couple of days, he'd said. "Don't get attached." He knew her heart. Yet a child was in front of her, in her home, right now. She reached out and drew Gibson close. "Ah, *pequeño*, I'm sorry, but you're not going back. These men are taking you back to your family."

"My family?"

"Si, your mother and father? They must miss you very much."

"But… but, I don't have a family."

"Of course you do!" She hugged him again. "That's why you're on this little adventure. To go see them."

"No," the boy said firmly. "I don't have a mother or a father. I'm not like other children." He reached up and touched the back of his neck with slim fingers. "Dr. Evans said that's what my mark means."

Carmen craned her head and brushed his hair aside. There, nestled at the base of his neck was a small, round, neon blue shotcode: a gene series tattoo. Further up, she spied the small, smooth bud of a flesh pink dermal jack behind his left ear. The boy was a clone. One with cyber-system capabilities. She looked over the side of his head, smoothing his hair and feeling his scalp underneath: there was no interface set, not even a small one. She sat back, piecing it all together.

Now they're growing children? She looked upwards. *Lord Jesus, what's happening here?* But her thoughts only bounced off the ceiling right back at her.

She knew all too well what kind of work Tam and his crew did. It had been called "left-hand work" when she and Alejo had started. It was dirty work, crap work that no one wanted. For decades, in the guise of fighting terrorism, Interpol and all the major national security agencies had been closing in on organized crime. Every boss was tired of extradition trials, lawyers, harassment, audits, SWAT teams, watching their money and influence drain away faster than blood from a butchered carcass. They grew frantic to survive, to stay in power, so they looked for the new need and followed the money. They found cover on the shady side of legitimate.

Decades of declining defense budgets and the rise of the private military industry was a tailor-made opportunity. Back then, the first freelance crews had been hired through organized crime syndicates. The muscle and transportation networks already in place, the Yakuza, the Triads, the Mafia families took contracts no above-board private firm would touch: anything, anywhere, for anybody, so long as it paid. For twenty years, she and Alejo ran blockades all across the Med and Black Sea, every assignment performed old school. Low-tech, sanitized surplus weapons, forged documents, brush pass hand-offs, dead drops. Payment to crews was always untraceable tangible goods: pharmaceuticals, gold, diamonds, narcotics. People made a lot of money, and a lot of people died.

Nowadays, every major business entity and nation on the planet hired "conflict-resolution specialists" for black contract work. Fancy terms for accounting; it was the same cruel game. The executives, the government ministers, the regional managers could now hide behind operational prudence, the legal terminology of disconnect that guaranteed plausible deniability. It was the commerce of felony and murder.

She caught Gibson staring at her, and smiled quickly. "Well then... you're going someplace new. You must have new friends, and you're going to meet them soon."

"What kind of new friends? Dr. Evans never said anything about new friends." Gibson's face knit in concentration. "He did tell me some important people would come to the labs, and we'd do new kinds of tests. But he said I needed to rest and be ready for them." He frowned at Carmen. "Is this a test?"

"No, no... this is not your doctor's test." She folded her hands back onto her lap. "But this is like a test, perhaps the hardest so far. In this one, you're going to have to be brave no matter what happens. Gibson, can you do that for me?"

"Dr. Evans said it wasn't safe for me to leave." He bit his lip and looked straight at Carmen. "There was shooting and explosions. They stole me. Why?"

Carmen took him gently by the shoulders, "Listen to me, little one. I'm not sure why you were taken, or where you will end up. But I promise no one is going to hurt you while you're in my home. You believe me?"

"Yes. I think so." Gibson frowned. "OK, I do."

"Good!" She hugged him quickly. "Thank you, Gibson. You're a very brave boy. Now tell me about the other tests you took. Were they hard for you?"

He drew his eyes away from Poet9. "Well, I'm not supposed to say anything... but no, they weren't very hard. They were on computers. In them, really."

"In them?" Carmen looked intently at his head again.

"Yes, in the cyber-systems. I'd log into networks the staff set up. Later they opened the base system for me, most of the departments anyway. And in the last month, I even went out into the Grid for them eight times."

"And did what?"

"I went to secure sites, to data mine, or re-script code. At first, it was hard, trying to understand it all, but after a few tries, I got it, and then it was easy. As easy as thinking. Sometimes security programs stop me though."

"ICE programs?" Carmen exclaimed. "What were you doing messing around with them? Security A.I.s are very dangerous. And you're much too young to be a data rat."

Gibson threw his head back and laughed. "The staff called me that a couple times. It got Dr. Evans mad, but they didn't care. He taught me code to get past security systems. 'Felix the Cat's magic bag of tricks' he called it. I use it all the time now. The staff was very happy the first time I cut my way through a firewall. They said I was the fastest so far."

The fastest so far... Carmen filed the comment away for later. For now, she smiled at him, crow's feet catching the corners of her eyes. "Then you are not only brave, but smart, eh?" She stroked his cheek. "You'll be fine."

"Ma'am, can I ask you a question?" the boy asked hesitantly.

"Of course!"

"You're a fundy, aren't you?"

"A what?"

"A fundy, a fundamentalist. One of those religious people. They pray all the time and blow things up. I've seen newsnet clips. At the lab, they talk about religion, but only as a joke. You don't seem like one of those."

"Well," Carmen laughed. "I pray and believe in God, but I stopped blowing things up when I became a Christian."

"So what were you praying for just then?" he asked.

"I was asking for help," Carmen said.

"For him?" Gibson pointed at Poet9.

"Yes, for him. For all of them, and you too."

Gibson stopped at that thought, nodded and pressed on. "Dr. Evans says religion is an irrational superstition, a product of people's wish fulfillment. There's no proof God exists."

"Little one, there's plenty of proof," Carmen said. "It's all around you if you know how to look. God exists, just not on a specimen slide."

"But you can't see God. You can't be sure He's there, listening to you."

"Let me ask you something... could you imagine the Grid before they let you into it? What it would be like? How vast and intricate it was? You couldn't see it, but it was there, right?"

"Well no, but they told me about it, and after the first time I logged in I knew it was real."

"Well, God is real the same way, and I experience Him when I log in. In prayer."

"Where, in your brain?"

"Yes, but mostly in my heart."

"Ummm… that's weird," the boy said.

Carmen laughed again. "Yes, I suppose it is."

A shadow fell over the two of them. Carmen looked up to see her son, Curro, standing beside the bed. "Dr. Kalahani made it in past the district patrols. He's at the door, mama."

"Well, show him in." She turned and winked at Gibson. "The doctor made it. See? God heard me."

CHAPTER SEVENTEEN

DARK EYES, UNBLINKING

Barcelona Metro Zone. Eastern Sprawl, Dock District: La Sentina neighborhood. 1:45 p.m. Day Two.

The knob trembled, and three heads turned simultaneously to watch the door open. The *shinigami* remained seated as Lieutenant Kaneda stepped through, struggling with a large knapsack. When the young officer kicked the door shut, he glared at the clones, and the three of them stared back, heads cocked, faces unreadable, dark eyes unblinking. The lieutenant dropped his gaze and suppressed a shudder.

Colonel Otsu had told him these clones would be different, some new kind deployed specially for this mission. He hadn't realized just how different they would be, and Lieutenant Kaneda wondered if they all felt like this. They looked normal, human, but something about them made his skin crawl, something vaguely reptilian. He couldn't put his finger on it.

He was astonished at how perfect they appeared: olive complexions, dark hair and Spanish features. No hint of makeup or surgery, the three of them looked genuinely native. One man was tall and broad, thick, like a heavy laborer, the other small and race dog thin, almost malnourished. Those two passed for characteristic sprawl dwellers.

The woman was another story. Perhaps there had been some kind of error, a comfort girl series spill over into the gene-coding. She was medium height, but full-bodied, with fine features and sensuous lips. Lt. Kaneda thought that even dirty and dressed in cheap worker's clothes, she was far too striking for the slums. And of the three, she was the most unnatural. Like a cobra; beautiful, hypnotic, and lethal. Maybe the executive who ordered their deployment did that for a reason…

The lieutenant forced the thought away. He had to stay on task. The colonel had ordered him to oversee the activities of this clone cell. It was imperative everything went smoothly, and it wasn't like these three were really human.

He cleared his throat, and tried to project command tone in his voice. "You going to sit there and watch? Or do mission parameters allow you to help me?"

The larger male slipped out of his chair and took the heavy backpack with one hand. He set it in the corner without a word.

The young officer gathered himself and wiped his brow. "Now, these are your accommodations. To maintain operational security, no one is to leave without my express permission."

The clones surveyed the apartment. It was little more than a concrete box, twice as large as a prison cell. Half the illum-tiles in the ceiling were burnt out, and the walls were thick with slathered coats of white paint. Bed pallets lay off to one side, and a pitted stainless steel sink, cooking, and fridge unit were bolted along the opposite wall. The closet at the far end of the room held a chemical toilet and cheap one-piece plasti-form shower stall, and the only window was a dingy square of acid rain frosted plastic that looked out onto the gray slab of the next tenement two meters away.

A bizarre, psychedelic cyclone of caricatured icons, astrological symbols and anarchist graffiti was drawn on one wall in black magic marker. It twisted up out of the corner by the floor and ended at the ceiling. The musk of stale sweat and ammonia was soaked into everything. The squalor meant nothing to the clones, and the three looked back at the lieutenant without comment.

The young officer cleared his throat again, "You shouldn't have any problems with your identities either. They've been inserted into the Barcelona database along with job covers. The area around here houses dockhands and migrant workers. Thousands of transients come and go from this district every week, so your arrival and disappearance shouldn't be noticed. As long as you don't do anything to attract attention, you should be fine."

The woman finally spoke, an odd, husky rhythm in her voice. "We'll be sure to maintain operational security." She glanced at the other two clones. They acknowledged her statement with the briefest of nods.

Lieutenant Kaneda let out a breath he hadn't realized he'd been holding. "Yes, that's good. It won't be for long anyhow. You're meeting with the contractors tomorrow night to discuss delivery and extraction. This operation should be over soon." He paused. "In fact, I'm not sure why you're here at all. My men and I can manage the situation."

"We're here to insure the mercenaries deliver the device they were contracted to acquire," the woman spoke again.

"My unit has coordinated covert missions before," the lieutenant said. "We can handle freelance contractors."

"Apparently not." The big man was staring at him. "The executive himself informed us that your unit failed. We will not fail."

Lieutenant Kaneda bristled. "The only reason your cell was deployed is your capability to blend in to the local population. It's unwarranted, but if the executive believes you can make the delivery go smoothly, then who am I to argue? In the meantime, you will follow my orders."

"We will not fail," the big man repeated.

The lieutenant ignored him and pointed at the heavy bag in the corner. "That's the first load of equipment. I want a hand getting the rest from the van downstairs. You," he motioned to the larger man, "will come help me bring the other bags up."

The large clone stood without a word and the two of them left. Once the dingy steel door had shut, the other two started going through the knapsack. Executive Hsiang himself had briefed them during their flight. For the next ninety-six hours, they were under his direct authority and could employ whatever means necessary to acquire the device.

Given the deadline, a direct solution was required, and once all the equipment was present, the three of them would outfit themselves accordingly. Simple, direct action, that's what the executive demanded. They would seize one of the mercenaries and force him to divulge the location of the device. Once they'd acquired it, they would sanitize any evidence leading back to the executive. That was their directive.

Footsteps scuffed in the hall outside, then someone began banging on the door with a fist. "Cleto! Cleto, open up! I know you're in there, you little pussy. Open the fucking door before I break it down." A muffled voice came through the metal.

The two clones slid silently to stand on either side of the door.

"Cleto, you monkey shit. I want my money! Open this fucking door and give me my fucking money right now!"

The door shook under more pounding. The two looked at each other and on a signal, the female clone flattened herself against the wall while the small man thumbed the lock and turned the knob. The steel door flapped open on a kick, and a broad, shaven-headed gorilla of a man sauntered in.

"Cleto, you're dead this time. I mean it." He stopped when he saw the small man. "Who the fuck are you? Where's Cleto?"

"Cleto?" the small clone asked.

The sprawl ganger shifted the bulk of his body and pulled a length of chain from inside his filthy denim jacket. "Yeah, Cleto. I asked you a question, shithead. Where is he?"

"There's no one named Cleto here,"

The ganger glanced around the room. "Well, I can fucking see that, you little dickwad. You're Cleto's friend or something, right? Cleto leave my money? Little junkie owes me." The big man stepped forward, closing in on the small clone. He didn't move.

The heavy ganger growled and rolled his shoulders. "You'd better smarten up, paco. You have no fucking idea who you're fucking with here." He puffed out his chest and jabbed a fat, dirty finger in the clone's face.

The *shinigami* looked up at him, his voice lowered to a whisper. "We're new here. We don't know this 'Cleto'. You've made a mistake and come to the wrong apartment."

"The fuck I did!" the big man roared. "I know that little shit's artiste scribble." He gestured with the chain at the drawings. "Fuck you! I didn't come all the way over here to be jerked around by some pussy-assed little fucker!" He glared around the room again. "Someone's paying me my money. If it ain't Cleto, then it's got to be you." He smiled all teeth. "So lucky fucking you." He reached behind him and slammed the door. "Now pay up!"

As the metal door screeched into place, the woman stepped away from the wall and waved her hand casually. The shaven head caught it out of the corner of his eye and jerked a step sideways against the possible threat. In that instant, the small man darted forward and slid up along his barrel chest. Reaching up, he grasped the ganger's chin and the smooth curve of the back of his head. There was a loud snap.

A look of surprise suddenly flitted across the big man's face. He realized, in the split second remaining, that he was looking at a woman directly behind him. She stared into his eyes as they went flat and the big ganger folded into himself onto the floor at her feet.

The door swung open again and Lieutenant Kaneda swept in, a two-fisted grip on a little Daewoo automatic pistol. "I heard a noise. What the—?" He froze, staring at the body. "Who's he? What happened?"

The female agent spoke first. "He forced his way in. He said he was looking for a previous tenant who owed him money."

"So you killed him?"

"He was a witness," the small male spoke up. "His presence compromised operational security."

"Operational secur—? Was there anybody else? Did anyone see him come in here?"

The big *shinigami* strode in behind him carrying two more of the military sacks slung over his shoulder. He took in the body with impassive eyes and set the packs down. "There weren't any others."

Lieutenant Kaneda turned on him. "What? How do you know?"

"We passed downstairs. I checked in the lobby, and in the street, while you were talking on your phone. He was alone."

Lieutenant Kaneda ran his hands through his hair. "Not even six hours in country…" The three clones saw his hands tremble as he holstered the pistol under his arm. "All right," he pointed to the smaller man. "You. You made this mess, so you're going to clean it up. You need to get rid of the body somehow."

"It is not necessary. The three of us are were ordered to focus on—"

"I'm the ranking officer!" Lieutenant Kaneda shouted. "And I say you can't keep a body here."

The three clones froze. "What about operational security?" the small man asked softly.

Lieutenant Kaneda stammered. "Exercise some, just get it done. I'll be back at 2200 hours and I expect this body to be gone."

As the young officer left the room, a silent understanding passed between the *shinigami*. Activated under Executive Hsiang's direct authority, he'd made a point to tell them he considered all local, corporate personnel and materials secondary to their mission objective. They must obtain the nanotechnology, and they could use whatever lethal force they deemed necessary. Those were his explicit orders.

They would not fail.

It was the end of another sweep and sniff operation in a filthy neighborhood south of the Barcelona UpCity. The sun was hot and high overhead, and Major Eames stood in the hatch of her command APC, the metal armor heating up like an oven plate. She pushed down her bone-deep weariness and swept the crowd with hard eyes.

This was the eleventh neighborhood her unit had searched in two days, and they were starting to blur together. All of it blurred together, in fact. God only knew how many times she'd driven down the similar trash-blown streets, past drab, decaying buildings splashed with the bright graffiti tags. Hell, she'd grown up outside the London Metro Zone, escaping a dead-end existence by enlisting in D-H Security Services on her seventeenth birthday. Except for a bit of local flavor, this place looked just like the old neighborhood. It was the same grimy, congealed mass, populated by sullen men smoldering in their impotence, snot-faced, scrawny children, and pinched, pleading mothers clutching their paltry belongings. Suffering Christ, it was Hell on the dole.

Bangladesh, Budapest, Brixton or Barcelona… it didn't matter; the sprawls were spreading, swallowing each other. Soon, there'd be nothing but one continuous slum covering the planet, punctuated only by an occasional walled corporate oasis. Everywhere a vast accretion of people, concrete, steel, and garbage, bordered by cold, empty oceans stirred by sluggish tides.

God damn it, she hated this place. She hawked, trying to spit the stench of rotting fruit, piss, and exhaust from the back of her throat. It didn't help.

She glared over the crowd again, saw it flex and ripple. Even not understanding the language, she recognized the running mutter of resentment. News was spreading and things were definitely getting worse. She'd deployed four platoons this time, and they'd cordoned the whole neighborhood into the parking decks near some central square so the search and sniff teams could sweep their buildings unmolested.

But nothing worked right. Even with all the credits they were floating around, the sprawlers grew more restless, less cooperative in each neighborhood. They'd grown defiant. Fights had broken out in the last three neighborhoods, and the Spanish troops were chafing under the contempt. Perhaps starting in the southern sprawl hadn't been the best idea. Those Basques had a long memory.

She rubbed her eyes to clear them. Someone—it sounded like a man— started shouting, and immediately a chant surged up. She scanned him, but all she caught was the tidal sway of grubby faces burbling on the riot edge of panic. A line of G.C. police moved forward, while troopers on top of armored vehicles pointed "Screamers", focused acoustic amplifiers, toward the crowd.

Major Eames gripped the lip of the hatch opening. *Christ on a crutch, not again,* she thought, and braced herself. But the tension deflated at the sight of the police and the threat of noise suppression. The Spanish colonel, Estevana, came up to the side of the vehicle.

"Report, Colonel?"

"Si, Major. Nothing unusual. Again. The typical assortment of drugs: some crank, about five hundred hits of slipstream, and three kilos of rage. Four handguns, two old military assault rifles, several boxes of anarchist propaganda. That's all, Major."

"And no hit with the sniffers, right?" Dawson-Hull allocated two full search teams with DNA samplers to lock onto trace genetic material, either from the asset or the unidentified blood found inside the lab.

"No, Major. Nothing."

"Any word from Interpol?"

"No ma'am. Not a thing."

She slammed her hand on the steel ring. "Someone has that blood on file. The infiltrators didn't get that good without a background. Somebody trained them, ran them, then cut them loose, so there has to be a trace out there. We need a break here. What about the Cross-Corporate Data Share?

"With all due respect, Major, most of the profiles there are bottom feeders: thieves, fanatics, anarchists. All loose cannons, dangerous to any concern. No multinational is going to profile a first-rate operative. Especially one they might contract."

"Yeah, you're right. Very well then." She waved wearily. "We have to keep moving. No arrests, seize all the contraband. Distribute the food and med packets along with the reward bulletins. Make sure they understand informants remain anonymous. Then tell the troops they can stand down for one hour before the next sweep."

"Yes, ma'am. At once." He saluted and started chattering into his radio. Diesel engines roared to life and black smoke swirled in the air. A line of army supply trucks inched forward into the central square.

She spit again and looked over the crowd one last time. The perimeter troops were shouting now, herding the crowds into rough lines in front of each supply truck. The mob shifted under orders, collecting around the tall drab vehicles. She watched them take their bribe bundles and trudge back to their ransacked homes. At the head of one line, a little blonde girl in a flower-print dress was staring directly at her armored personnel carrier. Small fires of contempt, unclouded by self-pity, burned in her eyes. Major Eames stopped and remembered being the same age, watching police patrols cruise past her building in South London, and she wondered if she ever looked like that.

CHAPTER EIGHTEEN

CONTINUITY OF SIGN

Barcelona Metro Zone. Western Sprawl District. 2:10 p.m. Day Two.

Hester stared at the map in front of him. Barcelona Metro's four districts were highlighted in blue, the massive Port Complex in gray. Where, o where had the little lamb gone?

He eliminated Old Barcelona first. Whoever stole the boy was good, but wouldn't have the time or money to go to ground in UpCity. So scratch one. The Port was busy round-the-clock, so no sense hiding there. Scratch two. That left the sprawls. Three major districts, eighteen sub-districts, twenty million plus people crammed into twenty-four thousand square kilometers. That's where he'd go, and if these contractors were half as good as they seemed, that's where they'd be.

Hester rotated the map to another angle. At least there wasn't a civil war going on, he thought. That would make this downright impossible. But where to start? That was the question. He needed continuity of sign, some evidence of the team's passage or intentions, to narrow down the search. Hester wondered for the fifth time why the boy wasn't chipped. But then, that would make this easy. At least the dark room lads had given him a tracker. The nanite-rich hemoglobin in the boy's blood would register, but only when he was within ten kilometers. *I suppose I should be glad they have such confidence in my abilities…* Hester sighed and rotated the map again.

The sat-link chimed in his ear. "Hester?"

"Yes, Mr. MacKinnon?"

"What's the situation?"

"On site, getting my bearings, sir. Any word on who rousted the Toulouse labs yet?"

"Still waiting on the report on the blood found in the lab, but there's a very short list of teams that capable," MacKinnon's voice answered. "Cross-reference those few with probable connections to Asian Pacific... and an Eshu International out of Belfast is on top. Not confirmed, mind you, but they're the most likely suspects."

"Understood, sir. Profiles available on Eshu International crew? I'm monitoring both Eames' task force and the Spanish Security Grid, and I'll integrate their chatter into the search parameters, but it'd be helpful to know who I'm up against. Maybe narrow the search down a bit."

"I'm forwarding their files now. Let me know if you need anything else. That clone must be picked up, alive, and healthy. Our property is the priority, and Brenton tells me there's very little time."

"All I need is to get close, sir. Once I'm in the neighborhood, the tracker will pick him up. I'll verify the boy's presence and take it from there. I won't let you down, Mr. MacKinnon."

"You never have, Hester. That's why I brought you in on this."

"Thank you, sir. I'll let you know as soon as I have something definite."

"Right, MacKinnon out."

Hester opened the personnel files for Eshu International and started scanning. "All right lads, if you're the toshers in question, there must be a reason you picked Barcelona. So what is it?"

That afternoon, Barcelona Metro authorities slammed a lockdown on the sprawls. Constant *policia* patrols, transport hubs under heavy restriction, checkpoints on all major roads, and a curfew at 23:30 until further notice made a sticky situation worse. Word through Alejo's contacts said a large contingent of Dawson-Hull troops were acting as "security advisors" to local law enforcement, and that they'd run dozens of no knock, sweep and clear operations in the south district. D-H was searching hard for Gibson.

It looked like they were gearing up to do the same here because I spotted the black bellies of surveillance drones circling in the sky like vultures, and I noticed heavy police concentrations at the local precincts. To top it off, the newsnets had begun streaming terrorist alerts every fifteen minutes, and Tam and I guessed those had at least ten million impoverished citizens peering out their windows eyeing every stranger for a shot at the government reward money.

Paranoia Lotto. Free this week! Play early. Play often.

Just when I couldn't think of another thing to make my time in Barcelona more difficult, Tam tapped me to make the run on a UpCity hospital to steal the cyber-equipment for Poet9. I love it when I volunteer.

I'd gone to check on Poet9, and found Tam and Doc K. in mid-conversation. Standing over him, they both looked pretty grim.

"How is he, Ibram?" I asked. "Is he… fused?"

Ibram Kalahani had been our resident sawbones for over ten years, ever since the last Middle East war. His tall, almost gaunt, frame housed one of the most brilliant minds in advanced medical technology, but the elderly Israeli doctor shook his head at my question. "I was telling Tam, I don't have the right equipment, but as far as I can determine, the breakers in the interface module tripped in time. His central nervous system was shocked from the blast, there doesn't seem to be any permanent damage."

"So he'll pull through. How long until he comes around?" I said. "It's getting hairier every hour, and I don't want to overstay my welcome."

"Devante is in a light coma. His body is protecting itself and trying to heal."

"That's good. For how long?"

"That's where it gets knotty. Cyber gear, especially that sophisticated, connects directly with his cerebral cortex. It's wired into the nerve bundles. That machine is part of him, so to bring him out of the coma, it needs to be reset. He's not going anywhere until that happens."

"So hit the button and reset it," Tam said.

"If it were that easy, you think we'd be having this conversation? That's an advanced Chiba-Essen series, a state-of-the-art military and corporate security interface module. I can't just run into CompWorld and pick up the softs over the counter. The unit needs specialized equipment. Equipment I told you I don't have here." Ibram answered.

"Where do we get it?" Tam asked.

I could tell by the look on Doc's face we weren't going to like the answer.

"Only two places I know of: locked up in a top-level prosthetics and microsurgery department in a corporate city hospital, or secured at an advanced cybernetic spec-ops trauma unit on a military base. Take your pick."

I was right. We didn't like the answer.

CHAPTER NINETEEN

Research Facility Five, Asian Pacific Consortium Black Lab.
Chishima Islands. 5:23 p.m. Day Two.

The wind was a moaning constant out of the Pacific, an icy wall of sound and force off the churning water that drove painfully into his body and stung uncovered skin numb. Completely alone on the surface of the island, Dr. Shoei leaned forward ever so slightly, relaxing in slow degrees, and allowed the force of the gale to keep him upright. Below, blue steel waves smashed onto black crags, turning to mist and hissing as they withdrew. The sound of their assault poured up and over the cliff edge, roaring in the air around him and joining the relentless howl.

He found it perfect.

None of his coworkers joined him in his weekly trips to the top. "Expeditions" he jokingly called them. After their first time, usually in the first month of their assignments at the facility, they never came with him again. Ever. They complained it was desolate and stayed below after that initial exposure. They choose to recreate in the gym, library, or V.R. Not even security accompanied him anymore. After all, where could he go?

But Dr. Shoei returned to the black rock surface of the island every week. This was his pilgrimage, and he, like a faithful *junreisha,* trod the same path, along the same promontory, to the same high cliff every time. There on the sharp overhang, the ocean and sky stretched away vast and empty beneath his feet, and the far horizon vanished in alloyed gray. There he was surrounded, subsumed by it all.

He had decided his fellow scientists were frightened. They were too conditioned to the frenetic hives of Tokyo or Osaka, Kobe or Nagasaki, to the endless rivers of people, vehicles, light, and noise. The harsh expanse unnerved them. To be honest, Dr. Shoei had felt far more alone in those warrens of steel, glass and concrete, the labs, universities, mega-cities, than he ever felt here. The others needed the comfort of commotion, but after his first time up top, he'd found himself craving the emptiness.

This was a primal solitude, a severity of penance, as if the wind were scouring out the static and chaff, blowing away the incessant demand and petty pressures, leaving behind a wilderness, stark and terrible, beautiful in its clarity. This was his chiseled *shuin* for another week below. The wind paused, and the doctor caught himself, straightened up and opened his eyes.

He looked down at his watch: ten minutes before he had to get back to the elevator.

Back to Yomi, he smiled ironically. Legend held that once one had eaten at the hearth of the dead, it was impossible to ever return to the land of the living. Dr. Shoei hoped it wasn't true.

He looked out over the ocean, to the mercury line of sea and sky. His worry brooded like the clouds. Three of his creations were out there in that world; flawed, erratic, awakened before their time by his own hand.

True, the activation order had come from an executive, but he had not refused. *Shinigami* had been loosed from the underworld, and he was ultimately responsible.

There'd been no reports about the mission in Barcelona, and Dr. Shoei smelled the wind as if it could bring their scent, the slightest quiver of knowledge from across the oceans. There was nothing but a far off moan.

The wind filled his ears as he weighed his thoughts. The Type Fives had not been ready. He must take action to rescue them. He'd have to file a protest with the Sendai Bureau, with Tokyo Head Office if necessary. He would request a recall. Asian Pacific's security division had some of the finest operatives in the world. Surely there were trained human agents who could perform the tasks Manager Hsiang required? Challenging the requisition order could be viewed as insubordination. Dr. Shoei knew full well he risked discipline or demotion. Termination, even. But in his heart, he knew fathers must sometimes atone for their children.

With that, the scientist turned and headed toward the hidden guardhouse with its deep elevator, the wind pushing him down the narrow trail.

CHAPTER TWENTY

ZION APOCALYPSE DUB

Barcelona Metro Zone, Sant Adrià de Besòs district. Callejón del
Apuro, "Trouble Alley". 9:45 p.m. Day Two.

I didn't think I'd make it out of the Garcías' cellar alive.
Carmen looked ready to shoot me. Actually, she would have shot Alejo
first, then me. All I did was make one little comment, just thinking out
loud, about how nice it would be to have a guide in Old B. to help me find
the hospital. Naturally Alejo suggested Curro. After all, he was capable,
trustworthy, and he knew the back roads from temp work at Global Express.
It made perfect sense, but Carmen overheard us and the atmosphere in the
cellar plummeted like a cold snap. I could feel her stare drilling into my
back, and I had the sudden sensation I'd stepped between a mother bear and
her cub.

Finally I turned around to face her, to make a joke and explain, but
Carmen was looking past us over at Poet9. He was still there pale and small
on the bed pallet in the corner, breathing shallow and in sync with the
autodoc. Right now, this was his only chance. I watched her soften, and
without a word, get up and go over to kiss Curro on his forehead.

She turned to meet my gaze with hard eyes and a thin smile. "You
bring him back." I nodded, and she went upstairs. Curro could make the run
with me.

"She's going to pray." Alejo said watching her go.

"I'd be praying if I was you." Tam said after the upstairs door clicked
shut.

"Oh I do!" he laughed, and got up out of his chair.

"Are we going in the stealth suits?" Curro fixed his eyes on at the
Mitsubishi armor in the corner.

Tam shook his head. "Suits are less than fifty percent charged, and
we're going to need them to slip out of the BMZ when we're finished.
You're going to do a B & E the old fashioned way."

"This gets better and better." I muttered. "We're going regimental."

Alejo waved us over to another stack of crates. "Hah! Not quite. Lucky
for you I kept a few of my things. For sentimental reasons," he winked.
"Curro! Come help your papa. This one here. And here."

Together, they started piling equipment on the floor in front of us. All of it old school but in pristine condition: thermal masking body gloves, formfit Kevlar tac-vests, night vision sets, gecko pads for climbing, electronic lock picks, even smoke grenades and knockout gas canisters. They set it all out carefully, as if on display. Then last of all, Alejo pulled out a plastic double pistol case, faded and worn gray at the edges.

"Now you shouldn't have to use them, but since this is important... for Poet9." He paused and ran his gnarled hand over the case gently. "I will let them out of the house. My babies," he said reverently, and clicked it open. Tam and I both stared. There, snug in blue foam, lay two custom Walther P99 silenced pistols.

"They're still bang on. Almost perfect condition." Alejo crowed. "I had new firing pins machined last year. And the barrels are new too. I even have four extended magazines for each, and it all goes in these leather shoulder holsters."

He held the case in front of him and offered it to us like a communion plate. I saw Tam hesitate, then delicately lift one from its cut-out. "Beautiful," he sighed.

I rolled my eyes, "Tam, you're such a gunporn wanker. No offense, Alejo, antiques are nice and all, but I'm bringing my sub-machine gun. Those belong in a museum."

Alejo and Tam both turned to me at the same time, looking like I'd farted in church.

"What? I'm a big fan of microchip targeting." I said.

Alejo snapped the case shut. "Bah! Such a heathen blasphemer. Why do I bother?" While Tam looked away shaking his head, Curro reached past and plucked the pistol out of his grasp. He deftly ejected the magazine and racked the slide to check the chamber, then picked up a clutch of spare mags and a holster.

"You bring that back to me. You hear me, Curro?"

"Yes, Papa. I'll bring it back."

"And listen to Jace. Do what he tells you. He is more the expert than you are in this and knows—"

"Papa, I understand." Curro said.

Alejo grabbed his son in a huge bear hug, and held him tight for several seconds. "This is for a good cause, to save a life. God's love go with you. Remember what I've taught you, and He will watch over you, bring you back safe to me and Mama."

"Yes, Father. I'll remember."

I leaned in. "Hey, Al. He'll be fine. It's just a little Breaking and Entering, right? I said I'd bring him back. Promise."

"I know, I know," he coughed gruffly. "Now...everything you need is here." He gestured over the two piles of gear. "After all...who breaks *into* a hospital, *que*?

Tam spoke up. "Pharmacy's the only place they'll have any real security. I think they will have a closed circuit system for monitoring patients, but it'll be a walk in the park. Toughest thing will be getting into the Old City itself. But once you're over the wall, all you have to do is avoid the patrols and it's a straight waltz down Ronda del Dalt. Easy in, easy out." He clapped me on the back.

"Easy, he says." I looked at Curro, who just shrugged and started stripping down.

"So, you've done this before?" I asked as he slid into a body glove. He only smiled a thin smile like his mother, and kept getting ready.

I turned to Doc Kalahani who'd been silent in the corner watching all this time. "So once we're in, then what?"

His thick eyebrows knit together. "You'll want to find the cybernetic surgery department. Check the storage near one of their O.R.s."

"How big is this cyber-surgical unit?"

"Shouldn't be too big." He held his hands up vaguely.

"How big?"

"There're several components. Each of them isn't that large."

"You don't know do you?" I stared at him.

"It's been ages since I was involved with cyber-surgery," Ibram said. "And with advances in technology, there's no way to know exactly what the components look like now. In my day, there were three main components. I can explain their functions, so you know roughly what kind of machines to look for."

"Outstanding." I said dryly and started suiting up.

Later that evening the sky slipped from red veined gold to the burnished mercury of under-glare smog. All the lights, bill boards, and holo ads mean there's no full dark in the city anymore, only hard shadows. Curro and I made our way to a nearby "red" district just outside the Old City Wall. It didn't matter the country, the city, the zone; brothels, bars, and auto-banks cropped up like weeds in the perimeter barrios. All the activity, what's two more scabs in a crowd? Slip down a dark alley and we could make our climb unnoticed.

Sure enough, the streets were thronging with people. You'd never know the curfew was just over an hour away. The place was a bedlam of house mix beats, drunken shouts, and neon holo-ads. Noise burst into the crammed streets as another swarm of pub crawlers spilled out of one venue to stagger off to their next stop. Lining the gauntlet were hawkers and hookers for every persuasion, the dealers and pimps and standing sentry in the alleys, all of them eyeing the clusters of rich kids down slumming for the night. Those drew together for mutual protection, drawing even more attention as they chattered flush-faced and colorful like schools of tropical fish going cross current in a swamp. Every now and then I spotted the shaved heads of mirror-lensed private muscle topping the crowd as they guarded their spoiled wards, herding them away from the more dangerous predators. Curro and I skirted the edges and threaded our way past the mass.

We passed one of the warehouse clubs, El Moderne 7, and out through the doors surged the chest thumping bass lines of Jahmdi Mel's *Zion Apocalypse Dub*. On cue we both sang the chorus, and laughed at each other for knowing it:

> *Visions of bliss.*
> *Paradise beckons.*
> *Gotta go strike a blow.*
> *Sins to be reckoned.*
> *Purify, rip the sky*
> *for one holy second*
> *I'm the finger of God.*
> *Resolute*
> *Absolute*
> *I'm the finger of God.*

Insanely popular, the strutting Moroccan rhythms immortalized the final Arabic attack on Israel. It was a bizarre epitaph: a dance mix death jingle for five million souls.

Curro pushed that thought further. "How'd you meet Dr. Kalahani? Mama likes him, said he's a good man."

"Your mother's right, Doc's good people." I paused. "He's Israeli, a military medical scientist with the IDF back in the day. He was on loan to the Americans, consulting with their D.I.A. and on his way back when Hamas glassed Tel Aviv. That was home. He lost everything: family, friends, work, all vaporized in one hot second as he sat at 35,000 feet." I shook my head, remembering the day news of the attacks broke over the net. "His flight got diverted to Belfast International, and Tam found him getting jumped by some skinheads in Aldergrove. He'd wandered out of the jetport, alone at night, in shock. He was just lying there getting beaten. Like he didn't care. There were five of them. He wouldn't have lasted another minute if Tam hadn't put an end to it. After, he carried him back to our place." I remembered Ibram those first few weeks; bruised purple black, swollen shut and shattered beyond words in the jigsaw confusion of anguish and loss. He didn't talk for a month.

"He stayed in the Belfast District. With us. Eventually he opened up a little clinic and assists at Royal Children's twice a week. They've offered him full sponsorship don't know how many times. Wanted to make him a department head and everything, but he keeps turning them down." I hopped over a pool of sidewalk vomit. "What's the name of this hospital again?"

"Sant Honorat. Big white buildings off the del Dalt, on Avinguda Tibidabo."

"You say you know a way in."

"Si. The garage is monitored for thieves but not the loading docks by the kitchen."

"And the OR's are one floor up in C and F wing?"

"Hoy! You boys looking for a good time?" We must have wandered too close to the mouth of an alley because two raccoon painted prostitots, both female, came clicking out on spike heels, aiming their bodies our way. Neither of them was older than sixteen, wearing little more than shiny black pleather straps and spray on glitter tops. "We know a great place to party." The one with lime green hair winked at me, a small sharp tongue darting out to lick a gash of goth blue lips. The other girl, with fire red hair, reached out towards Curro, but stopped short in a hurry.

"Curro?"

"Ria?" Curro was looking hard at her in the streetlight, not quite sure. "That you?"

We were standing still and recognized. Not good. I tugged gently at Curro's sleeve. He whispered back, "Wait. I got it."

The girl had changed, teetering on her shoes. She threw a quick pout, frowned down at the littered sidewalk. "Curro... shit! Look, I was kidding OK? Don't—" She approached him again, impossibly young now. He held up his hands.

"Ria. Hey. Don't worry. None of my business, right?"

"Yea, umm. Sorry. I mean, damnit. I didn't—" Ria latched onto her friend and started backing into the alley again. "Don't say anything. 'Kay? Please, Curro. I mean it, don't say a thing."

"No, no. No worries. Look, Ria." He glanced at me then lowered his voice conspiratorially. In a quick motion, he leafed a fifty Euro bill out of his jacket pocket and followed after them. "Tell you what Ria... this is yours for a bit of data."

"What data?" she asked, eyeing the folded bill in his hand.

"Nothing big. Nothing big." He gave her a nervous little smile. "I just figured you might know when the G.C. patrols are around here. Like on 2nd and 3rd streets. You know, you might have noticed."

He let the bill dangle a little. Her eyes flitted between his hand and an apartment doorway across the street. I'd already spotted the flashy punk hanging back in the deep recess, leaning on the lintel and watching us. Her pimp. I moved to block his view.

"Yeah. I might have heard something, y'know?"

"Like?" Curro stepped in closer.

"Well, down here they run about every hour and a quarter, depending. Last one just went by."

He handed the bill to her. It vanished. "So police cruise by every hour or so, depending on what?"

She rolled her thick painted eyes. "On how busy the watch commander is. Usually, he gets a cut of the action to let things slip around here. Other times, he takes it out in trade, y'know? Some nights, like if he picked up a couple girls, the patrols don't even come 'round."

"Thanks Ria. You're a sweetheart."

"I am." she said, turning her vamp back on. Lime green goth girl winked over her shoulder at me, and they disappeared back into the gloom.

I looked over to Curro once we made it out of the club crowds. "Smooth. Where'd that come from?"

"Papa gave it to me. He always says you never know when it might come in handy. That seemed like one of those times."

I wasn't asking about the money, but I nodded and we walked on. My estimate of Curro went up with every step. Alejo might be right. We wended past the last of the clubs without any more incidents. Four minutes later we slipped onto the narrow streets cramped beneath the shadow of the dividing wall. Outer clothes disappeared behind a dumpster, and together we fastened on the gecko pads and started climbing into the Exclusive Sector, the city of Old Barcelona.

COMPLICATIONS

CHAPTER TWENTY-ONE

THE INVASIVE NATURE

Barcelona Metro Zone, Sant Adrià de Besòs district. Callejón del Apuro, "Trouble Alley". 12:47 a.m. Day Three.

Tam heard the upstairs door nudge and click shut, then the soft pad of footsteps descending on the cellar stairs. One eyebrow raised, he peered over the top of the wrinkled, water-stained paperback he'd been skimming. From the doorway, Ibram Kalahani ducked under the low header beam and emerged into the pale light of the cellar room.

"I just came from the boy."

Tam looked up, "So?"

"He says his headache isn't really going away."

"So…"

"So I'm concerned."

"Ibram, look," Tam hunched forward in his chair, "the kid was grabbed by armed men in the middle of the night, carried through a firefight, bundled onto a getaway plane and now he's captive, hidden in a massive ghetto. I'm not surprised the kid's a little stressed. It's just a headache." He leaned back and turned over a crinkled brown page. "And that's not bad, all things considering."

"Tam, I think it's more than stress."

"So," Tam said, "give him something strong. I'm sure Carmen can get her hands on pain tabs."

The doctor rubbed his narrow, lined face. "She already did. I gave him one, and he's sleeping now. Carmen's up there keeping an eye on him, and she'll let me know if there's any change."

"OK then, what's the problem? Just keep the package healthy until we get him out. And keep track of whatever you use. I'll pay you extra when we get back to Belfast."

Tam settled back and started reading again, but Ibram remained in the same spot. "I'm not worried about the money." The tall thin Israeli looked down at him. "You going to tell me about him?"

"Who?" Tam didn't look up.

"Who do you think? The boy. Gibson." Ibram squatted down. "I won't be able to help him unless I know more."

"Ibram, just keep the pain tabs coming. He'll be fine."

The older man studied one of the dim cellar corners for a second. "All this is because of him, right?"

"All what?" Tam finally looked up, irritated.

The older man waved one slender hand in a circle. "Eshu International hiding in a sprawl basement, a district-wide lockdown, corporate troops riding shotgun on police patrols. Come on," He looked Tam in the eye, trying to stare him down. It didn't work. "Fine, we'll play confirm or deny. I'll ask questions, and you say if I'm getting warm, how's that?" A long forefinger poked Tam's knee.

"What for, Doc? You know the drill: don't ask, don't tell. It's better for everyone if it's just a routine snatch."

"There's nothing routine about that boy," he snorted. "Tam, he's not well. Not well at all. If I'm going to help him, I need more information."

"What are you talking about?" Tam frowned. "What's wrong with him?"

"I'm not quite sure. I have a couple theories. But I need to know... where did you get him?"

"You're serious."

The doctor nodded.

Tam pursed his lips, and after a moment, he blew out a long slow breath. "OK. We did a run for Asian Pacific into Dawson-Hull territory. Dropped into one of their research facilities outside Toulouse and picked him up. It got a little... hairy as we were pulling out. Poet got hurt, and we had to go to ground here. End of story."

Ibram nodded some more. "So, you're telling me APAC hired one of the best covert outfits available just to pull a kid out of a secure location. I'm betting it was a biotech lab?"

Tam gave a little smile.

"And they offered a larger than normal fee, am I correct?"

"Huge like a fairy tale," Tam said. "Practically a blank check as long as we got him. Why do you ask?"

"Wait. I'm not done. This kid happens to be a clone. And the series shotcode on the back of his neck is unlike any I've ever seen or heard of."

"So?"

"Now it's been a while, but I still have connections in the field. Let me put this together," Dr. Kalahani started counting off points on his long fingers. "First, not only is whoever made him breaking a couple dozen international laws, but he's a child. That alone is unusual because all clone series to date have been engineered for specific purposes. They're only de-tanked when fully mature. Second, this one-of-a-kind child clone has a cybernetic jack behind his ear."

"I noticed. What, you're a detective now, Ibram?"

"No, just a doctor examining a little boy with a headache. Don't be a smart ass, Tam." He looked narrowly at him and went on, ticking off the next point. "Finally, that jack implant isn't connected to any discernable interface device." He stopped to let that thought sit in the air. "I'd wager that boy Gibson is a nano-host."

"A what? I've never heard—" Tam said.

"I've played cards with you, my friend." Ibram stared at Tam, waiting. "He is, isn't he?"

Tam held his gaze as long as he could, then tossed the book aside and raised both hands in mock surrender. "Yeah. The contract didn't spell that part out though. We got hired to loot and scoot on a Nanotech Neural Network prototype. It was reportedly in final trials before public disclosure. We had no idea it'd be in a clone." Tam leaned forward in the chair and cocked his head to the side. "So how'd you suss it all out?"

The Israeli rubbed his hands over his face again, more slowly this time, and spoke quietly. "Eighteen months before the war, I was assigned to the Mossad bio-weapons division, consulting for a series of high-level strategic planning and response meetings. Things were heating up. We knew another attack was coming, we just didn't know what. Everyone was desperate for any lead over the Jihadists, however slim. Even though the Bruges Treaty had been signed and all the clone laws were in effect, we knew other nations were funding black labs, so all the Israeli intelligence services were pushing for cutting-edge cyber-ware and bioengineering. They were convinced those would be our new force multipliers. That initiative put nanotech at the top of our list."

The older man's voice caught in his throat at a memory, but he dismissed it like a foul odor with a wave of his hand. "Because it's so unstable, I remember one of the theories bounced around was to introduce nanites into a human embryo when the cerebral and central nervous systems were still in their formative stages. A number of scientists thought the human body and the nano-system could develop together simultaneously. Through a biomimetic process, the human host would adapt to the invasive nature of the technology to form a more resilient, symbiotic relationship. But that line of thought was rejected on moral grounds."

"Why? I didn't notice any Jihadists exercising restraint."

"Ah yes. That's the trouble with having something of a conscience in a civilized society; you cling to the desperate illusion that on some level everyone is going to act rational and remotely humane." He shook his head. "You see, cloning is already an ethical gray zone, so we decided that integrating volatile nanotechnology into unborn children was crossing too many lines in an already controversial area. Rather than pursue that approach, our engineers then began looking for ways to stabilize nano-systems for voluntary adult hosts."

"Apparently someone at Dawson-Hull didn't share your compunction," Tam said quietly.

"Apparently not. You say the boy is a prototype?

"That's what I understand."

"No wonder they're frantic. A viable nano-system will turn everything on its head. Of course they're storming around with corporate security and police," Ibram said. "But I'm worried about the boy."

"Don't be. No one's going to hurt him. Not us, certainly not the Garcías. You know we're not like that."

"I know." Ibram placed his hand gently on Tam's shoulder. "–Not who, what. The nanotech is the problem."

"What? How?"

"The very concept of nanotechnology is its fundamental flaw. It is foreign material, an incompatible system inside a human body. Even if D-H geneticists tweaked him to be even more receptive to the nanites, any equilibrium between Gibson's body and the nanites would degenerate over time. I'm afraid the nano-system is self-replicating inside him, shifting into a rapid, uncontrolled growth phase. Like cancer."

"Cancer?"

"It's killing him, Tam. Gibson's not having stress headaches. He's dying."

It was past midnight when the man called Hester slid into the small room and softly pulled the door shut. It was a decent hotel in a better location: the fourth floor on a corner overlooking the Plaza Del Ermitaño. This was as central as he could get in the northern sprawl called Sant Adrià de Besòs, and Hester thought it fortunate he'd made it in before the curfew. Not that it would have stopped him. Delayed him perhaps, but delays annoyed him because he prided himself on being prompt. His Dad always said neatness is a sign of professionalism.

He flipped on an e-paper map of the district. Neat lines divided the spread into a search grid of smaller irregular blocks. After several hours of cross-referencing the files from his boss and ransacking the Guardia Civil's criminal database, he followed a single tidbit of information north.

He squared away the rest of his gear, set the tracker on the nightstand, and went right to sleep. Tomorrow, he'd see how well his hunch played out.

CHAPTER TWENTY-TWO

ON THE CORPORATE GRASS

Barcelona Metro Zone, Old Barcelona, UpCity District. 2:05 a.m.
Day Three.

Curro and I made it to the hospital without a problem. We climbed down into Old B. in a commercial neighborhood, its wide streets lined with shuttered boutiques and tiny cafés. Being late on a weeknight, the avenue was empty, but I nearly blew it before we'd gone half a block. Our passing triggered several ad projectors, and for a minute, a gang of the brilliant and beautiful people catwalked and kissed all around us, inviting Curro and me to their tragically cool, carefree existence. They shattered in a static crackle like petulant phantoms when we ignored them, but an evil little part of me still wanted to shoot them.

As we got closer, we found ourselves in a subdued white-collar neighborhood with frosted glass and steel offices mixed with the occasional checker-lit hab-rise. Real people started appearing: couples, late shift workers on their way to and from jobs. We stayed out of their way, alert but not worried. The only real surveillance was the cameras on the traffic lights and at the building entrances. Not a single cop cruised by.

It's a little-known fact that there's a very limited police presence in the enclaves. Automated security blunts down on most felonies, and with everyone toting around the latest fashion in bodyguards or personal protection devices, street crime is almost nonexistent. UpCity cops are strictly call/response units. At the same time, your average enclave citizen is just too self-absorbed to notice a couple of dark shapes gliding by. Even if someone had caught a glimpse, I doubt it would register. The walls have been up for so long, most Upcity residents only see sprawlers on the newsnets or in movies, and the occasional scab cleared for service work might as well be invisible. They can't fathom a zone scab treading on the corporate grass. We made it to the hospital by three in the morning.

Sant Honorat's rear loading dock was lit by a single large floodlight bolted over the roll-down shutter. The only visible security was a number pad lock on the metal door next to the bay, and an ancient wall-mounted camera on the right stuttering its way through a half arc over the kitchen entrance. Admin must be touchy about hired help walking off with hospital food. The kitchen door opened, and we heard the chatter of the nightshift cooks drifting on the cool air. One of them stepped outside, flipped off the camera and lit up a cigarette. Alejo was right: who breaks into a hospital? When he finished his smoke and went back inside, I mugged the key pad and we were in.

Curro and I crouched in the corner of a long room that reeked of bleach and clean linen. Rows of washers were humming through their spin cycle. I flipped open my data pad and started thumbing through the hospital floor plans. I practically had to shout at Curro over all the noise.

"We found the laundry all right. It says here, there's an elevator right outside the door, and a stairwell about twenty meters down the hall. The high-tech surgical suites should be right above us, three operating rooms in a row." I tapped the tiny screen. "The supply closet is at the end, and it looks large. We'll check there first." I folded the data pad away. "If there is a God, I hope He's listening to your mom right about now 'cause here's where it gets interesting. You ready?"

"Sure. But look," Curro pointed. "Mama always wanted me to go to medical school."

Behind me, neat stacks of crisp green hospital scrubs sat on wire shelving. It took me a second, but I saw the gleam in his eyes, and a minute later, we were tucking our gear underneath the loose fitting garments. They'd conceal the odd bulge of weapons long enough for us to bluff our way past any casual glance. We looked the part, but the whole idea hit me as bold-faced madness. I was fitting a cloth surgical cap on my head. "This is crazy you know. We're making this up as we go along."

"'Walking on water' as Papa would say. Besides, crazy can be good camouflage, no?"

"If it's all you got," I said.

"It will be easy, no one expects us. Besides, Mama is praying... good things happen when she prays."

I rolled my eyes. "You know, when your father made a comment about 'air cover', I'd hoped for something more... substantial." I folded my Blizzard into its shoulder holster. "Of course, if this works, she could contract out as Fundy Tactical Support."

Curro laughed like a little kid. "Papa said you might get grumpy. We'll get this machine for your friend, you'll see."

"You're actually getting off on all this, aren't you?"

Curro nodded as he tied off a pale green top. "How do I look?" he turned in place. "Anything printing through?"

The shirt was two sizes too large on him, but it hung clean and smooth over the tactical vest. I frowned. "You look like a minty-fresh Jelly Baby. Other than that, you're clear."

"Now we go and see what happens." Curro winked just like his father used to. Scraps of memory skipped through me, and the phrase 'running on a wing and a prayer' came to mind. Alejo used to say that all the time too. I looked over. Curro stood waiting.

"Right. Because this is what you do for friends." I appraised the new medical intern, Curro García. "OK, you remember what we're looking for?"

"*Sí*. Dr. Kalahani says it's three separate units. One is the cranial imager, the second is the instrument rack, and third piece, the control unit, has four small screens on it. And we can't forget the cable linkage."

"Why do I feel like we're gonna have to steal a truck to scoot this thing out of here?" I let out a short sigh. "You ready?"

"Ready."

"We're on." I smoothed down the last of the wrinkles, and we stepped out into the corridor. By the time we hit the stairs, we had our best privileged enclave attitudes firmly in place, and we strode toward C-Wing, Advanced Surgical Unit with blue latex hands and sterile face masks, looking down our noses at every passing graveyard shift staffer. This late, the wing was quiet, and nearly empty, save a clutch of nurses at their station and lone white-haired custodian steering an antique floor polisher across the red and white laminate floor. The nurses barely glanced up, but the janitor switched off the machine as we approached.

"Can I help you?" he removed his hat and bowed slightly.

I started pressing him right away. "Only if you can access Storage. We need to run diagnostics on the equipment for tomorrow, and not only are we late, we're in a hurry. There someone around here with a key?"

"I've got a passkey, sir. But I didn't hear about any cyber surgery on for tomorrow."

I looked at his nametag. "I see, Mr.... Morales. Are you on the surgical team?"

"Well no, I'm just—"

"That explains it then. You weren't informed because you don't need to know." I let my irritation mount. "Now can you open up for us? Or do we need to find someone else?"

The arrogance clicked and the older man defaulted to subservient posture. He pushed the machine aside and started shuffling forward. "Of course, Doctor...?

"Anderson. And Torres." I waved him on impatiently.

"You're new here to Sant Honorat?" he tried smiling at Curro, whose brown eyes looked through him.

"Luckily for you we're temporary—consultants for tomorrow's procedure," I fired back. "Do you interrogate every doctor that comes in?"

"No, no, sir. Of course not. I'm just trying to be friendly. Been here forty years, and I try to know all the staff."

"Try being more productive and less talkative, Mr. Morales. And I'll try to forget your attitude," I said. "Now... Storage?"

"Yes, sir. Of course, sir." The three of us started walking.

The halls were deserted, the bright ceiling strip light enlarging the white space and the empty sound of our steps. We passed through double doors into the east surgical wing. "I'll wave the fob, but one of you will have to thumb in." The janitor smiled weakly at us.

"Thumb in? The locks are biometric?" I asked. We were at the door now.

"Last year, Administration ruled they want only medical staff handling the equipment. They said it cuts down on the chance of damage." Mr. Morales had pulled out his keys, a ring of numbered gray plastic tears, smooth as river stones. His head bobbed as he continued. "I've always been careful with hospital property. Always. I can still get in, but I don't want any trouble."

Curro and I passed a look, and he stepped in seamlessly, playing up his accent for the old man. "I'm sure you have, Señor Morales. Listen, my partner and I arrived late and Admin hasn't had time to input our profiles into the hospital database. We're behind schedule already. We're going to need you to open this for us."

The older man stammered. "No, No Dr. Torres, the policy is specific. I'm not allowed. Admin should only take a few minutes to update the computers. If you wish, I can take you right there and speak with Gizelle for you. She will take care of it right away."

He smiled again, nodding as Curro sidestepped toward the door, drawing the man's attention with him. I glanced back, double-checked for camera domes and wandering staff, then snatched the older man in a chokehold. He was out on an eight count. Curro lifted the key ring from the man's limp hand as I eased him down to the floor.

"Use his thumb and wave that thing. We've got about ten minutes. We need to be long gone," I said.

The biometric lock beeped to green and the door slid open.

"What will they do to him? He's a good man," Curro asked as we dragged the janitor in with us.

"I'm sure he is. But we're here for Poet9. Now hit the lights and look over there." I gagged and zip-cuffed the old man, but not too tight. They'd find him in the morning, alive.

We found all three units already on an equipment caddy. Trouble was they were big, and plugged into a fourth unit, which was just as big. We sure as hell weren't walking out with all this under our hats.

I threw a sheet over the first set. The janitor stirred. We were down to five minutes, tops, so I made a snap decision. "Forget that last one. Doc didn't say anything about a fourth piece. Just disconnect those cables—we're leaving it."

"But what if it's important?"

"What if it's not? We don't have time to figure it out. Now move—we won't do Poet9 any good in jail being mind-pharmed. Stuff they IV into you nowadays, you'd be hallucinating, making stuff up just to get them to stop. Leave it."

We started toward the door, pushing the covered equipment. It had the jutting twist of some neo-tribal totem waiting to be unveiled. "Guess I *am* going to have to steal a truck after all," I muttered.

Curro laughed. "How about an ambulance?"

CHAPTER TWENTY-THREE

FLIPPING THE SWITCH

Barcelona Metro Zone, Sant Adrià de Besòs district. Callejón del
Apuro "Trouble Alley". 5:13 a.m. Day Three.

"What do you mean it's not going to work?" I was mad. "The power supply unit? Ibram, we lifted the three parts you said, thank God, from the first place we looked. I thought you could just plug the thing in. Why didn't you say something about a special power unit?"

"Jace, it's an incredibly delicate procedure. There's not a lot of wiggle room when you're operating near the corpus callosum. It seemed obvious. You said it was connected when you found it. What other kind of hint do you need?" the doctor asked.

"Oh right! Like I deployed on neurosurgery ops back in D-W-C Metro. What the hell, Doc? Like I'd know. Explain the logic to me."

Ibram glared back at me and dropped into stern lecture mode. "Fine. There's zero tolerance for power fluctuations, so the electrical source needs to be an absolute steady constant. You can't just run an extension cord. Why the micron actuators that are inserted into the cybernetic interf—"

"OK, OK." Tam held up his hands. "We get it… very tricky. What's the solution?"

Alejo spoke up. "If it needs to be a direct constant, I can get a battery from a truck or boat? Will that work?"

Doc Kalahani thought for a minute. "Right idea but not enough voltage. We need lithium-thionyl chloride or lithium ion polymer. They're stronger and have memory circuits."

Tam spoke up. "English, Doc. Plain English please."

"Those are industrial or military grade batteries. They're not commercially available."

"Think we could get back in to the hospital?" Curro asked me. Crazy kid was willing to try.

"No. Not a snowball's chance in hell we'd get back in there. Not after what we did. We'd have better luck ghosting into an army base and stealing a tank." I looked up at Curro. "Which we're *not* going to do either."

It went quiet in the cellar room. The Triplets were upstairs with Gibson, and the only sound was Poet9's autodoc and the shifting of feet as we tried to wrap our heads around the problem. Carmen was standing next to her husband, deep in thought.

"That's it," she said, gesturing toward the near wall.

"What's it?" We all looked to where she was pointing. Our Mitsubishi suits were stacked in segments, hollow and stiff like the molted carapaces of giant black beetles.

"Your suits. You said their internal power was still charged around fifty percent."

Ibram tapped his finger against his chin. "Right type, but it'll drain them."

"Whoa, whoa. Drain them? Who said you could even use them? What about ditching this place? We're going to need them to get out of the BMZ. Remember?" I asked.

"We still have the Gaki in that old steel mill," Tam countered.

I pointed up to the ceiling. "D-H and Madrid have UAVs banging into each other up there now. They'll expect that. Fast movers'll be scrambled the second they get a skip pass on their screens. We won't make it fifty klicks, even in a Gaki."

A look passed between Alejo and Carmen. Alejo spoke up. "We have friends at the Docks. It won't be comfortable, but we can get you out."

"For a new creation in Christ, you still have a lot of old business associates. You two moonlighting for extra credits, or what?" Tam asked.

Carmen smiled at him. "This outfit smuggle Bibles into the Islamic Federation, brings persecuted Christians out. Same kind of work, different cargo. They can get the six of you out of the BMZ, no problem. All we have to do is let them know you're coming."

Tam looked over at Ibram. "You sure those batteries will work? I don't want to throw away our best shot at vacating Barcelona. Honestly... what are the odds?"

"You want guarantees you're in the wrong line of work." Ibram said. "But if I run the power from all six suits simultaneously, they should do the job. I'm fairly certain I can get inside his head to reset the breakers."

"Really?"

"Really."

Tam looked at me. It sucks playing your last card. I shrugged. "In for a penny, in for a pound. But it's your call."

"OK. Do it," he said.

It was early morning, the pitch-black pre-dawn, before Doc Kalahani managed to rig up the equipment for Poet9. All of us had filed down into the cellar to watch, to be there. Gibson woke up, insisted on coming too, and he held Flopsy's hand, a small boy with green eyes and a solemn face surrounded by albino giants. The boy's forehead creased with concern as he watched Ibram plugging cables, double-checking connections, minutely adjusting dials.

Devante was still on the bed pallet, small and pale, breathing slow and shallow. Ibram had set up the eight-pronged imager array, locking the armatures in place around his head. It looked like Poet9 was trapped in the clutches of a giant mechanical spider. Cyber-surgery was so delicate it was performed by remote. The array would generate a hologram of his head and brain box so the operation could be monitored in real-time 3D, viewable from every angle.

Doc wiped his forehead and made last-minute tweaks on several knobs before turning to us. "Don't touch anything near the Mitsu suits. That cable is spliced onto all six batteries. I modified the power points so they'll run the surgical suite. But there's a problem."

"There's a what?" Tam asked extra quietly.

"A problem."

"You've stripped the batteries out of our suits, ruined them to jury-rig all this, and now you're saying there's a problem?" Tam was perfectly still.

"Take it easy, it'll work. The problem is time." He held up a small, shiny black digital timer, the display set to ten minutes. "With all three machines, the drain is massive. Even at fifty percent, I calculate your suit batteries will only run them for ten minutes, twelve tops. That means I'll need a hand. I'm going to operate the imager to locate and focus on the correct areas, but someone needs to run the robotics controller."

I piped up, "I'll help. How hard can flipping the switch be?"

Ibram gave me his "my, you don't think much" look. "There are eight separate breakers connected to neural fiber bundles in different regions of his brain. They have to be switched open in the proper order. Once the imager warms up, I'll need at least three, maybe five minutes to locate and tag them on the display in the right sequence. That leaves all of five to seven minutes to remotely guide the micro-actuators to do the resets."

"Wait, wait, wait... five to seven minutes?"

"Once we have the machines running, can't we supplement the power with more batteries to buy more time?" Tam asked.

"Not unless you've got spare suit batteries you didn't tell me about. Different power sources would introduce variations. Can't risk it. Even a minor fluctuation during the procedure might kill him."

"So... what are we going to do? Other than hurry like hell, and hope we don't fumble something, or run out of power in the middle of poking around in Poet's head?"

Doc stood still looking at Poet, at the machines, then back at Poet again.

"Doc?" I asked.

"I'm thinking." Several seconds went by, and Ibram pursed his lips and let out a long breath.

"Well?" Tam asked.

"I guess we hurry like hell and hope we don't fumble something or lose power while we're poking around in Poet's head." He turned to face us. "This is the only chance he's got right now."

A leaden quiet dropped into place, the kind when you don't like any of the options, but you don't have any other choices.

I shook myself, and stepped forward. "OK, Doc. What do you want me to do?"

"Jace..." Tam said.

"I know—don't screw up."

He put his hand on my shoulder. "No. Good Luck."

I cracked my knuckles and swallowed. "Yeah... Seeing as how this mission's been going, I'd say we're due for some good luck."

Doc led me over to the robotics unit and started going over the control panel. "These switches here toggle the micro cables. They're numbered one through eight. These two knobs determine the speed and direction of whichever cable you've toggled. The small screens tell you when you're in proximity to the circuitry. All you have to do is get them to my marked positions. Once activated, the actuators will do the work and reset the breaker." He grabbed my hand, making me look up into his face. "It is vital you position all eight cables first, then activate them in sequence. Do you understand?"

"Go to your markers. Get the cables in place, then turn them on in the proper order. Got it."

Doc leaned close to me. "You sure you want to go through with this? If anything happens..."

"No. No, I'm good. I've got to try. Besides..." I tried being funny, "I can get lots of things done in five minutes."

He didn't smile, just looked at me with that sad long face of his, and then spoke to Tam. "I've removed the face plates off his C.I.U. Attach those fiber cables to the access points, please. Look for the small red ports. Screw them snug and smooth out the cables so there're no kinks."

I don't think I'd ever seen Tam be so gentle. He knelt down, and one by one, threaded the actuator cables to the side of Poet9's head. "Don't worry. We're coming, Devante," he whispered. He finished, rose to his feet and stepped back.

"Good." Doc went to the imager, his long fingers hovering over the power switch. "When we start, hit the timer." He glanced over at me. "While I'm tagging the micro-breakers, you start up the controller's operating program. Dials one through eight need to be lit green, the rest will stay yellow. All eight have to be ready when I say go. Understood?"

"Got it, Doc."

"Good. Now the hologram is going to appear directly in front of you in the air. I'll orient the image as you need. Ready?"

I nodded.

Doc Kalahani flipped the switch, and the three machines started humming. In front of me, a dozen screens blinked to life, twitching with tiny constellations of icons, numbered bars, and needles. The next second, a hologram of Poet9's brain flickered into existence.

Enlarged ten times, it spun in the air on the central axis between its left and right hemispheres then snapped in place as still as a vid freeze-frame. The brain surface was an organic mass of glowing folds and undulations, the topography of his cerebellum highlighted in electric-blue tracery. On the left side, the severe line and right angle schematics of the cybernetic interface unit appeared in a stark contrast of lime green. Where the brain and machine met was a blurred confusion of spider-web delicacy. I stood there blinking, astonished at the sight.

Doc was moving as fast as he could, but it was nearly a minute before I saw the yellow marker "One" pop up: a little flag deep inside the holo-image of that tangled zone. The timer next to Tam was shrinking white digital seconds into smaller minutes. At seven minutes twenty-eight seconds, there were three such flags.

Doc was starting to sweat. And mutter. "Things are buried. There're ones for each lobe and nerve bundle. C'mon, c'mon. I can't find—there they are."

Two more flags popped up. Six minutes seventeen seconds remaining.

"Jace, get ready. I. Just need. Three more."

The timer was dropping. Another flag, number six. Five minutes forty seconds. The holo of Poet's brain spun to a view up from underneath. Doc was searching for the other two. Five minutes twenty-two seconds. The holo shifted again. Ibram was sweating harder, blinking his eyes.

"Doc...?" Five minutes three seconds.

"I'm looking."

The air was stretched thin in the cellar. At four minutes twenty-nine seconds, flag number seven appeared and Poet's big blue brain turned to face me.

"Almost there. I need the last one at the corpus callosum." Four minutes thirteen seconds.

"Doc, you're not leaving me much time."

"I'm working as fast as I can here. This *is* brain surgery, remember."

Behind me, someone shuffled and I heard Gibson say, "Let me through please."

Four minutes five seconds. White digits were blurring the timer. The holo moved again, the last flag wasn't showing. Doc was muttering. Three minutes fifty-two seconds. Gibson was at my side.

"Let me help."

Tam grabbed at him. The movement made me jump.

"Damnit, Tam!"

"Hold on there, kid, this is very important—" Tam had Gibson's hand now, but the boy spun on him, his green eyes blazing.

"I know it's important. This is your friend and you're running out of time."

I tore my eyes off the timer and saw the needle on the power gauge trembling at twenty percent.

"I can help him." Gibson spoke again.

"Got it," Ibram said. Three minutes two seconds. Doc looked over at the timer. He looked close to weeping. "God help us."

I looked at Ibram, then down at Gibson. He was right beside me, holding up a jack cord in his small hand. My thoughts turned to sludge. Less than three minutes left now. My friend, Devante Galeno Perez was going to die under my hand. I was sure of it. I wanted to hit "Rewind", start this scene over, but there was no such thing. I heard Ibram's voice.

"Let him on, Jace. You know what Gibson is. He was made for things like this."

As if underwater, I heard Tam protest, saw myself step back and nod to Gibson.

"OK, kid. You're up." The white digits read two minutes thirty-seven seconds. Green eyes looked at me and gave me a small smile. The boy walked up to the controller and jacked in.

"Now, Gibson," Doc said.

At precisely two minutes, I saw the actuator fibers enter the holo image from the machine side. They were bright red lines like lasers sliding inwards; eight of them moving simultaneously, extending deeper into Poet9's brain. Gibson was motionless, eyes closed, in front of the machine.

Timer numbers continued whipping down toward zero. I saw Alejo bow his head in prayer, while Carmen started speaking in tongues. For me, something like yearning and fear, like desperation and a plea came from inside and lofted upward. I hoped it would make it past the spy drones that hunted us from the dark skies.

CHAPTER TWENTY-FOUR

THIN ICE

Barcelona Port Complex, Asian Pacific Consortium Trade Offices,
Bureau D. South Dock, Level Five, 7:59 a.m. Day Three.

Colonel Otsu stared out the tiny window in his office. Somewhere beyond the concrete slabs and steel girders, a new day was brightening over the Mediterranean Sea, and he was missing it. *You'd think they'd put the legation office somewhere with a view*, he thought. But security protocols dictated a double perimeter envelope to counteract possible electronic eavesdropping. After all, hard data on bulk orders of Ninja Heroes and Robo-Pets was highly classified. He craned his neck for a better view as a solid wall of hot pink "Hello Kitty" shipping crates slid past on automated forklifts. He sighed and turned back to his desk. Eight o'clock.

Right on time, the vid-link chirped and Lieutenant Kaneda's face appeared on the screen. "Tonight, sir," the young officer said without preamble. "We're meeting them tonight."

"Good. Where?"

"A historical building in the Northern District. A mosque."

"A mosque?"

"Yes, sir. Out of the way but still a public place. It's a preliminary meeting to work out the delivery details. I'll make sure we have the package in the next eighteen hours."

"Very good. And the clones?" the colonel asked warily. "Have they adjusted to mission conditions?"

A shadow passed over the lieutenant's face, but he answered quickly. "They are... odd, sir. But bio-forms are conditioned to obey. I don't foresee any difficulties."

"You watch yourself, Lieutenant. Those are prototypes." Colonel Otsu leaned forward. "I want a full report when this is over. The damned things are risky under any circumstances. To use this as some sort of trial run borders on reckless."

"Don't worry, sir. I'll handle it."

"I know, Lieutenant. That's why you're there. Report back after the meeting. I'll have the transport remain on standby in case you get the package sooner."

"Yes, sir. Kaneda out."

Colonel Otsu watched the screen go blank and let his mind churn. Mercenaries, corporate theft, clone units with maximum sanction on foreign soil… He'd heard that speed was the only safety on thin ice, but this situation was growing more precarious by the hour.

One day, he thought. *Twenty-four more hours, and if this isn't finished, I'll call Head Office. We can pull out before any lasting damage is done.*

Colonel Otsu sat back, still uneasy, but resolved. Then he remembered the lieutenant's face when he'd mentioned the clones and wondered if he shouldn't pick up the phone right then.

Asian Pacific Consortium N. EU Division Regional Offices, Amsterdam, Netherlands Region. 8:47 a.m.

Avery Hsiang frowned as the video link chimed. *Why do I pay Kanang if he can't accomplish simple tasks like field phone calls?* He made a note to dock the man's salary as the screen slid up from his desktop, a Directorate icon flashing in its center. Avery sat up and adjusted his tie. "Accept."

The screen brightened and the aged face of Senior Director Yoshio Tetsuo appeared. "Ah, Avery, my apologies for calling you direct. I wanted to catch you early before appointments pulled you away."

Avery bowed his head. "Director Tetsuo, my pleasure. How can I be of assistance?"

"An old matter has come to my attention, and I thought we might resolve it ourselves."

"Of course, Director Tetsuo, what matter in particular?"

"Ukraine. I was under the impression we had resolved the dispute, but my managers have alerted me to ongoing mineral and natural gas trading. The Board determined that region falls under my purview, yet it appears your agents are still operating there."

Avery nodded. "Director Tetsuo, my men are simply concluding existing commitments. Once those contracts are filled, I've ordered them to refer all contacts to your offices."

"That was seventeen weeks ago, Avery. An estimated forty million in net sales, and it's still continuing. How do you explain that?" the director asked.

Avery shrugged in wry apology. *More like fifty-three million, you decrepit relic.* "Strong ties, Mr. Director. My men are excellent at their job and want to insure their obligations have been met."

"Aren't they stretching that notion a bit, Avery?"

Avery bowed his head lower, smiling inside. "Director Tetsuo, you have my word my managers will notify you as soon as they have finished."

Yoshio Tetsuo eyes tightened. "Your subordinates violated clearly defined market boundaries and pursued local interests contrary to corporate guidelines."

"Director Tetsuo, borders in that region are historically fluid. It was an honest error—excusable to zeal. The parties involved were in need, but their petroleum requirements surpassed our initial projections. My agents are only interested in developing profitable opportunities for the Consortium. Ones, with all due respect, your managers failed to explore. Now those opportunities have been seized."

The older executive paused before continuing softly. "Manager Hsiang, it would be a shame to interrupt the upcoming Assembly's schedule with an issue thought long concluded. Ukrainian commodities are an inconvenient and unworthy digression in the face of far more pressing matters, wouldn't you agree?"

"I've always found the Board receptive to initiative and maximum production and profitability," Avery replied.

Unblinking, Senior Director Tetsuo smiled. "Yes. Yes, indeed. My sincere apologies for disturbing you at your work." The old head bowed slightly and his arm reached out on screen to cut the link. It paused halfway, and Yoshio Tatsuo looked up suddenly. "One further question if I may?"

"Of course, Director Tetsuo."

"You know, of course, I administer all branches of the Sendai Research Department." The older man lifted a small data pad up in front of him, squinting at it as if he found it difficult to read. "Oddly enough, I just received notice, as yet unconfirmed, that there has been an unauthorized deployment of Chishima products." Yoshio Tetsuo looked back up at the screen. "Use of clone units is always a delicate matter under any circumstance; but these were not standard types."

Avery got the sudden impression the director was scrutinizing him through the vid-link. He feigned a look of mild surprise. "No? What type was deployed?"

"According to Supervisor Shoei, three Infiltrator prototypes were authorized by Tier Two administrator codes. As a director, I can find no record of Board approval for clone deployment. Are you aware of any such requisitions within your division?"

The face of Director Tetsuo floated in the middle of the screen, and for a moment, Avery Hsiang stopped breathing. Then he blinked and forced a smile. "No, sir, but I'll look into it immediately. This is a serious matter. I understand those units are very promising, but still under development."

The senior executive nodded. "You are correct; they were not finalized, and it is a very serious matter. As I mentioned, the report needs to be verified before my office forwards it to the Board, so I am grateful for your assistance. Tetsuo, out."

The screen dimmed and disappeared into the desktop. *He knows. The old bastard knows. I have to finish this quickly.* Another chime startled him. It was his assistant, Kanang.

"What?"

"Mr. Hsiang? We just received a message from Barcelona, sir."

"And?"

"They say there's a meeting with the mercenaries in twelve hours, local time."

Avery Hsiang steepled his fingers in front of his face. "Excellent. Put me through to the clone cell immediately."

CHAPTER TWENTY-FIVE

STRONG MEDICINE

Barcelona Metro Zone, Sant Adrià de Besòs district. Callejón del
Apuro, "Trouble Alley". 3:05 p.m. Day Three.

Gibson whimpered as Carmen set another damp cloth on his head. It
was burning, feverish, and his body trembled under her touch. She
felt his skin with the back of her hand and dabbed a second cool
towel on his face and neck.

"Shhhh. Dr. Kalahani is coming with strong medicine right now. You'll
be all better soon, *pequeño*, I promise."

Gibson stirred. "I tried to go as fast as I could—"

"Don't you worry... you did good, very good. Hush now."

His eyes opened, bright with pain and questions. "It hurts. Why does it
hurt so much?"

"I don't know, little one. But you are a brave boy—you can make it.
The doctor will be here any second."

With that, the bedroom door opened and Ibram Kalahani slipped in. For
a brief second, the two towering backs of Mopsy and Cottontail could be
seen standing guard out in the hall. Ibram forced a wan smile at the boy, but
gave Carmen a worried look.

"How is he?" he asked.

Carmen cupped Gibson's cheeks in her rough brown hands. "Fine, fine.
He is strong, this one. After all that work, he needs a bit of medicine and
some rest. He'll be back on his feet in no time." She took two small white
pills from the doctor and helped Gibson take a sip of water. "There you go.
You'll be all better soon." She wiped his face again then looked back at the
doctor. "Close the door behind you. I'll let you know if there's any change."

Ibram Kalahani was rooted in place, looking down at Gibson's small
form with something like sorrow, and not a bit of awe on his long face. "That
was one of the most incredible things I've—" his voice choked, "I've ever
seen." He brushed at his eyes.

"Of course it was," Carmen tutted. "Gibson is special. Now enough
standing around. You're keeping him awake, staring at him like that. You
can congratulate him later."

"Yes, yes, of course. I'll let them know downstairs."

Carmen didn't bother to reply, instead busying herself smoothing the sheets around Gibson's shoulders. Ibram nodded and shut the door with a soft click.

"Carmen?" Gibson whispered after a moment.

"Yes, *pequeño*?"

"When will the medicine work?" His eyes were squeezed tightly shut, and a single tear trailed down the side of his face.

Carmen brushed it away and changed the cloth on his forehead. Her hand lingered several seconds in silent prayer. "Soon. Just a few minutes and you'll feel better. You lie still and let it work." She took his hand in hers and bent over him. "I'm proud of you, Gibson. You know that? You weren't afraid and you saved Devante's life."

"You mean Poet9?"

"Ha! I knew him before he started calling himself that. I met him when he wasn't much older than you are right now, so I can call him by his real name." Carmen smiled at a memory and patted the boy's hand. "And believe me, when you're older and some big hotshot, I'll still call you Gibson, eh?"

"Is Poet9, er, Devante really going to be all right?"

"Yes, thanks to you. Dr. Kalahani says he'll be back to normal in a couple days."

"I remember getting the cables in place," Gibson said. "I could see them in my mind, but my headache came back. When I switched them on, there was pressure, and a flash of light in my head. After that I don't remember."

"You fainted. Jace caught you, and Flopsy carried you upstairs. He likes you. All three of the boys do. Why, I had to kick them out of here to take care of you, they were so worried." She smiled down at him. "You did it, *pequeño*."

"Good," he said. "I'm glad."

"And now it's time you rest. I'm going to read to you. You listen and let the medicine do its work. OK?"

Gibson yawned and blinked twice. "OK."

Carmen leaned over and pulled a well-worn Bible from the side table drawer. She opened at Psalm 139 and read aloud until Gibson fell asleep.

Poet9 was sitting up with his head between his knees and a bucket on the floor, groaning every thirty seconds or so.

"You going to throw up again?" I asked, patting his back. I couldn't believe how glad I was to listen to Poet9 puking.

"Don't think I have anything left. I'm heaving up my testicles now."

"Charming. Good to know your near-brush with death didn't change your sense of humor. I'm glad you're back."

"So am I. I think." He wavered and let out another groan.

Doc K had come back down to the cellar and was speaking to Tam. "Devante will be weak, dizzy for a while, but it'll pass. I gave him something for motion sickness. He needs to keep food down, and rest."

"Rest? He's been in a coma. That'll have to do until we get back to Belfast. We're out of time."

"Any strain—" the doctor started.

"Ibram... every cop in Spain is looking for us and every hour we stay here puts the Garcías in more danger. Someone might have already noticed us. We're meeting APAC tonight, then we'll deliver our package and get the hell out of Barcelona."

Poet, head still hung down, raised his hand.

"What?" Tam asked irritably.

"So cyber-boy really saved the day?"

Tam hesitated, and Ibram started speaking rapidly. "It was remarkable. I've never seen anything like it. He interfaced in seconds, gaining complete simultaneous control over the unit. We never dreamed the technology could be so fast. There's no doubt he saved your life."

"Well, that changes things up," Poet9 said weakly.

"No," Tam said. "No, it doesn't. Don't even say that."

Alejo stepped forward. "Thanks for thinking of us, but I want to know what they're going to do to Gibson."

"Don't know, Al. Not my job description," Tam said.

"He saved Poet's life. And you are going to hand him over?"

"That's what the contract says," Tam answered quickly.

"And then what?" Alejo asked. "You tell me he's the asset. I see why now. I know your employers will crave what's inside him, yet Ibram tells me he might be dying. What will they do to him?"

Tam threw his hands up. "For God's sake, Al, what am I, the psychic hotline? How should I know? They might treat him like a Saudi sheik. They might have a cure. We're just the delivery guys, end of story."

"He's a little boy. Someone should take care of him."

"We have taken care of him," Tam retorted. "He's alive and in one piece. Now it's someone else's job."

"You know what I mean. When they find out he's sick, or he's not useful to them anymore, they'll throw him aside like a broken toy," Alejo said.

"What are you saying, Al? You got another idea?"

"You could not deliver him," Alejo said simply.

"Oh right. Tell Asian Pacific I had him a second ago, but now I can't find him? Then what, you and Carmen adopt him and live happily ever after?" Tam pointed out into the large cellar room. "You two going to start a sprawl orphanage now?"

"If that's what's needed. God would provide," Alejo countered evenly.

"Al, I'm not changing my mind here. This is business. Now you going to take us to the Mosque tonight or not?" Tam said.

"You're sure that's what you want?"

"What other choice do I have?" Tam said. "No one's going to say Eshu International dropped their side of a contract."

Alejo held Tam's gaze, then sighed heavily. "Very well, then. I'll take you."

CHAPTER TWENTY-SIX

BRIGHT TENSION SHIVERED

Barcelona Metro Zone, Sant Adrià de Besòs District. 6:57 p.m.
Day Three.

The meeting was to take place in an ancient Moorish mosque, down in the basement where they held illegal cage fights. There was no word on whom or what would be brawling that night, only that it was *lucha al final*, a fight to the finish.

"Aren't they all?" Tam muttered. No matter the headliners, this ranked as one of the strangest places for a corporate espionage tryst I'd ever heard of.

Tam and I had strapped the ceramic Boker blades on under loose-fitting clothes, and Alejo had picked out a steel-capped oak walking stick from another trunk. Alejo led us through the streets, and he started limping more dramatically about two blocks from the mosque. After all, who'd deprive an old man of his cane? The three of us hadn't been together in years, and I caught the edge of déjà vu as we came around the last corner.

It was the golden hour, right before dusk, and the mosque's dome was flaring blood red bronze as the sunset gleamed in the burnished, stretched reflection. People were streaming in from every quarter as the minaret speakers wailed and called to the faithful. Alejo didn't know if anyone actually worshiped there anymore, or if the mullahs traded the space for a piece of the betting action. All he could say for sure was that the Turks had overseen this particular racket as long as anyone could recall. The mosque was cleaned and vacated for every match, and the fights always coincided with Muslim holy days. This was a hell of a long way from bingo and bake sales.

We entered the main portal, no one greeting or guiding us, so we left our shoes on, and followed the queue through the building. As we passed the musalla prayer hall, Alejo translated the script chasing the underside circle of the dome.

"Let those who would exchange the life of this world for the hereafter fight for the cause of God; whoever fights for the cause of God, whether he dies or triumphs, on him We shall bestow a rich recompense."

Alejo pointed with his cane. "Old timers say there was a Jihadist madrassa here once. They say some of the cells trained here actually fought in the Final Push."

"And now it's an illegal blood pit," I said. "Those Wahhabists sure know how to put the 'fun' in fundamentalist." Alejo snickered, and Tam elbowed me in the ribs.

"They also boast that the girl came from here; the one who took out the American Embassy in Paris," Alejo said.

Tam raised his eyebrows. "'The Bride of Allah' came from Barcelona?"

"It's what they say. Her name and picture is on a plaque on the east wall."

"Na'ilah the Nuke," Tam snorted. "You can always get a fanatic to do something stupid."

That comment earned Tam glares from several men in the line. Not that he cared. It took three years, and a half a million dead to clean up Paris after her attack. The Jihadists counted on the decadent Western powers to cave in after playing the WMD card. They figured dead wrong. The whole world turned on them, and they were hunted down within a year. There had been some show trials in Brussels, but most of the terrorist cells and leadership had been executed on the spot in their caves like rabid dogs. Nothing delivers a "Guilty" verdict like a precision-guided cruise missile. Their "holy struggle" to return global civilization to the golden age of abject poverty and medieval superstition ended in that mushroom cloud.

Looking around at the crumbling stonework, the graceful arches and slender pillars fading in the interior gloom, I couldn't help get a little cynical myself. I caught Alejo looking at me sideways as we walked, a patient grin under his moustache. "Were you going to comment too?" he asked.

I held up my hands. "No, no, he didn't mean anything against you."

"I know what he meant."

I sighed. "Sorry, I know you're religious."

"Jace, you've known us for years. You knew us before Christ came into our lives, and you've known us since. Jesus is different. He is not religion."

"So you've said. I know it worked for you two. You *are* different. You've certainly changed. But religion's like nitroglycerine: handle it right and you can move mountains. Screw it up, and you'll kill yourself and everyone around you. Na'ilah point in case. Not everyone's the same, Al. Seems most people abuse it and do crazy things in the name of God. And that lowers the street cred, don't you think?"

"Of course, but the problem isn't God. People will wrap their wickedness in anything they can find." Alejo said. "None of that makes God any less real, or me any less responsible to Him."

"Yeah. I suppose."

"Hey. Don't argue with an old man, eh?" He gave me a fast jab in the ribs with his cane. "See? Beware the 'rod of correction'." The crowd was walking faster now. "God is a reality, Jace. You'll come around. You and Tam are both too honest not to."

I had to laugh at that. "I never thought honesty was one of our strong points, Al. Considering our line of work."

"Well, we'll have to work on that then, eh?"

Tam spoke up. "Not a chance in hell, Al."

Alejo only grinned back.

Eshu International and the Garcías had parted ways seven years earlier when they suddenly converted to Christianity in a major way. Before that, Alejo and Carmen would say they'd believed in God in a vague, general sense. Nothing definite or dogmatic. God was like stars at night: pretty to think about sometimes, but so far away He didn't really matter. Then one night in southern Sudan something happened that changed everything for them.

This was the same time the newly formed Islamic Republic was flexing their muscle, making their grab for the region. Saudi-backed paramilitary brigades were pouring across the Gulf of Aden to help the African people 'transition' to the new caliphate rule, and the Garcías had been turning a tidy profit by slipping past U.N. peacekeepers to smuggle arms to a rebel group near Eritrea. One night, as Alejo, Carmen, and several of their crew were on their way to swap ammo and AK-74s for diamonds, they came across a couple dozen schoolchildren fleeing down the highway, led by several nuns and a priest. Apparently, the Jihadists had just hit a series of Christian villages. Stopping to help, they packed the kids in on top of the crates and turned around to go back to their boat.

They never spoke in detail about what happened next. They only said that the Mujahideen doubled back for the survivors and caught up with them on a stretch of road overlooking the shore. Whatever happened that night, they gave up smuggling, sold their boats and retired the next morning. They still keep in contact with the priest and some of the children.

Carmen said prayer and God's love were the only weapons she needed now. Alejo had told us she mentioned our names every night, asking God to watch over Eshu International. Personal attitude about religion aside, it's hard to begrudge someone praying for you, and if there was one thing Tam and I did have faith in, it was that Alejo and Carmen were good people; the kind you'd want at your side when the pucker factor ratcheted up to ten. They'd never give us up. Their conversion had only made them better. And standing there in line that evening, hiding in a foreign city-slum, hunted by the police and corporate security, I found that realization very comforting.

We halted suddenly when the line of spectators bunched up in a large room. People stood at a doublewide doorway a few meters ahead, the line had stopped because of a security check.

We waited, and Tam and I gave the place a once over. There were no wands or doing pat-downs, no visible cameras, or sensors, just an old security scanner. I glanced at Tam, who rolled his eyes. A breech like this was big enough to drive a truck through.

A few more steps and I spied a skinny kid with spiked blue hair seated behind a folding table. He bounced and swayed to the music in his earbuds, barely glancing up from the console as groups passed through the detector frame. He reminded me of Poet9 ten years ago—smart but clueless. Flanking him were four, mirror shade, no-neck gypsies with poorly concealed Uzi bulges under their jackets. Guess the Turkish Mob was relying on old-fashioned intimidation to keep everyone in line.

I sighed. Amateurs.

The four guards tried to look tough when the three of us shuffled up to the scanner. Angry noise wafted up the dark stairwell in front of us, and I admit my fingers itched for the familiar grip of my Blizzard. We stepped through, and the blue-haired kid hit a button. The static tingle of electronics filled the air, and a bright tension shivered through me. I swear I felt the outline of Boker blades pressing on my skin. I held my breath. Seconds passed and nothing happened. The kid's head went on bobbing, the guards waved us through, looking over to the next batch of spectators. Tam caught me out of the corner of his eye again, and I saw him switch into ready mode. I nodded back, and we followed Alejo downstairs.

The basement turned out to be a large open hall, circular, windowless and clammy. Its center had been dug out for the pit, and concrete ledges dropped like steps in concentric levels down to the fighting cage. The wide, top level was crammed with shouting bookies and food vendors, while at the far end a makeshift bar sold drinks and cheap beer. The place was filling up fast. Clamor and sweat surged in the thick air, like the auger of violence in an impending storm. Mobs of men, and not a few women, kept streaming in, piling into plastic benches lining the ledges.

Sunk in the center at the very bottom, the hexagon shaped fighting pit was topped with rusted chain-link fencing and barbed wire. The first match hadn't been fought yet, so the sand on the arena floor was immaculate, raked smooth like a Japanese tea garden. On the six cement walls, a patchwork of painted sheet metal plates made a quilt of faded yellows, reds and blues, all dented, gouged and streaked with dried blood. Rough chiseled entrances with iron gates revealed passageways underneath the stands leading to and from the arena.

Taking it all in, the feverish seething of bodies, the noise, the murky light, the eager cruelty in the air, the place warped into an industrial version of Dante's Inferno.

Alejo caught me sweeping over the area. He gestured with his cane. "The passages down there go the separate chambers where fighters get ready. There are two main rooms—on the north and south sides—and old tunnels that lead to the metro tubes." He cast his eyes to the far side of the room. "Over there, see the yellow door? That's a utilities room where the Turks count the money, and keep an eye on everything. Those three guys, there, there, and at the door are armed. And so are the two bartenders. The counting room has a ladder to the street, but you won't get close to it any day there's a fight. Only other way in or out is the stairs."

"And you said this was a safe spot?"

"Safer. I said safe-er."

CHAPTER TWENTY-SEVEN

MAD BADMINTON SKILLS

Barcelona Metro Zone, Sant Adrià de Besòs District. 7:30 p.m.
Day Three.

The sun had just set, pulling the narrow streets into darkness. Lieutenant Kaneda squeezed the blue-gray Kia van into an alley across from the mosque and cut the electric motor. Lights glistened in primary colors through the slit windows of the wudu entry hall, backlighting the dark shapes of people on the streets. Several hurried up through the doors into the mosque. The lieutenant rolled down the window and immediately felt the slab weight of slum walls tottering above, the cram and stink of the zones closing in on him.

Filthy rat's nest. How can people live like this? He turned, leaned back into the small cargo interior and regarded the clone agents. The two of them were sorting through the contents of one of the large duffle bags. He cleared his throat. "There it is. Over there. We're told the building hosts illegal fights in the basement. You're to meet at least one of the mercenaries down there, so be on the lookout. Here is some currency for admission." He passed back a grimy pastel wad of old large denomination Euros. "Their man will be at the bar, the contact phrase is 'something to trade.' Understand? All you need to do is confirm his identity, and make arrangements to pick up the package. Tonight if possible, tomorrow if you must. The colonel has a transport on standby."

He paused, waiting for a response. The clones were sorting through the contents of a black duffle bag and didn't bother to look up.

"Do not draw attention to yourself.," the lieutenant continued. "Just get the information and set up the delivery. No more bodies." Instead of answering, the two clones drew weapons out of the bag's black nylon folds. Lieutenant Kaneda watched the female pocket two Daewoo semiautomatics.

"What are you doing? I said no more bodies."

"Call it contingency planning," replied her partner. "There are only two of us, and it's a tactical liability to be unprepared."

"Your friend is busy disposing of a body, that's why he's not here. The colonel wants this to be fast and off the radar. This is a meeting, not an assault." He bit off the words one at a time, as if talking to a child. At his tone, the clones froze and stared at him. Lieutenant Kaneda drew back and continued patiently. "That mosque is run by a local crime gang. There's bound to be armed guards. Some kind of security. A crowd. Your guns will get detected, and that will cause more problems." He breathed out a long sigh. "Problems we don't need."

"It's an illegal gambling operation. There are armed guards, and you're saying we go in without any weapons?" the large man demanded.

"Yes. It's a public place. All you're doing is talking. My orders are to set up del—"

"Our orders come from the executive himself," The woman interrupted. "We are to retrieve the item. Failure is unacceptable. We must guarantee this mercenary's cooperation."

"They are cooperating. They're the ones who arranged this meeting. I don't want you taking weapons. Am I clear?"

The female clone stared at the young officer, then shrugged, and passed a medical hypo-spray to the large man.

"What was that?" the lieutenant asked.

"A tranquilizer. We'll remove the subject for interrogation. You need to be ready when we exit the building," the large man answered.

"Look," Lieutenant Kaneda was almost pleading now. "These contractors know what's at stake here. They want to get paid. You're here to get the device. They want to give it to us. Simple. All you have to do is talk, not kill things."

"You are correct." The girl shifted in the back cargo area, facing the lieutenant directly. "It is very simple. This mission is crucial, and we've been ordered to take whatever steps necessary to ensure its success."

Lieutenant Kaneda ground his teeth. "Fine. Bring the spray. Now get in there and make contact."

The female clone hesitated, a mannequin smooth look on her stunning face. Abruptly, she smiled at the lieutenant and put the pistols back in the bag. "We'll take care of it."

Behind her, slick as black nylon, the large man slid an Isuzu machine pistol and a single Semtex micro grenade into an inner pocket of his jacket. "We will return shortly," he said. "Be ready."

Lieutenant Kaneda toggled a switch and opened the side cargo door. The agents hopped out and made their way across the street, two more dark creatures sinuous in the gathering night.

I leaned back into the damp shadows that clung to the wall. I'd stayed on the top level across from the entrance to watch the last of the spectators flow in. Tam stationed himself near the tumbledown bar with its busy swarm of bookies, while Alejo found a bench seat in my line of sight across from me in the first tier. We were ready, and the event was getting started.

On the pit floor below us, a goateed little emcee in a tuxedo ran around, working up the crowd like some evil circus midget. His voice was amplified incoherence as he bellowed into an ancient handheld mike. Somehow the crowd understood him, or maybe they just knew the routine, because they all roared on cue. The noise made me glance down at the first contenders.

Judging by all the chanting and stomping in the stands, the first guy who came out must have been local talent. The reigning champ was a thick, swarthy, pug-faced punk who strutted out of the northern tunnel. With his fists raised, he circled the pit, thrusting his groin at the painted women who screamed his name. I shook my head. *Hold the lines—we have a winner.* Even from the top floor, I could see the thick lattice of scars on his shoulders and head. He was the kind of fighter who led with his face.

He flexed his arms, all poser ape, and danced some cheap footwork pattern back to his side of the ring, rolling his shoulders like he was warming up. Someone handed him a short club studded with nails, and he swung it back and forth. He was low hit, street-trash muscle, but by the smirk on his thick face, he figured himself the alpha dog in this pen. He stood ready to piss on anyone who dared say otherwise.

The announcer then turned to the southern wall and gave another unintelligible shout, introducing the challenger. A small black man stepped out of a dark oversized sewer hole. At first, I thought he was old; his skin was the color of dark ebony, shiny and taut over a thin, almost emaciated frame. He was all knobby boned, with long muscles and hair frizzled dirty white from years of malnutrition. He hesitated in the lights, standing still in a half crouch as he adjusted to the halogen brightness and din of the crowd.

I looked closer and realized what he was: a Somali boy soldier, probably yanked from the garbage heap of a border camp somewhere in the bloody nose of East Africa.

The entire crowd jeered and hissed, the prejudice palpable as they threw a volley of contempt and beer bottles smashing onto the chain link canopy. Having come of age in the rabid playground of tribal wars, the Somali looked up unfazed and strode into the middle of the ring. In his left hand, he gripped a battered military folding shovel. A cheap Chinese knockoff, it was as scarred and beaten as he was, but the edge held a ragged gleam.

The local champ snorted in contempt and started complaining to the emcee with indignant sweeps of his thick arms. The crowd loved it and chanting swelled again. The African stood and waited for his rant to end. He knew there was no backing out of this fight. After a couple minutes, Pug Face stopped his little machismo jerk off and agreed to fight, even though this contest was beneath his skill. The crowd roared their approval, the victory as good as won for their boy. Last bets were called and there was a flurry of notes changing hands, but watching the skinny 'fugee, calmly assess his opponent, I knew where the smart money went.

The Asian Pacific agents emerged from the stairwell right then; a large man with a good-looking woman. I can't say spotting them was hard; we were expecting them. I caught the looseness of their limbs, the tightening around their eyes as they swept through the crowd, but something else gave it away. Space: body space all around them. Everyone else was jammed in tight as they passed through the doors, but the other spectators veered away from these two unconsciously. It was like they emitted a repelling field. No one jostled, or even spoke to them. They gave off mixed signals on a primal frequency.

Tam had made them straight away too, and he caught my eye from across the room. I tipped my beer to Alejo and loosened a Boker in my left sleeve. Tam moved towards the bar.

I tracked the two agents over my fight bill as they strode up to the bar. Tam eased in two stools down from them and ordered another drink. I started waving my betting sheet and drunk-stumbled toward the bookies clustered by the stairs, drawing them out like gulls to a carcass. I kept two of the better-dressed ones between me and the bar, and played Anglo ignorance, demanding translations of fighter's names, reps, and odds. The bookies chattered away while I kept one eye on Tam.

The bartender working his end was a shaggy-haired, foot soldier with muttonchops and missing teeth. He grinned wide and poured the girl a drink on the house. She smiled back, but it never reached her eyes. Despite the subliminals, the girl was definitely drawing attention. There were plenty of appreciative stares and a couple wolf whistles. The big guy didn't respond, let alone acknowledge them. He was certainly hefty enough to dismiss little dogs yapping, but his body language was way off beam. He wasn't acting arrogant or macho. He just stood at the bar tense and distracted, gripping his beer bottle like a life rope. Meanwhile, the girl stretched, arched her back slightly, and I saw the effects of her movement ripple up and down the bar. Heads were turning now, and at least four other men had zeroed in on her. These agents were drawing far too much attention, but they seemed oblivious. Our little appointment was starting to read very wrong.

My palms were itching.

I was going to signal Tam to call it off, but while everyone was eyeing the girl, he edged onto the stool next to the big man.

"The first ones are never good, eh?" Tam lurched, sloshing his beer.

"What?" The big man tensed, his eyes two flat black stones.

"The fights, you know. Opening bouts are just to get the blood up. Or spilt on the sand." Tam slurred a little, raising his beer toward the pit. "Fresh meat can't even fight properly any more than a couple minutes."

"Go away," the big man snapped, staring down at Tam. "I don't want your company."

"What'cha doing down here then, you pissy bastard?" Tam leaned past him and winked at the girl. "Your friend over there want company? Ain't got any credits left, but I got something to trade."

I saw the man start to grab Tam and freeze as the code phrase registered. It was so fast, I only saw him twitch. Sirens were going off in my head now. Other patrons missed it, either heading off to catch the first fight, or intent on the girl. In fact, one of her admirers had screwed up his courage and was angling towards her.

I took another step closer to the bar.

The suitor was an old ganger, long past his prime, the right side of his face tattooed in faded Bic blue. Hatchet mark gang signs and carbon copy tears ran down into gray stubble, and a doe-eyed saint peeked out of his shirt collar, her halo sagging in wrinkles. Lingering in a place like this, he was wringing the last dregs out of a fading street rep. My guess was it wouldn't be long before he wound up as a notch on some up and coming punk's shank handle.

Still, he must have been someone in his misspent youth because the patrons gave him wide berth when he moved. Almost as big as her partner, he displaced a skinny meth-head off a barstool and sidled up next to the female agent. He puffed out his chest and yelled.

"Armando, another drink for the lady here!" He eyed the big agent as he murmured to her, "Hey, *chica*. I've never seen you before 'cause I know I'd remember. First time to the fights?"

Her partner was ignoring him, intent on Tam, but she turned her head, appraising the old ganger as through a riflescope. He, in turn, missed it because he wasn't looking at her face.

The gangbanger went on. "Fights are exciting, but you can't see from here, *chica*. Tell you what… I've got a couple good seats down pitside. So close you'll get blood on you." He leaned in conspiratorially. "You want get closer baby?"

"No." She turned her back on him and started looking through the crowd. Anger flashed across the old ganger's face, but that's not what worried me. The large man was still staring at Tam like a snake. I pointed to a random name on my fight bill, passed a handful of faded Euros off to one of the bookies and moved closer to the bar.

"You have something to trade?" the big agent blurted out. Tam gave a slight nod and kept the drunk act going.

The old ganger eye-raped the woman long and low and made the mistake of insisting. "C'mon, baby. Don't be shy. No harm done. Just asking that's all." The booze must have upped his courage. "Your friend don't matter," he said. "He's ignoring you, see? I bet you want to get closer to me though." He pressed his crotch up against her back, smirking.

If I hadn't rolled my eyes at the ganger's play and looked over at Tam, I'd have missed it. The big guy was utterly unconcerned about what was happening with his partner. Instead, he dropped his right hand down into his jacket pocket. Tam missed it, leering at the drama with the girl as he waited for the guy to speak again. But the big agent was palming something, bringing his hand up toward Tams face.

I stepped toward Tam and yelled, "Hand!" and the sugar turned to shit in a split second.

The same moment, the old ganger had grabbed at the woman's butt, pawing hard, and rubbing up against her. Both she and Tam reacted simultaneously: Tam by pushing back off the bar and swinging his beer bottle at the upcoming fist, the girl by reaching down and grabbing the ganger's fingers.

Tam smacked the big guy's hand; she jerked her wrist. I heard the ganger's fingers break the same time a yellow medical hypo-spray flew through the air.

The ganger bellowed like an animal, but it was lost in the roar of the crowd as the bell rang and the fight started below. "Bitch!" he snarled, and raised his other arm to backhand her. I saw a blur and heard the snap of cloth as the female agent reached out and struck his windpipe with two rigid fingers.

Once.

Perfect.

The old ganger jerked upright and started gagging. The room around us was howling over the pit, so the bar patrons missed the blow, but they started backing away as soon as they spotted the ganger choking, going blue. He sagged to his knees and fell face first onto the floor.

Tam was backpedaling away from the big guy. The girl hadn't even turned to look at her victim. I shook my arm and the Boker knife dropped into my palm. Out of the corner of my eye, I saw one of the Turks coming towards us, his pistol out and raised. One of the ganger's buddies made a mistake and grabbed for the girl. She pirouetted into him, taking his arm in hers and made a right angle at his elbow, the wrong way.

The snap and scream made the Turkish bartender yank an old Russian Saiga 12 from under the counter. An automatic shotgun... This was a definite 'situation' now. Her partner spotted me reaching for Tam and whipped a flechette gun out of his jacket. A 3mm Isuzu Shredder.

Great! We'd brought knives to a gunfight.

I threw the blade anyway. The big man sidestepped easily and let it thunk into the bar.

Yep—bad all around. I ducked among the tables.

The female agent vaulted the counter and moved on the bartender. She hit him twice, and he dropped out of sight so fast it seemed the floor opened up and swallowed him. The Saiga appeared in her hands and the second bartender didn't even have time to raise his weapon before double-ought painted him all over the wall. Behind me, the fight was kicking into gear down in the pit. Everyone in the benches was on their feet, screaming for blood, but panic was spreading from our more immediate violence; shockwaves fanning out from our little epicenter.

The throng at the bar scattered as the first shots hammered over the skittering chimes of broken glass. The big guy was searching for me now, extending the Isuzu out in front of him. I popped up and spun a second blade, which sank in his forearm. A long burst from the Shredder cut a hooker next to me in half, and I glimpsed the female agent trying to track me through the criss-cross of darting figures. Half a second later, she gave up and opened fire in my general direction.

I slipped on a warm blood slick and scrambled away as shotgun rounds chased me over the drop into the second level. I'd lost sight of Tam and Alejo. I could hear the Turks reacting, shouting panicked orders. Someone was screaming close by, and above me, a pistol crescendoed. The Saiga barked twice then stopped. Fear was hemorrhaging into the crowd now, kick-starting a stampede. A worried moan rose, and I rolled under a bench to avoid getting trampled. People were rushing the stairwell when the heavy clatter of an assault rifle fired up. I dropped another knife into my hand and peered over the ledge.

The first level was littered with bodies and blood. There must have been a sale on Soviet relics because the female agent was still behind the bar, only now she was cranking off shots with a vintage Kalashnikov AK-47. There was a look of dead calm on her face. The zen of homicide. The Boss Turks on the far side had hustled themselves into the utilities room and slammed the door. Thinking this was a robbery or raid, their remaining no-necks surged forward, firing heavy pistols gangsta sideways.

Amateur night at the fights.

On my right, I heard the Isuzu buzzing and spotted Tam weaving cross current against the rush of spectators. The big guy was firing after him, off hand.

Another one of the Turk's guards came charging in from my left, shouting and firing toward the bar. He managed to kill three patrons. The girl never flinched and aimed his way. Right then, Alejo stood up and saved his life, dropping him with an uppercut of his cane. He stepped through the swing and snatched up the fallen gun one-handed.

"Down!" Alejo yelled to me. "Go down!" and he pointed his cane toward the fight pit.

He was right. The stairway up to the main floor was heaving with the crush of bodies trying to escape. Alejo knelt and began rifling through the guard's jacket. I heard the big guy's Shredder run dry. That gave Tam a spare second. I saw him twist and slide under the rail down onto the second level and roll hard toward the next drop. The man shouted something—in Japanese—as he snapped another coil into the Isuzu. The woman stepped out from behind the bar and both of them began closing in on Tam.

Alejo started placing rounds around the woman. He didn't hit her, but the shots drove her back behind the counter. He kept moving down the stairs, and she came up, spraying where he'd been. Her partner, surprised by Al's gunfire, spun and ripped two quick bursts, sending streams of tiny steel darts whining after him. The range was long, but I spun out two more blades at him: one slicing past his face, the other sinking into his shoulder. I heard a grunt as he doubled back out of sight.

Tag, creep. You're it.

I ran down the stairs.

On the bottom level, bystanders gripped each other, huddling by the walls and crying. Tam was already slinking down by the cage, staying out of sight and looking for the gate. Alejo was doing his best to back down the steps with his bad leg while keeping a watch up top. Around me swam sobs and snapped whispers while the moans of the wounded and dying drifted over the frenzied jabber from the top level. More shots rang out.

"We need to leave, Tam," I said.

"State the obvious. I'm working on it."

I had a Boker blade in each hand. Not that it mattered at this range, but it made me feel better—sort of. I stayed low and kept moving downward.

Sprinkled in special pit side stands, a few flush patrons had been caught slumming. They crouched fat and sweaty, fearful behind large cushioned chairs, their clinging-arm candy blondes sniffling out whimpers.

"Is it a raid? A raid?" one stuck his head up and wheezed at me. His Slavic Barbie escort was crying mascara black tears under a glittery tangle of peroxide and neon blue.

"No. Stay down," I said.

"I can't be here... I can't—" he burbled, and his head exploded like a melon. Wet tissue and gray matter spattered on my face. The bimbo went a shrill two octaves higher, then collapsed in a heap, vomiting. I veered off to one side, and Alejo blasted upwards until the clip ran dry.

"I'm out." He threw the Star .45 automatic down in disgust. Up top, two mannequin faces slid away from each other over the chipped yellow railing. The woman going west, the man south.

"Now would be good," Alejo growled at Tam.

"A minute ago would be better. They're flanking, and we're out of bang," I yelled.

I heard the jangle of chain link as Tam broke the lock. The three of us fled into the pit and made for the north wall. The emcee was gone, and the evening's entertainment stood opposite each other, un-bloodied and animal tense. Alejo yelled a warning in Spanish and waved for them to follow.

The two agents were gliding down opposite staircases two at a time. Closing in, they opened fire. Heavy rounds from the AK cut right through the steel fencing and it rent, sagging down onto the sand. The Shredder darts pinged and ricocheted off the links, sparking and veering crazy. Tam made it to the north tunnel, but Alejo and I were stuck center ring with the fighters.

I was right next to the African, and saw his reactions kick in at the sound of the AK. He dropped his shovel, swiveled out of the line of fire and skirted along the wall for the nearest hole. Pug Face froze, then flailed like a mad puppet as the 7.62mm rounds hit him. He came apart and went down in chunks. I turned to see the big guy stopped halfway, looping his good arm in an underhand toss. A small olive drab egg arced towards me.

Time dilates in combat. Sometimes fast-forward, sometimes underwater slow. This went slow. I dropped my hands, letting the blades slip onto the sand, then grabbed for the worn haft of the shovel. A chorus of AK rounds sang over my head, and steel dart splinters stung my face and neck. I watched the grenade as it sailed almost lazily and caught a tear in the fencing, then bounced straight at me. The girl was still firing, far away. Tam was yelling. I swung, smacked the grenade back with the flat of the blade, and turned away. The African kid was crazy grinning at me, two thumbs up. Mad badminton skills. Someone grabbed me from behind and the world exploded.

CHAPTER TWENTY-EIGHT

TRAWLING THE WAKE

Barcelona Metro Zone, Sant Adrià de Besòs District. 11:43 p.m.
Day Three.

It was nearly midnight by the time Major Eames arrived at the mosque. The sky was dull coal dark and low, and the rain had drizzled to a stop and charged the air with a dusty ozone smell. The streets glistened wet black, and she heard the police cordon beams sizzling in the damp. Colonel Estevana had called this one right: responding fast and strong, sealing off the streets around the crime scene and radioing for her and the task force. By the time she arrived, all the main avenues were blocked by military trucks and squads of Guardia Civil troops.

She'd snatched a couple hours sleep, so her mind was clear when she clambered out of the command track. Still, she ran up the mosque's stone stairs two at a time to get her heart moving faster, to bring focus in her thoughts. At the entrance, she felt the lurch of déjà vu. Three precise rows of lumpy, blood spotted sheets lay on the sidewalk; clumps of detained civilians were huddled around the CSI vans; an orderly queue of sterile white ambulances emerged from the fog, the spin of their lights rendered the tenements in the stark relief of metronomed lightning.

A little voice nagged in her head. *You're too late.*

She'd been at a dozen scenes like this before, most of them in the Balkans. She saw the same raw daze spreading over the activity, haunting it, suffocating it, as if even inanimate objects had been shocked mute from the explosive brutality.

Incidents like this, police were an afterthought: there to draw chalk lines and fill out paperwork. They'd called it "trawling the wake" back in Kosovo. "War is a beast," a gunnery sergeant once told her, a rabid thing blind with rage. It gets loose, only sane thing to do was stay the hell out of its way.

She drew a sharp breath, and the world synced back into place. Colonel Estevana approached from inside the mosque. "Something wrong, Major?"

"No. Too familiar, that's all." She regarded the older soldier. He had a deep-lined face, worn even more by the recent fatigue, and iron-gray hair under his command helmet. She'd been too hard on him the other day. *My God, was it two days ago*, she thought. He'd taken her browbeating and done his job regardless. Good man. He was more cop than soldier, but these days the line was blurred anyhow. She made a mental note to mention him in her reports. "Doesn't make it any easier though. What's the count?"

"To start," the colonel said, "we've got eleven bodies upstairs. All civilians, five with criminal records. Four must have been guards, we found machine pistols on them. There was some old scanning gear at the top of the stairs too. Strictly low-tech, mostly for show. The fifth victim was a wire head with priors. Hack and fraud, all Turkish and Russian gang related. He was probably the maintenance boy for the old system."

"What else?"

The colonel hesitated. "There're more bodies downstairs. In the basement. It's bad. Looks like they held cage fights down there. There was a crowd—" his voice caught and Major Eames glanced up.

Must be a horror show if he's choked up, she thought. "Take me there. I want to see for myself."

He nodded and walked back into the building. They followed police tape, blood smears, and the bustling ant trail of CSI geeks until they got downstairs. When she stepped out onto the main floor, she realized he was right. Bad didn't even start to describe it.

The air was rank, cloying with the stench of blood and bowels, and an acrid linger of gunpowder. Dozens of bodies were sprawled throughout the open room, tumbled on the stairs, draped over the railings like broken dolls. The cement floor was slick with dark fluid, wide swathes congealing into sticky black aspic sprinkled with spent brass casings. She clamped down hard before she retched. This wasn't a shootout: it was butchery.

Frowning, she nodded toward the room's center, where it dropped down to the pit. "How many down here?"

"Sixty-seven bodies so far," Colonel Estevana answered. "A couple of them just parts. Most are here on the top level, some in the lower stands, a few trampled on the stairs and down by the pit. There was more armed security down here; six as best we can tell. Two behind the bar, four on the floor. All had known histories with the Turkish mob. And this was certainly a gun battle; not bombers."

"You're sure?"

"Positive—No shrapnel, no explosion radials, no legs."

"Legs?"

"Usually all that's left of bombers—their legs."

"Right. Any live arrests?"

"No," he grimaced.

"So your people ID'd the local mobsters. How high were they on the organized crime ladder?"

"Bottom rungs. The guards have been identified as low-level muscle for the Arif Family, a Turk-Cypriot gang. There's no one higher up the food chain. The utilities room has an escape hatch leading to the street, and the door was locked from the inside. If one of the Arif's was in charge, my bet is they fled at the first shot and left their *gamberros* as rear guard. CSI already sniffed it. We're checking for definite matches against the Interpol VICAP database."

"Mob front like this… I take it there's no surveillance, right?"

Colonel Estevana nodded.

"What about witnesses? Someone must have seen something," Major Eames demanded.

Colonel Estevana consulted his data pad. "My men are interviewing people right now. Most everyone was gone by the time the first response arrived. Neighbors say everything was nice and quiet until people came streaming out like the place was on fire. No one would hear anything going on down here anyway."

"Your men find any survivors?"

He thumbed through more screens. "We only got six wounded from inside the building. Four are on their way to the hospital, two were treated in ambulances on site. They both mentioned a Spanish couple; a big guy with an attractive woman. And an Asian." A pause knitted his brow. "One of them also says he saw someone, an Anglo male, throwing knives."

"Throwing *knives*?" the major asked. "That's six different kinds of stupid if you ask me."

"With the scanner upstairs, maybe it's all he brought," Colonel Estevana said. "It must have been one of his we found stuck in the bar. You think the Asian suspect is linked to the Triads? Local crank dealers have been scuffling over turf and supply."

"No." Major Eames stepped carefully further out into the main room. "This isn't some street spat; it's a war zone." She looked back at the colonel. "Any clues on the shooters at all? Did the guards take down any of the attackers?"

He shrugged, pointed to the body of one of the guards. "No. Not unless one of the dead *gamberros* tried to off his boss. And that's not likely."

"Then you have any ideas who this big guy and his girlfriend might be? Local guns for hire?"

"No one this crazy," the older officer replied.

Major Eames' eyes hardened. "You have anything good to tell me? How about the CSI teams, you getting matches on the Guardia Civil database?"

"There were too many people in the main area for sniffers to sort out. We're waiting on prints and DNA matches off the weapons we picked up. And there's a problem with the weapons..." his voice trailed out.

"What about them?" Major Eames asked.

"Well, there's lots of brass—10mm, old 12-gauge, 7.62. Typical gang guns. The bad thing is the CSI team found flechettes everywhere. And indication of an explosion."

"You said it wasn't a bomber."

"It wasn't," the colonel replied. "There was Semtex residue down by the pit, and plastic casing fragments. CSI says it was a micro-grenade."

Major Eames' eyebrows went up. "That's not mob stash. Both the Shredder and Semtex are on the banned list. They're tagged with mandatory minimums just for looking at them funny." Suspicion jangled at the back of her mind. "Those are strictly military issue, or Corporate."

"Corporate? You think someone hired professionals?"

"C.E.O. orders a grudge hit on a low-rent fight pit? No to that one too. And this," she gestured with her hand at the scene all around them, "isn't too professional. Psychopathic yes, but definitely not professional."

Colonel Estevana stared out onto the main floor. "This, this can't be deliberate, can it? This has to be some kind of deal gone wrong."

"Something went wrong for sure. Why? Over what? And what happened to the attackers? If they're not under sheets, then they escaped. But how'd they get out? With the last of the crowd?" She looked over at the colonel, who nodded grimly toward the center of the room.

Eames stepped warily toward the railing and peered down the circular, stepped levels towards the caged arena itself. The fencing was shredded, crazy canted in tangles and heaps, acting as a steel link shroud for another butchered corpse. The cage door was ajar, broken open. "What's down there?"

"More problems. My men had just started searching under the stands when you arrived. They found an old steel security door on the north side. Looks like it had been locked shut years ago, but it'd been pried open, and at least several people got out that way."

"And…?" Major Eames felt heat rising in her voice.

"Major, the passage goes to the maintenance system for the Tube network. And into the sewers. I re-tasked the sniffer team, but it's a maze of tunnels down there that go on for hundreds of kilometers. The trail went cold after two hundred meters."

"God. Damn. It! This keeps getting better." Major Eames let out a heavy sigh. "There any other bad news you want to fill me in on?"

Colonel Estevana shook his head.

Jessa Eames spoke her thoughts out into the room. "This is just too goddamn weird not to be connected to our boy. I need to know how." She stared at the wall across room. Like gathering smoke, hunches coalesced in her mind, phantoms of suspicion that wisped a fraction beyond her grasp. Like faces in a line up, she tried to focus, force identity to them, but they vaporized under her scrutiny, leaving only a hazy dread.

Enough mystic bullshit.

She made a decision. "I'm concentrating our search in this district, starting from this neighborhood. We'll keep the zone-wide checkpoints and general surveillance, but I'm authorizing round-the-clock Predator and Death Star overwatch. If anyone tries to bolt, we'll know immediately. This is definitely linked to the boy. Let's tighten the screws and see if anything pops."

She looked around the large room one more time. "'Cause I get the feeling we're not the only ones looking for him."

The man called Hester stopped threading his crossbow and watched the Late Breaking Newscast with growing interest.

"Yes Jen, the scene here can only be described as chaos. There's blood and bodies everywhere. Newsnet 5's exclusive sources with the Guardia Civil say the mosque you see in the distance was treacherously attacked during evening prayer services. An unknown number of gunmen shot down nearly a hundred worshippers, sending the rest fleeing into the streets. District leaders are outraged by this latest incident of gang violence and called for increased security patrols in the zones. North District ombudsman Cameron Salazar decried this "massacre at the mosque" saying it was further proof of deliberate negligence and discrimination on the part of the Montevedo Administration towards the zone populace. It remains to be seen whether this act is linked with the recent reports of a new Basque narco-terrorist group operating—"

He shut off the hotel wall screen. "North it is," he said out loud and started packing gear into a small backpack. Last of all, he detached the stock and slid the crossbow next to several other favorite weapons.

When he finished, he switched the nanite tracker on, its dull blue LED screen slowly brightening as it powered up. "Time to see how well you work, luv." Setting it on silent mode, he tucked it in his shirt pocket, turned off the lights, and stepped quietly out the door.

CHAPTER TWENTY-NINE

SHARP JABS EVERYWHERE

Barcelona Metro Zone, Sant Adrià de Besòs district. Callejón del Apuro, "Trouble Alley". 4:44 a.m. Day Four.

I came to on a cool rush of chemical well-being. It was dark, and my body remote. A very familiar numb, I drifted in the sea of painkillers. Couldn't quite lock exact memories down, but I'd been here many times before, so I was content to lie still, soaking it in. *Just visiting—like a vacation*, I thought, and felt the endorphins tug a grin at the corners of my mouth.

"He's coming around."

Now that voice sounded familiar. I tried to place it, but it became another item I couldn't grip. It was all so far away. Somewhere inside I figured this was a good sign: the fact that I recognized the voice. And that no one was hitting me.

Time to try and move then.

I shifted my head, felt my brain slosh inside my skull. Nausea, pain spiked through the happy padding. I groaned. It got muffled seconds later by the drifty analgesic billows, but whatever happened must have been bad.

"Take it easy." Hands on my shoulders. I was on my back. "Give it a minute."

The accent... it was Ibram. Doc Kalahani was here. A recognizable sound filtered in: the beep of an autodoc somewhere nearby.

I'd definitely been here before.

"OK." I kept my eyes shut. "Tell me again what happened."

"They tried to off us, that's what happened!" That was Tam. Loud, and yelling from my right. Alejo interrupted him from somewhere on my left.

"We got out. That's the important thing. Jace, you batted back a grenade, remember?"

"No, but I can feel it."

"The explosion bought us time to get away from those two assassins," Alejo went on. "Good thing you had that jacket. The concussion only knocked you down. Tam and I carried you through the underground."

"Thanks for that." I tried moving again. That only earned me more sharp jabs everywhere. I breathed in hard. "What's that smell?"

"Sewers. We had to go through the sewers the last few kilometers before we got home."

"A trace? They get a trace?" I asked. Things were clicking in place now. I remembered the mosque. The cage in the basement.

Tam muttered, but Alejo spoke again. "No one came after us in the tunnels, if that's what you mean. Good thing too. Except for a couple knives, we were empty handed. Sniffer sets might pick us up at first, but once they hit the sewers, it's gone for sure."

"Damnit, Jace. APAC tried to off us! Some corporate twat issued a D.N.R. and tried to bury us. Us!" Tam again, still loud, his voice edged with anger.

"You don't know that for sure." Ibram's accent came from behind me.

"The hell I don't! You weren't there! They were shooting at me! Christ sake, they were shooting at everyone." Tam was getting louder, and my head was pounding.

"Hey, could you not do that?" I asked.

Carmen spoke up. "I thought you went to arrange for delivery and an extraction."

"So did I," Tam snarled.

"Looks like someone wanted to renegotiate the terms," Ibram said.

"Bullets do make a very definite statement," Carmen murmured.

"Major goddamn ballistic counseling is what that was. They were cutting anyone down to get at us. Who the hell did Asian Pacific send after us?" I could hear Tam pacing back and forth now.

"More like *what* did they send? They weren't human," Alejo countered.

Ibram spoke up again. "You sure they were APAC? What about the Turks? You said they ran the place. You trust them, Alejo? Would they try to pinch the product?"

"Trust them? No. But they knew nothing, and no one was following us. Besides, they wouldn't jeopardize their normal business, not like that."

My brain was getting back on track. I piped up. "It had to be APAC. They're the only ones who knew about the meeting."

"See? See? I knew it!" Tam started in again. "Bastards are trying to burn us, sending agents in heavy like that. We need to wave Rao, and have him tell those—"

"Tell them what? To screw off 'cause we're fencing the product to some other Corp?" I croaked.

I felt a hand lift my head up. Long fingers, it had to be Ibram. He brought a cup to my lips and the water went down cool, spreading clarity in my veins. I opened my eyes and the Garcías' basement swam into gritty focus.

"Yes!" Tam roared. "They broke the contract! Hell, they violated the terms. Corporates can't burn contractors without due cause. We were there to deliver! We were keeping our end. We always keep our end." I could see the veins standing out in his neck. That was a bad sign. He wasn't just angry, he was scared.

Tam pointed at me. "Once word of this gets out, no outfit in the system will work for them. I'll make Rao flash every other contractor. Asian Pacific won't even have trash pickup."

Our situation had boiled over Tam's mind. He was afraid APAC had just cut us loose and slammed the door. Eshu International out in the cold meant we were exposed, expendable, and fair game to anyone we'd ever done a run against.

I tried to sit up, but dropped that idea like a hot rock. My head was killing me, especially when I tried to think. Or move. Or breathe. I lay back, but some dim notion nagged at me.

"Hold on. Maybe I'm slaphappy, or Ibram dosed up the patches, but it doesn't tetris. Why would APAC issue a burn notice? We got out of Toulouse clean. The kid's still viable." More aches were surfacing all over my body, but I reached over and pulled the autodoc's derm-tab off my forearm. I managed to look around before I sank back. "Hey… where is he, anyway? And where are the Triplets?"

Carmen pointed up. "Still sleeping upstairs. I don't want him to see or hear any of this." She smiled at me. "You know the Triplets won't let him out of their sight now?"

I was going to answer, but Tam was in a rage. He spun on me. "What was that that flew out of the big guy's hand?"

"Looked like a mister to me. A med spray."

"Was he trying to snatch me? And they started shooting when it went south?"

"Well that's obvious."

"Maybe the kid's not viable like they thought? They found something out and now it's a cut and run," Tam muttered.

"Why not just wave Rao and call us in then? Why try to grab you?" Poet9 spoke up. "Contract has standard abort clauses. We'd be sniveled, but so what? No need for an eraser. You're right: burning us without due cause would jeopardize all Asian Pacific contracts. Their gray and black ops would grind to a halt."

Alejo sat in his chair, a bandaged hand stroking his moustache. "And if the child isn't still valuable, why do we have this news story about terrorists going after the Docks, and Dawson-Hull Corporate Security ransacking the entire BMZ sprawl?"

Tam wasn't answering. I could tell he didn't like the situation, the questions, or any of the possible answers. "We could call another company," he finally said. "The Americans… M.S.I. projects have dumped the last three years. They'd snatch him in a microsecond. At least we'd get paid something and be undercover. We could lay low on the other side of the globe."

I tried laughing at him. "There's a reason Microsoft Systems International is called 'Messy'. They'd have us running ops in Venezuela like a bunch of wet-work thugs, putting counterinsurgency hits on Amazon Indians or something. We wouldn't last six months."

"We could drop the mission altogether. Give Gibson back," Poet suggested.

"Right! You want to wave to Dawson-Hull and say 'We found your top secret clone boy wandering the streets and wondered if you wanted him back. There a reward?' What the hell is wrong with you?"

"Our offer still stands," Alejo said.

"Jesus Christ, Al," Tam snapped.

"Look, you're praying already," the old Spaniard smiled.

Tam ignored him. "What are we going to do?" he asked me.

"I have no idea."

"Well, you'd better decide on something fast," Doc said.

I looked up at him. "Why?"

"You going to tell them?" Ibram was looking at Tam.

He scowled back. "Fuck me. I'm lost here. You tell them." Tam threw up his hands and walked away.

Everyone turned to Ibram. "Gibson's headaches, they're a symptom of a bigger problem. I think the technology inside him multiplies when it's activated."

I sank back onto the pillow. "This just gets better and better."

"If it's inside him, isn't it active all the time?" Poet9 asked.

"Technically, yes, but it's not functional until he interfaces. I don't know how unstable the nanites are, or how advanced the problem was before you grabbed him, but I'm not surprised he passed out after operation. Instantaneous multitasking like that would put a massive strain on the neural network."

"What are you saying, exactly?" Carmen demanded.

Ibram paused before answering softly. "I'm saying the nanites are killing him."

"Is there a cure?" She got to her feet. "You know how to make him better, *si*?"

"Carmencita, sit down," Alejo tugged at her.

"Don't *'Carmencita'* me. A boy is dying in my home, and you want me to sit down?" She glared at Ibram. "How long have you known?"

"Suspicions, that's all. I filled in the blanks after examining him and talking to Tam. Nothing is certain yet."

"First he's dying, now you're not sure. Which is it, Ibram?" This was the second time in twenty-four hours I was glad Carmen wasn't within reach of a gun. "The companies grow children for experiments now? Inject them with these nanites?" She stamped her foot. *"Jesús se vuelve ahora."*

"What does it matter? I thought you people believed they didn't have souls?" Tam threw back at her.

"I don't think that's gonna help, boss," Poet said.

"How do you know what I believe?" Carmen snapped. "Have you ever read a Bible? Of course he has a soul."

"Who doesn't have souls?" I asked. "What are you going on about?"

"Clones. Gibson. Isn't that what the True Life riots were about?"

"*Basura y humos*! He's alive. He saved Devante's life. It matters to me if he dies. And it should matter to you."

"Don't make this my fault."

"You kidnapped him," Carmen said. "And brought him here."

"Poet was hurt," Tam shouted. "You're the only people we could trust. How could I know what they'd done to him?"

"You could have left a little boy alone, that's what you could have done."

"Carmen!" Alejo's voice cracked like a whip. "What's done is done. They're here. And now we help find an answer." He looked at Tam. "Remember… when the time comes, we can get you out of the BMZ."

"Hey," Poet9 said. "Changing the subject here… Doc, you think there's a cure for whatever they did to Gibson?"

Ibram shook his head. "I don't know. I need time and equipment, neither of which I have here. I have no idea how the nanites integrate with his neurology, how far along the deterioration is, how widespread the growth is."

"But there's a chance."

Ibram shook his head. "Ahhh… in theory, yes. But I can't promise anything without hard data."

"Good enough for me." Poet9 looked over at Tam. "Screw the sushi eaters, I owe the kid. I say we help Gibson."

"We're not voting here, Poet," Tam said. "Stop being stupid for five minutes and think. The Triplets are shoot on sight. You, me and Jace have jackets that'd get us mind raped and strapped on the next Space Mountain ride to Luna… if we survived custody and interrogation. We've stayed alive because we made ourselves useful. We had coverage. But left in the cold, you think the suits wouldn't terminate us given half a chance?"

"Seems like they're trying to do that now," I said. "The whole 'coverage' thing got shot to hell by our two new friends. This isn't business as usual anymore."

"He's right, boss. If we can't go to APAC, and you won't drop the contract, what are we going to do?" Poet9 asked.

The cellar got real quiet. I heard the floorboards creaking upstairs, people around me breathing, heard my heartbeat in my ears, all waiting for an answer.

"I don't know," Tam finally said.

For a second I thought he was going to cry.

CHAPTER THIRTY

TORN

Gibson: Something's wrong.

It's dark and there's yelling downstairs. Voices rumble up through the floor, broken and sharp-edged, and for a moment, I don't know where I am. But then the door opens and light spills in with the Triplets and I remember. They've been waiting in the hall for me to wake up.

This last headache was the worst one yet. Most of the pain is gone, but I'm weak, and it feels like someone is squeezing my head. Something's different inside. Mopsy has to help me up.

We go into the kitchen. They move quietly for such big men. The floor is cold and my hands feel huge. We listen together at the basement door.

I hear Poet. He's awake, but now Jace is hurt. Tam sounds lost, and Carmen is angry. There's been more shooting and everything is confused. The tall doctor with the sad face says I'm dying. My interface is killing me.

I want to shout "No," but my head pounds and I think he might be right. The net is where I'm free. I fly as fast as thought, and am alive there. But the headaches always come after, and I think what he says is true because I'm torn inside. Leaking, and each drip pulls a tiny bit of me away.

They shout about souls. Is that what I feel slipping away?

Where is it going?

What will happen when it all leaks out?

It's dark and there's yelling downstairs. The pain is in my chest now and my eyes are blurry. Mopsy holds my hand.

Something's wrong, and it's because of me.

CHAPTER THIRTY-ONE

COMPLICATIONS

Barcelona Port Complex, Asian Pacific Consortium Trade Offices,
Bureau D. South Dock, Level Five. 10:17 a.m. Day Four.

Colonel Otsu glanced at the communications monitor for the fifth time in the last thirty minutes. "He's over two hours late. Anything on our other dedicated channels?" he asked his secretary.

"No, sir, nothing yet."

"Sit-reps are every eight hours. Lieutenant Kaneda has missed two already."

"Colonel, with the emergency measures imposed, there's bound to be complications. Guardia Civil and Dawson-Hull patrols, network jamming... Weather sats report an incoming storm. It could be as simple as a dead battery. He's a capable officer. I'm sure he'll arrive soon."

"Capable officers don't miss sit-reps. Remind me where the meeting was last night."

His secretary thumbed through the screens on one of her data pads. "A mosque in the Sant Adrià de Besòs zone up north."

Mr. Hsiang's face flashed in the colonel's mind. *'shinigami designation. Highly valuable prototypes...'*

"'Complications'..." The word tasted flat in his mouth. "Did the Chishima Labs forward any details about these clones?"

"Only that their appearance had been imprinted for the region," his secretary answered. "The lieutenant said he'd provide more details after the meeting with the mercenaries."

"But he hasn't. All the more reason for concern then. The executive made it abundantly clear this operation warrants our absolute cooperation, and he's not a man who takes disappointment well." Colonel Otsu took in a deep breath. "Send out a plain clothes detail to locate and assist the lieutenant. Have them start with the safe house, and if he's not there, track his chip. This situation is feeling even more... tenuous than usual. I want him and those clones found."

"Yes, sir." His secretary was halfway out the door when she paused, touching the earbud on her right side. Frowning, she turned back and brought up the video on one of the large flatscreens on the office wall. "Sir, I think you're going to want to see this."

A news report about a shooting in the Northern District came on.

Asian Pacific Consortium N. EU Division Regional Offices, Amsterdam, Netherlands Zone. 11:11 a.m. Day Four.

"Complications?" The word hissed through Avery Hsiang's clenched teeth like steam from a ruptured pipe.

The female agent looked back at him from the screen, unfazed. "Our initial contact didn't go as planned. The mercenaries were uncooperative, and we're continuing our search."

"How soon will you have the device?" Avery demanded.

"That's impossible to determine at this point."

"Impossible to determ—?" Avery choked, an incandescent rage blinding his thoughts momentarily. He bit down and tasted blood. "I gave you simple orders: get the device from the mercenaries! Now you're telling me you can't?"

The *shinigami* looked directly at Avery, her eyes cold and flat like two black stones. "Dawson-Hull has mobilized significant resources to regain possession of their item," she explained slowly. "They have the full cooperation of the Spanish government and police force, and have the entire area of operations under civil lockdown. There's heightened surveillance, armed patrols, and tight travel restrictions."

"Excuses!" Avery screeched. "You're supposed to obey, not justify your failures."

"We won't fail."

"You did. You told me—"

"We need Maximum Sanction," the agent interrupted.

"What?" Avery paused. "Why?"

"Our new plan requires use of Trade Legation resources."

"They're already at your disposal. Colonel Otsu was ordered to render you every consideration," he snapped.

"We need him to effect an intrusion into the Dawson-Hull Communications Net for us."

"Impossible. That's a direct action against a corporate entity."

"Isn't direct action what you ordered, Executive?" the agent replied.

"Not to the point of corporate conflict."

Avery could have sworn the agent smirked. "You risked that the moment you contracted the Toulouse infiltration."

Avery's eyes narrowed. Like it or not, this cloned bitch was correct: the die was cast and there was no retreat now. Failure would be finish him once and for all. But his talk of Maximum Sanction had been more a goad to Otsu than an actual consideration. "And this intrusion will achieve what?" he finally asked.

"It will get you the device, Executive."

"When?"

"Thirty-six hours at the latest," she said.

Avery Hsiang tapped out a simple alphanumeric code on his keyboard. "Bring me the N3."

"We will not fail," the agent replied, and the screen went blank.

CHAPTER THIRTY-TWO

GRAVEYARD ANGEL

Barcelona Port Complex, Asian Pacific Consortium Trade Offices,
Bureau D. South Dock, Level Five. 11:50 a.m. Day Four.

"You want what?" Colonel Otsu sat back in his chair, unsure he'd heard the female clone correctly.

"In order to locate the mercenaries quickly, we require access to the Dawson-Hull tactical communications net," she said from the monitor. "We've penetrated the Barcelona police channels, but that only provides half the conversation, and half the information."

Colonel Otsu was stunned. "You've hacked the national police band, and now you want me to initiate an intrusion into a corporate security net. What for? You were supposed to arrange for the delivery last night. What happened at that mosque?"

"The meeting didn't go as planned," the woman said in a dead voice.

"Didn't go as planned? There're reports of shooting all over the news."

"The mercenaries were uncooperative."

"This is supposed to be a routine pickup, not a hostile takeover," the colonel practically shouted.

The woman shrugged. "We are revising our method: with Dawson-Hull and Spanish authorities mobilizing significant manpower, it is far more effective to let them lead us to the item and intercept it. But we need complete access to their communications, and only the Trade Legation has the computing capacity to decrypt Dawson-Hull's communications. "

"If Madrid finds out and traces it back, every Asian Pacific concern in the region will be threatened. The company would be PNG'd, our offices closed down. The loss would be incalculable. Mr. Hsiang would not be pleased if—"

"The executive is concerned about the device. I will inform him as the situation demands."

"As the situation demands...?" Colonel Otsu was dumbfounded. Action like this was outright provocation that could spark worldwide reprisals and corporate censure. "Dawson-Hull counter-intelligence would detect an attack in days, if not hours. My unit would be ejected from the country, the entire Legation closed down. I need authorization from Tokyo for something like this."

"I'm not interested in what might happen to you. As for authorizations..." the girl tapped her keypad, and a secondary window opened on Colonel Otsu's screen. "The 'Maximum Sanction' designation subordinates all local corporate resources to my cell for the duration of the mission. That includes you, Colonel. All information regarding this mission is classified 'black' until further notice. Now get us into the Dawson-Hull Net."

Colonel Otsu felt the air grow thick. The Tier Two codes in the pop-up window were authentic. Hsiang had actually done it. Clone units had been given Maximum Sanction... This dirty little incident had just moved light years past the usual black-ops squalor.

He drew two labored breaths before speaking again. "I need twelve hours to effect the intrusion."

"You have eight. In the meantime, we've extrapolated several possible locations for the mercenaries from the police chatter, all of them in the northern Sant Adrià de Besòs district where the mosque was. We're going to investigate. Keep transportation on stand-by in case we're successful and locate the device." She reached forward to sever the connection and the movement jogged the colonel's memory.

"Lieutenant Kaneda... where is Lieutenant Kaneda?"

The girl turned back to the screen, her beauty as frozen and lifeless as a graveyard angel. "The officer was killed due to the confrontation with the mercenaries. But don't worry, we disposed of the body."

With that, the screen went black.

Barcelona Metro Zone, Sant Adrià de Besòs district. Callejón del Apuro, "Trouble Alley". 2:18 p.m. Day Four

Hermano swayed to one side and cuffed his runny nose. His eyes were watering hard from that last shot of Orujo. He let out a deep belch, and vomit rose, burning the back of his throat. He blinked hard, swallowing it down. Then with a satisfied grunt, he rubbed a meaty fist-edge on the filmy glass and squinted through the smear for the hundredth time. Behind him, the bottleneck clinked against a glass again, and he heard his cousin mutter something.

"They're over there I tell you. You wait, wait and see," Hermano growled back over his shoulder.

His cousin Gaspar sat in rumpled militia uniform in Hermano's favorite chair; a dumpy, soiled heap of baby blue spilling over the torn and faded paisley.

"You'd better be right, Mano. I have been waiting—waiting all morning." He slurped noisily from his glass. "I didn't come all this way for nothing, you know," he added importantly.

"Where else do you have to go?"

"I have my duties. I'm the third officer on watch tonight."

"Ha. There are only three of you on nightshifts anyway."

"No matter!" He heaved forward, muffled gas sounding in the seat cushion. "I am a man of importance in this district. I am authorized, authorized, you know? I have a pass card even. For when my official duties take me to UpCity." Gaspar's piggish face reddened with cholesterol and umbrage. "What do you do? Drive a forklift on the Docks, bah." He frowned.

Hermano scowled but held his tongue. He doubted they ever let fat Gaspar anywhere near Old Barcelona, let alone gave him a pass card. He may not have a uniform, but at least Hermano worked a real job, a man's job, instead of taking bribes and shaking down venders and hookers for small change. Hermano despised Gaspar and his kind almost as much as Anglo supervisors like Mr. Vandarm.

A thought rattled around in Hermano's brain: maybe he should kick Gaspar out. Worthless pig. He'd throw his pompous militia ass right out of his flat. He turned around, squinting hard at his cousin now, images of Gaspar red-faced and puffy sitting startled on the sidewalk, Hermano on the stoop shaking his fist in righteous anger while his neighbors looked on impressed. Hermano's chest swelled with pride. His cousin looked at him suddenly, and he deflated.

Slug though he was, he was still a district militiaman, and as such, he could cause trouble for Hermano if he bent his little mind to it. Besides, Hermano needed him to verify the claim, get the reward money; and Gaspar—as family—would only take half. He let his face soften and tried a different tactic. Hermano spread his hands and smiled sheepishly.

"But, Gaspar, you've been watching the girls more than that apartment." He gave a clumsy wink.

"I have to make sure none of them are suspicious," he grumped.

"And drinking all my booze." Hermano wagged a thick forefinger.

"Sharpens my police instinct." Gaspar tapped his head and sloshed his drink in cadence.

"Empties me out more like it."

"If you're right about *la cuadrilla del narcótico*, Hermano, you won't have to worry about it," Gaspar intoned piously, farting again as he leaned back in Hermano's chair.

Did he have to do that? Hermano grimaced.

Gaspar, oblivious, went on, "Think about the reward. Besides," he waved his hands again, spilling more of Hermano's liquor. "Even if it's not them, I'm sure we can find some reason to detain the whole bunch." Gaspar's face brightened and Hermano saw a thought emerge in his cousin's mind. "Perhaps they even have money to stay out of jail, eh?"

Hermano nodded silently, clenching inside. He turned back to the window and stared sullenly across the street. Behind him, his cousin let off another muffled explosion.

CHAPTER THIRTY-THREE

Barcelona Metro Zone, Sant Adrià de Besòs district. 4:30 p.m.
Day Four.

Hester stood at a metro stop a block away from the mosque. The area was still cordoned off, but he had a clear line of sight to the entrance. The place was swarming with police and news crews—far too many people around for him to get in and rummage for clues. *Maybe tonight*, he thought, and he was eyeing the tenement balconies nearest to the mosque's roof when the link in his ear beeped.

"Hester."

"Mr. MacKinnon?"

"Have you located them yet?"

"Nothing solid yet, sir, but I've got eyes on a lead as we speak. Local fuss: gunners in a mosque, bit of a bloodbath… seemed a bit sketchy so I popped over to take a look." Hester checked the time. "I was going to brief you later this afternoon—"

"Never mind that. There've been some new developments." Director MacKinnon's voice spoke inside Hester's head. "My source inside Asian Pacific reports that in his eagerness to get his hands on our item, their man crossed a line and attracted some unwelcome attention. Evidently, he requisitioned several combat bio-units from their black labs on his own authority. Atrocious violation of procedure. All sorts of red flags went up."

Hester moved out of the metro shelter and started down the street. "Next you'll tell me he sent them here."

"Well, I thought you'd want to know. They're covert ops prototypes; infiltration and wet-work conditioning, but untested. And apparently a bit on the psychotic side."

"All right, sir, but other than psychosis, what is the clones' recognition feature?"

"That's another challenge," MacKinnon said. "Their scientists didn't code any of the customary distinguishing marks into this series. In fact, they've apparently developed a way to imprint racial types on top of a base physiology. They can program their appearance to whatever they need and slip them into a local population. I'm told these things can look like anyone.

Clever work, I'll have to speak to Brenton about that. I hate playing catch up."

"You're saying on top of the contractors, I have to watch out for three crazed Spaniards in Barcelona now?" Hester asked. "That doesn't narrow it down much, sir."

"I understand. That's why I called. You need to stay on your guard."

Hester frowned. I *thought this was too easy*. "Yes, sir. Trouble usually comes in threes. Is there anything else?"

He heard a rather joyless chuckle. "Indeed. Because of those clones, Yoshio Tetsuo, a member of their Board of Directors was alerted. Not a fan of Hsiang, there's a very strong chance he's going to intervene, if he hasn't already. We were counting on Hsiang's monumental self-interest to circumvent normal security procedures, but Tetsuo is a senior director, and far more circumspect. We don't have time for that sort of thing. Long and short of it is that you need to be prepared to take matters into your own hands. Do you have a problem with that?"

Hester considered what that meant. "No, sir. But if this Tetsuo is such a concern, why not drop breadcrumbs for these clones? Kill two birds with one stone."

"Because killing is the issue. Mr. Hsiang's attitude toward the contractors is less than generous, and with him unaware the nanotechnology utilizes a host, I'm concerned all our hard work and preparation would get caught in the crossfire. We're too close, I can't risk it."

"Very good, sir."

"I knew I could count on you." The voice of Director MacKinnon paused. "How's our dear major getting on?"

"Tearing through the sprawl with her crunchies on. Not ladylike at all."

"But you'll keep an eye on her as well?"

"Of course. She's already here with me in the neighborhood."

"She's off limits, Hester. I want that boy to stay in one piece, so do whatever's necessary, but don't let her come to any serious harm. You're creative. I'm sure you can think of something."

"Already have, sir."

"Good. MacKinnon out."

The link went silent, and Hester recalled details from the news reports. Two shooters, seventy-eight killed, six wounded. *That right there is a bit on the psychotic side… in fact, it's well over the line.* A familiar wariness edged into his mind.

With one last backward glance at the mosque, Hester checked the time on his watch and started walking faster.

CHAPTER THIRTY-FOUR

GROWING MADNESS

Barcelona Metro Zone, Sant Adrià de Besòs district. Callejón del Apuro, "Trouble Alley". 5:15 p.m. Day Four.

Tam, Poet and I were in the cellar that evening sorting through our gear when Alejo walked in.

"Can you stash them for us?" Tam asked, pointing at our Mitsubishi suits. "We'll come back later when things have cooled down."

Alejo nodded. "No problem. So you're definitely leaving then."

"WeatherNet says there's a storm coming, so as soon as your friend at the Docks is ready, we'll be off. Jace will go back to that café tomorrow and let Rao know what's happening. Best thing all around."

"And the boy?"

"Gibson's coming with us," Tam said too firmly. "The captain will have to take payment after we get back to Belfast. Think he'll have a problem with that?"

Alejo waved that thought aside and looked directly at Tam. "You can leave him here. We'll look after him."

Tam focused on the spare magazines for his Tavor rifle. "Thought we'd had this conversation already... Thanks, but no. You and Carmen have stuck your neck out far enough. I don't want to risk any more trouble for your family."

"You going to shop him to some other corporation?" the old Spaniard asked.

"Sorry?"

"You heard me."

Tam sighed. "Al, drop it, will you? Take off the Jesus-colored glasses for a second; you must remember how things work in the real world."

"Boss..." Poet9 interrupted. "You might want to cut him some slack."

"It's OK, Devante," Alejo said evenly. "I do remember, Tam... that's why we came to faith; it was the only thing left that made sense."

"If it works for you, what can I say, right?" Tam started disassembling the short bullpup assault rifle.

"It would work for you too. If you'd ask."

"Well I'm not."

Alejo's eyes narrowed. "What's your problem with God, Tam?"

"No problem here. He leaves me alone, I leave Him alone."

"There is a problem, but I have no idea what it is." Alejo settled into his old leather chair. "You say you trust us, yet when I talk about Him, you slam shut like a broken window."

"Let's not go there. It's your home, and I don't want to disrespect you."

"You're leaving soon," Alejo grinned. "Humor me."

Tam worked the bolt on the weapon several times before answering. "It's dangerous," he said finally.

"What is?"

"Religion. The Bible."

"'Dangerous' is a strong word."

"Yeah well, dangerous is the right word. Life's a ten-ton bitch that'll run you over first chance it gets. Fables and wishful thinking only set people up to be blindsided."

"Tam, you've turned cynical in your old age," Alejo said.

"Very funny. Turned realistic is what I've done." Tam shook his head. "Look... Carmen can read Gibson all the Bible stories she wants, but it won't change anything. The sooner he figures that out, the better chance he has with whatever shit APAC or D-H throws at him."

"If he lives through whatever's inside him."

"Yeah well, Ibram's got some ideas on that front," Tam replied.

"Of course. After all, you can't sell damaged goods."

"Now who's being cynical?"

"I'm being nostalgic," Alejo said. "Remembering how things work in the real world."

"So what would you have me do here, Al?" Tam snapped. "Risk my life and my team for a clone? They'd just grow another one."

"Tell me, what do you think would have happened to the Triplets back in Africa if we'd left them, eh?" Alejo asked quietly. "Did you see tools you could use? The bounties for turning them in? Or did you see three cornered, starving human beings?"

Poet and I both felt that question hit. I didn't look at Tam, but I heard him after a minute. "Al, you and Carmen have always taken care of us, from back in Libya." He laughed softly. "I swear to God—if He's really up there—there's no one I trust more in this world. But I'm not going to lose everything I've worked for, bled for, fought for, hoping Jesus will reach out of the sky and give me a 'happily ever after'. I'm doing this the only way I know how. It's a foregone conclusion."

Alejo held Tam's gaze for a several seconds. "Sometimes a conclusion is just a place where you stop thinking," he said at last.

Barcelona Metro Zone, Sant Adrià de Besòs district.
6:40 p.m. Day Four.

It started with the sound of broken glass.

Major Eames was handing a data pad back to one of the section leaders when a window shattered somewhere behind her. Just a minor key jangle that floated down out of the maze on tenements on the thick air: a fleeting high note to the chorus of yelling troopers, the bass growl of truck engines, fading wails of faraway sirens, and the running babble of the crowd. She barely heard it.

"Finish that last section, buildings seventeen through twenty-one. Drag the people out if you have to. And make sure the sniffer teams go over every inch of this place. I want definite readings."

"Yes, ma'am." The young sergeant saluted then ran off.

As he disappeared, she turned towards this latest congestion of grimy concrete apartments, her face creased and as hard as a clenched fist. Just another sprawl neighborhood, she thought, more filthy than usual, if that were even possible.

Her eyes flicked everywhere, double-checking the operation as it played out in what was now almost tedious repetition. The Guardia Civil units herded lines of scrawny, dirty civilians away from the buildings while the techies with security details moved in to systematically ransack their homes. Same shit, different district.

She couldn't help wondering for the hundredth time what the hell was going on.

It wasn't like she had a problem inflicting blunt trauma, but going after one person in the sprawl was like trying to find spit in the ocean. Sledgehammer ops never finesse well, but at this point, she and her men were generating nothing from the population but sullen hostility. Why in Christ's name did London keep her kicking down doors and making a big scene rousting Barcelona's sprawl scabs? Orders are orders, but this was morphing into a major cluster.

She looked over the crowd, picking out the small round faces of children sleeping in their parents' arms.

This asset, a boy… Didn't all corporate personnel have an RFID implant? So, if old man MacKinnon and the rest of her bosses thought he was so goddamn important, why not just turn on his chip and triangulate? Satellite imagery and a scalpel of ninja boys would double-tap the baddies and have him back inside ten minutes.

On the other hand, if the kid wasn't chipped—why not? Major breech in basic security, right there. Somebody could go up against the wall for that screw up.

Or was it intentional? Were the suits hiding him for some reason?

Suspicion twitched at the edge of her mind, but her radio beeped and the thought skittered away before she could get a good grip on it.

"Yes?"

"Team B reporting in, Major. Building sixteen is negative."

"Sixteen clear, acknowledged. Hurry it up and move to seventeen. We're running out of daylight. Command out."

Clear. What the hell else is new? It'll take a million years to find the kid like this. As she rubbed her forehead, someone in the apartments in front of her started yelling a Spanish phrase over and over again.

"Van a matarnos. Ayuda! Ayuda! Van a matarnos."

Her instinct picked up and suddenly the radio squawked again.

"—ninth floor. Guy threw a brick a minute ago, and now he's running. We're in pursuit. He disappeared into seventeen. Toward the roof. Repeat: Roof of building seventeen."

Major Eames snatched up the mike. "This is Command. Take him alive. Non-lethal, soldier. I want a fast and quiet takedown. Repeat: non-lethal. I don't want a panic down here. Do you copy?"

The radio chattered terse and harried with several soldiers' voices, but the team leader rang out over them, "—opy that Command. Scab bastard's fast, but we're on him. We got him now!" She heard the heavy breathing, the triumph in his voice just before the radio cut off in the density of concrete landscape. *They'll corner him,* she thought. *Probably some creepy meth dealer bolting out of his dingy kitchen lab; the troopers'll beat the living—*

A single gunshot rang out, its magnum echo running once around the buildings before it fell onto the street. As the thunder faded, like a single living creature, the crowd turned around and looked up toward building seventeen. Then on cue came a scream. A young girl's scream: long, piercing, terrified, fluttering high in the air like a nervous bird. Ice hit Major Eames' veins, and she looked up.

"Son matanza nosotros. Ayúdeme!" They're killing us. Help me.

A second gunshot rang out, answered this time by the clatter of military assault rifles. Major Eames looked over in time to see the cordon of Spanish policía step back several paces, uncertain. She opened her mouth to yell, but the command was drowned out by a worried groan that rose from the civilians massed on the plaza. As the sound grew louder, the crowd turned toward the thin line of police, a thousand faces tensed in the headlights of her command track.

The sound stopped abruptly, as if everyone paused to draw a collective breath. Major Eames reached down and felt for her side holster, but as she tore the velcro flap, the moment tipped over. Someone in the mob reached out and grabbed one of the police officers. He jerked back and stumbled into one of his fellow troopers. Riot batons came up, the mob heaved forward, and the pressure snapped like a storm front.

Major Eames found her voice. "Hold your ground! Control them! Control them! Put your guns down. Guns down, God damn it! No shooting!"

She watched in growing horror as the mass of people surged like a wave, roaring rage and fear. At first, they recoiled when they struck the thin line of lexan shields. The piston steady truncheon blows and the blue sparking arcs of shock sticks crumpling the leading edge. Bodies started piling up, trampled or dragged back, but the dark front of frenzied arms and legs kept coming, kicking, punching, pulling, clawing. Major Eames watched as the uniforms were driven back step by ragged step.

Merging with the bedlam, every police radio erupted with frantic babble as troopers began pleading for orders, direction, back-up. Each of the armored police tracks began broadcasting rapid-fire commands at the crowd, six different loudspeakers blaring out distorted noise, as if their sheer volume could contain the mob.

Heedless, she sprang up onto her command vehicle and started shouting on the radio, struggling to prevail over the chaos and confusion. She saw the first of the troopers get pulled down by the crowd. Then another. She shook the mike in her fist, furious.

"Hold the line! Stay together! Control them! Control them!"

Someone on the police channels was screaming for permission to fire. Major Eames watched a dozen rifles come up.

"No! Do not fire! Secure those weapons, God damn it! I repeat: do not fire!"

A volley of litter flew through the air. Several troopers fell, others were pulled down by the crowd. G.C. policía started falling back in clumps.

"Hold that line for Christ's sake!"

More junk, bottles and stones this time, arced in. The police line was breaking. People started running towards her and the row of tracked carriers. Major Eames was still shouting into her mike when an assault rifle buzzed and the first swath of civilians was cut down. The rest of the Spanish troopers opened up a second later.

The man called Hester looked on the growing madness for several minutes, then clambered down the rear fire escape of building seventeen.

CHAPTER THIRTY-FIVE

OUT FOR BLOOD

Barcelona Port Complex, Asian Pacific Consortium Trade Offices, Bureau D. South Dock, Level Five. 8:05 p.m. Day Four.

Colonel Otsu stared over his desk out of the narrow office window. The day had faded hours ago and taken his hope with it. Earlier that morning, Executive Hsiang had granted unconditional authority to three untested, psychopathic clones who had then demanded what amounted to an act of war with one of the largest financial entities on the planet.

Communication networks were the most common targets of cyber attacks and corporate espionage; consequently, they were the most heavily guarded. The Dawson-Hull Conglomerate maintained round-the-clock surveillance on their electronic infrastructure, and he doubted they'd have even one full day before their countermeasures detected a 'pry and spy' penetration. Yet here in the Legation's Command Center, Asian Pacific technicians were working feverishly to effect just such an intrusion.

The situation was crumbling under his hand like rotted silk, and he was powerless to do anything but watch.

His office doors slid open and his secretary entered. "How much longer?" he asked without looking up.

"Ten hours. Twelve at most. Overnight trade and transactions will be cut to a bare minimum. Decryption is pulling most of the system's capacity."

"It doesn't matter, when this is discovered, every Asian Pacific venture around the globe will be suspect. Trade will come to a screeching halt."

"Perhaps the cell will get the information they need before we're detected," she suggested.

"They'd have to know exactly what they're looking for, and know precisely when that information is being transmitted." Colonel Otsu rose to his feet. "No, the clones will sift signals until they get what they need. And then it will be far too late. London and Madrid will be out for blood."

"What are you going to do?" his secretary asked.

"I have half a mind to commit seppuku."

She frowned. "You're not serious."

"That was a joke." The colonel tried to smile, but despair clung to him like a wet blanket. The only thing worse at this moment would be if Avery

Hsiang called for yet another update. On cue, the corporate link chimed and the desk monitor slid up into view, an executive icon flashing.

"Fantastic," he muttered. "Come back in an hour with a status report," he ordered his secretary.

Returning to his desk, Colonel Otsu steeled himself and accepted the call. The screen brightened and he was sat back, startled.

"Colonel Otsu, what is going on in Barcelona?" Director Tetsuo asked.

Barcelona Metro Zone, Spain. New European Union. 11:25 p.m. Day Four.

"How the hell should I know what's going on?" Major Eames waved the communiqué at Colonel Estevana. "All it really says is 'keep looking'."

She'd got the final count an hour before: 278 civilian dead, ninety-three wounded, most of them in critical condition. Five square blocks cordoned off, her troops stunned and confined nearby, Jessa Eames' world was in chaos.

The newsnets had dropped the mosque story like a hot rock and were streaming video from the plaza: the bodies torn and scattered like shreds of clothing around the reporters, the sightless staring faces of children awaiting identification, fire trucks hosing blood down the street drains, the mingled scent of blood, shit, and outrage. Scab bloggers had already picked up the riot, labeling her *"El Carnicero de Barcelona"*, the Butcher of Barcelona, and no less than a dozen government ministers in Madrid were screaming for her head on a stake right now. *Suffering Christ*, she realized, *this'll rank up there with Las Tres Vergüenzas. I've made history.*

She read the end of the statement again: "*...a thorough investigation pending, but while the Board considers the incident shocking and deeply regrettable, even so, all members deem the matter secondary to the critical objective of recovering the personnel asset. As such, you are hereby assured of the full and continued support of all corporate resources in the unremitting pursuit of said objective.*"

Dawson-Hull's official response had come lightning fast, and there was not a word of reprimand. Jackson MacKinnon and the rest of the Board had to be applying seriously heavy leverage to keep the Spanish from lynching her on the spot.

Who was this kid?

What was this kid?

She looked at the paper again, then up into Colonel Estevana's face. "Our orders stand."

"What?"

"The boy. They still want the boy."

"Why?" he cried. "Is he worth that?" His arm swept back toward the plaza.

In the distance, survivors fell to their knees before the neat rows of bodies, halogen poles creating ghastly halos around the frenzy of their ink-black anguish. Jessa Eames swallowed back something brittle.

"I'm sorry. I have no idea. But there's blood in the water and we have to keep moving." She looked back at the older Spanish soldier. "Tell the men I want them suited, booted, smooth, and strapped in fifteen. Intel finally worked up some solid leads here in the north. We've got to finish this."

CHAPTER THIRTY-SIX

SUITABLY DESPERATE

Barcelona Metro Zone, Sant Adrià de Besòs district. Callejón del Apuro, "Trouble Alley". 5:58 a.m. Day Five.

The morning sky was heavy with storm clouds gathering on the last dregs of night. Carmen entered the bedroom quietly, but she hadn't taken three steps before green eyes were peering up at her.

"What time is it?" Gibson asked.

"Still early, *pequeño*. Go back to sleep. I'll get you before it's time to go."

He noticed a book in her hand, along with some clothes and an old backpack. "What's that?"

"A Bible. I want you to have it. I marked the Psalm you liked so you have something to read on your trip."

"OK." Gibson closed his eyes. "When are we leaving?"

"We'll take you to the Docks tonight. Our friend wants to be underway before the worst part of the storm hits."

"There's a storm coming?"

"Yes, off the hot sands of North Africa. Happens every year. But don't worry, the ship you'll be on is different. It's—"

"Carmen?"

"Yes, little one?"

"Why were you mad last night?"

"Me?"

"Last night everyone was yelling and you were mad. Why?"

"Bah! The foolishness of adults... it's settled now. Don't you worry." She took one of his hands. "Try and go back to sleep. You have a big adventure today, and you'll need your strength." She turned to leave, but he held on to her.

"Carmen, I think my soul is leaking."

"What do you mean? Why do you think that?"

"Because I can feel it. After the last headache, after I helped Devante... it's like it's draining out. But I'm scared because I don't know where it's going."

Carmen started to speak, but her voice caught, and she knelt on the floor by the bed. "Don't be frightened. Everything's going to be OK."

"It doesn't feel OK," he said in a small voice.

"It is though. God loves you." She smiled. "And so do I."

"Yeah but where's it going?"

"Perhaps God wants to take your soul back to Himself."

"He's taking my soul away?"

"No, no, not in a bad way. He wants you to be safe *with* Him."

"Why doesn't He stop the leak and let me stay here?" Gibson pleaded.

"Maybe He will. The headache will go, and you'll get all better." Carmen cupped his face in her hands. "But everybody passes from this life someday, *pequeño.*"

"But I don't want to leave."

"I understand, really I do. But that's not up to us. Each of us gets a turn to walk in God's purposes, and no more. That's why life is precious. That's why *your* life is precious."

"Precious? How am I precious?" Gibson turned his head away. "Dr. Evans said I was the fastest one yet, but what about all the others before me? What about the ones who will come after? I'm like an appliance that's only valuable if it works right."

"Stop that foolishness," Carmen said. "You are precious. You're precious to me. You're precious to God. You risked yourself and saved Devante's life. So stop."

Gibson was silent for a long time. "I didn't want this," he finally said in a quiet voice.

"No, but this is what you have. And you can face it with God, or without Him." She placed her hands on his shoulders. "He's a prayer away, Gibson."

"I don't know how to pray," Gibson scoffed. "All I do is jack in and run the net."

"Faith is like the net, remember? You have to go and find out for yourself, but when you do, God promises you'll find Him when you look for Him with all your heart. Here." She placed the Bible on his lap. "Look at Psalm 139 again while I get your medicine."

She rose and slipped out the door. Behind her, Gibson opened the small black book and started reading.

Barcelona Metro Zone, Sant Adrià de Besòs district. 6:40 a.m. Day Five.

"Three hundred?" Jackson MacKinnon's voice was crystal clear inside Hester's head. *Uplink tech is getting better every mission*, he thought. "You started a riot and three hundred sprawlers end up killed?"

"I had to slow things down, sir. I'd mentioned the major was in the neighborhood."

"Yes, but a hundred wounded?"

"Well, I wasn't doing the shooting, sir."

"That's not what I meant, Hester," his boss grumbled. "You say Eames is unharmed?"

"Of course, sir," he replied. "And all the Special Deployment units are intact. Beg your pardon, but speaking of the major, why don't you just yank her chain and call her off? That way this Eshu outfit come out of the cold unscathed."

"Too obvious," Director MacKinnon said. "It has to appear to be a close thing. Asian Pacific's man is a monumental paranoid, as well as ruthlessly ambitious. He can't have the slightest hint of suspicion. I'll spin your little commotion to serve our purpose. A little brutality will make us look nicely desperate. Just locate our asset, and no matter what mischief you instigate, I'll keep Major Eames chasing her tail."

"Very good, sir. Any preference on the mercenaries' final disposition then?"

"No. Not really. If Toulouse is anything to go by, I'd say they're a highly skilled outfit. Shame to waste talent, but left-hand work is contracted precisely because it's disposable. Still... if they survive Eames and Asian Pacific, I'm confident we could put them to use somewhere." Director MacKinnon paused. "If you get a chance, see if they'll come around. If they sign on, I'll make sure the lads in the dark room have a chat with them. But... to be perfectly clear; they are secondary to our package getting into Asian Pacific's hands."

"Will do, sir. Deadline?"

"Yesterday. This one has the latest version of nanotech, but Brenton and his lab rats can't say with any certainty how long it will remain stable. According to our profile on Hsiang, he's angling for a seat on their Board, and the psych boys say there's a very good chance he'll want to show off, give a demonstration and play the hero. That is precisely what we want. The nano-host platform needs to remain viable until then. It is vital this little venture goes off as planned, Hester."

"And the clone afterwards? Termination?"

"No, no. That will take care of itself: planned obsolescence. Labs are already working up the next version. We might even get a breakthrough there as well. Regardless, I need this one in the wog's hands still functioning. Am I clear?"

"Crystal clear, Mr. MacKinnon. I'm on my way to a probable location right now."

"Perfect. I'll be in touch."

"Yes, sir."

COLLISION

CHAPTER THIRTY-SEVEN

BLACK SNAKE LINE

Barcelona Metro Zone, Sant Adrià de Besòs district. 8:25 a.m.
Day Five.

Major Eames caught herself as the armored car lurched and weaved through the broken streets. A large pothole slammed everyone in the troop compartment sideways and caused her data pad to smack her in the face. Gears grinding over the ripe profanity, the vehicle shuddered back up to speed and they headed toward the suspect's location. Colonel Estevana swayed side to side next to her, holding an overhead handgrip.

She focused on the pad's small screen. "You've confirmed this is the place?" Live feed from a Predator UAV focused on one of the large anonymous tenements jammed in a maze of streets and alleys.

"Yes, Major. One of the district militia is watching the building. The suspects keep to the bottom floor and don't seem to go out much. He says they're in there now."

"Other people in the building?"

"We estimate two to three hundred. They're all on the upper floors. Many are working jobs, day labor, so that number's probably cut in half this time of the morning."

"OK." She faded the screen and stuck the pad back on the velcro patch on her vest. "My men will block the stairwells and breech the apartment. Make sure the sniper team is on the roof, and have your squads seal off the intersections. Every exit and window out of the building needs to be covered. I don't want a stray dog leaving without permission." She punched in a code on her forearm PDA. "I've ordered another Pred on station as eyes in the sky, so smile pretty for the folks back home. Remember: the boy is solid gold— everyone else is target practice. Am I clear?"

"*Si,* Major."

She looked out one of the large vision slits and watched the backdrop of soot-black, cracked cement slid by. Sprawl stench forgotten, she felt the iron-wired twinge of adrenaline singing in her veins as they rushed closer. Her troopers were rolling hard, and with a little luck this would be the jackpot. Grease the scabs, grab the boy, and go home. A good day in her book.

She grunted with satisfaction as call signs for the Spanish units sounded out over the radio. All units were on location, tightening the noose.

"One minute!" the driver called out.

Run and gun. I got a green light, baby.

She breathed in slow, filling her lungs and calming her heart rate. The trucks gunned their engines one final time and roared around a corner, then cut their motors to coast in silence the last 300 meters.

The urgent call of "Go, Go, Go!" filled their headsets, and even before the vehicles jerked to a stop, hatches swung open and troopers leapt out. Civilians scattered as her men ran to the main entrance. Jessa Eames joined herself to the primary breeching team as they went straight into the main lobby.

Inside, a dog was barking, and somewhere up above a chorus of brats squalled, the tinny wails carrying down the moldering stairway. In the dingy gloom, a hunched row of black armored troopers scuttled into position on either side of a green wooden door.

Eames took anchor position—fifth and last one in—and her vision tunneled. Everything went snapshot still and she breathed in the coiled moment.

5, 4, 3, 2, 1...

The tiny LED on everyone's wrist blinked from yellow to green. The point man lashed out, the door blew in, and the black snake line surged forward.

The lead trooper flowed through the shattered frame shouting. She heard shotgun blasts and as she brought up her pistol, his body flew backwards onto the floor.

More blasts and the second trooper in line snapped upright, head deformed, blood jetting in an arc through the face visor. He too dropped backwards out of sight.

She suddenly heard the furor of automatic weapons fire, frantic shouts and counter-commands from the rear of the apartment, as if someone had just turned on the sound. The second breeching team had entered the apartment.

Another step and something ticked in her mind: the buzz of a full auto flechette gun. There was no chance to pin it down; muscle memory and training had her committed in fast-forward.

Another step and an explosion rocked the floor, its pressure pushing past her. The third trooper fell.

She was three steps from the door. The soldier right in front of her, Corporal Kellerman, tried to jump over the bodies, but stumbled as he broke left into the room. Major Eames could hear men screaming now, the sound of auto fire, flechette buzz, ripping through the apartment. Murder crackled in the air. She bared her teeth and swung around the splintered doorpost, gun up and tracking for targets.

The room was filled with smoke, but the bodies of three civilians were sprawled on a worn sofa. Training recorded it: one woman and two men. Bullet holes in the center of their heads. One man was missing the fingers on his right hand, his throat cut, Pollock arterial spray on the walls. Déjà vu: torture and execution.

Her pistol jerked, frantic for a target. Nothing. Kellerman had stayed on her left, covering the kitchen, so she stepped toward the bedroom hall looking for someone to kill.

Suddenly, another flurry of cries erupted in her headset, answered by a roar of gunfire. A second later, a figure popped into her peripheral vision: a large Spanish man had come out of the kitchen with an auto shotgun.

She twisted around for a shot, but he was inhumanely fast. The AA-12 fired and Kellerman came apart. Finger still on the trigger, the big man pivoted, slamming twelve-gauge rounds across the wall toward her.

Off-balance. Bright muzzle flashes. She wouldn't get her pistol up in time.

Screaming, she pulled the trigger anyway. "Burn in Hell!"

She let herself drop, hoping to fall below his line of fire, but two rounds hit and the impact spun her around. Agony spiked deep in her chest, and she landed face down behind a broken chair.

Biting back the shock, she spied him through the shattered chair legs. He was moving towards her when a second person, a woman, stepped out into the hall and spoke in what sounded like rapid-fire Asian. He answered in the same language, and surveyed the living room.

Jessa Eames froze.

After a moment, he followed after the woman and was gone.

Warmth was spreading under her, soaking into the filthy carpet, and she couldn't catch her breath. She'd seen the big man's face before he'd turned away. There was no flush of fear, no panting or rage. Nothing but dead calm.

A stray thought clicked in place right before she blacked out: there'd been Shredder darts in the fight pit in that basement.

These were the shooters from the mosque.

In his apartment, Hermano stumbled in from the bathroom and found his chair empty. He was confused until he spotted Gaspar staring out the window holding another bottle of Orujo. Hermano knew it was his last one and was about to say something until he noticed his cousin was staring intently out into the street.

"What? What is it, Gaspar?"

"Could be some action on the other side," he mumbled back.

"You see one of the *terroristas*? I told you. See? Didn't I tell you?" Hermano lurched toward the kitchen window, trying to see if the police were arresting people. This meant payout time. He elbowed Gaspar. He wasn't about to let his fat cousin ruin his view, or claim all the reward, but Gaspar didn't budge.

As Hermano stood by the sink, he heard the shrill scream and giggle of girls outside. In front of him, Gaspar grunted and licked his lips. "Hot action indeed. You think their mothers know they dress like that?" Gaspar turned back to leer at him, reeking garlic and booze breath all over Hermano's face. Then he peered out the window again, sniggering.

"Fah!" Hermano turned away, disgusted. Staring at girls not much younger than his daughters: cousin or no, this was the last straw.

I'm throwing him out, he thought. *I'm going to report this fat slug for extortion, and take the reward myself.*

He took a deep breath to clear the Orujo fog and braced himself. He would kick Gaspar out, but he couldn't decide if he should shove him first, or yell an insult.

Behind him, there was a sound like a spring releasing and Gaspar's lecherous giggling turned into a gurgle, as if he were choking.

Serves him right. Pervert.

Hermano decided he should yell first, but then he heard the bottle smash on the floor. Gaspar dropped his last bottle? *Clumsy and a pervert.*

He was really mad now, but when he looked, his cousin was doubled over, clawing at his own neck with pudgy sausage fingers.

Maybe it's a seizure... or a heart attack, Hermano thought. That worried him because Hermano didn't want to get blamed somehow. Gaspar's motions became feeble, and a cold fear gripped Hermano's tiny mind. He hoped he wouldn't have to drag him out of his apartment into the back alley. He crept closer. Gaspar's hands fell away and he sagged to his knees.

Hermano pulled up short and stared. A dull metal shaft was sticking at a right angle out of the side of Gaspar's neck. It had black feathers on the end. Gaspar jerked his purple-blotched face toward Hermano, terrified piggish eyes looking up at him. He was pleading, his mouth moving; but no sound came out except a nasty gurgling. Hermano saw blood now, just a little seeping down the shaft. Rooted in place, Hermano stood there watching, unable to look away.

All of a sudden, the reek of excrement filled the air. Gaspar's bowels had released and a dark stain formed on the front of his pants. Hermano saw his cousin's eyes pop open wide, and then fade as the light went out behind them. With a final sigh, Gaspar slumped to the floor.

Hermano's mind was stuttering: he didn't understand what had just happened. He looked at his cousin, to the window, then back to his cousin again. Had someone thrown that thing, that arrow, through the window? As he bent over for a closer look, he heard the sharp twang sound again, and like lightning, a searing pain flared in his own throat. He staggered and caught himself on the sink. He reached up carefully and felt feathers. There was an arrow thing in his neck now. He tried to yell, but the only sound that came out was that hideous burble. He looked around frantically for his phone. It was gone.

Frantic, he tried to pull the thing out, but it wouldn't budge. He felt himself leaking out, getting weaker, and after a helpless minute, he slumped to the ground. His fading eyes caught movement in the hall darkness inside his front door. Someone was there, he didn't know who.

His last thought as he collapsed was: I *just went to the bathroom. At least they won't find me with a load in my pants—fat bastard—*then he flopped onto his cousin's body in an awkward embrace.

When he was sure they both were dead, the man called Hester stepped out of the hallway. He touched his hand to his ear and murmured a command that muted the chatter from the communication nets he'd been monitoring. Looking around, he found it odd both the Barcelona police and Dawson-Hull Security had tagged this location as a low priority lead and left it under surveillance by this militia buffoon and his friend. Hester considered himself lucky.

Sifting through the Spanish and Dawson-Hull communications, Hester had compared them with the files Mr. MacKinnon had sent. He'd noticed an interesting correlation and followed a hunch. Apparently, a former ship captain and suspected smuggler named Alejo García had been mixed up in a lot of mischief in North Africa and the Med around the same time a certain Tam Song had started a freelance career with a Canadian vet named Jace Manner. It seemed the two outfits had crossed paths more than once back in the day. After Alejo García had retired from the sea, he'd settled in the Barcelona Metro Zone, and oddly enough, his current residence was listed in the building right across the street.

In several quick motions, Hester pushed the bolts through the necks of the two men, wiped them clean, then disassembled his crossbow and slid everything back into his pack. Once that was finished, he stepped around the two bodies and went up to the window at the sink. Peering past the dirty curtains, he spotted a gaggle of teenage girls in skimpy summer wear, all clustered in front of the massive flat-front tenement across the street. Scattered cars and trucks zipped by. This was a relatively quiet block, almost a family neighborhood, he thought wryly. As Hester moved in for a better view up the avenue, his shirt pocket abruptly started pulsing more rapidly. He smiled and patted the small tracker.

Yes. He'd struck it lucky indeed.

CHAPTER THIRTY-EIGHT

OBLIGATIONS

Barcelona Port Complex, Asian Pacific Consortium Trade Offices,
Bureau D. South Dock, Level Five. 9:07 a.m. Day Five.

"And where are these contractors now, Colonel?"

"We have no idea, Mr. Director. My liaison officer was killed, and the clones have been unable to reestablish contact."

"I can see why that might be a problem, after this mosque incident," the director said dryly. "The Type Fives suffer from a lack of imagination, among other things. And now they're demanding access to the British security force's communications net..."

"Yes, sir," the colonel answered.

Director Tetsuo frowned. "Given all these *precarious irregularities*, why didn't you contact Head Office?"

Colonel Otsu bowed his head. "Director Tetsuo, the executive stated this mission was critical to corporate interests. My unit is assigned to his division, and I assumed he was working in the Consortium's best interests."

"You can assume executives work in their own best interests, Colonel. Your loyalty is commendable." The aging director stroked his chin. "As dubious as the objective was, you're telling me the team Hsiang hired actually obtained the prototype?"

"Yes, sir, our last communication indicated they were ready to turn it over. The meeting in the mosque was supposed to arrange for delivery," Colonel Otsu answered.

Yoshio Tetsuo's face crinkled with concern. "And now you say there's been some sort of riot in the same district?"

"Yes, now we don't know if the two incidents are related, but Guardia Civil troops were already engaged in a massive hunt for the mosque gunmen, in addition to supporting Dawson-Hull Special Deployment units. They've placed the outer districts under civil lockdown."

The director gave a smile that didn't reach his eyes. "Avery Hsiang is not known for subtlety, but this is extreme." He waved a small wrinkled hand. "No matter, the oversight of Barcelona Trade Legation was transferred to my office last night. Until this matter is concluded, you are to report directly to me."

Colonel Otsu bowed again, "Yes, Director. What are your orders?"

"Two items. First, you are to make contact with the mercenaries. At once. Asian Pacific cannot afford to break faith with private companies at any level, even black commerce. Get a hold of their handling agency and provide whatever assurances you deem necessary. We will honor our obligations."

"At once, sir."

"Regardless of how improbable the nanotech system is, Dawson-Hull has reacted swiftly with considerable force. Invoking the Crisis and Cooperation Act is itself an extreme contingency." The director stroked his chin and continued. "I have to put aside my reservations on the remote chance this prototype is genuine. If this Eshu International has the device, we must get it before Dawson-Hull retrieves it."

"I'll make every effort to contact the mercenaries, Director. And the second order?"

"The Type Five clones are to be returned to our Chishima facility. When they contact you again, have them cease all activities and report to the Legation. This is a Tier One directive that overrides their previous orders, and they are to comply immediately."

Colonel Otsu hesitated. "And if they refuse?"

"Then kill them, Colonel," the director said sharply. "I suspect this entire operation is nothing more than a mirage formed out of Avery Hsiang's febrile ambitions. He has single-handedly managed to jeopardize the Consortium's global enterprise chasing a technological fantasy. He'd better pray those bio-units are not apprehended, and that we obtain this supposed nano-system. We are engaged in damage control here, Colonel. This debacle needs to end as quickly and quietly as possible."

"Yes, sir. And if Executive Hsiang contacts me again?"

Colonel Otsu watched as the aging executive reached over and made a small notation on a piece of paper. "I will attend to Executive Hsiang," he answered simply.

And the world changes at the stroke of a pen, Colonel Otsu thought. The director was speaking again.

"I appreciate an officer with perspective and a finely tuned sense of duty. You have my gratitude." Yoshio Tetsuo inclined his head slightly. "Good luck, Colonel. Contact me as soon as you've heard from the mercenaries."

The connection cut and the screen faded to gray. Beyond the narrow slit of his office window, past the Dock's tangled superstructure, the sky was dark and lowering. A major storm was brewing and he had to move fast before it arrived in full force.

Colonel Otsu picked up his phone and called for his security officers.

Barcelona Metro Zone, Sant Adrià de Besòs District.
Guardia Civil Medical Clinic. 2:30 p.m. Day Five.

Curtains. White curtains and machines. That was all Jessa Eames could see. Stacks of whirring, beeping metal boxes with tiny screens enclosed her bed like field emplacements, all of them back-dropped by tall bleached creases. *In the hospital again*, she thought.

She tried to sit up, but she was weak. Her chest was tight, wrapped and stiff like a block of wood. She raised her right arm and saw wires and tubes coming out of it. Her hand was tingling pins and needles, so she clenched and unclenched her fist slowly to make it stop.

Pain means you're alive. Alive is good. She concentrated and tried her left arm next, but nothing came into view. In fact, from her left shoulder down, everything felt numb. That was probably not good, she thought. Her head fell back on the pillow.

People were murmuring outside the curtain walls. She licked her lips. "Hello?" she croaked. "Who's out there?"

The voices stopped abruptly, the curtains parted, and a tired looking Colonel Estevana stepped in. The dark circles under his eyes looked more like bruises and fatigue etched heavy lines on his face. "You look like I feel," Jessa Eames managed to say. "Report?"

"Major, I think it can wait. You've been injured and—"

"I figured that when I woke up in this bed." She tried smiling to offset the interruption. "I want to know what happened. Tell me what happened."

"You survived, which is a start," the colonel smiled back.

"The shooters. Did... did you get them?"

He shook his head quickly. "No. They escaped."

She closed her eyes and nodded. Somehow she'd figured that. "How many?"

"Three. There were three of them," he answered.

"No," she said. "How many of the men were hit?"

"Twelve, all killed. Both entry teams and one of the perimeter details. Two civilian bystanders were also killed when the suspects stole their vehicle." The colonel's face clouded with anger, and there was frustration in his voice. "We tried to pursue, but it happened so fast, so perfect, like they knew where we were. They were machines."

Jessa Eames only nodded again. She remembered the man's speed, the brutal accuracy as her troopers died one after another with assembly-line precision. She closed her eyes and pictured the flat, unconcerned look on the man's face, as if killing were as common as lacing up boots.

Of course they escaped. She tried sitting up again.

"No, no." The colonel placed his hands gently on her shoulders. "The doctors say you aren't going anywhere for a while."

"How bad am I?"

Colonel Estevana looked down at her. "Major, I'm not a doctor. They should be the ones—"

"Just tell me."

"Well, your vest plate shattered, but it stopped the chest shot. You've got broken ribs, cuts, one ugly bruise. Your arm…" he paused. "Your arm wasn't so lucky. Shotgun almost tore it off. The doctors patched you up as best they could, but you'll need extensive surgery just to keep it."

"Good thing I'm right-handed then."

"What?"

"I can still shoot." She licked her lips again and managed to grin. The colonel returned it, but his face remained tight.

"What else?" Major Eames asked. "Sniffer teams get anything in the apartment?"

"Nothing. The people there were small-time traffickers, into drugs, prostitutes. All with records, strictly bottom of the food chain. No connection to contract mercenaries at all."

"What about the other two priority leads?"

"I sent units to pick them up. One group has gone missing, the other's in lockup now."

"Missing?"

Colonel Estevana nodded grimly.

Major Eames sat up and winced. "And the other one?"

"Just more thugs and junkies, but judging from this morning, it probably saved their lives."

"Yeah well, no good deed goes unpunished." She frowned at her left arm. "One of them had a flechette gun. I heard it. Those shooters, they were at the mosque." It wasn't a question. She looked over at Colonel Estevana.

He nodded back. "Reports indicate it's the same weapon, yes. Why?"

Her head was pounding. She concentrated to get the words out. "How did these guys know about our lead? And what did the mosque have to do with our boy?"

"We don't know. Security's been tight, and I've got every available unit looking for them, but there's a major storm coming off North Africa. Satellite cover is dropping to zero and all the UAV's are grounded. We'll have to find them the old-fashioned way."

"This gets better and better. You got any good news for me?" she spit out a laugh.

The colonel held up a data pad. "More tips are pouring in, all in the northern district. We did get one break: a fingerprint match off one of the pistols in the mosque shootout. The prints belong to an Alejo García, former ship captain, smuggler. He's an old-timer now, but very busy in his younger days. His jacket is about three inches thick. It seems he was wanted all over the Med."

He thumbed through to the next screen. "Middle East, North Africa and Southern Europe. Even a couple warrants in the Black Sea. This García fellow was slippery as an eel. No one could ever pin him for any real time. He supposedly retired. Saw the light—got religion and the love of a good woman and all that." He stopped suddenly and looked at Major Eames. "Connection is… his last known address is under surveillance by one of our militia members as a possible terrorist hideout. It had been flagged as low priority, but it might be another lead on the boy. Then again could be an angry neighbor who owes him money."

"But you're saying he was in the mosque? A shooter?"

"One of the guard's pistols at least."

Major Eames stared up at the tiled ceiling. It didn't help. The little white squares were blank and monotone. She tried putting her thoughts into the little blank boxes, but her head was throbbing, fuzzy from sleep and morphine. Images of the fight pit in the mosque started mixing with the riot in the plaza and the raid on the apartment. Screams and shouts and shots. A dead man with no fingers and thick blood swirling down storm drains. She looked back at the colonel.

"OK. Do everything you can to find those shooters from the apartment. Nail them to the fucking wall, just make sure they're alive enough to strip-mine their brains down to the core. And you'd better bring that García in for questioning. With three psychopaths somehow having a line on our intel, it'll be for his own protection more than anything else. Some other party is definitely hunting this kid, and we've got to recover him before they get their bloody hands on him."

"Of course, Major. Anything else?"

"Yes," she lowered her voice. "Get me a beer and a couple cigarettes, will you? This place is killing me."

Colonel Estevana saluted and slipped through the curtains.

CHAPTER THIRTY-NINE

Asian Pacific Consortium N. EU Division Regional Offices,
Amsterdam, Netherlands Zone. 3:13 p.m. Day Five.

Already tense, Avery Hsiang's irritation ratcheted up several more notches when the thin, bearded face of one of the male clones appeared on the screen. He didn't bother to hide his contempt. "Your cell leader, the girl. Where is she?"

"She's occupied," the agent said.

Avery waited for an explanation, but the small man only stared back with a bored expression and dark, dead eyes. "Occupied with what?" he snapped.

"Monitoring the Guardia Civil communication channels for more leads, Mr. Executive. You still want the device, correct?"

Avery's rage flared. This *thing* could ill afford to be insolent. It owed its very existence to his orders, orders it had yet to accomplish, and if there was one thing Avery loathed, it was ingratitude. "Of course, I still want it," he said acidly. "How close are you to getting it?"

"We've intercepted a number of priority leads, and have exhausted two options so far."

"But you still don't have it. Why is that?"

"It's difficult to pinpoint the mercenaries' location with only half the information."

"What about Colonel Otsu? I placed his men at your disposal. Send them out."

"We don't need more personnel getting in the way. We need accurate data."

"If you hadn't blundered the initial meeting, I wouldn't have to listen to these excuses," Avery hissed.

The dead eyes went sharp. "We didn't blunder anything, Executive. Number Three is using the Legation. She ordered a decrypt on Dawson-Hull communications channels. Once that's done, we should have the device in short order."

"She did what?" Avery said. "First a gun battle, and now a cyber-attack on corporate communications... what don't you understand about *covert operation*?"

"Given your timetable, she considered it an acceptable risk," the clone replied.

"Acceptable to whom? They're already searching for you. What if you run into the police at one of these leads?" Avery demanded.

"We eluded them in our last encounter," the small man said with a shrug. "We'll do so again."

Avery's composure fled. "Last encounter..." he sputtered. "You ran into the Spanish police?"

"They were Dawson-Hull armed response teams. There were no survivors."

Avery sat back in his chair, stunned. These things, these clones, had killed British corporate security troops in an open confrontation? These things were leaving a trail right back to his office. He was about to explode when the intercom beeped.

"Mr. Hsiang?"

He stabbed the button with his finger. "I thought I told you no interruptions."

"Yes, sir, I know, sir. It's just that there are some men here to see you," his secretary said.

"Some...men?" Avery asked icily.

"Four of them. From Head Office. They say they're here on Director Tetsuo's authority."

At the sound of that name, the world slammed to a halt and collapsed inwards. *He knows*, Avery thought. *That old vulture knows.*

Avery forced himself to look back at the monitor. The thin agent sat there with a bemused look in his face, waiting.

A tight fury jolted through Avery. *Not now... I'm on the edge of triumph.*

Two sharp raps at the door startled him. Had Tetsuo even ordered them to break down the door, barge into an executive office and seize him like some common sprawler? The decrepit bastard had gone too far.

Is the scent of fresh blood rising in the updraft, Yoshio? Am I prey kicking out the last of its life in the dust?

The Honorable Tetsuo is making a fatal error if he thinks I'm helpless, Avery thought.

"Mr. Hsiang, sir?" his assistant pleaded.

"Tell them..." Avery heard himself speak.

"Mr. Hsiang," a different voice spoke over the intercom. It didn't plead. "Open the door."

The moment teetered.

Avery dragged his gaze back to his screen, back to the thin face, still insolent, still waiting. Perhaps he'd made a mistake releasing them, but he could deal with that later. Right now, they were instruments of his will, there in Spain.

Old Tetsuo was a fool. Suspicion is one thing; proof is quite another. There'd be nothing left to incriminate Avery.

More hammering at the door.

He gathered himself. "You will wait. I'll be with you momentarily."

"Executive Hsiang, I insist—" the new voice demanded, but Avery cut off the intercom with another stab of his finger and looked up at the screen. "Change of plans. I'm enacting Directive Two, the erase order. I want all evidence of my involvement eliminated."

"The erase order," the small clone repeated deliberately. "Number Three is confident we're closing in on the objective. The deadline—"

The intercom beeped again and more knocking erupted from the black paneled doors—louder, sharper, obstinate.

"Mr. Hsiang, sir? Sir?" his secretary was back on the intercom, wheedling, cringing. Avery ground his teeth. When this was over, he would ruin this worthless excuse of a man. He was nothing but dead weight.

The doors were shuddering now.

"Directive Two!" Avery bit off the words. "Find the mercenaries, and erase everything. There must be no one left. No one. Do you hear me?"

The agent let out a little sigh, as if condescending to a child's petulance. "Yes, Mr. Hsiang. Erase order confirmed. Barcelona cell out." The small man gestured and the screen cut to black just as the doors burst opened. Four large Internal Affairs men strode into Avery's office.

He stood to face them. "What do you mean breaking in here? Do you have any idea who I am?"

Three of them fanned out in his office, drawing neural stunners as they took positions around the desk. The fourth man wore old-fashioned spectacles and carried a single page Council Directive. He halted in front of the desk and held it up. Avery saw the black and gold icon winking across the top of the smooth cream paper.

"Yes, Mr. Hsiang, we do." he said smoothly and began to read the charges.

As they put restraints on his wrists and led him out, the one in spectacles leaned close. "I hear the view of Earth is quite impressive from Luna Penitentiary, Mr. Hsiang."

CHAPTER FORTY

NEW DEVELOPMENTS

Barcelona Metro Zone, Sant Adrià de Besòs district. Callejón del Apuro, "Trouble Alley". 5:25 p.m. Day Five.

The man called Hester stood at the kitchen sink and watched the figure steal out of the dark sliver of an alley across the street. It joined the crowd and started walking up the crowded avenue. A younger man, lean and fit, clean-shaven, dressed like a street thug. Even though he hunched over, there was no mistaking the way he scanned the area and moved through the flow of people without breaking stride. Hester smiled, it was nice to see talent even in the little things. He amped up his vision and focused in on the side of the man's face; strong resemblance to Jace Manner of Eshu International right there, he thought. The tracker in his pocket was still humming.

Hold the phones, I'd say we have a winner.

Now he could nudge everything over the edge like Mr. MacKinnon wanted.

Barcelona Metro Zone, Sant Adrià de Besòs District. Guardia Civil Medical Clinic. 5:48 p.m. Day Five.

Major Eames motioned to Colonel Estevana. "Help me up."

She struggled to sit up in the hospital bed, but he stood there shaking his head. He was sure she was crazy. Her face was drawn and haggard, and when she'd yanked the bio-monitor lines off her good arm and chest, a shrill chorus of electronic alarms sounded. She'd almost made it to her feet when a doctor and nurse rushed through the curtains.

"No, no, no, Major. Rest. You have to rest," the doctor said. "You must stay. Your wound hasn't even begun to heal." He looked at the Spanish colonel. "Tell her."

The older soldier frowned. "Major, the doctor is right. Your office contacted me, and *Señor* MacKinnon ordered me to continue the search. Don't worry, I will find the boy, and these killers. Please, rest."

"You're not replacing me yet, Estevana," Jessa Eames growled. "I can still function, so I can still command. Now help me."

The doctor tried to gently push her back down onto the bed, murmuring something fast and low in Spanish to the nurse. She reached into the front pocket of her outfit and brought up a hypo-spray.

Major Eames locked eyes with her. "Touch me with that thing, I'll break your arm."

The younger woman couldn't speak English, but the hard look and the tone stopped her in mid-stride. She cast imploring looks first at the doctor, then at the colonel.

"I must insist," the doctor started. "Your arm will start bleeding again. You cannot risk—"

"I can't risk blowing the mission over this. Bind up the arm tight and give me a handful of twenty milligram Percs. And antibiotics. I'll be back when this is over. You can yell at me then."

The major stood up, clenching her jaw, deep breaths hissing through her nose. She wobbled, but kept a white-knuckle grip on the bed rail.

"Please," the doctor pleaded. "You must be tired."

"Losers quit when they're tired. I'll quit when I'm done. Now help me or get out of the way," she snarled.

The doctor looked to Colonel Estevana, who could only shrug, then spoke to the nurse in rapid Spanish. She nodded curtly and slipped out through the curtains as the doctor turned back to Major Eames.

"She will get the medicine you want. If you check yourself out, I will not be responsible for any problems. You are doing this to yourself. Against my advice."

"I know, I know... it's all my fault. I'm used to that."

Hester stood by the window listening to the rumble and grind of traffic, waiting for Jace Manner to return when the link in his ear beeped.

"Hester."

"I'm never going to get anything done if you keep calling, sir."

"Have you located them yet?"

"Yes, in fact. I've got eyes on the contractors now." Hester checked the time. "I was going to brief you later tonight—"

"Never mind that. There've been some new developments. No doubt you've heard about Major Eames."

"Yes, sir. Channels were frantic this morning; reports about a raid going spectacularly bad. They said a number of Special Deployment troopers were killed and an officer was badly wounded. The major did survive, correct?"

"Yes, she did. That Jessa is a hard case. But that's not why I'm calling. You need to intervene."

"Why, sir? The Spanish colonel is in the lead, and he's pulled off almost twenty units to hunt for those three shooters. Whoever they are, they did everyone a favor and drew off a lot of heat."

"Just the opposite I'm afraid," Mr. MacKinnon said.

"I'm listening, sir."

Jessa Eames swallowed back the pain and focused on the Colonel's face. "Report on the search?"

"Major. Let me handle details like that. The medicine you're on—"

"God damn it, Estevana, I can still function. And as of right now, this isn't finished. Now report."

He let out an aggravated sigh. "Major, I have half the force combing through thousands of leads looking for the boy, and now the other half is after the three shooters. I flashed a shot of them to the newsnets taken from a traffic cam, but it's far away and grainy. Even enhanced, they look like anybody. Satellite coverage is still zero and the storm's only getting worse."

"And the good news?"

He fixed his gaze on the major. "Honestly? None of it's good. There're five million sprawlers in the northern district alone, over twenty million around Old Barcelona. Those three could be anywhere by now, even out of the country."

Major Eames shook her head. "No. They haven't skipped town. I don't know if they're the scabs we're after, or somebody else crashing the party, but they're connected to the boy somehow. He's still here, so they're still here."

"Are you sure?" the colonel asked.

"Nope. Just a feeling." She looked up him. "What about the old guy from the mosque? The pistol-packing sea captain, where is he?"

The colonel checked a data pad. "I dispatched two units to pick him up. They have orders to bring him and his family straight to our precinct for questioning."

"Perfect. I want to know the minute they get him. Now get my bars, a clean uniform and some armor. I want to be there when he arrives. I need to ask him some questions in person."

Hester crossed the street and caught up with Jace Manner halfway down the block. Approaching him from behind, he stayed several paces back in the crowd until Jace reached the alleyway that ran alongside the building. Hester saw him slip into it and vanish from view without leaving a ripple in the flow of pedestrians. *Well done*, he thought. He settled his pack on his shoulders, took a microsecond to adjust his eyes, then followed him in.

The narrow concrete cut was dark and cramped, sitting like a crevice at the bottom of two hulking buildings. There was scarcely room for one person to thread his way among the stacked debris and battered trashcans. The stench of mold and rotting garbage was thick, and the street noise was muzzled down to a low growl. Hester trailed silently behind, ignoring everything except the dark shape of the man before him.

After a moment, Jace Manner slowed down and Hester caught the flick of Manner's wrist, the dull glint of metal that slipped down into his palm.

Ah well, so much for being coy, he thought, and drew the magnum from the small of his back. Jace was half-turned, the knife arm coming up and around when Hester stepped up and leveled the pistol at his head.

"Don't."

Jace stopped in mid-motion.

"Good lad. Now drop it."

"Who the—?" Jace started to speak.

"Drop. It." Hester repeated. "Or this ends poorly right here."

The knife clattered to the pavement.

"Excellent choice," Hester said. "Who I am isn't important. But you, you're Jace Manner, and I believe you have something that belongs to my boss."

CHAPTER FORTY-ONE

Barcelona Metro Zone, Sant Adrià de Besòs district. Callejón del Apuro, "Trouble Alley". 6:08 p.m. Day Five.

The small wiry guy dipped his head toward the Garcías' cellar door. "Tell them we're coming in."

We both stood outside in the murk and filth of the alley, glaring at each other. Aside from his light Irish brogue, I noticed he remained professionally out of my reach, and neither his gaze nor a nasty-looking magnum wavered from my head.

OK, this is bad.

I tried stalling. "Why?" Not sure exactly what that could accomplish, maybe I did it for my ego's sake. "You pointing that thing makes me think you're not all that friendly." I fought to keep my hands at my sides. "I'm not sure my friends would be happy to meet you."

He flashed a grin. "I'm not here to hurt you."

"Says the man with the gun."

"Look, mate, if this were a snuff, you'd have never even seen me. I hate drama. But here I am, in the flesh, because we need to chat, and there's not much time. No joke. Now," he nodded toward the steel door again, "quit hedging and let's get a move on. And as we go in, I'll thank you to leave the door wide open and keep four paces ahead." He gave me a little half smile. "I want you on your best behavior too. These rounds are mercury tipped," He inclined the pistol a degree and gestured me forward. "Hate to have to use one."

Bad to worse.

I turned and knocked, and we went in.

Tam, Alejo, Doc and Poet9 were still there where I'd left them. As we came down the steps, they were all laughing at something Poet said. The mood took a definite twist when we walked in though. I have to give credit to Alejo. He may have gotten older, but as soon as we came into the light, he had a pistol up and ready so fast I'd have sworn he'd already been holding one.

"Who are you?" he demanded. "Coming in my home like this?" One of his custom Walthers was leveled and rock steady. The only problem was I was in the way.

"Says he's here to talk." I shrugged. "Al, you mind? People pointing guns gives me a rash."

Alejo didn't move.

"Talk?" Tam asked. "Who are you?"

"I told your friend that's not important. This is a professional courtesy, Mr. Song, so I'll get straight to it… I need you and your crew to deliver the boy to APAC right now," the small man said evenly.

"Boy? What are you talking about? What boy?" Tam started edging his way along the table toward our gear.

I heard the small man sigh. "The clone you nicked from E.C.I Toulouse. They call him 'Gibson'. I want you to gear up, take him and get out of here."

"We don't know anything about Toulouse," Tam responded slowly. "Tell me who you are."

Behind me, the small man tutted impatiently. "Stop. Jig's up, Mr. Song. You can keep yapping, asking questions I'm not going to answer, or you can shut up, take my advice and deliver your package. My appreciation for freelance talent only stretches so far."

"Leprechaun or not, I say he's Asian Pacific," Poet9 interjected.

"Way to go, Poet." I mumbled. "Real discreet."

Poet threw me an exasperated look. "What? He's got a gun. He knows."

"Hey," I called over my shoulder, "is it OK if I turn around?"

"Of course," he said.

When I looked back, he was addressing Poet9. "Very sensible, but I'm not with Tokyo. Give it a think as you pack, and I bet you'll figure it out," the small man winked. "Besides, from what I've heard, some slant-eyed executive already red-dotted you. Sent a couple gunners your way, am I right?"

"What did I tell you?" I said to Tam.

"Why are you listening to him?" Tam asked me. "Why is anybody listening to him?"

"Who are you working for then?" Poet9 asked.

"More questions, more wasted time. Let's just say I represent someone who wants the boy make it to Tokyo sooner rather than later. Your arrest would spoil the itinerary."

"Our arrest? You're full of shit," Tam said. "We're clean."

"Not for long. G.C. is on their way."

"How could Guardia Civil know about this place? No one knows Gibson's here," Alejo scoffed.

The small man shook his head. "Mr. García, the terrorist alerts had neighbors eyeballing your building for the last three days. I took care of them, but it's you they want. It seems someone at G.C. has taken a keen interest in what you were doing at a certain mosque two nights ago. You're to be brought in for questioning." He checked an old-fashioned digital wristwatch. "I'd say you've got maybe twenty minutes before the vans show up."

Alejo still had his pistol up. "And you know this how?" he asked in deadly earnest.

"Connections." The small man tapped his ear. "I've got a shunt on their nets."

"You lie. They don't have any traces to me," Alejo said.

"How about prints on a pistol? Apparently you were naughty and shot at someone." The small man raised one eyebrow. "That good enough for you?"

The old pirate thought for a second then muttered darkly under his breath. "That guard's gun..." He lowered the Walther.

"Hold on," Tam said. "You stroll in here with that hand cannon, spouting all this. How do we know we can trust you?"

"Trust is an occupational hazard in your line of work," the stranger smiled. "But you're still breathing, and that has to count for something. Besides, I'm telling you to *leave*. I *want* you to make your delivery. Now, between the lockdown and the search teams, APAC's UpCity offices are out of the question. That leaves their Trade Legation at the Docks. Chop, chop. Time to be going."

Doc K spoke up from the corner. He'd been silent the whole time, and he addressed the small man slowly, his accent drawing out each word.

"If I read between the lines here, Dawson-Hull knew about Tam's mission and somehow wanted Gibson to be stolen."

The stranger turned to face him. "I don't believe I know you," he said. "You are?"

"A doctor."

"You have a name?"

"Yes. But it's not important," Doc said, and pressed him further. "So London actually wants Asian Pacific to have the boy... and you're here to insure everything goes smooth. Why?"

The smaller man made a slight bow to Ibram. "Wheels within wheels, I'm afraid. There are other men behind the curtains with their hands on the levers and knobs. I'm just the messenger."

"Does it bother you that you're gambling with a child's life here?" Doc asked pointedly.

"Did you hear what I just said?" the stranger replied.

"That boy's dying. Whatever they did to him is killing him."

The small man gave Ibram an amused look. "These chaps nick a classified bio-unit from a secure research laboratory, and you're lecturing me on morality?"

"Gibson isn't a 'unit'. He's a child. A boy."

"Wrong. Gibson is a biological platform for proprietary technology, engineered and produced exclusively for that purpose. The seventeenth in a series, no parents to speak of, he has no rights. He's not a citizen; he's corporate property, doctor. And the corporation can dispense with their property as they see fit."

"Gibson's a human being. You can't trade life like some commodity. What's wrong with you?" Ibram fired back.

The small man rolled his eyes. "See here, if we're getting principles, the same thing goes on every day all over the planet. Sweat shops, child soldiers, sex slaves, drug mules, cubicle drones, on and on. You get my point. And those are real lives, doctor, not test tube ones. Millions of them. Your problem here is that you've got front row seats and you don't like the view."

"What about God?" Alejo interjected. "You invade my home with a gun and this nonsense. The Bible sets out right and wrong—"

"Ah, sorry..." the small man held up his hand. "No opiate of the masses for me. A lot less baggage if you're a strict utilitarian. Beside," he winked at Alejo, "a 'gun and nonsense' have got plenty of things done in the past. Speaking of which..." He squinted at his watch again. "I should stop with my sermon."

"Why did Dawson-Hull want Gibson kidnapped?" Doc demanded.

"No more questions." The man faced Tam. "You in, or out?"

"I'm supposed to believe that APAC still wants the boy, even though they tried to off us?"

"That's the simple version, yes."

"We could be walking into a trap."

"But you're not," the small man said impatiently.

"I'll make you a deal," Tam said.

"A deal?" The stranger flourished his pistol in a rapid figure eight and looked around the cellar. "Looks to me like your hand is played out, and you don't have any chips left on the table."

"A deal," Tam insisted. "If G.C. is really on their way, Al and his family need to disappear. We'll take the boy, no fuss, but you have to get the doctor here and the Garcías to the outer arm of the North Dock. They have a friend who can get them out of the country."

"Do I look like a relief worker to you, Mr. Song?"

"You look like one of those quiet types who could snap and become a serial killer," Poet9 said.

"Very funny, but I'm not in a position to—"

"You're in a position to barge in here and chat us up," Tam cut him off. "You're in a position to tap secure comms. Your bosses deployed you solo, so you're not some noob spook. You've got weight, and I want you to use it."

"I'm only here to insure the asset gets to Asian Pacific intact."

"And we'll get him there. After all, we lifted him out of Euro Cybernetics. That has to count for something." He gave the smaller man a thin smile. "This way everyone gets what they want, right? You shepherd Doc and the Garcías to safety, and Jace and I will bring Gibson right to APAC's doorstep ourselves."

"We will?" I asked.

"Yes," he glared at me.

The stranger's head bobbed from side to side as he weighed Tam's proposition. After a moment, he looked straight at Alejo. "We leave in five minutes. Meet me in the alley. Pack light, and here, take one of these." He shrugged his backpack around to the front, unzipped it and held out a silver canister.

"What is this?" Alejo asked.

"A fogger. Set it upstairs in a main area. I'll leave one down here for that big room. When you're ready, hit the black button on the bottom. The black one. Not the red."

"What does it do?" Alejo asked.

"After ninety seconds, it releases a bio-reactive aerosol," the smaller man said. "Don't be close when it sprays. You breathe it in, you'll be sick for days. Once it's dispersed, it stinks like hell, but it'll muck up every DNA trace in your home in ten minutes."

Alejo eyed it. "Not explosive?"

"No. It's not a bomb."

"I didn't know they made things like that." Alejo frowned.

"You're not supposed to."

"And it works?" Alejo asked dubiously.

"I use them," he replied. "Remember. The *black* button."

Alejo plucked it from his hand and started upstairs, calling for his wife.

"Against my better judgment, I'm making an exception for you, Mr. Song," the stranger said. "You understand my obligation ends if you fail to meet your side of the agreement?"

"We hold up our end. Always. Look, Mr... you have a name yet?" Tam asked.

"Hester," the small man said. "You can call me Hester."

"Well, Hester, seems we'll have to trust each other here. You've got my friends—I've got your package. I intend on making that boat," Tam replied.

"I could care less about your intentions. I want results. See that Gibson arrives at his destination. In one piece."

"Same here with my mates," Tam answered.

Hester nodded back.

Suddenly Carmen started shouting upstairs. We all looked at each other.

"Guess he told her," I said.

CHAPTER FORTY-TWO

NO TRANSLATION NEEDED

Barcelona Metro Zone, Sant Adrià de Besòs district. Callejón del Apuro, "Trouble Alley". 6:22 p.m. Day Five.

"You trust the little creep?" I asked Tam as soon as the door scraped shut.

"About as far as I can throw him, which wouldn't be far unless it was off a cliff." Tam pulled his Tavor TAR 21 out of a crate. "But he knew about Toulouse, the mosque, the pistol, he found us in the middle of the BMZ sprawl for God's sake." He looked back at me. "We were going to the Docks anyway. Mr. Hester there just sped things up. You got in touch with Rao, right?"

"Yeah. He knows we're leaving. He'll be waiting for us."

"Good. This might work out. We've got a shot at salvaging something out of this cluster."

"You're not thinking of bringing Gibson to APAC?"

"We could end up getting paid."

"We could end up getting dead," I said.

"I told Poet9 to take the Triplets and meet us at the Docks. My guess is they'll lurk on the sidelines and watch our backs."

"Answer the question. We're responsible for—"

"For ourselves, for the Garcías, to stay in business and stay alive," Tam finished. "That's the bottom line. Why'd you think I made a deal with him?"

"What about Gibson?"

"What about him? They probably have some way to extract or stabilize the nanites."

I shook my head. "This is cat food, Tam. We're running blind here."

"Yeah well, you got a better plan, I'm all ears," Tam said. "We're going to have to improvise."

"You mean make it up as we go."

"Yep," Tam shrugged. "Gather up what you need, get Gibson and switch on Shorty's fogger thing. I really hope they work. Maybe Al and Carmen can come back when this blows over. I'm going to grab everything I think we might need. Meet me down here with the kid."

As I looked around the cellar, that bad feeling I had in Toulouse pounced on me like an angry, errant ghost. I crossed the room to the crate

Tam had been going through and brushed my fingers over the metal receiver
of my SMG. Maybe I thought it was an iron charm that warded off malicious
spirits, or maybe I hoped the prospect of violence would be therapeutic.
Either way, it didn't work.

So much for magic.

I left the Blizzard in the crate. I didn't want to get Gibson while waving
a gun around. I went upstairs, and as I opened the door into the García's
apartment, a bad case of guilt hit me. The clutter and bustle of life was
everywhere, but the place had the shocked vacancy of abrupt interruption.
I was like a thief walking through the stillness of their home.

This was our fault. If we hadn't brought Gibson, they'd still be here,
happy and content. The image of the two of them in an interrogation cell
reared up and kicked me in the stomach. I shook it away, but for all intents
and purposes, we'd just trashed their life here.

I found the boy in the hall near one of the back bedrooms standing in
the doorway like he'd been waiting for me. He looked thinner, smaller in his
jumpsuit, and his hair was damp and slicked back out of his face as if
Carmen had made a last-minute effort to neaten him up. His green eyes had a
fevered shine to them that was even brighter against his pale skin. He
watched me as I approached. I tried on a smile.

"Is it time to go?" he asked.

"Yes. Tam and I are taking you with us, to a new home."

"But not with Carmen and Mr. Alejo?"

"No. Not with them," I said. "Different people, some place new.
They'll be nice like them though." I saw him looking at me as I'd lied.
I changed the subject. "You OK? I mean we need to hurry, but if you want
something to drink, some food, I'll get—"

"No. I'm ready," he said, He was still scrutinizing me, but now there
was a sad little smile on his face. Guilt and more guilt. He slipped a slim,
leather bound book into the side cargo pocket of his pants. An old printed
copy of the New Testament. *Great*, I thought, *now I've got God pissed off at
me too.*

"You sure?" I said.

"Yes."

"We've got to go downstairs and meet Tam."

Gibson nodded and started past me toward the cellar. I turned and kept
my head down to hide my expression, working my way back through the
house toward the kitchen.

My hand was on the doorknob when I remembered the fogger. I'd seen
it in passing on a low table somewhere. If it really worked, Spanish Security

wouldn't have enough evidence to hang on the Garcías. "Wait here. I'll be right back," I said, and headed back down the hall.

Sure enough, the silver canister was perched on a coffee table in the living room. I had just picked it up when I caught a noise at the front door. A scrape, a muffled voice, the click of a door handle being tested.

Damn. I dropped into a crouch.

The door splintered open and the first pair of Guardia Civil uniforms rushed in fast and low. Guns up, they shouted out commands in Spanish. No translation needed. I raised my hands. A second pair of assaulters swept in right behind them, and the next thing I knew, I was facedown eating carpet with a knee in my neck, a Beretta 10mm in my face, and zip cuffs cinched on my wrists.

Hauled to my feet, I saw one of the troopers dragging Gibson into the room, the shoulder of his jumpsuit bunched up in a gloved fist. Through the floorboards, I could hear a crash and more yelling in the basement. No gunshots answered back. One of the Guardia Civil men started jabbering on his radio while the first pair swept through the rest of the house. Sirens howled out in the street.

We were busted.

CHAPTER FORTY-THREE

SUSPECTS

Barcelona Metro Zone, Sant Adrià de Besòs district. 6:48 p.m.
Day Five.

Major Eames leaned back against the armored flank of the command track and let out a stuttered, pained breath.

"You're sure you're all right, Major?" Colonel Estevana asked. "I can take you back to the hospital."

"No, I'm fine," she lied and winced as she used her other hand to tug her wounded arm closer into her body. "Christ, but they wrapped this tight. I didn't want it in my way. That didn't mean I wanted them to cut the circulation." She swallowed one of her Percs with a swig of bitter coffee and finished strapping up her tactical vest.

"Dr. Rodidos says if you keep at this, you could lose that arm completely." The colonel looked worried.

"My guess is it's a loss anyway. I'd rather have a working prosthetic than a broken original. How long will it take us to get to Central?"

"Traffic control is clearing a hole for us, but in these we're still a good thirty-five minutes out. I can call for a chopper if you want, but that'll take another twenty."

"No. The tracks are fine. What's the status on the García pickup?"

The Spanish soldier picked up the comm-set and began speaking in rapid Spanish, listening to the responses. He looked up after a moment. "Two teams have secured the premises, but they say the suspect wasn't present."

"They roust the right address?"

"Of course they did, Major. The team leader says they swept the entire place but there's no sign of him." The radio squawked again. "He reports they did find what looks like a large cache of weapons and equipment in a basement directly below the suspect's apartment."

"What kind of weapons and equipment?" she asked slowly.

The colonel spoke again then translated the answer. "He doesn't know for sure. They haven't gone through most of it. Seems to be old, but in good shape." There was another static filled exchange before the colonel spoke up again. "He also says there were three civilians present when they entered the apartment. No IDs on any of them."

Major Eames snorted. "Who? Unlucky neighbors?"

"He doesn't know. They don't scan. He says they aren't chipped."

"What?" Major Eames sat up. "Aren't chipped? He snapped any video? DNA sample them?"

The colonel translated Major Eames' questions again. "Not yet. He's detained them pending further orders. He says there are three males: two adults and a boy. The men are definite military types. They were geared up, and it looked like they were on their way out."

Major Eames gripped the colonel's sleeve with her good hand. "The boy, what's his description?"

"Small. About nine or ten years old, with dark hair and green eyes. Looks sick."

"Jesus H. Christ! It can't be," she said in awe. "Tell the team leader to hold off on the pictures and bio-samples. I want those suspects brought straight to your station now. We'll do a thorough DNA profile there and check for gene matches. We might have just hit the lottery."

"I'm sorry, what? How?"

Major Eames stared at the colonel. "Damned if I know. Leave a unit to secure the place, but I want him to bring those three back personally. He's to run over anything that gets in his way. And get a tech team at that location five minutes ago. Are there any other units in the area?"

The colonel looked puzzled. "Yes, several but—"

"Get them there now. I want that neighborhood sealed off. And put an escort on that van. Make sure it gets back to Precinct. I'm not taking any chances."

"Chances on what, Major?"

"My ten million to one odds going bad." She pounded on the side of the track and stepped toward the rear ramp. "Now get this heap moving."

As the hatch clanged shut, the air turned heavy. Deep thunder rolled out of the southern horizon, and a cold drizzle began to fall. The storm was unfolding in the lowering gray skies.

Tam and I sat with Gibson in the back of the police van out on the street in front of the alley. The tempo of raindrops was picking up on the metal roof, and somewhere far off, I heard thunder crack and rumble. The storm was kicking into gear.

The back doors were still open and the Guardia Civil sergeant was standing outside jabbering away on his radio. Every sentence or two, he'd peer in, scrutinizing the three of us, and it seemed he was answering questions, growing more attentive every second. Someone higher up the police food chain was bending his ear and had taken a definite interest in us.

I looked over at Tam. "I think we just made Spain's security database."

"They haven't sampled us yet," Tam said, and just then one of the other troopers walked up to the van with the ID kit.

"Spoke too soon."

This situation was morphing into a right huge cluster in record time. First the Hester character and now this: if Spain got our pictures, prints and DNA on file, we were well and truly hosed. We'd never run ops for anyone again—if we lucky enough to see the outside of a prison cell that is.

The trooper was climbing in with us when the sergeant interrupted with a curt order. He stepped down and looked questioningly at his commander. The sergeant gestured impatiently and called out to two of the others, who came over at a jog. He issued more orders, the troopers peeling off one by one, and waved his clenched fist in a circle above his head. The van's engines started up. We were going for a ride.

As the rear doors slammed shut, Gibson piped up. "Are these the new friends I was supposed to meet?" I swore I saw a little grin flit across his face.

"You're funny. No, we weren't planning on meeting these guys," I answered.

"I didn't think so."

With that, the interior light went dim and the van lurched into motion. The three of us sat swaying on the metal benches as it gained speed down the street.

"So much for our ocean cruise," I said to Tam. He just shrugged and leaned back with his eyes shut. I fixed my gaze on Gibson and tried to think.

The thing about being taken prisoner is that if you want to escape, you have to take your shot in the early stages because the further up the chain you go, the tighter security becomes, and your chances get trampled like pilgrims on hajj.

The assaulters had kicked in the doors so fast neither Tam nor I had a chance to stash anything useful. And if things were this miserable in the first stage, I wasn't too optimistic about any chances later on. I tried to console myself by thinking at least the rest of them got away. Poet would know enough to get the Triplets, Doc and the Garcías back to Belfast. Jaithirth and Dengler could get them work with a new team. Sure as not, they'd bounce them over to Black Friar and help them keep their edge. I tried to imagine them working with someone else, but I cut that thought short. It was too depressing to consider.

I looked around morosely in the bad light, then leaned back and closed my eyes too. Yep, this was one of those moments when slashing your wrists actually seems like a reasonable solution. You can plan for capture in your mind a hundred different times in a hundred different ways, but it's still a kick in the kidneys when it comes. Most everyone says they're never going to talk, that they'd die before they spill their guts, but it's not true. Training, preparation, deep conditioning for resistance, but in the end it's all hollow. Everyone talks—it's only a matter of when.

Whether you're talking straight up old-school physical torture, fancy mind games and deprivation, or the latest in chemical and physiological interrogation technology, it's only a question of how long you can stall them and how badly you want to suffer. And depending on where you were and who nabbed you, you could face any or all of the above options. Eventually, you'll tell them anything they want to know and more.

All of us at Eshu International had agreed a long time ago that if anybody was caught, we'd stall as long as we could to give the rest of us a chance to escape and evade. Tam and I had been trained, and the Triplets were inured to resist. All of us had rehearsed cover stories. They were emotional and realistic, so that when we 'broke', it would seem authentic and throw any pursuit on a false trail. That would at least buy a little time for whoever survived.

I looked over at Gibson, who despite his fever was taking the experience in with an eager curiosity. He had his own problems, but at least they wouldn't touch him. I'd be lucky to get a cell with plumbing.

We'd been traveling some five, maybe seven minutes, with sirens warbling constantly, and I could feel the spurt and stop as the Spanish police negotiated sprawl traffic. Suddenly, the sirens barked twice and there were shouts and muffled voices coming through the front wall. The driver was leaning on the horn when we stopped short.

"Traffic jam?" I whispered.

"Could be, but why isn't their traffic control clearing a path?" Tam was interrupted by the sound of gunfire. "Shit! Get down!"

I fell onto the grimy metal floor and curled up below the bench. Tam urged Gibson down next to me.

"Bet that's not on their schedule," Tam said.

"Triplets?" I asked.

"Dunno. Sounded old, heavy and slow. Listen."

Sure enough, the deep hammering sound of an assault rifle wafted through the armored walls of the van. "Cover him." Tam nodded at Gibson, and I had him lay down flat on the grated floor. I knelt over him, shielding him as best I could.

The gunfire outside grew louder, closer. Suddenly, I heard a second and third weapon join in. The volume of fire was definitely rising, and a neat line of indents materialized on the sidewall of the van.

"I hate it when this happens," Tam said. "Stay down!"

There were frantic shouts, and the burp of small-caliber SMG fire from the cab. The engine roared and the van accelerated briefly, swerving to the right, only to smash to a halt. The three of us slammed into the forward wall, tangling up in a heap on the floor. I was wedged under a bench, stuck with my cuffed hands behind my back. Two more rows of pockmarks appeared across the metal wall.

"Gah! If this is the Triplets," Tam said. "I'm going to beat them with a stick."

I heard one of the troopers in the cab yelling, screaming some Spanish phrase over and over. I felt the vehicle start forward, but then came the crump of grenades and our van flipped onto its side. We lay there, dazed, as smoke started seeping into the back with us.

"This is not good," I coughed.

"I didn't think so," I heard Gibson say.

"Whoever it is, we need to be ready to move." Tam had gone all crisp and businesslike. "Gibson, when I say go, I want you to stay with Jace and run as fast as you can. You understand me?"

"Yes."

"Good. We're going to get out of here."

The three of us were untangling ourselves, struggling to sit upright, when a sharp burst of auto fire went off right outside the cab. We froze and everything fell quiet. Acrid smoke and tension filled the compartment as we all watched the back doors and waited. The seconds started dragging. Still nothing moved. Gibson muffled a cough, and we could hear the muted cacophony of rainfall, car horns and approaching sirens.

"Now would be a good time," Tam said, and as he spoke, one of the doors wrenched open with a savage jerk. The jumble of slick wet roadway and wrecked cars was framed in the gray half-light of the sidelong doorframe. I was waiting to hear Poet's voice, or see one of the Triplets reaching in.

Suddenly a head popped into view. It was a woman's head, looking in at us. The face was familiar. Then I saw her eyes: it was the woman from the mosque.

"Not quite who I was expecting," I heard Tam say.

CHAPTER FORTY-FOUR

Barcelona Metro Zone, Sant Adrià de Besòs district. 7:01 p.m.
Day Five.

"Stopped?" Major Eames sat up. "What do you mean they stopped? Why?"

Her command track, a Grizzly IFV, swayed from side to side, the turbo whine of the engines growling as it tore down the roadway. The trooper in the comms seat, PFC Banner, put one hand up to his headset and yelled over the noise. "Dunno, ma'am. Happened all of a sudden. They're saying something about a blocked intersection." He listened again. "He says there's cars smashed up, people hurt. I'll get him rerouted—damn!"

"What?"

"That sounded like gunfire. They... shit! They're being hit. Someone's bushwhacking them."

"Get me that location, trooper." She turned to Colonel Estevana. "Order all units to drop everything and converge on that van." She stabbed a glance back at the private. "You find them yet?"

"Isolating them now." He flicked through digital displays faster than she could register them, freezing on one with a glowing green dot. "There. Main artery coming out of Sant Adrià near the Dock."

Major Eames shouted at the driver. "Get us there! Now!"

"Yes, ma'am."

The diesel turbines snorted and wound up to a relentless howl as thirty-four tons of ceramic and steel Chobham armor accelerated. The vehicle heaved upward briefly then settled like a massive bull in full charge.

Private Banner kept listening and looked over at Major Eames. "Ma'am. Sounds like a major shit storm. This guy is losing it big time. His partner's dead, and he keeps saying there're three of them. Three of them. And..." he clutched his headphones again, twisting the dial on his set. "Ma'am, I lost 'em."

They both looked up on the screen. The green dot was still winking at them. "Vehicle's still intact."

"God. Damn. IT!" Major Eames ground her teeth. "Get everyone there. All G.C., Grupo Especial, and D-H Special Deployment teams.

I want that area sealed. These scabs aren't sliming out of this one. Get this thing moving faster!"

It was another time drag: I saw her eyes tighten and her body shift as the chopped muzzle brake of an AK-74 snaked around the corner of the doorframe. Gibson was right behind me and Tam yelled something. I felt him scramble to shield the boy with his body. I drove myself forward towards the woman, my hands still fastened behind my back. I'm not sure what I meant to do, but I wasn't dying cowering in a corner.

I didn't hear any sound, just saw the rifle come up in stop motion slowness, its black wire stock fixing itself to her shoulder like a choppy training video. I was almost on her when real time kicked in. There was a rapid smack as three rounds punched through the van door right by her head in a picture perfect-tight group. Grit and splinters hit my face and her eyes widened in surprise as she darted back and disappeared. I slammed into the doorjamb and careened out of the van face first into an oily puddle. I lay there panting in the open in the middle of the road.

The place was chaos. Stained, tar-brown buildings towered over a narrow intersection where five roads met. Cars were burning, overturned, and black smoke was spilling up into a low and churning sky. Rain was falling, soaking the bodies spilled on the road, hanging out of shattered car windows all around me. I could see the traffic stretched out, jammed tight in every direction. The rancid snap of diesel and low tide was in the air. We were near the Docks.

On my right, the Mosque woman was ducked down behind the crumpled fender of a grimy black and yellow taxi. The big man from the basement was next to her, and two cars over I spied a small scraggly rat-faced man. All three had old Russian assault rifles. I scuttled frantically on the asphalt, cursing the flex cuffs, trying to get out of their line of sight.

Thankfully, they had more immediate concerns. The heavy clatter and flash of their fire was directed at someone off the roadway on my left, and I could hear the fast chatter of a Heckler & Koch assault rifles answering back. I made it behind one of the van's back tires when I spied a large figure with a pale face and short white hair dart out from behind a corner of a building.

Poet9 had come with the Triplets.

The three attackers were stuck behind the cars. Caught off guard, they recovered fast, but anytime they raised a head, the Triplets kept them from moving any closer toward us. They were giving us a chance to get clear. Near one of the muddy brown buildings, I spotted Poet9 running toward me.

"Here! This way, to me. Move!" he shouted. The distant wail of sirens was growing louder, more shrill. I banged on the dented roof of the van beside me. "Tam! Grab Gibson. Cavalry's here and we gotta go now!"

They scrambled out the back of the van on their knees, and together the three of us made our way toward a side street where Poet9 waited.

"Where's Al and Carmen?" Tam looked around.

The thin Mexican shrugged. "Last I saw, the leprechaun guy was taking them to the Docks. I don't trust that *poco bastardo*, but I had to make a choice," he said as he cut us free. "I made a good call coming back to you, eh? *Madre Santa de Dios*," he gestured toward the wreckage of the road. "They don't like you much."

Tam rubbed his wrists. "Yeah well, we've met before... when you were napping. I don't think they're with Hester, or whatever his name is, but I don't want to stick around to find out for sure. You got a ride out of here?"

Poet9 shook his head. "We'll have to hoof it. I got a weird wave from Jaithirth. He says Tokyo's singing a different tune, playing all nice now. They want their package after all, and are waiting for us. What's up with that?"

"Wish I knew," I said. Shots whined overhead. "We need to color ourselves gone, Tam."

"We were on our way to the Docks anyway," Tam said firmly, then grabbed Poet's comm-link and radioed the Triplets. "Asset is secure, but we need to keep him that way. We're moving out on foot. Cover our retreat. Eliminate the threat if possible, but disengage when necessary. Rendezvous is on the bottom level, very end of the South Dock in thirty minutes. Repeat: Lower level, tip of the South Dock in thirty minutes. Confirmed?"

The exchange of fire was growing more furious, but Cottontail's voice sounded calm. "The boy is safe?"

"Come again?" Tam asked.

"The boy... is he safe?"

"Roger," Tam said. "He's fine. Gibson is A-1. Confirm orders."

"Engage and cover. Rendezvous Barcelona Port Complex, Bottom level, end of the South Dock." There was a pause. "Mr. Song, sir?"

Tam was handing the radio back and stopped. "Yes?"

"You're taking him some place safe?" Cottontail's voice sounded plaintive, even over the tiny speaker.

Gunfire and thunder rattled the air all around us, but Tam, Poet and I all looked at the mike. The Triplets spoke among themselves in a simple argot, a strange hybrid of child-like babble and military acronyms. It was rare that they spoke more than two sentences to anyone else. Ever.

Tam opened his mouth to fire back a sharp answer, to reinstate tactical discipline, but he caught himself and keyed the mike gently. "Affirmative. He'll be safe. I need you to keep hostiles off our back. We need to protect Gibson."

"Roger. Protect Gibson. Out."

"Picked an odd time to come out of his shell, eh?" Poet said, peering around the side of a mailbox. The gunfire between the Triplets and the mosque shooters was growing more vicious by the second, and there was a chorus of sirens accompanied by a swarm of flashing lights converging from every direction. It looked and sounded like every cop in Spain was headed our way. Poet9 handed Tam and me pistols with spare clips. Then he tossed me a Gerber combat blade.

"One of your favorite things," he winked. "Docks are that way." His big black Walther 11 pointed down one of the long, narrow streets.

Thunder tore through the dark sky, and a single dagger of lightning flashed. Cold rain was falling in sheets now, soaking us through. I looked over at Gibson, huddled up against the yellow mailbox. His head was down, and he shivered in the wind, looking smaller, paler than even a few moments before. My heart sank. *We're going to be the death of him*, I thought.

He glanced up and his green eyes shined back at me. "Is it time to go yet?"

I only nodded.

Behind us, the swelling sound of gunfire and bitter sirens was dwarfed by the rage of the black storm. I lifted Gibson into my arms and the three of us took off, running toward the leaden horizon.

CHAPTER FORTY-FIVE

Barcelona Metro Zone, Sant Adrià de Besòs district. 7:13 p.m.
Day Five.

Combat Unit 5905, the one they called "Cottontail", watched his master/leaders disappear down one of the long side streets. The rain was falling harder now and the second-in-command, Jace, was carrying his new friend. It made 5905 feel sad to see the boy go. He and his brothers all liked Gibson, but the master/leader, Mr. Song, said they were taking him someplace safe so that was good. Cottontail felt a little better.

Another round of shots came from behind the smashed taxi and clawed into the brickwork, sending a spray of dust and splinters onto his head. That was close. The stinging made him think about his orders: cover their retreat then disengage to rally at the Dock. But Mr. Song's also said they had to protect Gibson. That was the priority. It seemed these hostiles wanted to take the boy away, maybe to someplace bad and hurt him, and that made 5905 mad. He radioed his brothers and they agreed: they wouldn't let anyone hurt Gibson.

5905 popped out from behind the corner and put a three-round burst precisely over the hood of the battered cab, right where the larger man had been kneeling half a second ago. But he'd already moved.

5905 frowned. These hostiles were fast, very fast, and much more proficient than regular targets. He saw his brothers firing, trying to pin them down and keep them away from the street Mr. Song, Poet9, Jace and Gibson had just taken.

But these hostiles were smart too. They'd recovered from the surprise of the ambush quickly, and one of them, a woman, had already shifted right, angling toward the long road. The other two concentrated fire on 5901 to keep him from cutting her off.

Another spatter on the brickwork and several rounds cracked past Cottontail's head as the larger man dashed between the cab and the overturned van. He was moving right too.

Whoever these three were, they were good enough to be dangerous. The tactical problems were multiplying by the second.

Two of them were near the side road now, and Cottontail could hear the local police coming. Lots of them. He glanced up. The storm would interfere too, cut down on visibility, mask noises and scent. At least it kept security choppers out of the sky.

Cottontail radioed his brothers again. It was time to get away from this intersection, and there was only one option left. On his signal, they'd fire and funnel the hostiles down the long road. They'd be between them and Mr. Song, but that way they could narrow the kill zone and move away from the Spanish security forces at the same time. Cottontail and his brothers would just have to eliminate them before they reached Mr. Song.

A flash of movement, the small man was moving now. Cottontail fired and he saw him flinch as if hit, then ducked down. Cottontail grinned.

He hadn't been this challenged since Africa.

Barcelona Port Complex, Asian Pacific Consortium Trade Offices, Bureau D. South Dock, Level Five. 7:25 p.m. Day Five.

Colonel Otsu looked up as his secretary strode through the door holding out a data pad. "The mercenaries are on their way, sir. We just received flash traffic from their agent in Belfast stating they were headed this way right now."

"This is confirmed? They're bringing the device to us?"

"It's authentic. The codes were verified, but the message only stated they were coming to the Docks. It also said the asset required immediate medical attention."

"What? An asset? It's supposed technology, not personnel." He took the data pad and scrolled through the screens. Nothing in this operation was going as expected. Between the Dawson-Hull Security force, Hsiang, Tetsuo, the *shinigami* clones, and now this, there were far too many radical contingents here for his comfort. His secretary cleared her throat.

"Yes?" he didn't look up.

"Colonel, we are receiving reports of a massive traffic accident closing the E-15, as well as gunfire north of here. Intercepts indicate the Spanish police are heading this way in pursuit of a suspected 'terrorist' group, and that Dawson-Hull Special Deployment units are involved as well."

"And you think this *terrorist* group and our mercenaries are one and the same," he said.

"That would be an unusual number of coincidences," she replied.

Colonel Otsu nodded, considered the narrow slit of his window for a moment then tapped the intercom button on his desktop. "This is Colonel Otsu. I'm ordering a Code Orange Alert. All automated defense systems are to go to standby status. All security personnel are to report to their perimeter defense stations immediately. Use of deadly force is not authorized at this time. All units are to remain on Standby status until further notice. Out."

An alarm started to sound, and the Colonel looked up at his secretary. "Make sure the mini-sub is prepped and ready for immediate departure. This storm should provide excellent cover for it to get into international waters."

"Yes, sir."

"I'll be at the command and communications center. I need our security details alert. If those agents are coming here with the British on their trail, they are to be secured and safe, not shot. I'm going to credit both Madrid and Dawson-Hull with enough sense not to violate corporate sovereignty and risk an international incident. Even if there's pressure for an inspection, it'll have to be cleared past Tokyo first. We can stall long enough to get the asset and the mercenaries out of country. Let me know when the sub is ready."

"Of course, Colonel."

As the doors hissed shut, Colonel Otsu gathered his jacket and turned toward the window again. The horizon line was lost in the far dark of boiling silver gray, a thin strip of churning sky washed-out by the glare of floodlights. Motion brought his attention in closer. The Dock's automated cargo systems continued to run unceasing and oblivious in a complex ballet of crisp, seizured jerks as crane arms loaded, unloaded, sorted, moved and stacked. Chains of mini-trains laden with color-coded crates zipped by in every direction, chasing each other on overhead loops and conveyor tracks. Several wavered slightly, buffeted by powerful winds that gusted through the level, funneled by the maze of duracrete columns, steel gantries and support beams. In the distance, Colonel Otsu spied a huge wave heave up and shatter, reaching past the railing with soaking fingers before dragging itself back out.

His grandfather used to call storms like this "Fujin's Fury", telling his family the mythical demon prince had stirred up the waters for battle. A lifelong fisherman, Colonel Otsu remembered the scent of open air and brine clung to him for years after he'd retired. His grandfather had also been a devout Shintoist, and insisted tempests mirrored crisis and strife in the spiritual world, the turmoil so great it was reflected in the physical one. He always claimed hurricanes heralded momentous change.

That was many years ago, and Colonel Otsu didn't believe in deities or spirits, but as he stepped outside, he couldn't shake the impression of inchoate rage. The wind screamed, and the sky and sea battered at the Port Complex as if they sought to tear it down and pull it into the depths.

Fury and turmoil were fitting descriptions indeed.

CHAPTER FORTY-SIX

ANGLES, DARK WITH FOG AND SMOKE

Barcelona Metro Zone, Port Complex District. 7:25 p.m. Day Five.

The storm was swelling into a full-blown hurricane, the downpour a relentless drumbeat on the roof of the Grizzly Command Track. Major Eames clenched her teeth against the throbbing in her arm and leaned forward to pester Private Banner again.

"What the hell? Why aren't we moving?"

Traffic had slowed, stuttered, and finally stopped about seven kilometers out from the intersection where the police van had been ambushed. A quadruple line of standing cars and trucks stretched out on the highway in front of her convoy, disappearing as black inkblot shapes in the gray curtain of rain and fog.

"Ma'am, no one's moving. The roads are clogged in every direction going in. Spanish emergency service is putting heavy choppers in the air to get EMTs to the accident, but they're having a hell of a time getting airborne in this weather."

"I need boots on the ground now. Bring up a map showing the area from here down to the B-Port."

Private Banner clicked twice and a street map of the city northeast of the massive Port Complex sprang up on his screen.

She leaned over his shoulder and began pointing with her good arm. "I want all Dawson-Hull Special Deployment units mobilized to seal off the area around the Dock. Stop everything that moves. Order units there, there, and there—and every other street or alley that spills out at the water. Especially those on either side of that long one those fugitives were heading down. My money says they're going to either to hand the boy off, or hitch a ride out of town." She singled out the circuit splay of lines stretched out over the Mediterranean. "That Goddamned Port is a maze of layers that runs for klicks. They make it there, they can hide for days. Or worse, cower inside some company's sector, protected by extraterritorial status. I'll be damned if I let that happen!"

She looked over at Colonel Estevana. "I want your men to secure the intersection where the van was ambushed. Have the Grupo Especial units fan out and go after whoever's there. Maximum sanction. Any hostiles, I want their heads on a platter."

"Si, Major," said the colonel, and he bent over his radio.

Jessa Eames peered through a vision port in the side of the armored compartment. "Driver, turn this rig left and go through those barriers." She yelled. "Opposite lanes are empty, sort of. We'll go on that side. Fire up the 30 mike-mike and punch through if you have to." She tapped PFC Banner on the shoulder. "Tell the tracks behind us to stick close. Oncoming traffic will just have to get the hell out of out our way."

Private Banner started speaking then clutched his headset again. "Major, the emergency services net is getting a stream of calls about gunfire in the streets. Seems to be moving toward the Docks."

"All the more goddamn reason to get units there. If you're in the Spanish Grid, can you pull down any cam shots on the attackers?"

"Working on it," he replied, and his fingers flew over the keys. In seconds, four grainy images tiled up into the corners on his screen. "Enhancing now. Timestamp says they're about twelve minutes old. Spain's gear is total junk, but in this one you can see two shooters behind the taxi. They're firing at someone off to the side. In this picture, the van's already trashed. That's the back of it there, on its side. Here and here," Private Banner highlighted one area, "you can see a third shooter. A scrawny male."

Major Eames looked closely. In the first image, she could make out the figure of a large man crouched behind the hood of a car, and a woman near the trunk was clearly firing an AK-74 at someone off screen.

"Those two are from the apartment raid." Colonel Estevana spoke up. "And that means the mosque too."

A chill spiked through Major Eames. She tapped Banner's helmet. "Find who she's gunning for. Get anything from those side streets heading southeast?"

There was another staccato rush of key strokes, and a succession of low-res pictures marched past, all blurry angles, dark with fog and smoke. He stopped on one abruptly. "Got 'em. There's three, like a matching set. See? There... near the parked truck and behind that corner. One of them is firing. See the head and torso? That looks like an H&K G-40."

"Zoom in and enhance."

The image clicked and expanded, pixels resolving to a rough clarity until they filled the pop-up window. Major Eames focused on the profile and froze.

"Suffering Christ," she said. "That better not be what I think it is."

"What?" Private Banner asked.

"Look at the size of it, the face, the pale skin. That's a Pretoria clone."

"Shiiiiit!" Private Banner breathed out.

"That's impossible," Colonel Estevana said. "U.N. commanders accounted for all General Mambi's forces after Victoria Falls. They said they rounded them up and had them destroyed."

"The latte brigades can't find their own arse with two hands, Colonel." She nodded at the screen. "And that sure as hell looks like someone missed a couple."

Private Banner spoke up. "Major, that's not good. The UNdies were scared shitless of them. They were filling ditches with bodies and torching 'em just to make sure they were really dead."

"Yeah well... From what I heard, I might have too if I'd have tussled with them." Major Eames leaned over. "Private, put a warning out on the tac-net and tell the boys to stay frosty. I hope like hell I'm wrong, but this thing's morphing into a real freak show."

As PFC Banner started talking into his comm-set, the rapid crack, crack, crack of a 30mm chain gun filled the IFV's interior, blasting a four-meter-high section of the highway barrier into chunks and dust.

We ran through empty streets, the storm and gunfire had cleared the way. Tam and Poet9 were the lead, and I followed up with Gibson in my arms. Freezing rain was beating like a lunatic's rage, drenching us through to the skin, but he was warm to the touch, and I could feel his heart fluttering like a bird. The winds tore at us, and dense curtains of water snaked out of the fog, slamming down on the roadway with such force they threatened to drown us. I hunched over Gibson, trying to cover him, but it didn't work.

"Sorry, kid," I murmured in his ear.

"It's OK. We almost there?"

The road crested ahead, and all I could see was the wind-whipped sky between the narrow gaps of buildings, but the stench of fuel and tide rot was heavy in the air. I guessed we were maybe two blocks away from the Port.

"Yeah, just a little more. We're almost there."

"Good." He nestled back into my shoulder.

Tam and Poet9 had stopped to catch their breath.

"*Madre de Dios*, could this get any worse?" Poet9 panted out, wiping his eyes clear.

"They could catch up," Tam said, jerking his thumb back down the street. "And then we'd find out."

I slowed my own breathing and listened, trying get a fix on any pursuit, but it was impossible. This storm wanted to sit at the big hurricanes table, and it tossed the noise of weapons and sirens around like kites in a gale. All I got were soggy echoes coming from everywhere, dismal and confused.

Tam nodded at Gibson. "Is he gonna make it?"

"We gotta get out of this."

He peered back down the street, then up further on toward the sea. "Let's move. We're one step ahead, and we need to stay that way. We'll stop in the next block and work up a way to get onto the Docks."

None of us spoke, just ran straight into the mouth of the storm chased by the clamor of approaching violence.

On the next block, we ducked down a side street lined with cheap two-story prefab units. All of them were weathered hard, their battered façades covered with peeling paint and weeping rust stains. Each building had two large, second-story windows on the left and right that stared seaward, dark and vacant, over a large garage door covered with steel roll-down shutters. Some of them had been welded shut, others stuck half-open, or torn and gaping. In the gloom, the row of buildings looked like decapitated heads, executed heretics on display for the opening segment of a jihadist webcast. We ducked through the broken mouth of the nearest one and got out of the rain.

I set Gibson down against the back wall on the first floor as Poet9 and Tam went upstairs. "You hanging in there OK?" I asked Gibson.

He was dripping wet and shivering, but he nodded back at me. The fever shine in his eyes was brighter.

"Where're Carmen and Mr. Alejo?"

"Probably already at their friend's boat. Why?"

"There was shooting again, and I don't want them to get hurt." He gave me a long look. "Are those people after me?"

I lied. Again. "No. It's us—me, Tam, and the others they want. I think. But don't worry, we'll take care of them and get you somewhere safe." I hunted around for anything remotely dry and warm to cover him with but came up empty. Except for scattered trash, hanging shreds of insulation, and fistfuls of empty purple crank vials, the place was a stripped-out concrete box.

Through the window, the shadowy arms of giant cranes loomed in the sky, and the massive skeletal form of the multilevel Docks was outlined in blinking yellow lights. Under the sound of the storm, we could hear the heavy throb of machinery from deep inside. Directly across the street, a tall reinforced cyclone fence topped with triple strands of barbed wire and security cam nodes marked the start of the Barcelona Port Complex. A guardhouse sat ten meters inside the gate, and beyond it, stacks of shipping containers created a maze of alleys off a central road.

Poet9 came down the stairs, obviously anxious to go.

"Tam thinks going straight up to the gate is best. We don't have time to find another way in. He'll cover us from upstairs until we reach the guardhouse, then you and I'll have to get past the rent-a-cops they got camera sitting. He'll be on our tail as soon as we disarm the guards." He nodded at the pistol in my belt. "Stay behind me. I'll carry Gibson. The sight of a sick kid should get us close enough so you can take them down. Try and look wet and miserable, OK?"

"No problem there." He turned to leave. "Wait. Where's the Bible smuggling sea captain?"

"That's the very end of South Dock, at the bottom level."

"You think Al's friend is going to risk his ship in this?"

Poet9 rolled his eyes. "Umm, no, now that you mention it." He paused and lowered his voice. "Tam says if he's not sailing, we're heading to the APAC Legation. We're going trust the Japanese to pull our fat out of the fire."

Somehow I knew that was coming, but it didn't make me feel any better when he said it.

He picked up Gibson, and the three of us slipped out and started across the broad street. We kept our heads down against the rain and stumbled through puddles toward the gate. I saw one of the guards lift off a stool and scrutinize us through the window, then lean over to his partner. We kept walking.

He ambled to the door, stuck his head out and started yelling. He probably thought we were laborers looking for shift work, or beggars wanting to scrounge through their dumpsters. Almost there. Keep yelling, pudgy. We're two soggy scabs with a kid, nobody worth getting wet for, and certainly not a threat.

We were almost to the other side of the street when I felt something. I can't say how; the storm was in full gear. Maybe I heard the rumble under the roar of rain. Maybe I picked up the tremble in the roadway, or it could have been that my brain recognized the distant shapes materializing in the fog before I actually understood what they were. Whatever it was, my body tensed up for a fight, and my vision switched to high-def clarity.

The guard started waving us away with a disgusted look on his face. I plastered a pathetic look on mine, and as we reached the sidewalk, I moved out from behind Poet9 and started walking faster. Five more steps and we were through the gate. The guard swore and stepped outside into the rain. Hands on his hips, he was telling us in no uncertain terms to piss off, or else.

My hand curled around the railing in front of him as two Dawson-Hull armored tracks charged up the avenue. Poet9 broke into a run, holding Gibson close to his chest. He ducked behind the nearest stack of shipping containers and got out of sight. I leapt up the steps and slammed into the startled guard.

I drove him back into the booth flailing and slipping, swearing in a panic, and he fell, clipping his head on the edge of the countertop. His mouth clicked shut, and he slid onto the floor, out cold. The charge carried me into the little room where his partner sat in his chair stunned, clutching his coffee cup and a pastry. He looked down at his friend then back up at me. He didn't even reach for the gun on his hip. I whipped the pistol out from under my shirt and pointed it at his forehead.

"Incluso no piense en él a mi amigo." *Don't even think about it, my friend.*

He nodded at me, open-mouthed, crumbs on his chin.

Behind me, Poet9 was shouting toward the storage unit just as the thick shapes of the two APCs ground to a halt in the street. The roar of their engines was deafening, and their turrets activated, the long barrels of the 30mm chain guns slashing through the air like probing antenna. Even before they stopped, back hatches clanged open and gray and red uniformed Dawson-Hull troopers spilled out and around the flat armored sides, yelling as they filled the intersection.

Tam shot out of the small building like a bat out of hell, a low dark shape slicing across their front, heading for the gate entrance. It took a second, but one of them spotted him and shouted a command. Rifles went up.

I shoved the seated guard aside and slammed the emergency lock-down button on his console. A braying two-tone klaxon erupted, and a row of nasty tire spikes fanged up out of the grating across the entrance. Half a dozen yellow caution lights began spinning as the tall steel gates started sliding shut with a grinding squeal. All the troopers flinched instinctively at the noise and light, weapons ready for a threat. Tam ran faster. The gates were closing rapidly. I could hear them squealing in their metal tracks.

"Halt! Stop, stop or we'll shoot. Freeze scab motherfucker! Drop him. Drop him!"

The first shot rang out.

The two gate edges were barely a meter apart when I saw Tam take two huge steps and jump. The guttural coughs of tri-bursts skipped around the street as the troopers opened fire, but Tam was diving low and sideways through the air. He cleared the tire spikes as the two gates clamped shut behind him, landing in a spray of muddy water. He rolled off to one side, and after a couple seconds, stopped flat on his back.

Poet9 was the first to reach him. He was still carrying Gibson. "You all right? You all right?"

Tam lay there, eyes open to the sky, Poet9 on his knees beside him. Suddenly the wiry North Korean groaned and sat up with a wry smile on his face.

"I really need that vacation."

CHAPTER FORTY-SEVEN

HEADSHOT CLEARANCE

Barcelona Port Complex, Asian Pacific Consortium Trade Offices, Section D. South Dock, Level Five. 7:55 p.m. Day Five.

When Colonel Otsu arrived in the Command Center, warning lights were flashing at every workstation, reflecting off the tense faces of the technicians. A klaxon blared over the androgynous voice of the security grid, which kept repeated its decision to bring the perimeter defense turrets online.

"Someone shut that thing up," the colonel ordered, and the audio fell silent.

A massive screen hung over the main console, filled with the face of Captain Murata, the Chief of Security. Colonel Otsu could see one of the Dock's loading platforms stretched out in the background, and the storm raging beyond that. "Report. What's going on out there?" he demanded.

"Sir, we just received a general All-Port alert."

"Because of the storm?"

"No, sir. An emergency lockdown went into effect seven minutes ago."

"Who triggered it?"

"It came from landside, Colonel. The north eleven gate. "

"Someone trying to rob the place again?" Colonel Otsu asked.

"I don't think so, sir. The surveillance feed shows four suspects—three adult males and a child—rushing a gate's guard station. No trucks, no guns I could see. Not even the Russians are that crazy. The really strange thing is two units of corporate troops arrived on the scene at the same time. Soon after, someone there hit the alarm."

"You're sure those troops were corporate, not Spanish nationals?"

"Yes, sir. The Dawson-Hull logo is plastered all over the vehicles. From the uniforms and gear, it looks like they're Special Deployment Branch."

"Were they chasing those four?"

"Yes, sir," said the captain.

"Did they get in? The four I mean."

"Yes, sir. Barely."

"And the British?"

"Stuck standing outside in the rain, sir. It appears the intruders headed straight onto the South Arm. I put the men on standby. Your orders, Colonel?

"You're doing fine, Captain. I want you to track those four people. I have reason to believe they're headed our way."

"They won't get past us, Colonel."

"No. If I'm correct, those are free agents who've been working for us. It's vital they reach here safely."

"Sir, I can use the Dock security, get a fix on their position, and have a squad there in ten minutes."

"Captain, this is a complicated situation that just got more difficult. London only let Special Deployment out of their cage when they're dead serious." Colonel Otsu frowned. If he assisted the agents directly, he would implicate the Consortium, and there was no way he could risk a public confrontation with Special Deployment troops. However, if he failed to act and the agents were caught, he'd be held responsible for the mission's failure. He chose the middle ground. "I want your men ready to protect and assist them once they reach our sector, but under no circumstances are your men to leave the boundaries of the Legation. I repeat: do not leave Asian Pacific jurisdiction. I can't risk giving Dawson-Hull a reason to enter our sector."

"Yes, Colonel, but if they can't find one, I think they might invent it."

"What do you mean?"

"More D-H troops keep coming, sir, from everywhere. They're all over the Dock feed in the streets. The lockdown might have shut them out, but I see multiple heavy units taking up positions at all points landside. It looks like they're sealing the Docks off from the rest of the city." The captain glanced off screen momentarily. "I've got breeching teams assembling outside north gates eleven and fifteen. There's also a report of a tug launch from the shore headed our way. It looks like they're gearing up for an assault, Colonel."

"Keep your men focused, Captain. I'm turning over control of the automated defense system, but don't activate it yet. I don't want it targeting those four fugitives."

"Yes, sir." Captain Murata saluted.

"Have them escorted directly to me in the Command Center once they arrive. Afterwards, you're free to conduct whatever tactical response is necessary to keep our interests secure. The British might get livid for losing them, but they're not crazy enough to violate corporate sovereignty laws. All we need is those agents to keep it together and get here in one piece."

Major Jessa Eames stood outside the Barcelona Port Complex in the pouring rain feeling thoroughly pissed on as well as pissed off. She glared at the garish orange and black security barrier that blocked the gate opening as if she could bore a hole through its duracrete sections. Surrounded by the frantic chatter of a dozen radios and the incessant commotion of troopers and technicians, she was in full swing of what her men called her 'rip' mood; as in "rip someone's face off". The scurrying personnel did their best to stay out of her line of sight and keep busy elsewhere. Someone had to update her, so one of the Special Deployment sergeants took a deep breath before approaching.

"We haven't got the override code yet, Major," he started.

"Fucking break it down then! Do I have to tell you everything? I want those scabs nailed. Get your men in there, on the Docks, ten minutes ago, Sergeant. What's so hard to understand here?"

"Major, needless destruction of Port infrastructure could jeopardize—"

"Letting that asset get away jeopardizes any career plans you had with Dawson-Hull, Sergeant. Rig up some C4 and open those fucking gates!" she roared. "You clear on that?"

"Yes, Major, perfectly clear. Right away."

"Now we're going somewhere. What's the status on the boats?"

The sergeant chewed his lip. "Storm's whipping the water out of control, ma'am. One boat barely made it to the start of the South Arm, and the captain of the other is refusing to launch. Teams Six and Seven were on the first boat. They're spreading out now. Two and Five are standing by at the lower tug dock awaiting further orders."

"Suffering Christ, find me a captain with some balls! I want the other teams out there. The South Arm has to be isolated. My guess is those scabs are running for the APAC sector, and even money says the Japs are taking in strays today. I need their entire Legation surrounded. Make it happen."

"Yes, Major, right away." A hasty salute and the sergeant ran off.

"Major?" Private Banner popped his head out of the command Grizzly's turret hatch clutching the communications handset. "I've got a Priority wave from London. Director MacKinnon's office. He's asking for you."

Jessa Eames bit off a snarl and grabbed the comm. set. "Major Eames here."

Jackson MacKinnon's clipped tones sounded loud and clear. "Major Eames, I was informed you'd been seriously wounded. While it's good to hear your voice, why are you in the field and not in the hospital?"

"I'm just earning my pay, sir. We've located the asset. It seems he was snatched by some black ops freelance outfit. We tracked them to the Barcelona Port Complex and are in pursuit right now. It looks like they're heading for the Asian Pacific Legation."

There was a slight pause before Director MacKinnon's spoke again. "Exceptional work as usual, Major. You say they've brought the boy to the Docks?"

"Yes, sir, but don't worry. I've got units closing in. We'll have him back by nightfall."

"You're certain the boy is there? These mercenaries definitely have him?"

"Yes, sir. We think he's unharmed, and I don't think they've crossed into the Jap's territory yet," Major Eames answered. "I'll get him, sir."

"Very good, Major." Jackson MacKinnon's voice took a direct, authoritative tone. "In light of this, I want you and your men to stand firm around the Consortium's Legation there at the Port Complex. I cannot authorize deadly force, but no one enters or leaves. I'm going to call an emergency session of the Board here in London. We will contact Tokyo and lodge a formal complaint, and request an immediate inquiry. Our U.N. staff will apply pressure from there." Director MacKinnon paused. "Outstanding work, Major. You've certainly earned your pay. Now, I'm ordering you to report back to the hospital. I can't have my finest security commander disabled."

Jessa Eames stared at the comm-set. "I've got them in my sights, sir. We can get the boy back. Today."

"Of course you can. I don't doubt that for an instant," Jessa Eames' superior responded. "This mission was important, which is why I specifically selected you for command. The Special Deployment units have exceeded my expectations. Again. You have done your job, and now I will do mine."

"Yes, sir. Thank you. But, Mr. MacKinnon, the situation is very fluid… if we cut them any slack, APAC will find a way to slip the asset out of the country. We have to strike now before they can consolidate."

"Your concern is valid on a tactical level, Major, but the situation is far more than *fluid*; it's positively volatile. These new developments with the freelance mercenaries convey the entire situation beyond your area of expertise. This is the realm of corporate affairs, Major. Rather sensitive corporate affairs at that."

"Mr. MacKinnon, I can get him," the major urged. "All I need is an hour, two at the most. I have to move on it now, though."

"Major Eames, if those mercenaries have the boy in the Asian Pacific sector, they are officially under their jurisdiction. I won't have an inter-cartel incident on my hands because your forces trespass and break several dozen international laws."

Jessa Eames implored her boss. "Sir, I doubt the fugitives have crossed over Consortium lines yet. And with all due respect, we've already got an incident. Let me go in and finish the job. The Spanish authorities are standing off. It's only D-H men here, sir. Let us go in. They won't be able to prove a thing."

"That asset is designated Tier Ultra. *Ultra*, Major. That means he's critical to the company's global strategic interests." Director MacKinnon was lecturing her now. "I'm not even sure I'm afforded that designation."

Major Eames fell silent for a moment, then spoke softly, urgently into the comm-set. "Sir, speaking frankly… if he's that valuable, then we can't let him fall into another's corporation's hands. Grant Headshot Clearance, Mr. MacKinnon. I'll have him eliminated before Asian Pacific gets him."

"Major Eames, I appreciate your candor, but the asset *must not* come to any harm whatsoever. I'm giving you a direct order: seal off the Asian Pacific Legation. That is all. You and your men have performed excellently. Now I will handle the balance of the situation from here. MacKinnon out."

There was a faraway click as the line cut off. Jessa Eames looked down at the comm-set and clenched in her fist... something wasn't right. MacKinnon wasn't acting like the ruthless old bastard she'd known for years. She turned and threw the headset back to Private Banner. The sergeant had returned and was standing off to the side, waiting to speak with her.

"What is it?" she snapped.

"Breaching teams are ready, Major, and the second tug just launched. They'll be out on the South Arm in fifteen minutes."

"It's about time. Have them link up with Six and Seven and cut all access to the Asian Pacific Legation. I want eyes on every walkway, stairway, elevator, and conveyor into or out those levels. If London wants babysitters, we're going to clamp down Asian Pacific like they've had an Ebola strike. I want those gates open in five minutes, and I don't care how it's done. We're going in."

CHAPTER FORTY-EIGHT

HOSTILE PARTIES

Barcelona Port Complex, South Dock, Level Two. 8:15 p.m.
Day Five.

We ran through the Port Complex for twenty minutes, trying to get as much distance between ourselves and the gate as possible. Gibson had started wheezing when we reached the junction to the South Arm. I was last in line, and I could see him draped over Poet's shoulder, his face flushed and sweaty. Every now and then, his eyes jolted open, and he'd look around before sinking back into exhaustion. I could even hear his breathing over the distant crash of the storm and the surrounding buzz and rattle of machinery. We'd come to the bottom of another set of steel grate stairs when Poet9 called for a break.

"Boss, I can feel the heat coming off him through my clothes," Poet9 called out. "*Madre de Dios*, this place is huge. How much farther?"

"Eight sections total. Al's friend is at the very end." He pointed at a thick numbered column. "We're only in three, and we've got to go down another four levels."

I brushed Gibson's hair aside and put my hand on his forehead. "He's burning. The little nano-cancers must have kicked into high gear. They're eating him up inside."

Tam glanced back down the Dock. "OK, one minute, but he's got to hang on." He sighed and looked at me and Poet. "APAC is Section Four. What do you think about going straight there? They've got medical staff."

"They got crazy people with guns too," Poet9 said. "Weren't we bringing him with us?"

"Look at him. You think he's going to make it back to Belfast?" Tam asked. "And what about Al and Carmen? They're with Hester."

"Screw the leprechaun. We can take him."

"How you going to feel when he dies if APAC could have saved him?"

"You don't know that. You're making a case for a payday, is all," Poet9 said. "We owe the kid... I owe him, anyway."

Gibson was unconscious again, breathing loud and ragged. One look at him, and I knew we were kidding ourselves if we thought we could save him. Something tore in my gut when I realized that, but I said it anyway. "How many people want us dead now, Poet? I'm losing count. Tam's right; he's sick and we're targets. APAC might be his best bet."

"We can make it," Poet spoke up. "We've weaseled out of worse before—"

"You think the Brits made it in yet?" I interrupted him, jerking my thumb over my shoulder. "I'm surprised they didn't smash the wall down right then and there." Poet started to protest again, but I cut him off. "Madrid won't want to waste cell space on us. Those D-H lads want our heads on stakes, and I'm still not sure who that Hester guy is working for. That makes three hostile parties."

"The mosque," Tam added.

I threw up my hands. "Right... how could I forget? Make that four. It's a cast of twisted characters with dangerous intent, and we're not doing Gibson any favors dragging him around with us." I ended gently. "We have to bring him to APAC."

Poet's face clenched, and he held the boy tighter but kept silent. We were out of choices.

As we moved out, I leaned in close to Tam. "You think Shorty's telling the truth that APAC sent that woman and her two friends?"

He laughed and shook his head. "I'll have to ask next time I see her."

"Nah, just shoot her."

"Love to, but I sure as hell hope the Triplets have them bagged and tagged already."

The one they called Cottontail was down to one last magazine for his rifle. He peered into the street, searching for the three *abiku*. Their former Zulu drill sergeants had used the word for General Mambi's enemies, and at some point in the last thirty minutes, he and his brothers had resurrected it for the hostiles. It meant 'child-eating demon'.

They'd chased them through the furious storm for thirty minutes, trading shots down the long street, and getting closer to the Docks with every stride. Soon, they'd be down to their pistols, and after that they'd need new weapons. From the sounds of the police all around, Cottontail didn't think that would be much of a problem.

It was the *abiku* that troubled him. They were modified, conditioned, and good—dangerously good. After forcing them out of the intersection, he and his brothers had been unable to kill even one of them yet. Worse, 5902 had been hit in the shoulder and 5903 was bleeding from several grazes on his legs. They were still combat effective, but for the first time in almost a decade, 5905 felt concern.

The female seemed to be the leader, and she'd had one of the men always rotating back to shoot and delay pursuit. It was a page straight out of the tactical manuals, performed flawlessly. Cottontail decided that was their strength, and their weakness. It didn't matter the *abiku* had been spliced, hardened and wired; he and his brothers had experience. They would improvise, think around the drills, and that, Cottontail decided, was their edge.

His brothers were trading careful shots with the bigger man now, so he ran to the next doorway. The structures in this neighborhood were plain and dilapidated, and crouched behind flaking concrete, he realized the street was ending. Up ahead over the slight rise in the road, the muffled glint of flashing lights bounced off the faces of the buildings. Sirens were growing louder by the second. Cottontail smelled a rotting tang of seawater, and the multi-tiered shape of the Port Complex rose darkly in the gray gloom. This was where they were supposed to meet the Mr. Tam and the others.

5902 fired from behind a lamppost, two sharp cracks down the street and the big man stumbled. He recovered immediately, but ran off favoring his right side. Cottontail grinned like a schoolboy. Things were looking up, and the promise of new weapons was just around the corner.

Gibson was one child they weren't going to get. He and his brothers would slay these *abiku.*

CHAPTER FORTY-NINE

Barcelona Port Complex, South Dock, Section Three. 8:33 p.m.
Day Five.

Poet shifted Gibson gently and looked around, "Hey – where is everyone? Workers, I mean."

Tam shrugged. "My guess is management sent everyone home with the storm. As long as no one's around, we can stick to the marked walkways and move faster." He gestured toward the machinery and conveyors on the main floor. "Otherwise, we'd have to play duck and dodge out there, and those things can pulp a person without slowing down for a second."

"I'd really feel stupid if I got killed by a case of jockey briefs," I said.

"Me too. Let's keep an eye open for an elevator."

We got down to another level, one of the sorting areas. All around us, the B-Port's automated systems were in motion keeping the flood of commercial goods flowing. Bolted to the floor and hanging from the ceiling, a network of conveyor belts and monorail skiffs whirred incessantly, bearing endless lines of cases and cartons of every size and shape. Every one of them passed under a series of infrared scanner eyes, and hydraulic arms clattered back and forth, diverting each box according to the codes on the manifest chips. It was the electric pulse of profit.

The four of us followed white outlined walkways through the stacks of shipping containers. Painted in bright primary colors, their corrugated steel walls formed a labyrinth of corridors, dead ends, and random clearings, and everywhere the stark tribal hieroglyphs and animistic icons of company logos were stamped like primitive finger-painted ciphers. Between the flickering lights, the moan of funneled wind, and the drip of moisture off the low ceiling, I felt like I was trapped in an Ogilvy and Mather rendition of the Lascaux Caves.

Another five minutes and two levels down, we came to the Personnel Area at the end of Section Three. The floor was wide open, with only four conveyors running through it. Two routing stations stood roughly at the center, a bank of vending machines stood next to toilet stalls on one wall, and there were a dozen forklifts and loader exo-suits were parked opposite them. At the far end, next to another set of stairs, a wide freight elevator stood open-mouthed and lit behind a chain-link fence.

Gibson stirred on Poet9's shoulder. His eyes fluttered open. "Where are we?"

"You keep resting. We're almost there." Tam pointed. "That's a sign for the APAC Legation."

"Mmm, OK," he mumbled, and fell back into a fitful sleep.

We were about to get in the elevator when voices drifted up from the floor below, radio crackle and the tone of command and instructions. We froze.

"Sounded English to me," Poet9 whispered.

"D-H troops?" I looked at Tam. "How the hell…?"

"Beats me. A boat? Swimming lessons? Either way they're between us and the Japanese. And if they made it there," he pointed down, "five credits says they're closing in behind us too."

Poet9 glanced over my shoulder. "Why don't we hop on the elevator and skip them altogether?"

Tam shook his head. "It's slow, wide open and empty. There's no cover. They'll shoot us like fish in a barrel as we go past. We have to get past them. Fast."

I pulled out the Beretta Poet had given me and slid the Gerber into my left hand. "Time to get sneaky devious."

"Poet, hang back out of sight with Gibson until we call," Tam said. "We need you, you'll hear us yell."

Poet unholstered his Walther 11. "Got it, boss. Either of you want to borrow Grace?"

"Grace?" Tam looked puzzled.

"I told you he named it," I said.

"You named your pistol *Grace*? Isn't that a little… blasphemous?" Tam looked at Poet9.

"No way." The small hacker hefted the big black magnum and gazed at it. "She saved my life three times on that last run in Morocco. Three times. I wanted to do something special, so it was either that or Baldomero."

"Baldomero?" I coughed.

"After my father. He was big and loud and could kick the crap out of anybody."

Tam just shook his head.

"I'll take her," I said.

He handed it over along with four spare clips. I passed the Beretta back to him.

"Be nice to her," Poet9 said seriously. "And if you need to take a long shot with her, pray and it'll hit."

"Oh stop, Poet. You're sounding like Al now," Tam hissed.

"Hey, it worked in Morocco. And whatever works..."

Tam shooed him off toward the row of forklifts. He turned to me. "You ready?"

"Whenever you are."

I glanced back at Poet9 and Gibson. The skinny Mexican winked, put his hands together, and mouthed the words, "Pray. Pray."

I grinned and slipped after Tam.

The next level down was another sorting area, so Tam and I had plenty of crates and noise to cover us. Problem was it worked for the D-H troopers too. We knew they were there, but we didn't see them until we were almost on top of them.

We were crouched by a monorail when Tam spotted the first one ten meters away.

There was four of them kitted out in Special Deployment red and gray combat armor, the Kev-flex pads bulking them out. They'd paired up behind cover on either side of the main walkway to the elevator, and I could see the cool blue of their reflective goggles moving slowly back and forth over the floor. They were carrying brand new FN F2000 assault rifles. Sharp, suited up and armed to the teeth, they were definitely a cut above the standard issue security mannequins. Tam and I were clad in soggy jogging suits, clutching pistols behind a crate of toys from Hasbro International.

Another line of boxes whizzed by my head. "This is a little too *asymmetrical* for me. Plan?"

Tam closed his eyes. "Go black, split left and right, come around on their flanks. We've got to get close."

"I was afraid you'd say that."

"Sorry to bore you," he flashed a tight grin. "See you on the other side."

I nodded and as the next string of boxes went by, we separated.

Even with all the crates and machinery, getting close was the main issue. The brutal fact was we needed to be right next to them to punch through the weak spots in their armor. I checked the Walther 11 one last time, rolled to the next stack of crates and took a deep breath.

I started shutting everything out: sight, noise, smell, the sensations of cold and damp, the weight of the pistol in my hand, the itch of clothing against my skin. I concentrated until the noise and motion around me dropped away and all I heard was my heartbeat and the slow bellows of my breathing. I focused on those two until I found their rhythm, and dense gray filled in from the edges.

Once I'd fastened myself in that place, I counted down from twenty, turning things back on. Every sensation was sharper, more distinct. I smelled the thick stench of hydraulic fluid, the musk of mold, and the iron tang of rust, the stale breezes of cardboard and plastic boxes. I could hear the rattle of the spindle bearings on the conveyors, the thrumming of the electric motors, and the thin drips of rain sweat off the walls. I tuned in the rubber texture and finger grooves on the pistol grip in my right hand, the knurled haft of the knife in the other. My muscles slid and coiled beneath my skin, electric.

Last of all, I opened my eyes. In the dim light, all the edges were traced in a thin black line, each object separate and specific. My mind was clear and hard as I gathered up the facets of my surroundings and hid myself inside. I was ready to run. Tam was already in motion on the other side of the room, so I rolled to a crouch and slipped off to my left.

The trooper on the outside left had taken a position near an aluminum repair bench about five meters behind of his partner. He was supposed to provide flank security, but he never looked to the ocean side once. He figured any attack would come straight across the floor. Someone said once you should never interrupt your enemy when they're making a mistake, so I circled around and kept the wind and waves at my back.

A minute later, the Gerber opened his throat and he was on the floor. I sighted the Walther on his partner's head, waiting for a Tam's signal.

A split second later, I heard the flat pops of a 9mm double tap and rose up to shoot, but the trooper had ducked. Radio squelch cut through the air.

"Top, this is Six-Two, Six-Two. We have contact, our position. Repeat. Six-Two has contact our position."

"Contact Six-Two confirmed. Hold on. Units en route."

There was a yell and more shots from the far side of the elevator cage: 9mm followed by the stutter of an F2000. My guy popped up and turned, looking for his backup. He spotted me instead.

I came at him straight on, emptying Poet's Walther. He peeled off sideways, firing his rifle on the move. We both missed. As I reloaded, he began backing away, loosing tri-bursts in my direction to keep my head down. The gunfight was building on the other side too. Tam and I had maybe five minutes before their backup arrived.

I scrambled low and chased him around the back of the elevator shaft to the other side. Staying behind containers, he kept out of sight, and closed in on Tam and the other D-H trooper.

I focused in on the sounds. There was no gunfire, but I could hear Tam and the other trooper scuffling somewhere straight ahead of me. No sign of my target. I made a mad dash between stacks and ended up next to an open white walkway running alongside a conveyor. Framed at the far end, Tam and the second D-H trooper were wrestling, hammering at each other in a mad flurry of blows and kicks.

I ran forward and dropped to one knee, waiting. Between the distance and the tangle of them fighting, I had no shot.

The brawl seesawed back and forth until Tam threw the D-H soldier down on the conveyor belt. A line of crates smashed into him and snatched his body out of sight. As Tam was gulping for air, the final trooper I'd been hunting stepped directly behind him, that nasty little rifle sighted up on his shoulder.

Instinctively, I uttered three words, raised the Walther and fired a single shot.

The second trooper spun and fell.

Tam turned around at the sound, startled.

I held up Poet9's pistol. "Grace works for me."

CHAPTER FIFTY

ORDERS

Barcelona Port Complex, Gate Five. 8:55 p.m. Day Five.

Major Eames stood next to her Grizzly Command Track staring at the Port Complex. Her men had sealed off the all landside entry points to the huge structure, and radio reports poured in as various units checked in. The pain in her arm and shoulder had subsided into a deep, dull ache, and she let it throb, hoping it would put an edge on her thinking. She still couldn't wrap her head around London's orders to stand down. Suddenly, Private Banner called out from the top hatch.

"Major, I've got no signal from the units at Gate Eleven."

"What the—? Get someone there and find out why."

"Yes, Major. Ahh, ma'am? Six Two just called in a hostile contact on the Tac-net."

"Six-Two? What's their position?"

"On the Docks, ma'am. Deployed at South Arm, Section Three, Level Six. Right outside the APAC sector."

"Current status?"

"They're not answering, ma'am."

"Christ on a crutch!" she shouted. "Scabs are there already. Are they really that good, or do we just suck?" She stared furiously at the Docks, then up at Private Banner, who still held the radio. "That's the way it is? Fine. Order all units to close on the APAC Legation."

"Major?"

"You heard me, Banner. Do it. Now," she spit out. "One of my units has been attacked, and we are moving to assist."

"All of them? What about Director MacKinnon's orders, Major?"

Major Eames stared hard at the young soldier. "There's an old saying about permission and forgiveness, Private. I'll worry about MacKinnon, you worry about me. It'll take days to get the U.N. moving on this, and then all the suits will just dick around and deny everything. They'll sit there on their fat arses while their lawyers shout at each other across a round table. Goddamn waste of oxygen if you ask me."

She scrutinized the tactical display on her data pad. Three other combat teams were in position out on the South Arm. "I didn't come all this way to lose the asset now. We're going in, and I'm going to pull him out of there if

I have to tear down every building in the Jap sector to do it. Now get 'em moving!"

The elevator lurched to a stop on Level Six, Section Four, and I swung back the gate. As we stepped onto the floor, a group of soldiers burst out from behind a duracrete barricade, running towards us.

Poet9 tensed, but Tam spoke up. "Yellow and black. They're Asian Pacific. We're here."

Two full squads of Japanese corporate security surrounded us, weapons facing outward for defense. An officer stepped forward, snapped to attention and saluted Tam.

"Welcome to the Asian Pacific Trade Legation, Barcelona. I am Captain Murata, chief security officer. Please be assured from this point on, you are all under our protection. My commanding officer is expecting you, and I have orders to provide you with whatever assistance you deem necessary."

Poet9 brought Gibson around off his shoulder. The boy's face was ashen, his breathing labored, and for a second I thought he'd died. "Are we there yet?" he croaked out.

Tam, Poet9 and I almost laughed aloud with relief. "Yeah. Yeah, kid. We're here."

"He needs a doctor right away," Tam said to the captain. "Where's your medical station?"

Captain Murata barked out a command in Japanese, and two soldiers ran forward with a stretcher. "I was to escort you to the Legation's commander, Colonel Otsu, as soon as you arrived. The clinic is next to the Command Center. I suggest we go now."

As the two soldiers gingerly placed Gibson on the stretcher, Captain Murata gave a slight bow and gestured for us to follow.

"*Dios santo en cielo, gracias,*" Poet9 breathed, and we started after them.

Cottontail thought the storm was raging like a rabid thing, cruel, blind, and savage. Cold rain fell in torrents, pounding down like fists, drenching everything flat and numb. Tantrums of icy winds lashed out of the clouds, clawing at him and his brothers, slicing and shoving from every direction. Ahead of them, a massive, multi-layer shape sat heavy and black behind a curtain of churning gray, and despite the hurricane, the stink of fuel and rot was heavy in the air. They'd reached the end of the long avenue and were standing in front of the Barcelona Port Complex South Arm Dock.

The Port entrance itself was blocked by a massive orange and black barrier, a large "11" stenciled in white block letters on chipped duracrete. The *abiku* were nowhere to be seen, but the bodies of eight corporate soldiers lay scattered like rag dolls in the street. An armored personnel carrier was skewed up on the sidewalk, greasy black smoke sputtering out its vents and forward top hatch, sly, hungry flames flickering inside the troop compartment. Its back ramp was bent, and the rear door was slamming back and forth in the frigid gusts, clanging like a broken bell.

Cottontail recognized it as a standard corporate-issue transport, a Dawson-Hull "Grizzly" Armored Personnel Carrier. He scanned the bodies and realized all the soldier's rifles were missing, and on the right, there was a large tear in the chain-link fence. Not only had the hostiles re-armed themselves, but they were inside the B-Port Complex.

Cottontail checked his own G3 assault rifle. He was down to his last five rounds. His brothers checked their own weapons; 5901 held up five fingers, 5902 held up four. Fourteen rifle rounds between the three of them, nowhere near enough to stop this enemy.

The voice of his old Zulu drill sergeant screamed in his mind. *Action— not thought! Action!* They were losing time and distance standing here. Cottontail frowned. "Search and salvage. Most fast," he ordered.

His brothers moved among bodies as he turned to double-check the long avenue and watch for *policia*.

Three minutes later, 5901 and 5902 came back clutching a handful of pistol magazines, two small caliber back-up pistols, and a plastic emergency kit filled with magnesium flares. Cottontail looked up from the meager finds and inspected his two brothers. Both were wounded. 5902, the one named Mopsy, was favoring his left leg, two AK rounds having passed through the meat of his thigh. 5901, or Flopsy, was bleeding heavily from the right side of his face, head and ear. 5905 figured it looked worse than it was. Head wounds bled a lot. "Tend that," he commanded. 5901 tore a length of sleeve and tied it around his head to keep the blood from dripping in his eyes.

Cottontail himself was relatively unscathed. There were numerous bloody scratches from splinters and concrete chips on his hands, shoulders, and neck, but none of them serious. Both his brothers kept glancing from his face to the Dock, their eyes sharp and bright. They were eager to pursue. 5905 grinned. They were functional, and that was the key. *You are the weapons! Not the guns.* Day and night, the Zulu instructors had beaten that mantra into them. *Does the weapon still function? Yes? Then you can still fight. And if you fight, you can kill. Now go kill.* That was all that mattered.

Mr. Tam had given them orders; Gibson needed to stay safe. The little guns would have to do. Cottontail nodded, and the three of them ran across the street and slipped through the fence. The chase was still on.

CHAPTER FIFTY-ONE

Barcelona Port Complex, South Dock, Section Three. 9:00 p.m.
Day Five.

It was another twenty minutes before Major Eames could set up her command post. Her men had secured the entire section next to the APAC Legation, and she stood a mere thousand meters away from a main entrance, looking over the tactical display.

A 3D schematic was projected in the air, the Legation boundaries highlighted in neon yellow, Consortium units in red, her own in green. She thumbed the track ball and the image spun to a different angle.

"All teams good to go?" she asked one of the lieutenants.

"Yes, Major."

"ECM geeks hack their defense systems yet?"

"They're mugging their grid now. In the meantime, we've set up jammers at the assault points. That should snow-blind the sensors long enough for our troops to disable their turrets. If you're hell bent and hot to trot, Major, we won't have a better chance than right now," the officer replied grimly.

She frowned at the holo-display one last time. "Go."

The lieutenant tapped his comm-set. "All units, green light on the assault. I repeat: weapons are free and you are green to go. Commence assault now."

Tam, Poet and I had stepped off another elevator when a siren started blaring. Captain Murata and the two soldiers with the stretcher halted in mid-stride and looked at each other.

"Is that bad?" Poet asked. "It sounds bad."

"What's that mean?" I looked to the captain.

He threw me a grim look and got on his radio. The two soldiers set Gibson down and brought their rifles up. Automatic weapons fire erupted behind us.

"*Dios santo*, not again," Poet muttered.

Captain Murata issued several sharp commands and signed off. "We're under attack. Dawson-Hull Special Deployment are jamming our automated systems and threatening to breech our lines." He pointed to a group of low white structures in the center of the next section. "The Command Center is right over there, the large building on the ocean side. Report there first, and ask for Colonel Otsu, he will see to it your friend gets proper treatment." He bowed low. "I must return and conduct the defense." With that, he and his troops ran off.

Poet smiled down at Gibson on the stretcher. "Trouble just follows you, doesn't it?"

Tam and I picked up the handles, and Poet9 drew Grace. Together, we set off toward the squat, white metal and black armorglass building.

Cottontail and his brothers caught up with the three *abiku* on a middle floor in Section Three. A sorting area, it was nestled deep in the South Dock's interior, brightly lit and dry, away from the storm's fury. One of the large conveyors had thrown a roller, hurling a cargo segment into the elevator cage, smashing the wire gate shut with a pile of containers. The rest of the floor remained in motion; infrared readers bobbing and blinking, crates whizzing past in every direction at random intervals. 5902 spied the scrawny rat-faced male leading the woman and her larger partner toward the stairs.

Using hand signals, Cottontail directed his brothers to the left. He'd given them all the scavenged pistols and spare magazines in return for the remaining rifle rounds. Speed was their only chance now. They had to press the attack, pull them close, and finish them quickly. To draw out lions, hunters staked a buck in a clearing as bait. To kill these enemies, Cottontail decided his brothers were blades, and he would be the bait.

Cottontail fired as the *abiku* were in the open space in front of the floor's maintenance station. The big man recoiled, clutching his side, and the other two scattered, seeking cover. His brothers had started moving fast, silent and low the moment he'd raised the rifle, and they disappeared down an aisle between two sorting gates.

Cottontail ran forward, firing his rifle until he was ten meters away, then dove behind a stack of metal crates directly in front of them. He had their attention now. The only way off the floor was in the open toward the stairwell down, or past him back to the stairs leading up. Seven shots left in the rifle, two magazines for his pistol, and then it was fists and feet; not very menacing, but the *abiku* would have to kill him before they went any further.

His brothers couldn't spring the trap until they moved on the bait, so Cottontail popped up and fired two more rounds near where the big man had stumbled. No response. He had to flush them out, so crouched behind the crates, he scrutinized the maintenance station.

Tucked in between two thick support pylons, the back wall was lined with lockers, and there were tools littering several workbenches. A rack of oversize wrenches and man-sized crowbars stood nearby, and pyramids of blue plastic lubricant drums squatted on the floor like an obstacle course. Nothing but junk. On the right, the battered, empty skeleton of an exo-suit loader slouched next to its propane gas fueler.

You are the weapon. There is always something you can do, a Zulu sergeant screamed in his head. *Always something you can use. Find it!*

Cottontail felt the hard cylinders of the magnesium flares rolling against his thigh and smiled.

Suddenly, one of the conveyor belts next to his head rasped, and a line of canary-yellow crates sang by his head. The bed of steel rollers rattled down the line and the three agents attacked.

Spraying their weapons on full-auto, the two men stayed behind a rack of steel shelves while the woman sprang forward on his right. Cottontail shifted and crawled below the metal-rimmed side of the conveyor platform as rounds buzzed and sparked around him. Frantic to catch up with Mr. Tam and Gibson, they were trying to pin him down and rush the stairs. Cottontail didn't signal his brothers yet.

He waited for a microsecond pause between bursts, then leaned out and fired twice at the men. As they snapped out of sight, he put his last three rifle rounds into the propane tank. He threw the rifle down as another length of boxes raced by and crawled closer.

The two fired again, this time zeroed on his position, and Cottontail felt a round burn through his shoulder, another crease his ribs. He could tell the woman was creeping up on his right, but the men were still too far away. He couldn't spring the trap yet.

Ignoring the blood warmth spreading down his side, he drew his pistol, a slab-sided Russian MP-443 "Grach" 9mm. He frowned. He wasn't sure his shots had penetrated the propane tank.

When the rattling ceased, he jumped up, fired off a full clip, and ran alongside the conveyor to a juncture where several tracks merged. Another bullet seared into his hip. He lunged down at the intersection, panting, and craned his head to listen. There, behind the two men, he caught the telltale hiss of the propane tank leaking.

All three *abiku* started moving in for the kill. The two men stepped out from behind the shelves, and Cottontail spied the cold-eyed woman's legs making scissoring shadows beneath the machines. *Any second now.*

Footsteps on concrete two meters in front of him. His large hands were slick with blood, shaking with adrenaline and blood loss, but he reloaded his pistol and dug two flares out of his pocket.

The leg shadows on his right knotted and paused.

Now.

Cottontail twisted the igniters and the flares blossomed white and sizzled. He signaled his brothers—a sharp, ululating whistle—rose to his full height and hurled them straight into the exo-loader bay.

He was staring into the face of the large man, his rifle on his shoulder, his dark eyes flat like pebbles, his mouth black and open to yell.

Like a mamba snake, Cottontail thought.

The tank exploded in a long belch of flame and a flurry of pistol shots erupted behind the two men. His brothers were moving in.

They would deal with the men. Cottontail spun to face the woman.

Stunned, eyes wide at the explosion, she snapped off a tri-burst past his head. One round clipped his ear, hot blood splashing down his neck.

On either side of a large conveyor, Cottontail and the female *abiku* opened fire and dove to one side. Each missed the other. Rollers rattled, and Cottontail lost sight of her as another length of boxes sped by.

Half a clip left, two flares in his pocket, he moved toward the raised bed of the conveyor belt, every nerve taut. Behind him, gunshots bickered over the cackling flames. His brothers had their hands full. *At least she won't find an exit there*, he thought. *She'll have to go up a level and find a way around.* Cottontail's foot nudged something solid: one of the massive crowbars had been left on the floor. He hefted it in his other hand like a spear and kept hunting.

The rollers rasped again, and a line of neon green crates dropped out of the ceiling onto the conveyor at the same moment the woman emerged behind him. She'd doubled back after all.

Cottontail only had time to empty the last of his pistol rounds into the air, but it was enough. The woman flinched, and in that sliver of hesitation, he jammed the crowbar between the conveyor rollers and wrenched down with all his strength. The entire segment of crates went airborne, a vivid lime steel python that slammed into the woman and smashed her back into a duracrete column. Warning sirens warbled and every the belt on the floor skidded to a stop.

Panting, Cottontail heard two pistol shots behind him, followed by an ululating whistle.

The *abiku* were dead.

CHAPTER FIFTY-TWO

CHERNOBYL PACKET

Barcelona Port Complex, Asian Pacific Consortium Trade Offices,
Bureau D. South Dock, Level Five. 9:11 p.m. Day Five.

"Status Report," Colonel Otsu snapped.

"Multiple units attacking from Sections Three and Six. They're jamming the turrets and have gotten past the Legation boundaries on both sides. Captain Murata reports his men are falling back. He requests backup."

"Get the automated systems back online, now! Murata has to hold. I've got nothing else to give him. You," he pointed to one of the technicians, "notify Tokyo and forward the camera feed. They need to see this."

The Command Center was frantic; lights, alarms, all the technicians yelling, scared, talking at once. Colonel Otsu was stunned. He couldn't believe the British had dared to assault them. Such foolish, reckless desperation... over what? He didn't even know if the mercenaries had arrived safely.

The sounds of the battle came over the speakers, gunfire and shouts adding to the din in the large room. One of the windows shattered, the black armorglass showering down in daggers.

"They're here," one of the technicians shouted. Colonel Otsu frowned. The tactical map didn't show any Dawson-Hull units this close. He was about to order them to activate the storm shutters when the smell of rotten apples and garlic filled the room.

His throat closed and his face started to twitch. That, mercifully, was the last thing he remembered.

The doors slid open as Tam and I stepped up to the Command Center, but no one greeted us. There was a conspicuous absence of guards and secretaries in the reception room. The place was neat and orderly, and empty. Behind the counter, a heavy security door was locked open, and I heard the sound of the storm wind howling from the room beyond.

"OK. This feels wrong." Poet brought his magnum up in a two-handed grip. "What… what the hell's that smell?"

"Shit," Tam muttered.

"More like bad apples." Poet9 looked back at us. "Oh…"

Tam nodded toward the open door. "In there. Jace, hold Gibson. Poet, you and I go first."

Tam drew his Beretta, and he and Poet stepped cautiously into the Asian Pacific Consortium's Command and Communications Center. "Jace," he called out after a moment. "You're going to want to see this."

I stepped through the vault-like door and stared.

Storm winds were gusting through a large shattered window. The lights were on, computers humming away. A dozen large screens ran live feed from the security cameras showing Asian Pacific and Dawson-Hull troopers fighting at various locations. Except for the bodies and the broken window, the scene was perfectly normal.

It looked like the entire staff was there, all of them sitting in their chairs or slumped over workstations. There was no blood, or signs of a struggle. An older man, a uniformed officer, was crumpled on the floor in the middle of the room.

Tam pointed at his shoulder insignia. "There's our colonel."

"OK, this is officially creeping me out," I said. "What do we do now?"

Poet9 stepped forward and listened. "The mainframe's up. We're tapped straight into the APAC network here." He unzipped his jack cords.

"Are you serious?" Tam asked. "You're splicing now?"

"Think they'll mind?" Poet9 nodded toward the bodies. He holstered Grace and sat down at the main console. "Watch the door, amigos. I'm going to sift their logs and find out what happened."

"You're not exactly who I had in mind for the interface," a voice lilted out.

We all drew on the voice, and the man called Hester stepped out of the corner. He had an IMI Blizzard in one hand and a silver canister in the other.

"What are you doing here?" Tam asked.

"Is that my SMG? I hate it when people take my stuff," I asked.

"No, Mr. Manner, you just have good taste. And I'm just doing my job, Mr. Song." He gave a slight mocking bow towards us. "Congrats on making it here with the boy, by the way. I knew you could do it."

"Where's Alejo and Carmen, and Ibram?"

"At their friend's boat. A very unusual one it is too. You kept up your side, I kept up mine."

"What are you doing here then?" I repeated Tam's question.

"Tying up a couple of loose ends."

"I hope you don't mean us," Tam said quietly.

"If I did, you'd never have seen me coming. Lucky for you, I've a soft spot for talent. I'm talking about him." He nodded my way, at Gibson.

"What about him? He's dying. We've got to get him next door to a doctor," Poet9 interjected.

"I'm afraid there's no time for that right now," Hester shook his head. "I need him to jack in."

"What? That's why he's sick in the first place," I said. "Cyber-connectivity. The more he does it, the faster it kills him."

"I know," Hester nodded sadly. "Nonetheless."

"Are you listening?" Poet9 yelled. "Interfacing. Only. Makes it. Worse. Look at him, he needs a doctor now."

"My mission is more important."

"What mission? What are you talking about?" Poet said. "You got what you wanted. We delivered him. He needs a doctor, you heartless bastard."

"Guilty as charged, Mr. Perez. Frankly, I'm surprised he made it this far. The whole project has been a bit dodgy from the start, and…" Hester held up a small device in his hand, "he's dangerously close to having a Fatal Cascade Event. I can't risk that happening just yet."

"What project? And what's a Fatal Cascade Event?" Poet9 demanded.

Hester shrugged. "The boy is one of an exclusive clone series, gene-tailored to accommodate developmental nanotechnology."

"We got that part," I said. "We saw it work. He saved Poet's life."

"Yes, it does work… to a degree. Our biotech division has developed nanite technology to a functional stage, but only for extremely limited durations in the specially modified biological platforms. Gibson is the latest modified host for the latest version of the prototype nanites."

"If it works, why let us snatch him?" Tam asked.

"Because the program has cost the Conglomerate billions so far, and there's no guarantee the technology will ever fully mature. However, London did see an opportunity in its temporary stability."

"How?"

"They 'leaked' news of successful trials to a certain regional administrator in a rival corporation who is known for his ambition and rash judgment. The Board trusted his base nature to take its course."

"And that's where we came in," Tam said.

"Got it in one. At least Avery Hsiang gets high marks for an excellent choice of talent."

"If you really work for D-H, why is Special Deployment after us?" Poet9 demanded.

"Drama. We had to make it convincing, didn't we?" Hester gave one of his little smiles.

"So this was a bloody charade? Hsiang contracted us on the information you gave him. You devious bastards," I said. "But what the hell good does it do you?"

"Trade secrets, I'm afraid."

"Answer the damn question!" Tam said.

Hester glanced at the video screens. The Special Deployment troops were closing in. "Gibson's neural network has a little extra code meshed with the interface system: a Trojan virus that will download once he's logged into their mainframe. Once it burrows its way in, D-H intelligence gets a back door into the Asian Pacific Intranet; every file, every memo, every spreadsheet, projection, every dirty little secret."

"Flipping brilliant," Poet murmured.

"As a topper, the lab rats worked in a *Chernobyl Packet*. Trigger it, and Asian Pacific's entire cyber-infrastructure melts down. London will be able to eliminate a major rival in one simple key stroke."

"Or hold them hostage indefinitely," I said.

"Right. And now that we're all on the same page..." Hester regarded us intently, "my boss needs him to jack in. He might be under the weather, but as far as I can tell, he's still got enough left in him for one more go. Now," he pointed at me with the Blizzard, "bring him over to the mainframe, would you?"

None of us moved. "And if we refuse?" Tam asked.

"After all we've been through together? I'd be very disappointed, Mr. Song."

I held out Gibson in my arms. "Look at him, Hester. He won't survive another jack-in," I said.

"Nonetheless, I insist. It needs doing."

It was silent in the room for several long seconds except for the sound of gunfire carried through the open window.

"Piss off," Poet finally said. "I won't let you kill him." Grace was in his hand.

"Then we have a proverbial Mexican stand-off, don't we? No pun intended." Hester waggled the silver canister at him.

"I said, piss off." Poet9 spit out the words. "I'm not going to let a little kid die for your cloak and dagger *boludeces*."

Hester held out the silver canister again. "Novichok agent."

"Novi-what agent?" I said.

"Novichok. It means 'newcomer' in Russian. That smell? It's a fourth generation nerve gas developed under Putin and Medvedev. I hit the *red* button, you spasm so hard you actually break your own back." He looked around the room.

"You don't have the balls to do yourself just to get us," Poet sneered.

"Try me."

"Screw you, Hester." Tam raised his Beretta. "Gibson deserves better than to give his life for a hostile takeover."

Tension silted up in the room, building with every gust that clawed through the shattered glass.

Tam's eyes tightened, Poet was chewing his lip, and I hunched over Gibson, turning toward the heavy door. Hester's smile froze.

"Stop." Gibson spoke out. Green eyes looked up at me. "Bring me over," he whispered.

"What?"

"Bring me over to the computer." His words were small and coming from far away.

"Voice of reason, that is," Hester said and pointed. "The one with the fiber optic links."

The barrels of Tam and Poet's pistols dropped slightly, and I carried the boy past Poet9, his body small and light, fragile as bird's bones. He was sweating, but when I set him in the chair, he shivered as if it was arctic cold. His hands trembled as he pulled out his jack cord.

"You don't have to do this," I whispered in his ear.

"Yes, I do. I don't want anyone dying for me." He plugged in.

"Gibson," I started to speak, but he put his hand on mine and looked into my face, his eyes bright with a strange look of calm. "Jace, it's OK. I'm not scared."

He turned back, closed those eyes, and his little fingers hurried over the keyboard.

Gibson started his run.

Gibson: It always begins the same way: tumbling in the black nowhere until a horizon line forms and suddenly I'm on the cliff. That's another thing that's the same every time: the feeling of standing at the edge of a vast deepness that drops away beneath my feet.

My head hurts, pounding sharp spikes with every heartbeat, and I can't see the lines. The skeletons and spider webs aren't forming. Everything stays dark, and my head hurts, but somehow I can hear Carmen reading.

Where can I go from Your Spirit? Or where can I flee from Your presence? If I ascend into heaven, You are there; If I make my bed in hell, behold, You are there.

There: one bright white-hot dot shining in the empty black like the last star in the universe.

Even there Your hand shall lead me, and Your right hand shall hold me. If I say, "Surely the darkness shall fall on me," even the night shall be light about me;

I'm there with a thought, and instantly the other structures spring up, emerging like a magician's trick conjured by my movement. One shape in particular floats high above me; an inverted pyramid spinning on its point.

There's a delicate webwork of a thousand million strands connecting at that single spot.

That's where the man wants me to go.

I step into the light and flow with the data, picking up commands and pass codes as I go, and I strike the needle-pointed nadir half a second later.

A blink and a check, and I'm inside. One of their own.

But I am not.

The data flow is massive, and I am overwhelmed, caught in the torrent flowing upwards. I cannot control it. I cannot think to move. The pounding is worse, and the undertow of information pulls me in. I can't breathe. I... I...

Indeed, the darkness shall not hide from You, but the night shines as the day; the darkness and the light are both alike to You.

Pain stabs in my head, and I'm me again.

I am carried into the dense sphere of core programming, and the throbbing gets sharper, faster. I lurch to a stop, stuck, spinning in place, and through the pain I feel things shredding away, peeling off. They scurry and burrow, disappear under the immense white skin, under the glare of root codes and routines.

The pain drops away and I'm hollow, sick. I've been ripped open and the leak is pouring out. Where does it go?

Suddenly there's a name in my mind: Hsiang. There's one last thing I need to do.

I pull myself away and start searching. Here in this center, nothing is closed to me. It unfolds at my touch like flowers, every password and encryption naked and open in this hive. I'm searching, but the sick feeling is spreading. I'm slower, slower with each heartbeat. All I need is one file, one strand of information. I grab gleaming handfuls, but they slip and spill. Everything is blurry at the edges. I'm running out of time.

There it is. And there... I've changed things. I let the strand go.

The data glow is dimming and I can't move. The thought of Carmen makes me sad, but I don't have the strength left to cry. The net light blinks twice then winks out altogether.

It's finished.

I am alone in the black.

Suddenly there is light, impossible light bursting from every direction at once. Light so bright it presses on my skin, fills me. I squeeze my eyes and can't turn away.

There are strong arms around me, lifting me. I hear words and suddenly the brightness dims. I can open my eyes.

I am not alone.

I will praise You, for I am fearfully and wonderfully made; marvelous are Your works, and that my soul knows very well.

Carmen was right.

Hester watched as Poet9 went over and checked Gibson's pulse.

"He's dead. Satisfied?" Poet9 said.

"Only that my job is done," the small agent replied.

"Shithead."

Two explosions went off outside the Command Center. We all looked up at the security monitors to see Dawson-Hull troopers closing in. Hester leapt up onto the window frame.

"Where do you think you're going?" I asked.

"My bosses will contact you once you're back in Belfast. I'll put in a good word. I'm sure they can find a couple of odd jobs that need doing."

"What if we don't want a paycheck from your Savile Row bastards?" Tam called out.

Hester shrugged. "Your choice. But it's a shame to waste talent. Accidents happen, and I'd hate to see you left out in the cold."

"Hey," Poet yelled. "They're your guys. Think you could lend us a hand?"

Hester looked over his shoulder. "If you can't get out of this on your own, it saves my Savile Row bastard bosses the trouble of ringing you up, doesn't it?" With that, he climbed through the window and disappeared out of sight.

Poet gritted his teeth. "I should have shot him."

I looked over at Gibson's tiny body. "Maybe you should have."

There was another explosion, followed by the chatter of automatic weapons and the whine of ricocheted bullets off metal. Every screen showed nothing but Dawson-Hull Special Deployment troopers.

"We need to vacate before someone finds us and thinks we killed all these people," Poet said.

"There a back way out of here?" I asked Tam.

"Hell if I know."

We took cover outside the main door behind a row of electric carts. The British were closing in fast and furious from all directions, and every APAC soldier we could see was either dead or surrendering.

Poet9 peered over a hood. "They've got a whole damn army out there."

"Everything but tanks," I said.

"A tank would be good right about now," Tam agreed.

Then out of the distance, over the noise of gunfire, we heard the roar of a heavy engine and the rumble of a large vehicle headed our way.

"If it wasn't for bad luck…" Tam said.

"We'd have no luck at all," Poet and I both finished.

The three of us stared, and there, coming down the main avenue into the Legation was an ancient, steel-sided, six-wheel garbage truck. And it was headed right for us.

"What *is* that?" I asked.

It tore through the fence and pulled up right in front of the Command Center. Rounds were sparking off its thick plate sides and cab. It sat there, the driver gunning the engine. Suddenly the passenger door flung open.

"Come on. Hurry, hurry," Alejo yelled.

"Are you nuts?" I managed to say.

"Hey! You can always get a fanatic to do something stupid, right? Now get in here. We've got a submarine to catch."

The three of us dove for the door.

EPILOGUE

Alejo drove like a mad Spaniard, barreling through fences, over barricades and dividers, right through the middle of the assault. Nothing stopped that old truck and in less than ten minutes, we'd screeched to a halt on the bottom floor at the very tip of the South Arm. We were right at the water level and the floor was swamped knee deep with waves crashing into the sides of the Dock some twenty meters overhead.

Alejo's Bible-smuggling friend was the captain of an old decommed Russian sub: an Oscar II class nuclear leviathan. No wonder the Islamic Federation had such a hard time stopping him. We slipped down through a hatch and in five minutes we were below the waves and headed out to sea.

Between the extraordinary quiet, the kindness of his crew, and the encased calm of the sub, it was like we'd fallen into another world. He took five days to bring us all the way back to the coast of Ireland. We made it ashore one foggy night and have been laying low in our apartments in Belfast ever since.

The Triplets killed the three APAC agents. We found out later they were some kind of secret clone Executive Hsiang sent after us. The Dawson-Hull commander in Spain, a nasty piece of work named Eames, had the bodies burnt, but only after emptying full clips into them just to make sure. From what we can tell, Cottontail drew them into a trap using himself as bait. There's mention of an explosion, and he smiles when he talks about killing the cold-eyed woman. Flopsy and Mopsy killed the other two. They were despondent when I told them about Gibson. They still won't say his name, but I think they're getting past it.

Doc Kalahani took that position in Belfast Children's Hospital. He comes around for a hot cuppa once or twice a month, checking up on us, telling stories about the kids in his ward. He smiles more these days. Al and Carmen are somewhere in the Bloody Nose of Africa, Somaliland I think, doing humanitarian work among the refugees. We get an e-card from them every month. Funny, they lost everything but seem happier than ever, if that's even possible. Curro on the other hand is here in Ireland with us. He runs errands, does chores, and Doc K. got him some shifts at the hospital. He says there's nothing for him back in Barcelona, and he hates the heat in Africa. Personally, I think he's angling for a spot on our next mission. Tam told me the other day he's seriously considering bringing him along, as logistics support, mind you. Alejo found out and wants us to teach him everything we know. Carmen says we better not or she'll come after us. Regardless, Tam has Jaithirth putting out feelers for our next contract.

We've got some stipulations next time around.

Not that we're hurting for credits. Not at all, in fact. It seems Gibson got creative when he was in the APAC Grid. When we finally checked, our bank accounts showed twice the amount we expected. On top of that, the Garcías mysteriously ended up with a substantial amount of Asian Pacific stock. More of Gibson's handiwork. They sold it all straight off, cashing out before D-H could pull the plug.

So far, there's been no obvious bloodletting in the corporate arena. I guess London's still rifling through the Consortium's database, grabbing everything that's interesting. At Eshu International, we've got one eye watching the skies for fallout.

Belfast smells like wood smoke, fog, and old stones. Tam and I have spent the last month replacing lost and broken equipment, repairing gear, generally healing up and thinking a lot. I even picked up a Bible and read a bit of it. I told Al, which Tam thought was a huge mistake, and now he and Carmen forward these devotionals to me. Tam calls them "holy spam".

I keep meaning to go through them and look up the scripture references, but I'm still "buffering" as Poet9 would say. Tam swore he's going to wait until he's at least forty before he even thinks about looking into the "God thing".

I think of Gibson every now and then. The other day Carmen told me he'd asked her if he had a soul after that night we argued in the cellar. I'm sure he did. A good one too. And wherever he is, I have the feeling he's safe and happy.

I can't prove it. Call it instinct.

FINISHED?
IT'S NEVER FINISHED.
Read on for a Sneak Peek at the next Eshu International novel

SHIFT TENSE
Coming Fall 2011

More Information at the author's blog:
Hot Space Station Justice
(http://CCGlazier.wordpress.com/)

SHIFT TENSE
Fall 2011

CHAPTER TWO

TINKERBELL PAYLOAD

Latvian coast, Merger of Baltic Nations. 50 km south of Ventspils.

Pitch black at two a.m., a winter storm was shrieking off the Baltic Sea while I dangled upside down like a giant origami bat.

Fifteen empty meters under me, scrawny I-beam at my back, swarms of ice chips pinged off my faceplate like glass slivers. A single abrading note sang through the skeletal metal around me, and I couldn't move a muscle.

Sometimes I hate my job.

Twenty minutes to extraction, I had been climbing a small crane to provide top cover when a Soviet-era KA-50 "Werewolf" assault chopper dropped out of the sky so fast I slipped in a rush to disappear. That's why, blood rushing to my head, I was hanging off a ladder clutching eight girthy kilograms of Vychlop .50 cal sniper rifle and trying very hard to look like a piece of machinery.

Rotors loitered behind me in the brittle air, suspicious and sadistic. The prying white of a searchlight snapped on, hard shadows suddenly lurching back and forth.

One minute.

I blinked away eye spots and exhaled slowly. The armored vest tightened around my chest, gathered under my arms like it wanted to slither off and wrap around my head.

Two minutes.

My knees started screaming from being locked around the ladder rung.

Three minutes.

My chest and shoulders glazed stiff with icy build-up. My stomach muscles trembled as the sweat ran inside my helmet from my neck into my eyes.

Shadows expanded, the shredding closed in. Lingered.

Four minutes. Five.

Sometimes I really hate my job.

Then, as fast as it came, the copter darted off and began probing the trees along the dirt road from town. The engine roar faded, the wind came back. My heart started again.

"Oh, oh. Oryol is *sumamente* pissed," Poet9's voice sang in my helmet.

"The explosion woke up the whole damn place." Tam snapped.

"You told Mopsy to stop the van."

"I didn't mean with a rocket launcher."

"Well, there must have been eight Ivan's in it." Poet9 tried to sound reasonable.

Tam sighed. "Which is why that Werewolf will be back. They're not sure if we've left yet."

"Hey," I gasped. "Can I. Move now?"

"Oh... yeah. Sure." Tam answered

I unfolded carefully. "You want me up or down?" I set the heavy rifle on a beam next to me, wiped the ice off and tugged my body armor back into place. "We'll need the Finger of God if company's coming."

"Not with that thing in the air. Find cover on the ground. Triplets will watch the road. I need you to help Curro with the ladies and hustle them into the boat when it arrives. We need to vacate the premises right fucking now."

"Speaking of the ladies ..." I started climbing down.

Curro's soft Spanish lilt came over the radio. "The ladies are here under the dome with me. Daughter's a little scared, but Mom's got it under control. We're ready when you are."

Curro was hunkered down under a tiny thermal-masking pop-up in a clump of trees some twenty five meters away from the shore. The "ladies" were our objective for this run: the wife and young daughter of a Ukrainian micro-robotics engineer who'd gone over the wire to Microsoft International. Somehow the Americans had finagled our services from Dawson Hull, our usual employer, and that's why we were hiding with his family by an abandoned fishing pier on the Latvian coast on a winter night being chased by Russian security.

Now I know DH hadn't grown a conscience and gotten all family friendly. There must have been some heavy boardroom deals to send Eshu International on an errand for the Americans, but our swift and silent extraction had turned into a smash and grab, so it wasn't the best time to speculate on corporate relations. Our immediate concern was to get them - and us - out safe.

My boots touched gravel and a siren started wailing in the distance. Security at the RSC Energia campus must have checked the apartment and connected the dots. I jogged away from the crane, keeping an eye on the road. "The Ravens up?"

"Oh yeah, " Poet9 breathed. "All three. Carrying surprises, too."

I knelt behind a small tin-roofed shed near the longest of the three piers. "Not again." I heard Tam say.

"You'll love it. Pure genius." Poet9 answered.

"So where's our ride?" I asked.

"Coming. I sent the ready signal." I could almost hear Tam's finger stroking the trigger.

"Oh, *muy bueno*" Poet9 snorted. "Can anyone say 'blue screen of doom'? DH should have let us do our own exit, instead of relying on the Microsofties. We have a perfectly good STAB of our ---"

"You're not helping." Tam interrupted. "Curro, I'll call once we see the boat. Stay under wraps until then. No heroics."

"Si."He answered.

I had just found a decent spot out of the knifing wind when Cottontail's voice sounded out. "Contact. Two vehicles approaching on the dirt road. One truck and one SUV."

"Raven Two has three more vehicles less than five minutes behind 'em." Poet9 added.

Tam was already up and sprinting toward the Triplets. "Activate mines. Engage vehicles when ready," he said crisply. "Poet, maintain the Raven feeds. Jace, be ready for that boat."

"Roger that."

Tam vanished into the tree line and I ran to a small rise next to a garage. More like a trash pile, it wasn't the best position, but it gave me a little height, and some sickly scrub brush provided a hint of cover. Most important, I had a clear shot up the road. I watched Poet9, his massive Walther in one hand, lug the Raven's Boss Box over to where Curro was hiding, then I flicked on my rifle's optics and sighted on the approaching headlights.

A small Korean cheap-jeep blossomed in my scope. Light colored, it charged toward us, bouncing and swerving like a thing possessed. The Russian muscle wanted their principles back. Behind it, I could see an old Mercedes panel truck struggle to keep up. The jeep slewed around the bend spraying sand, righted, then shot forward straight towards the first pier.

And exploded.

Mine one.

The big truck slammed to a halt. With the wash-out compensators in the scope, I could see figures leaping out of the back, fanning out to either side, their body shapes swimming in the green-white glare of burning jeep. They ran forward then scuttled back from the flames. No survivors there.

If we were very lucky and the Russians very stupid, the jeep had been carrying their officers.

The men from the truck dropped out of sight and assumed defensive positions. Ten seconds. Thirty. No shots, no motion. Seemed no one wanted to take the chance and knock on our door.

Then someone started barking orders. Either there'd been an officer in the truck or some Alpha-type wanted a promotion. So much for luck. Eventually, six of the Russian security soldiers appeared, wary, unwilling to leave the protective bulk of the Mercedes.

I found the loud one in the back and settled crosshairs on his torso. Real commissar type. He was bellowing, urging the rest of them forward with big slashes and chops of his arms. My finger took up half the slack. I waited for Tam's signal.

There was motion on either side of the road: things scurrying through the grass. I squeezed the trigger as the spider mines went off; the boom covered by a rapid ***Crack-Hiss***. The officer tumbled back and suddenly there was screaming.

Claymores with legs, Tam calls them. With the brain of a gerbil, Poet9 always added.

Screams turned to moans turned to wind again. I swept the area through the scope. Flames were the only thing moving. Ten, maybe twelve men had just died, and I was the only one of us who fired a shot.

Poet9 updated us. "Raven One has zero movement in killbox, but Raven Two has those three other vehicles coming fast. There's a fourth one leaving town. Cossacks are riding hard."

"Raven Three?" I asked.

"No contacts on the water."

"Helicopter?" Tam demanded.

"No sign of it."

"Screw the helicopter. Where's. The. Damn. Boat?" I demanded.

"It's coming." Tam snapped back.

"Three vehicles have stopped half a klick out. Figures dismounting." Poet9 said. "*Carajo*. Fifteen. No, twenty plus, coming our way. And we're out of mines."

Tam muttered something foul in Korean then ordered the Triplets forward. Cottontail spoke one short, sharp word in his Zulu combat argot, and the three big clones ghosted into the woods.

I chinned the video from Raven One, and the Oryol boys popped up on my helmet's H.U.D. Twenty one of them were spread out in a skirmish line, trotting along the road in a hurry. These guys wanted the ladies back something fierce. Most sported compact AK-9 assault rifles but I spotted at least four Pecheneg LMGs and a RG8 40mm grenade launcher. What Oryol Security lacked in finesse they made up in blunt force trauma.

The Ivans were about a hundred meters from the curve in the road when three grenades exploded, followed by the deep stutter of H&K G46s. "Contact." Cottontail said simply.

The Russians' response was almost immediate. Definitely not mall security wash-outs. They reacted fast and vicious, opening up with everything they had. Continuous muzzle flash washed out the drone's video, so I cut the feed and waited. The chainsaw roar ripped through the night for a full minute then fell silent all at once.

Cottontail's voice sounded in my helmet a second later. "Repositioning to beta."

I smiled.

I brought up Raven One again, and this time the view was from behind the Russian troopers. Sixteen figures were now creeping toward the bend.

Not bad. Not good, but not bad. And they were heading straight to our Nightingale.

An old trick out of the Spec Ops black bag, a Nightingale Device is a one meter by one and a half meter mesh net rigged with firecrackers and cherry bombs. Add a remote detonator, press 'play' and it looks and sounds like a platoon unloading on full auto.

The Russians were around the bend, four teams leapfrogging down the road in angry spurts. They had blood in their teeth and they knew we were still here.

Seventy five meters from the first pier, Cottontail spoke again. "Engaging, beta"

First, the Nightingale erupted on the right and the Oryol teams swung into it like it was another ambush, furiously unloading into the woods again. I saw bushes and small trees collapsing. Thirty seconds into their response, the Triplets hit them from behind, Another five went down, and the rest scattered like leaves in a gale.

One team made the mistake of taking cover behind what was left of the jeep. The Vychlop slammed into my shoulder twice before the other two scurried back to the Mercedes.

The Nightingale stopped, allowing the Russians to regroup and focus on the Triplets, but they were wary and off-balance, and our Killer Bunnies picked them off steadily. A no-neck with the grenade launcher was thumping out 40mm rounds, but Tam's Tavor 24 coughed sharply and he stopped.

Things were definitely looking up. Now if that boat would just show up ...

Eyes still on the road, I spotted the bounce of approaching headlights the same moment Poet9 sang out. "Fourth vehicle coming fast."

A large black van swung around the Mercedes truck and blew past the burning jeep.

"Kill it." Tam ordered.

A Bumblebee rocket screeched out of the woods and caught the van in the rear. It exploded Hollywood-style, flipping end over end and tumbled to a halt, blazing in smaller pieces.

Each of the Bunnies carried a single-use RPO-M thermobaric launcher. Made to crack hardened concrete bunkers, using them to radically disassemble vehicles was definite overkill. Whatever works though...

"Raven Three has water contact coming our way." Poet9 spoke up."Our ride's here."

"Better late than never." Tam murmured. "Disengage and fall back to third pier. Curro, Poet, get the women into the boat."

I stayed on my garbage heap and kept my eyes glued on the road, but no one was moving up there. That last display must have gutted Oryol's slavic zeal.

As the thrum of outboard motors grew behind me, Poet9 emerged from hiding and ran across the road. He was still jacked in to the Ravens' controller and waving his oversized pistol. Curro followed more slowly, sheltering the mother with his body. He'd given her his jacket, and she was carrying her young daughter in her arms. They went past me and headed to the end of the pier.

Almost there.

Tam and the Triplets loosed a final round of grenades and tri-bursts. Still no response. Not like Ivans to widdle their knickers, but far be it from me to interrupt when my opponent is making a mistake. Tam and the Triplets broke from the tree line at a dead run straight towards me.

Still no motion up the road.

The Triplets settled into position around me and Tam tapped my shoulder as he ran past. I got up and followed him down the pier.

The Microsoft boat was a Code X clone: chiseled long and low, with a cabin bulge at the rear. It was covered in mimetic smart-camo, so its surface flashed with the heave of moonlit waves. Curro and Poet9 had already helped the two women down the ladder. The wiry Mexican was still jacked in, but he flashed a smile up at me. "Home free, homie". I gave him a thumbs up - I was spending my percentage already.

"We're leaving." Tam called over the radio, and the Triplets rose out of the shadows and ran towards us. They were halfway down the pier when the Werewolf returned and all my sugar turned to shit.

"Drop it." Tam ordered. Flospy skidded to a halt, tugged the launcher tube off his back. A thread of fire lanced up into the sky straight toward the helicopter.

And missed.

That Russian pilot executed one of the most incredible feats of flying I'd ever seen. The twin rotor assault chopper literally spun in a three-sixty and sidestepped the rocket. It came around facing us head on again fifty feet from its original position. I'd never been so impressed and horrified at the same time.

The searchlight snapped on again, this time accompanied by a quick belch of its 30mm gun. The water geysered directly in front of us.

Остановка! Halt.

God. Damn. It.

Tam, the Triplets, and I froze like mystics with a peek at apotheosis. And between the roar of the storm, the helicopter's engine, the bright light, and the threat of instant death, it was like God speaking doom out of a tornado.

All of a sudden, another sound barged in on that weirdly sacred moment, so normal as to seem profane: the loud buzz of fans. It seemed to swoop in from all around us, and I heard three tiny pops before it vanished. A split second later there was a soft grinding noise.

It grew louder, and louder.

The searchlight dipped. Righted itself, then dipped again.

The grinding morphed into a rasp, and the Werewolf's nose dropped. The engine began to shriek.

The five of us stared, still rooted in place, as the pilot began to struggle for control. The helicopter dropped down, began to wobble back and forth like a drunk. The shriek became a grating howl, and suddenly the helicopter reeled up and away, lunging toward land.

"Go, go, go!" Tam shouted, and the five of us jumped into the boat. Twin Ilmor Formula One engines snarled to life and we shot into the frigid darkness on the Baltic Sea.

As the shoreline fell away, I started breathing again for a second time that night.

"What just happened?" Tam said out loud. "What was that?"

I stared at Curro. "Your mom praying again?" He only laughed.

"All you need is trust and a little bit of pixie dust." Poet9 warbled. "Knew it would work."

The Triplets turned in unison. "Peter Pan!" they boomed out, big grins on their faces.

Tam blinked twice. "Whiskey Tango Foxtrot is 'pixie dust'?"

"Mostly sand, with metal shavings and chaff to spice it up. Slight drag on the Ravens' aerodynamics, but when that chopper came back, I stuka-ed it and blew all three at the rotor assembly."

My jaw dropped. "Sorry?"

"I was worried RSC Energia might have their own drones over the facility, and seeing as missiles are too obvious, I rigged each of the Ravens with a Tinkerbell payload." Poet9 explained. "Each Raven had two kilos of pixie dust in a fiberglass canister. Stuff will wreck any drone engine."

"You know it would work on the chopper?" I asked.

"Nope." He shrugged. "But I figured it was worth a shot."

"Holy shit." Tam said slowly.

I looked over at Curro again. "Your mom is definitely praying."

"For God's sake, don't tell her about tonight, ok?" Tam pleaded. Curro laughed again, and handed a mug of tea to the mother.

I looked over at the two women. Both of them wrapped in blankets, the daughter was fast asleep and her mother was brushing hair out of her round, little face. She saw me looking and smiled back at me. Everything was right in their world now. They were warm and safe, going to be reunited with a loved one in a better country, for a better company. This one turned out alright.

Sometimes I love my job.

Seven hundred fifteen horsepower throbbed steadily under our feet, launching us further into the deep black of the Baltic night. Finding a Code X stealth boat anytime was a task; throw in a storm like this and the Russians would never trace us. Ever. This run was over.

Poet9 spoke up. He had jacked in to the boat's main console. "I told Rao we were clear, and he's relayed that to the Microsofties. Balance will be in the bank tomorrow." He unplugged the cable from the Interface Unit on the side of his head. "And he says not to get too comfortable. D-H is sending Hester around tomorrow to brief us on our next job."

I looked out at the storm swirling past the windows. "I hope it's somewhere warm."

ACKNOWLEDGMENTS

To Shelley Singer who kicked me out of the house, to the folks at TED who shoved me in the deep end, to Mark Hooper who fished me out, to Matt Dengler who's been there through it all, to Marc Giller and Neal Asher for answering a newb's emails, to James Strickland for the very first blurb, to Alejandro Martinez for the awesome cover, to Dee who prayed, to Paul Ward of Matakishi's Tea House who had it looking far better than it was, and to all the readers who suffered through the early drafts; you have my eternal gratitude.

Patrick Todoroff, 2010

Soli Deo Gloria

CPSIA information can be obtained at www.ICGtesting.com
Printed in the USA
267768BV00001B/4/P